'Brilliantly tense, beautifully written new mystery thriller . . . possibly the most joyously readable crime writer in the world right now' *Heat*

'If you haven't been caught by Coben's intelligent, gripping thrillers yet, this will hook you' *Daily Mirror*

'His trademark is twists that you don't see coming and his writing is not just exciting but also thought-provoking' *Daily Mail*

'*Caught* is a superb thriller . . . Coben's trademark scenes of legal cut-and-thrust are as gripping as ever; his ability to wring the drama out of the most mundane of potential criminal scenarios is, after all these years, remarkable. Furthermore, the fact he manages to create an ending that is both moving and convincing is testament to the enviable fact that he has never written better' *Evening Standard*

'Coben's characters are believable archetypes, his dialogue honest and pleasingly familiar . . . as always with Coben, it's the fun of the switchback ride that counts' *Financial Times*

'[An] excellent thriller . . . Coben's plots are always ingenious but that is never the point of them, so much as the emotional turmoil into which his characters are plunged by what happens to them and by what they do' *Independent*

'An absorbing page-turner, the theme of which is endurance and forgiveness' *Literary Review*

'Harlan Coben has been a first-division writer for some years now, and *Caught* finds him at the top of his game . . . The sheer unputdownability of his books means this is a quick and deeply satisfying read' *Sunday Tribune*

By Harlan Coben

Play Dead
Miracle Cure
Deal Breaker
Drop Shot
Fade Away
Back Spin
One False Move
The Final Detail
Darkest Fear
Tell No One
Gone For Good
No Second Chance
Just One Look
The Innocent
Promise Me
The Woods
Hold Tight
Long Lost
Caught
Live Wire
Shelter
Stay Close
Seconds Away
Six Years

Harlan Coben is one of the most exciting talents in crime writing. He is an international number one bestseller, gracing the charts of the *Sunday Times* and the *New York Times*. His books are published in more than forty languages and there are more than fifty million of his novels in print worldwide. Harlan lives in New Jersey with his wife and four children. Visit his website at www.harlancoben.com

Caught

HARLAN COBEN

An Orion paperback

First published in Great Britain in 2010
by Orion
This paperback edition published in 2011
by Orion Books,
an imprint of The Orion Publishing Group Ltd,
Orion House, 5 Upper St Martin's Lane,
London WC2H 9EA

An Hachette UK company

Reissued 2013

A CIP catalogue record for this book
is available from the British Library.

Printed and bound in Great Britain by CPI Group (UK) Ltd,
Croydon, CR0 4YY

The Orion Publishing Group's policy is to use papers
that are natural, renewable and recyclable products and
made from wood grown in sustainable forests. The logging
and manufacturing processes are expected to conform to
the environmental regulations of the country of origin.

www.orionbooks.co.uk

For Anne
From the luckiest guy in the world

Prologue

I knew opening that red door would destroy my life.

Yes, that sounds melodramatic and full of foreboding and I'm not big on either, and true, there was nothing menacing about the red door. In fact, the door was beyond ordinary, wood and four-paneled, the kind of door you see standing guard in front of three out of every four suburban homes, with faded paint and a knocker at chest level no one ever used and a faux brass knob.

But as I walked toward it, a distant streetlight barely illuminating my way, the dark opening yawning like a mouth ready to gobble me whole, the feeling of doom was unshakable. Each step forward took great effort, as if I were walking not along a somewhat crackled walk but through still-wet cement. My body displayed all the classic symptoms of impending menace: Chill down my spine? Check. Hairs standing up on my arms? Yep. Prickle at the base of the neck? Present. Tingle in the scalp? Right there.

The house was dark, not a single light on. Chynna warned me that would be the case. The dwelling somehow seemed a little too cookie-cutter, a little too nondescript. That bothered me for some reason. This house was also isolated at the tippy end of the cul-de-sac, hunkering down in the darkness as though fending off intruders.

I didn't like it.

I didn't like anything about this, but this is what I do. When Chynna called I had just finished coaching the inner-city fourth-grade Newark Biddy Basketball team. My team, all kids who, like me, were products of foster care (we call ourselves the NoRents, which is short for No Parents – gallows humor), had managed to blow a six-point lead with two minutes left. On the court, as in life, the NoRents aren't great under pressure.

Chynna called as I was gathering my young hoopsters for my postgame pep talk, which usually consisted of giving my charges some life-altering insight like 'Good effort,' 'We'll get them next time,' or 'Don't forget we have a game next Thursday,' always ending with 'Hands in' and then we yell, 'Defense,' choosing to chant that word, I suppose, because we play none.

'Dan?'

'Who is this?'

'It's Chynna. Please come.'

Her voice trembled, so I dismissed my team, jumped in my car, and now I was here. I hadn't even had time to shower. The smell of gym sweat mixed now with the smell of fear sweat. I slowed my pace.

What was wrong with me?

I probably should have showered, for one thing. I'm not good without a shower. Never have been. But Chynna had been adamant. Now, she had begged. Before anyone got home. So here I was, my gray T-shirt darkened with perspiration and clinging to my chest, heading to that door.

Like most youngsters I work with, Chynna was seriously troubled, and maybe that was what was setting off the warning bells. I hadn't liked her voice on the phone, hadn't really warmed to this whole setup. Taking a deep breath, I glanced behind me. In the distance, I could see some signs of life on this suburban night – house lights, a flickering television or maybe computer monitor, an open garage door – but in this cul-de-sac, there was nothing, not a sound or movement, just a hush in the dark.

My cell phone vibrated, nearly making me jump out of my skin. I figured that it was Chynna, but no, it was Jenna, my ex-wife. I hit answer and said, 'Hey.'

'Can I ask a favor?' she asked.

'I'm a little busy right now.'

'I just need someone to babysit tomorrow night. You can bring Shelly if you want.'

'Shelly and I are, uh, having trouble,' I said.

'Again? But she's great for you.'

'I have trouble holding on to great women.'

'Don't I know it.'

Jenna, my lovely ex, has been remarried for eight years. Her new husband is a well-respected surgeon named Noel Wheeler. Noel does volunteer work for me at the teen center. I like Noel and he likes me. He has a daughter by a previous marriage, and he and Jenna have a six-year-old girl named Kari. I'm Kari's godfather, and both kids call me Uncle Dan. I'm the family go-to babysitter.

I know this all sounds very civilized and Pollyanna, and I suppose it is. In my case, it could be simply a matter of necessity. I have no one else – no parents, no siblings – ergo, the closest thing I have to family is my ex-wife. The kids I work with, the ones I advocate for and try to help and defend, are my life, and in the end I'm not sure I do the slightest bit of good.

Jenna said, 'Earth to Dan?'

'I'll be there,' I said to her.

'Six thirty. You're the best.'

Jenna made a smooching noise into the mouthpiece and hung up. I looked at the phone for a moment, remembered our own wedding day. It was a mistake for me to get married. It is a mistake for me to get too close to people, and yet I can't help it. Someone cue the violins so I can wax philosophical about how it is better to have loved and lost than to never have loved at all. I don't think that applies to me. It is in humans' DNA to repeat the same mistakes, even after we know better. So here I am, the poor orphan who scraped his way up to the top of his class at an elite Ivy League school but never really scraped off who he was. Corny, but I want someone in my life. Alas, that is not my destiny. I am a loner who isn't meant to be alone.

'We are evolution's garbage, Dan. . . .'

My favorite foster 'dad' taught me that. He was a college professor who loved to get into philosophical debates.

'Think about it, Dan. Throughout mankind, the strongest and brightest did what? They fought in wars. That only stopped this past century. Before that, we sent our absolute best to fight on the front lines. So who stayed home and reproduced while our finest died on distant battlefields? The lame, the sick, the weak, the crooked, the cowardly – in short, the least of us. That's what we are the genetic by-product of, Dan – millenniums of weeding out the premium and keeping the flotsam. That's why we are all garbage – the dung from centuries of bad breeding.'

I forwent the knocker and rapped on the door lightly with my knuckles. The door creaked open a crack. I hadn't realized that it was ajar.

I didn't like that either. A lot I didn't like here.

4

As a kid, I watched a lot of horror movies, which was strange because I hated them. I hated things jumping out at me. And I really couldn't stand movie gore. But I would still watch them and revel in the predictably moronic behavior of the heroines, and right now those scenes were replaying in my head, the ones where said moronic heroine knocks on a door and it opens a little and you scream, 'Run, you scantily clad bimbo!' and she wouldn't and you couldn't understand it and two minutes later, the killer would be scooping out her skull and munching on her brain.

I should go right now.

In fact, I will. But then I flashed back to Chynna's call, to the words she'd said, the trembling in her voice. I sighed, leaned my face toward the opening, peered into the foyer.

Darkness.

Enough with the cloak and dagger.

'Chynna?'

My voice echoed. I expected silence. That would be the next step, right? No reply. I slipped the door open a little, took a tentative step forward. . . .

'Dan? I'm in the back. Come in.'

The voice was muffled, distant. Again I didn't like this, but there was no way I was backing out now. Backing out had cost me too much throughout my life. My hesitation was gone. I knew what had to be done now.

I opened the door, stepped inside, and closed the door behind me.

Others in my position would have brought a gun or some kind of weapon. I had thought about it. But that just doesn't work for me. No time to worry about that now. No one was home. Chynna had told me that. And if they were, well, I would handle that when the moment came.

'Chynna?'

'Go to the den, I'll be there in a second.'

The voice sounded . . . off. I saw a light at the end of the hall and moved toward it. There was a noise now. I stopped and listened. Sounded like water running. A shower maybe.

'Chynna?'

'Just changing. Out in a second.'

I moved into the low-lit den. I saw one of those dimmer-switch knobs and debated turning it up, but in the end I chose to leave it alone. My eyes adjusted pretty quickly. The room had cheesy wood paneling that looked as if it were made from something far closer to vinyl than anything in the timber family. There were two portraits of sad clowns with huge flowers on their lapels, the kind of painting you might pick up at a particularly tacky motel's garage sale. There was a giant open bottle of no-name vodka on the bar.

I thought I heard somebody whisper.

'Chynna?' I called out.

No answer. I stood, listened for more whispering. Nothing.

I started toward the back, toward where I heard the shower running.

'I'll be right out,' I heard the voice say. I pulled up, felt a chill. Because now I was closer to the voice. I could hear it better. And here was the thing I found particularly strange about it:

It didn't sound at all like Chynna.

Three things tugged at me. One, panic. This wasn't Chynna. Get out of the house. Two, curiosity. If it wasn't Chynna, who the hell was it and what was going on?

Three, panic again. It had been Chynna on the phone – so what had happened to her?

I couldn't just run out now.

I took one step toward where I'd come in, and that was when it all happened. A spotlight snapped on in my face, blinding me. I stumbled back, hand coming up to my face.

'Dan Mercer?'

I blinked. Female voice. Professional. Deep tone. Sounded oddly familiar.

'Who's there?'

Suddenly there were other people in the room. A man with a camera. Another with what looked like a boom mike. And the female with the familiar voice, a stunning woman with chestnut brown hair and a business suit.

'Wendy Tynes, *NTC News*. Why are you here, Dan?'

I opened my mouth, nothing came out. I recognized the woman from that TV newsmagazine . . .

'Why have you been conversing online in a sexual manner with a thirteen-year-old girl, Dan? We have your communications with her.'

. . . the one that sets up and catches pedophiles on camera for all the world to see.

'Are you here to have sex with a thirteen-year-old girl?'

The truth of what was going on there hit me, freezing my bones. Other people flooded the room. Producers maybe. Another cameraman. Two cops. The cameras came in closer. The lights got brighter. Beads of sweat popped up on my brow. I started to stammer, started to deny.

But it was over.

Two days later, the show aired. The world saw.

And the life of Dan Mercer, just as I somehow knew it would be when I approached that door, was destroyed.

When Marcia McWaid first saw her daughter's empty bed, panic did not set in. That would come later.

She had woken up at six AM, early for Saturday morning, feeling pretty terrific. Ted, her husband of twenty years, slept in the bed next to her. He lay on his stomach, his arm around her waist. Ted liked to sleep with a shirt on and no pants. None. Nude from the waist down. 'Gives my man down there room to roam,' he would say with a smirk. And Marcia, imitating her daughters' teenage singsong tone, would say, 'T-M-I' – Too Much Information.

Marcia slipped out of his grip and padded down to the kitchen. She made herself a cup of coffee with the new Keurig pod machine. Ted loved gadgets – boys and their toys – but this one actually got some use. You take the pod, you stick it in the machine – presto, coffee. No video screens, no touch pad, no wireless connectivity. Marcia loved it.

They'd recently finished an addition on the house – one extra bedroom, one bathroom, the kitchen knocked out a bit with a glassed-in nook. The kitchen nook offered oodles of morning sun and had thus become Marcia's favorite spot in the house. She took her coffee and the newspaper and set herself on the window seat, folding her feet beneath her.

A small slice of heaven.

She let herself read the paper and sip her coffee. In a few minutes she would have to check the schedule. Ryan, her third grader, had the early Hoops Basketball game at eight AM. Ted coached. His team was winless for the second straight season.

8

'Why do your teams never win?' Marcia had asked him.

'I draft the kids based on two criteria.'

'That being?'

'How nice the father – and how hot the mom.'

She had slapped at him playfully, and maybe Marcia would have been somewhat concerned if she hadn't seen the moms on the sideline and knew, for certain, that he had to be joking. Ted was actually a great coach, not in terms of strategy but in terms of handling the boys. They all loved him and his lack of competitiveness so that even the untalented players, the ones who were usually discouraged and quit during the season, showed up every week. Ted even took the Bon Jovi song and turned it around: 'You give losing a good name.' The kids would laugh and cheer every basket, and when you're in third grade that's how it should be.

Marcia's fourteen-year-old daughter, Patricia, had rehearsal for the freshman play, an abridged version of the musical *Les Misérables*. She had several small parts, but that didn't seem to affect the workload. And her oldest child, Haley, the high school senior, was running a 'captain's practice' for the girls' lacrosse team. Captain's practices were unofficial, a way to sneak in early practices under the guidelines issued by high school sports. In short, no coaches, nothing official, just a casual gathering, a glorified pickup game if you will, run by the captains.

Like most suburban parents, Marcia had a love–hate relationship with sports. She knew the relative long-term irrelevancy and yet still managed to get caught up in it.

A half hour of peace to start the day. That was all she needed.

She finished the first cup, pod-made herself a second,

picked up the 'Styles' section of the paper. The house remained silent. She padded upstairs and looked over her charges. Ryan slept on his side, his face conveniently facing the door so that his mother could notice the echo of his father.

Patricia's room was next. She too was still sleeping.

'Honey?'

Patricia stirred, might have made a noise. Her room, like Ryan's, looked as if someone had strategically placed sticks of dynamite in the drawers, blowing them open; some clothes sprawled dead on the floor, others lay wounded midway, clinging to the armoire like the fallen on a barricade before the French Revolution.

'Patricia? You have rehearsal in an hour.'

'I'm up,' she groaned in a voice that indicated she was anything but. Marcia moved to the next room, Haley's, and took a quick peek.

The bed was empty.

It was also made, but that was no surprise. Unlike her siblings' abodes, this one was neat, clean, anally organized. It could be a showroom in a furniture store. There were no clothes on this floor, every drawer fully closed. The trophies – and there were many – were perfectly aligned on four shelves. Ted had put in the fourth shelf just recently, after Haley's team had won the holiday tournament in Franklin Lakes. Haley had painstakingly divided up the trophies among the four shelves, not wanting the new one to have only one. Marcia was not sure why exactly. Part of it was because Haley didn't want it to look like she was just waiting for more to come, but more of it was her general abhorrence of disorganization. She kept each trophy equidistant from the others, moving them closer together as more came in, three inches separating them, then two, then one. Haley was about balance. She was the good girl, and while that was a wonderful thing – a girl who was ambitious, did her homework without being asked, never wanted others to think badly of her, was ridiculously competitive – there was a tightly wound aspect, a quasi-OCD quality, that worried Marcia.

Marcia wondered what time Haley had gotten home. Haley didn't have a curfew anymore because there had simply never been a need. She was responsible and a senior and never took advantage. Marcia had been tired and gone up to sleep at ten. Ted, in his constant state of 'randy,' soon followed her.

Marcia was about to move on, let it go, when something, she couldn't say what, made her decide to throw in a load of laundry. She started toward Haley's bathroom. The younger siblings, Ryan and Patricia, believed that 'hamper' was a euphemism for 'floor' or really 'anyplace but the hamper,' but Haley, of course, dutifully, religiously, and nightly put the clothes she'd worn that day into the hamper. And that was when Marcia started to feel a small rock form in her chest.

There were no clothes in the hamper.

The rock in her chest grew when Marcia checked Haley's toothbrush, then the sink and shower.

All bone-dry.

The rock grew when she called out to Ted, trying to keep the panic out of her voice. It grew when they drove to captain's practice and found out that Haley had never showed. It grew when she called Haley's friends while Ted sent out an e-mail blast – and no one knew where Haley was. It grew when they called the local police, who, despite Marcia's and Ted's protestations, believed that Haley was a runaway, a kid blowing off some steam. It grew when, forty-eight hours later, the FBI was brought

11

in. It grew when there was still no sign of Haley after a week.

It was as if the earth had swallowed her whole.

A month passed. Nothing. Then two. Still no word. And then finally, during the third month, word came – and the rock that had grown in Marcia's chest, the one that wouldn't let her breathe and kept her up nights, stopped growing.

PART ONE

Chapter 1

'Do you promise to tell the truth, the whole truth, and nothing but the truth, so help you God?'

Wendy Tynes said that she did, took the stand, looked out. She felt as though she were onstage, something she was somewhat used to, what with being a television news reporter and all, but this time it made her squirm. She looked out and saw the parents of Dan Mercer's victims. Four sets of them. They were there every day. At first they'd brought photographs of their children, the innocent ones of course, holding them up, but the judge had made them stop. Now they sat silently, watching, and somehow that was even more intimidating.

The seat was uncomfortable. Wendy adjusted her position, crossed then uncrossed her legs, and waited.

Flair Hickory, celebrity counsel for the defense, stood, and not for the first time, Wendy wondered how Dan Mercer had the money to afford him. Flair wore his customary gray suit with thick pink stripes, pink shirt, pink tie. He crossed the room in a way that might be modestly described as 'theatrical,' but it was more like something Liberace might have done if Liberace had the courage to be really flamboyant.

15

'Ms. Tynes,' he began with a welcoming smile. This was part of Flair's style. He was gay, yes, but he played it up in court like Harvey Fierstein in leather chaps doing Liza jazz hands. 'My name is Flair Hickory. Good morning to you.'

'Good morning,' she said.

'You work for a lurid tabloid TV program called *Caught in the Act,* is that correct?'

The prosecuting attorney, a man named Lee Portnoi, said, 'Objection. It's a TV program. There has been no testimony to support the allegation that the program is either lurid or tabloid.'

Flair smiled. 'Would you like me to present evidence, Mr. Portnoi?'

'That won't be necessary,' Judge Lori Howard said in a voice that already sounded weary. She turned to Wendy. 'Please answer the question.'

'I don't work for the show anymore,' Wendy said.

Flair pretended to be surprised by this. 'No? But you did?'

'Yes.'

'So what happened?'

'The show was taken off the air.'

'For low ratings?'

'No.'

'Really? Why then?'

Portnoi said, 'Your Honor, we all know the whys.'

Lori Howard nodded. 'Move along, Mr. Hickory.'

'You know my client, Dan Mercer?'

'Yes.'

'And you broke into his house, didn't you?'

Wendy tried to hold his gaze, tried not to look guilty, whatever the heck that meant. 'That's not really accurate, no.'

'It's not? Well, my dear, I want to make sure that we are as accurate as humanly possible, so let's back up, shall we?' He strolled across the courtroom as though it were a catwalk in Milan. He even had the audacity to smile at the families of the victims. Most made a point of not looking at Flair, but one of the fathers, Ed Grayson, stared daggers. Flair seemed unfazed.

'How did you first encounter my client?'

'He came on to me in a chat room.'

Flair's eyebrows went skyward. 'Really?' Like it was the most fascinating thing anyone had ever said. 'What sort of chat room?'

'A chat room frequented by children.'

'And you were in this chat room?'

'Yes.'

'You're not a child, Ms. Tynes. I mean, you may not be to my taste, but even I can see that you are a rather luscious female adult.'

'Objection!'

Judge Howard sighed. 'Mr. Hickory?'

Flair smiled, waved his apology. This was the kind of thing only Flair could get away with. 'Now, Ms. Tynes, when you were in this chat room, you were pretending to be an underage girl, isn't that correct?'

'Yes.'

'You then engaged in conversations designed to entice men into wanting sex with you, isn't that also correct?'

'No.'

'How's that?'

'I always let them make the first move.'

Flair shook his head and made a *tsk-tsk* noise. 'If I had a dollar for every time I said that . . .'

A smattering of laughter rippled through the court-room.

The judge said, 'We have the transcripts, Mr. Hickory. We can read them and decide for ourselves.'

'Excellent point, Your Honor, thank you.'

Wendy wondered why Dan Mercer wasn't here, but that was probably obvious. This was an evidentiary hearing, ergo, there was no requirement to attend. Flair Hickory was hoping to persuade the judge to throw out the horrible, sickening, stomach-turning material the police had found on Mercer's computer and hidden throughout his house. If he could pull this off – everyone agreed it was a long shot – the case against Dan Mercer would probably vanish and a sick predator would be out on the streets.

'By the way' – Flair spun back toward Wendy – 'how did you know it was my client on the other end of these online conversations?'

'I didn't at first.'

'Oh? With whom did you think you were conversing?'

'I didn't have a name. That's part of it. I just knew at that stage that it was some guy who was trolling for sex with underage girls.'

'How did you know that?'

'Excuse me?'

Flair made quote marks with his fingers. '"Trolling for sex with underage girls," as you put it. How did you know that was what the person on the other end of the conversation was doing?'

'Like the judge said, Mr. Hickory. Read the transcripts.'

'Oh, I have. And do you know what I concluded?'

That got Lee Portnoi up. 'Objection. We don't care what Mr. Hickory concluded. He isn't giving testimony here.'

'Sustained.'

18

Flair moved back to his desk and started checking through notes. Wendy looked over at the gallery. It helped her resolve. Those people out there had suffered greatly. Wendy was helping them find justice. Much as you could pretend to be jaded or claim that it was just her job, it meant a great deal to her – the good she had done. But when she met Ed Grayson's eyes, she saw something there that she didn't like. Something angry in his stare. Challenging maybe.

Flair put the papers down. 'Well, let me put it to you this way, Ms. Tynes: If a reasonable person were to read those transcripts, would they definitely, without a doubt, conclude that one of the participants was a luscious, thirty-six-year-old, female news reporter—'

'Objection!'

'—or might they conclude that it had been written by a thirteen-year-old girl?'

Wendy opened her mouth, closed it, waited. Judge Howard said, 'You can answer.'

'I was pretending to be a thirteen-year-old girl.'

'Ah,' Flair said, 'who hasn't?'

'Mr. Hickory,' the judge warned.

'Sorry, Your Honor, couldn't resist. Well, Ms. Tynes, if I were just reading those messages, I wouldn't know that you were pretending, would I? I would think you were indeed a thirteen-year-old girl.'

Lee Portnoi threw up his hands. 'Is there a question in there?'

'Here it comes, sweetie, so listen up: Were those messages written by a thirteen-year-old girl?'

'Asked and answered, Your Honor.'

Flair said, 'It's a simple yes or no. Was the author of those messages a thirteen-year-old girl?'

Judge Howard nodded that she could answer.

'No,' Wendy said.

'In fact, as you said, you were pretending to be a thirteen-year-old girl, correct?'

'Correct.'

'And for all you know, the person on the other end was pretending to be an adult male seeking underage sex. For all you knew, you were talking to an albino nun with herpes, correct?'

'Objection.'

Wendy met Flair's eyes. 'An albino nun with herpes didn't show up looking for sex at the child's house.'

But Flair would have none of it. 'What house would that be, Ms. Tynes? The house where you set up your cameras? Tell me, did an underage girl live there?'

Wendy said nothing.

'Please answer the question,' the judge said.

'No.'

'But you were there, correct? Perhaps whoever was on the other side of your online communications – and we really don't know who that was at this point – but perhaps that person had seen your news' – Flair said it as though the word 'news' itself tasted bad in his mouth – 'program and decided to play along so he could meet a luscious thirty-six-year-old TV star. Isn't that possible?'

Portnoi was up. 'Objection, Your Honor. These are matters for the jury.'

'True enough,' Flair said. 'We can argue the obvious case of false entrapment there.' He turned back to Wendy. 'Let's stay on the night of January seventeenth, shall we? What happened after you confronted my client at your sting house?'

Wendy waited for the DA to object to the word 'sting,' but he'd probably figured that he'd done enough. 'Your client ran away.'

'After you leapt out with your cameras and lights and microphones, correct?'

She again waited for an objection before answering, 'Yes.'

'Tell me, Ms. Tynes. Is that the way the majority of men who come to your sting house react?'

'No. Most of the time they stick around and try to explain.'

'And are most of those men guilty?'

'Yes.'

'Yet my client acted differently. Interesting.'

Portnoi was up again. 'To Mr. Hickory, it might be interesting. To the rest of us, his shenanigans—'

'Yes, fine, withdrawn,' Flair said as though he couldn't be bothered. 'Relax, Counselor, there's no jury here. Don't you trust our judge to see through my 'shenanigans' without your guidance?' He fixed a cuff link. 'So, Ms. Tynes, you turned on the cameras and lights and came jumping out with your microphone and Dan Mercer ran away, is that your testimony?'

'It is.'

'What did you do then?'

'I told my producers to follow him.'

Flair again feigned shock. 'Are your producers police officers, Ms. Tynes?'

'No.'

'Do you think private citizens should engage in chasing down suspects without the aid of police officers?'

'There was a police officer with us.'

'Oh, please.' Hickory looked skeptical. 'Your show is pure sensationalism. Tripe tabloid at its worst—'

Wendy interrupted him. 'We've met before, Mr. Hickory.'

That slowed him down. 'Have we?'

'When I was an assistant producer on *A Current Affair*. I booked you as an expert on the Robert Blake murder trial.'

He turned to the spectators and bowed deeply. 'So, ladies and gentlemen, we've established the fact that I'm a media whore. Touché.' Another smattering of laughter. 'Still, Ms. Tynes, are you trying to tell the court that law enforcement was in favor of your journalistic twaddle to the point of cooperation?'

'Objection.'

'I'll allow it.'

'But, Your Honor—'

'Overruled. Sit down, Mr. Portnoi.'

Wendy said, 'We had a relationship with the police and the DA's office. It was important for us to stay on the correct side of the law.'

'I see. You were working together with law enforcement then, weren't you?'

'Not really, no.'

'Well, which is it, Ms. Tynes? Did you work this entire sting on your own without the knowledge and co-operation of law enforcement?'

'No.'

'Okay, fine. Did you contact the police department and DA's office before the night of January seventeenth in regard to my client?'

'We contacted the prosecutor's office, yes.'

'Wonderful, thank you. Now, you said that you had your producers start chasing my client, is that correct?'

'That's not how she worded it,' Portnoi said. 'She said "follow."'

Flair looked at Portnoi as though he had never seen a more annoying gnat. 'Yes, fine, whatever – chase, follow, we can discuss the difference another time.

22

When my client ran, Ms. Tynes, where did you go?'

'To his residence.'

'Why?'

'I figured that at some point, Dan Mercer might show up there.'

'So you waited for him there, at his residence?'

'Yes.'

'Did you stay outside his residence while waiting?'

Wendy squirmed. They were coming to it now. She looked out over the faces, locked on the eyes of Ed Grayson, whose nine-year-old son was an early victim of Dan Mercer. She could feel the weight of his stare as she said, 'I saw a light on.'

'In Dan Mercer's house?'

'Yes.'

'How odd,' Flair said, his voice set on full sarcasm. 'I never, not once ever, heard of anyone ever leaving a light on when they weren't home.'

'Objection!'

Judge Howard sighed. 'Mr. Hickory.'

Flair kept his eyes on Wendy. 'So what did you do, Ms. Tynes?'

'I knocked on the door.'

'Did my client answer?'

'No.'

'Did anyone answer?'

'No.'

'So what did you do next, Ms. Tynes?'

Wendy tried to stay very still when she said the next part. 'I thought I might have seen movement through the window.'

'You thought you might have seen movement,' Flair repeated. 'My, my, could you make your wording any more vague?'

23

'Objection!'

'Withdrawn. So what did you do then?'

'I tried the knob. The door was unlocked. I opened it.'

'Really? Why would you do that?'

'I was concerned.'

'Concerned about what?'

'There have been cases in which pedophiles have done themselves harm after being caught.'

'Is that a fact? So you were worried that your entrapment might cause my client to attempt suicide?'

'Something like that, yes.'

Flair put his hand to his chest. 'I'm touched.'

'Your Honor!' Portnoi shouted.

Flair waved him off again. 'So you wanted to save my client?'

'If that was the case, yes, I wanted to stop him.'

'On the air, you've used words like "pervert," "sicko," "depraved," "monstrous," and "scum" to describe those you entrap, is that correct?'

'Yes.'

'Yet your testimony today is that you were willing to break into his house – in truth, break the law – to save my client's life?'

'I guess you could say that.'

His voice not only dripped sarcasm but seemed to have spent days marinated in it: 'How noble.'

'Objection!'

'I wasn't being noble,' Wendy said. 'I prefer to see these men brought to justice, to give the families closure. Suicide is an easy way out.'

'I see. So what happened when you broke into my client's home?'

'Objection,' Portnoi said. 'Ms. Tynes said the door was unlocked—'

24

'Yes, fine, entered, broke in, whatever pleases Mr. Man over there,' Flair said, fists on his hips. 'Just stop interrupting. What happened, Ms. Tynes, after you *entered*' – again stressing the word beyond all measure – 'my client's home?'

'Nothing.'

'My client wasn't trying to harm himself?'

'No.'

'What was he doing?'

'He wasn't there.'

'Was anybody, in fact, inside?'

'No.'

'And that "movement" you maybe saw?'

'I don't know.'

Flair nodded, strolled away. 'You've testified that you drove to my client's house almost immediately after he ran out with your producer chasing him. Did you really think he'd have time to go back home and set up a suicide?'

'He would know the fastest route and he had a head start. Yes, I thought there was time.'

'I see. But you were wrong, weren't you?'

'About what?'

'My client didn't go straight home, did he?'

'He did not, that's correct.'

'But you did go into Mr. Mercer's home – before he or the police arrived, correct?'

'Just for a brief moment.'

'How long is a brief moment?'

'I'm not sure.'

'Well, you had to check every room, right? To make sure he wasn't swinging from a beam by his belt or something, correct?'

'I only checked the room with the light on. The kitchen.'

'Which meant you had to, at the very least, cross through

the living room. Tell me, Ms. Tynes, what did you do after you discovered that my client wasn't at home?'

'I went back outside and waited.'

'Waited for what?'

'The police to show.'

'Did they?'

'Yes.'

'And they had a warrant to search my client's home, correct?'

'Yes.'

'And while I realize that your intentions were noble in breaking into my client's home, wasn't there a small part of you that worried about how your entrapment case would hold up?'

'No.'

'Since that January seventeenth show, you've done an extensive investigation into my client's past. Other than what was found at his home that night by the police, have you found any other solid evidence of illegal activity?'

'Not yet.'

'I will take that as a no,' Flair said. 'In short, without the evidence found during the search by the police, you'd have nothing tying my client to anything illegal, isn't that correct?'

'He showed up at the house that night.'

'The sting house where no underage girl resided. So really, Ms. Tynes, the case – and your, uh, reputation – is all about the material found in my client's home. Without it, you have nothing. In short, you had the means and a compelling reason for planting that evidence, did you not?'

Lee Portnoi was up on that one. 'Your Honor, this is ridiculous. This argument is for a jury to decide.'

'Ms. Tynes admitted entering the house illegally without a warrant,' Flair said.

'Fine,' Portnoi said, 'then charge her with the crime of breaking and entering, if you think you can prove it. And if Mr. Hickory wants to present absurd theories about albino nuns or planted evidence, that is his right too – during the trial. To a jury in a court of law. And then I can present evidence to show how absurd his theories are. That's why we have courtrooms and trials. Ms. Tynes is a private citizen – and a private citizen is not held to the same standard as an officer of the court. You can't throw the computer and pictures out, Your Honor. They were found during a legal search with a signed warrant. Some of the sickening photographs were hidden in the garage and behind a bookshelf – and there was no way Ms. Tynes would have planted those in the brief moments or even minutes she may have entered the dwelling.'

Flair shook his head. 'Wendy Tynes broke into the home for, at best, specious reasons. A light on? Movement? Please. She also had a compelling motive for planting evidence and the means – and she had knowledge that Dan Mercer's house would be searched soon. It is worse than the fruits from a poisonous tree. Any evidence found in the house has to be thrown out.

'Wendy Tynes is a private citizen.'

'That doesn't give her carte blanche here. She could have easily planted that laptop and those photographs.'

'Which is an argument you can make to the jury.'

'Your Honor, the material found is absurdly prejudicial. By her own testimony Ms. Tynes is clearly more than a private citizen here. I asked her several times about her relationship with the prosecutor's office. By her own admission, she was their agent.'

Lee Portnoi turned red on that one. 'That's ridiculous,

Your Honor. Is every reporter working on a crime story now considered an agent of the law?'

'By her own admission, Wendy Tynes worked with and in close proximity to your office, Mr. Portnoi. I can have the stenographer read it back, the part about having an officer on the scene and being in touch with the prosecutor's office.'

'That doesn't make her an officer.'

'That's just semantics, and Mr. Portnoi knows it. His office would have had no case against my client without Wendy Tynes. Their entire case – all the crimes my client is now accused of – stems from Ms. Tynes's attempt at entrapment. Without her involvement, no warrant would have been issued at all.'

Portnoi crossed the room. 'Your Honor, Ms. Tynes may have originally presented the case to our office, but by those standards, every witness or complaining party who comes forward would be considered an agent—'

'I've heard enough,' Judge Howard said. She slammed her gavel and rose. 'You'll have my ruling by the morning.'

Chapter 2

'Well,' Wendy said to Portnoi in the corridor, 'that sucked.'

'The judge won't throw it out.'

Wendy was not convinced.

'It's a good thing in a way,' he went on.

'How do you figure?'

'The case is too high-profile for the evidence to get tossed out,' Portnoi said, gesturing toward opposing counsel. 'All Flair did in there was show us his trial strategy.'

Up ahead of them, Jenna Wheeler, Dan Mercer's ex-wife, was taking questions from a rival TV reporter. Even as the evidence mounted against Dan, Jenna had remained a staunch supporter of her ex, claiming that the charges against him had to be bogus. This position, both admirable and naïve in Wendy's view, had made Jenna something of a pariah in town.

Still farther ahead, Flair Hickory held court with several reporters. They loved him, of course – so had Wendy when she'd been covering his trials. He took flamboyant and brought it to a whole new level. But now, on the other side of those questions, she could truly see how flamboyance could be close bedfellows with ruthlessness.

Wendy frowned. 'Flair Hickory doesn't hit me as being anyone's fool.'

Flair got a laugh from the fawning press, slapped a few backs, and started to walk away. When Flair was finally alone, Wendy was surprised to see Ed Grayson approach him.

'Uh-oh,' she said.

'What?'

Wendy gestured with her chin. Portnoi followed with his eyes. Grayson, a big man with close-cropped gray hair, stood close to Flair Hickory. The two men stared each other down. Grayson kept inching closer, moving into Flair's space. But Flair held his ground.

Portnoi took a few steps toward them. 'Mr. Grayson?'

Their faces were inches apart. Grayson swiveled his head in the direction of the voice. He stared at Portnoi.

'Is everything okay?' Portnoi asked.

'Fine,' Grayson said.

'Mr. Hickory?'

'We're peachy, Counselor. Just having a friendly chat.'

Grayson's eyes locked on Wendy's, and again she didn't like what she saw. Hickory said, 'Well, if we're done here, Mr. Grayson . . .'

Grayson said nothing. Hickory turned and left. Grayson came toward Portnoi and Wendy.

'Is there anything I can do for you?' Portnoi asked.

'No.'

'May I ask what you were talking to Mr. Hickory about?'

'You can ask.' Grayson looked at Wendy. 'Do you think the judge bought your story, Ms. Tynes?'

'It wasn't a story,' she said.

'But it wasn't exactly the truth either, was it?'

Ed Grayson turned and walked away.

Wendy said, 'What the hell was that?'

'Got no idea,' Portnoi said. 'But don't worry about

him. Or Flair either. He's good, but he won't win this round. Go home, have a drink, it'll be fine.'

Wendy did not go home. She headed to her TV news studio in Secaucus, New Jersey, overlooking the Meadowlands Sports Complex. The view was never soothing. It was a marsh, swampland, groaning under the weight of constant construction. She checked her e-mail and saw a message from her boss, executive producer Vic Garrett. The message, maybe the longest Vic had ever sent by e-mail, read: 'SEE ME NOW.'

It was three thirty PM. Her son, Charlie, a senior at Kasselton High School, should have been home by now. She called his cell because he never picked up the home phone. Charlie answered on the fourth ring with his customary greeting: 'What?'

'Are you home?' she asked her son.

'Yeah.'

'What are you doing?'

'Nothing.'

'Do you have homework?'

'A little.'

'Did you do it yet?'

'I will.'

'Why not do it now?'

'It's just a little. It'll take me ten minutes tops.'

'That's my point. If it's only a little, just do it and get it over with.'

'I'll do it later.'

'But what are you doing now?'

'Nothing.'

'So why wait? Why not just do your homework now?'

New day, same conversation. Charlie finally said that he would get to it 'in a minute,' which was shorthand for 'If I say in a minute, maybe you'll stop nagging me.'

31

'I'll probably be home about seven,' Wendy said. 'You want me to pick up Chinese?'

'Bamboo House,' he said.

'Okay. Feed Jersey at four.'

Jersey was their dog.

'Okay.'

'Don't forget.'

'Uh-huh.'

'And do your homework?'

'Bye.'

Click.

She took a deep breath. Charlie was seventeen now, a senior and a total pain in the ass. They had ended the hunt for college, a suburban activity parents engage in with a ruthlessness that would make a third-world despot blush, with an acceptance to Franklin & Marshall in Lancaster, Pennsylvania. Like all teenagers, Charlie was scared and nervous about this huge change in his life, but not nearly so much as his mother. Charlie, her beautiful, moody, pain-in-the-ass of a son, was all she had. It had been the two of them alone for twelve years now, single mom and only child rattling around in the great white suburbs. The years flew by, of course, as they always do with children. Wendy didn't want to let Charlie go. She looked at him every night and saw pain-in-the-ass perfection and, as she had since he was four, wished, Please just let me freeze him here, this age, not one day older or younger, let me freeze my beautiful son here and now and keep him with me just a few days longer.

Because soon she'd be alone.

Another e-mail popped up on her computer screen. Again it was from her boss, Vic Garrett: 'WHAT PART OF "SEE ME NOW" DID I LEAVE OPEN TO INTERPRETATION?'

She hit reply and typed: 'Coming.'

Since Vic's office was across the hall, this whole communication seemed rather pointless and irritating, but such is the world we live in. She and Charlie often texted each other within their own home. Too tired to shout, she'd text: 'Time for bed' or 'Let Jersey out' or the always popular 'Enough on the computer, read a book.'

Wendy had been a nineteen-year-old sophomore at Tufts University when she got pregnant. She had gone to a campus party and after having too much to drink, she hooked up with John Morrow, a jock of all things, starting quarterback, and if you looked him up in the Wendy Tynes dictionary, the pure definition of 'not her type.' Wendy saw herself as a campus liberal, an underground journalist, wearing tourniquet-tight black, listening exclusively to alt rock, frequenting slam poetry readings and Cindy Sherman exhibits. But the heart doesn't know from alt rock and slam poetry and exhibits. She ended up actually liking the gorgeous jock. Go figure. It was no big deal at first. They had indeed hooked up and then just started hanging out together, not really dating, not really not dating. This had been going on for maybe a month when Wendy realized that she was pregnant.

Being a thoroughly modern woman, what happened now, Wendy had been told her entire life, would be her decision and her decision alone. With two and a half years of college left and a budding career in journalism on the way, the timing, of course, could not have been worse, but that made the answer all the more clear. She called John on the phone and said, 'We need to talk.' He came over to her cramped room and she asked him to sit down. John took the beanbag chair, which looked so comical, this six-foot-five-inch hunk trying to get, if not comfortable, at least balanced. Knowing from her tone that this was something serious, John tried to keep his face solemn while holding himself steady, making him look like a little boy playing grown-up.

'I'm pregnant,' Wendy told him, beginning the speech she'd been rehearsing in her head for the past two days. 'What happens now will be my decision, and I hope you will honor that.'

Wendy continued, pacing the small room, not looking at him, keeping her voice as matter-of-fact as possible. She even closed her prepared statement by thanking him for coming today and wishing him well. Then she finally risked a glance in his direction.

John Morrow just looked up at her with tears in the bluest eyes she had ever seen and said, 'But I love you, Wendy.'

She had wanted to laugh and instead she started to cry and John slid off that damned beanbag chair and onto his knees and proposed, right there and then, with Wendy laughing and crying, and despite pretty much everyone's misgivings, they got married. No one gave them a chance, but the next few years had been bliss. John Morrow was sweet and caring and loving and gorgeous and funny and smart and attentive. He was her soul mate with all that entailed. Charlie was born during their junior year at Tufts. Two years later, John and Wendy scraped up enough money to put a down payment on a small starter house on a busy road in Kasselton. Wendy got a job at a local television station. John worked toward his Ph.D. in psychology. They were on their way.

And then, in what seemed like a finger snap, John died. Now the small starter house held just Wendy and Charlie and a great big hole to match the one in her heart.

She knocked on Vic's door and leaned her head in. 'You rang?'

'Heard you got your ass reamed in court,' her boss said.

'Support,' Wendy said. 'That's why I work here. The support I get.'

'You want support,' Vic said, 'buy a bra.'

Wendy frowned. 'You realize that made no sense.'

'Yeah, I know. I got your memo – check that, your many and repetitious memos – complaining about your assignments.'

'What assignments? In the past two weeks, you've had me cover the opening of an herbal tea store and a fashion show featuring men's scarves. Just put me on something quasi-real again.'

'Wait.' Vic put a hand to his ear, as though straining to hear. He was a small man except for the enormous bowling-ball gut. His face might be called 'ferretlike,' if the ferret was really ugly.

'What?' she said.

'Is this the part where you rail against the injustice of being a hottie in a male-dominated profession and say that I treat you like nothing more than eye candy?'

'Will railing help me get better assignments?'

'No,' he said. 'But you know what might?'

'Showing more cleavage on air?'

'I like the way you're thinking, but no, not today. Today the answer is, Dan Mercer's conviction. You need to end up the hero who nailed a sick pedophile rather than the overreaching reporter who helped free him.'

'Helped free him?'

Vic shrugged.

'The police wouldn't even know about Dan Mercer if it wasn't for me.'

Vic lifted the air violin to his shoulder, closed his eyes, began to play.

35

'Don't be an ass,' she said.

'Should I call in a few of your colleagues for a group hug? Maybe join hands for a rousing rendition of "Kumbaya"?'

'Maybe later, after your circle jerk.'

'Ouch.'

'Does anybody know where Dan Mercer is hiding?' she asked.

'Nope. No one has seen him for two weeks.'

Wendy wasn't sure what to make of that. She knew that Dan had moved away because of death threats, but it seemed out of character not to show in court today. She was about to ask a follow-up when Vic's intercom buzzed.

He held up a finger to quiet her and pressed the intercom: 'What?'

The receptionist's voice was low. 'Marcia McWaid is here to see you.'

That silenced them. Marcia McWaid lived in Wendy's town, less than a mile from her. Three months ago her teenage daughter Haley – a schoolmate of Charlie's – had purportedly sneaked out of her bedroom window and never returned.

'Something new in her daughter's case?' Wendy asked.

Vic shook his head. 'Just the opposite,' he said, which, of course, was much worse. For two, maybe three weeks, Haley McWaid's disappearance had been a huge story – teenage abduction? runaway? – complete with NEWS-FLASH and scrolls-across-the-screen and bottom-feeding 'experts' reconstructing what might have happened to her. But no story, even the most sensational, can survive without new food. Lord knows the networks tried. They had touched on every rumor from white slavery to devil worship, but in this business 'no news' was truly 'bad

36

news.' It was pathetic, our short attention span, and you could blame the news media, but the audience dictated what stayed on the air. If people watch the story, it stays on. If they don't, the networks go searching for the new shiny toy to catch the public's fickle eye.

'Do you want me to talk to her?' Wendy asked.

'No, I'll do it. It's why I get the big bucks.'

Vic shooed her away. Wendy headed down the end of the corridor. She turned in time to see Marcia McWaid in front of Vic's door. Wendy didn't know Marcia, but she'd seen her in town a few times, the way you do, at the Starbucks or school car-pickup lane or local video store. It would be a cliché to say the perky mom who always seemed to have a kid in tow now looked ten years older. Marcia didn't. She was still an attractive enough woman, still looked her age, but it was as though every movement had slowed down, as if even the muscles that controlled facial expression were coated in molasses. Marcia McWaid turned and met Wendy's eye. Wendy nodded, tried to give a half-smile. Marcia turned away and entered Vic's office.

Wendy went back to her desk and picked up her phone. She thought about Marcia McWaid, that ideal mother with the nice husband and beautiful family and how quickly and easily that had been snatched away, how quickly and easily any of it could be snatched away. She dialed Charlie's phone.

'What?'

The impatient tone actually comforted her. 'Did you do your homework yet?'

'In a minute.'

'Okay,' Wendy said. 'You still want Bamboo House tonight?'

'Didn't we already have this discussion?'

37

They hung up. Wendy sat back and threw her feet up on the desk. She craned her neck and checked out the butt-ugly view from her window. Her phone rang again.

'Hello?'

'Wendy Tynes?'

Her feet fell back to the floor when she heard the voice. 'Yes?'

'This is Dan Mercer. I need to see you.'

Chapter 3

For a moment, Wendy said nothing.

'I need to see you,' Dan Mercer said again.

'Aren't I a little mature for you, Dan? I mean, I'm old enough to have a menstrual cycle and breasts.'

She thought that she could hear a sigh.

'You're very cynical, Wendy.'

'What do you want?'

'There are things you need to know,' he said.

'Like?'

'Like nothing here is as it seems.'

'You're a sick, twisted, depraved perv who has a genius for a lawyer. That's how it seems.'

But even as she said it, there was just the slightest hesitation in her voice. Was it enough to warrant reasonable doubt? She didn't think so. Evidence doesn't lie. She had learned that often enough both personally and professionally. The truth was, her so-called woman's intuition was usually crap.

'Wendy?'

She said nothing.

'I was set up.'

'Uh-huh. That's a new one, Dan. Let me jot that down and grab my producer, have him put one of those news scrolls on the bottom of the screen. "Newsflash: Sicko Says He Was Set Up."'

Silence. For a moment she feared that she'd lost him, that he had hung up. Stupid to get all emotional. Stay calm. Talk to him. Make friends. Be nice. Get information. Trap him maybe.

'Dan?'

'This was a mistake.'

'I'm listening. You said something about being set up?'

'I better go.'

She wanted to protest, scold herself for going too far with the sarcasm, but something about this felt like classic manipulation. She had danced his tangos before, several times, in fact, starting with the first time she tried to interview him last year for a piece about his work at the shelter, almost a year before he'd been caught on camera. She didn't want to cave, but she didn't want to let him go either.

'You were the one who called me,' she said.

'I know.'

'So I'm willing to listen.'

'Meet me. Alone.'

'I'm not crazy about that idea.'

'Then forget it.'

'Fine, Dan, have it your way. See you in court.'

Silence.

'Dan?'

His voice was a whisper that chilled her. 'You don't have a clue, do you, Wendy?'

'A clue about what?'

She heard a noise that might have been a sob, might have been a laugh. Hard to say over the phone. She gripped the receiver tighter and waited.

'If you want to meet me,' he said, 'I'll e-mail you the directions. Two PM tomorrow. Come alone. If you choose not to show, well, it was nice knowing you.'

And then he hung up.

Vic's office door was open. She took a quick peek and saw him on the phone. He held up a finger to give him a second, said a gruff good-bye to whomever was on the phone, and hung up.

'I just heard from Dan Mercer,' she said.

'He called you?'

'Yes.'

'When?'

'Just now.'

Vic leaned back, put his hands on his paunch. 'So he told you?'

'He said he was set up and wanted to meet.' She saw the look on his face. 'Why? What else is there?'

Vic sighed. 'Sit down.'

'Uh-oh,' Wendy said.

'Yeah, uh-oh.'

She sat.

'The judge handed down her ruling. All evidence found in the home is thrown out, and because of the prejudicial nature of the press and our TV airing, she threw out all charges.'

Wendy felt her heart sink. 'Please tell me you're joking.'

Vic said nothing. Wendy closed her eyes, felt the world closing in around her. She got it now, how Dan had known that she'd definitely show up at the meet.

'So now what?' she asked.

Vic just looked at her.

'I'm fired?'

'Yep.'

'Just like that?'

'Pretty much, yeah. Bad economy. The suits upstairs are laying people off anyway.' He shrugged. 'Who better to ax?'

'I can think of many.'

'Me too, but they're not damaged goods. Sorry, sweetie, that's just the way it is. HR will handle severance. You need to pack your stuff today. They don't want you back in the building.'

Wendy felt numb. She teetered to a standing position. 'Did you at least fight for me?'

'I only fight when I have a chance to win. Otherwise what's the point?'

Wendy waited. Vic looked down and pretended to be busy.

Without looking up, Vic said, 'You expecting a tender moment here?'

'No,' Wendy said. Then: 'Maybe.'

'Are you going to meet with Mercer?' Vic asked.

She turned back toward him. 'Yes.'

'You'll take precautions?'

She forced up a smile. 'Man, I just had a flashback to something my mom said when I was starting college.'

'And from what I know, you didn't listen.'

'True.'

'Officially, of course, you don't work here and have no standing. I should advise you to keep a safe distance from Dan Mercer.'

'And unofficially?'

'If you could figure a way to nail him, well, heroes are easier to rehire than goats.'

*

The house was silent when Wendy got home, but that meant nothing. In her youth, her parents would know she was home because her music would be blaring from the ghetto box in her room. Nowadays kids used headphones or earbuds or whatever they called them 24/7. She was fairly confident that was where Charlie was right now, on the computer, earbuds firmly in place. The house could catch fire, and he would have no idea.

Despite this, Wendy shouted at the top of her lungs, 'Charlie!'

There was no answer. There hadn't been an answer in at least three years.

Wendy poured herself a drink – pomegranate vodka with a splash of lime – and collapsed onto the worn club chair. The chair had been John's favorite, and yeah, that was probably creepy, keeping the chair here and collapsing in it with a drink at the end of the day, but she found it comforting, so tough.

How the hell, Wendy had wondered before today, would she pay for Charlie's tuition on her current salary? Now that wasn't a concern because there was simply no way. She took another sip, glanced out the window, pondered where she would go from here. Nobody was hiring and as Vic had so delicately pointed out, she was damaged goods. She thought about what other kind of job she could do but realized that she had no other marketable skills. She was sloppy, disorganized, ornery, not a team player. If she took home a work report card, it would read, 'Does not play well with others.' That worked as a reporter going after a story. It worked almost nowhere else.

She checked the mail and saw the third letter from Ariana Nasbro and felt a sharp pang in her gut. Her hands began to shake. No need to open the letter. She had read the first one two months ago and nearly vomited. With two fingers, she held the envelope as though it had a stench, which it did when you thought about it, walked into the kitchen, and stuck it into the bottom of the wastebasket.

Thank God, Charlie never checked the mail. He knew who Ariana Nasbro was, of course. Twelve years ago, Ariana Nasbro had murdered Charlie's father.

She headed up the stairs and knocked on Charlie's door. Naturally there was no reply so she opened it.

He looked up, annoyed, pulled off the headphones. 'What?'

'Did you do your homework?'

'Just about to.'

He could see that she was put out, so he flashed the smile, so like his father's that it stabbed every single time. She was about to launch into him again, about how she'd asked him to do homework first, but really, who cared? It was pointless to get caught up in all that minutiae when her time with him was flying by so fast and soon he'd be gone.

'Did you feed Jersey?' she asked.

'Uh . . .'

She rolled her eyes. 'Never mind, I'll do it.'

'Mom?'

'Yeah?'

'Did you pick up the food at Bamboo House?'

Dinner. She had forgotten.

Charlie rolled his eyes, mimicking her.

'Don't be a smart-ass.' She had decided earlier not to tell him her bad news yet, to wait for the right time, but she still found herself saying, 'I got fired today.'

Charlie just looked at her.

'Did you hear me?'

'Yeah,' he said. 'Sucks.'

'Yep.'

'You want me to pick up dinner?'

'Sure.'

'Uh, you still pay for it, right?'

'For now, yeah. I think I can handle that.'

Chapter 4

Marcia and Ted McWaid arrived at the high school auditorium at six PM. Because the old cliché that 'life goes on' could not have been more true, tonight, despite the fact that Haley had now been missing ninety-three days, was opening night of the Kasselton High School production of *Les Misérables,* featuring their second child, Patricia, in the roles of Onlooker #4, Student #6, and the always-coveted role of Prostitute #2. When Ted first heard about that, in the life they'd known before Haley had vanished, he had made constant jokes about this, how proud he was to tell his friends that his fourteen-year-old daughter would be Prostitute #2. Those days were long gone, a world and time lived by other people in another land.

A hush fell over the auditorium when they entered. No one knew how to act around them. Marcia got it but was beyond caring.

'I need some water,' she said.

Ted nodded. 'I'll save us seats.'

She headed down the corridor, stopped briefly at the fountain, then continued. At the next turn, she made a left. Down the hall, a janitor worked a mop. He wore earphones, his head gently bobbing to a song only he could hear; if he noticed her, nothing on his face showed it.

Marcia started up the stairs to the second floor. The lights were dimmer on this level. Her footsteps clacked and echoed against the stillness of a building that during the day knew so much life and energy. There is no place more surreal, more hollow and empty, than a school corridor at night.

Marcia looked over her shoulder, but she was alone. She hurried her step because she had a destination in mind.

Kasselton High was big, nearly two thousand kids in four grades. The building was on four levels, and like so many high schools from towns with constantly growing populations, it ended up being more a series of pieced-together add-ons than anything resembling a cohesive structure. The later additions to the once-lovely original brick showed that the administrators had been more interested in substance over style. The configuration was a mishmash, looking more like something a child had made by mixing wooden blocks, LEGOs, and Lincoln logs.

Last night, in the scary quiet of the McWaid home, her wonderful husband, Ted, had laughed, really laughed, for the first time in ninety-three days. How obscene the sound was. Ted stopped almost right away, cut himself off in a choking way that became a sob. Marcia wanted to reach out, do something to comfort this tortured man that she so loved. But she simply couldn't.

Her other two children, Patricia and Ryan, were handling Haley's disappearance okay on the outside, but kids adapt more easily than adults. Marcia tried to concentrate on them and shower them with attention and comfort, but again she simply couldn't. Some probably figured that she hurt too much. That was part of it, but there was more. She neglected Patricia and Ryan because all she worried about right now, her sole focus, was on Haley – bringing her back home. Then, after that, she would make it up to her other children.

Marcia's own sister, Merilee, the popular know-it-all from Great Neck, had the nerve to say, 'You need to focus on your husband and other children and stop wallowing,' and when she said that word – 'wallowing'! – Marcia wanted so much to punch Merilee in the face and tell her to worry about her own damn family and that her son Greg was taking drugs and her husband, Hal, was probably having an affair and to shut the hell up. Patricia and Ryan would hopefully get through this, Merilee – and you know what? Their best chance at being okay wouldn't be by having a mother who made sure that Ryan's lacrosse stick pocket was properly broken in or that Patricia's costume was the right shade of gray. No, the thing that would make them fine and whole, the only thing, would be to bring their older sister back home.

When that happened, and only when that happened, would the rest of them have a chance to survive.

But the sad truth was, it wasn't as though Marcia spent all day looking for Haley. She tried, but a horrible exhaustion kept creeping in. Marcia wanted to stay in bed in the morning. Her limbs felt heavy. Even now, making this odd pilgrimage down the corridor was difficult for her.

Ninety-three days.

Up ahead Marcia could start making out Haley's locker. A few days after the disappearance, some friends started decorating the metallic front like one of those curbside shrines you see when someone dies in a car crash. There were photos and wilting flowers and crosses and notes. 'Come home, Haley!' 'We miss you!' 'We will wait for you.' 'We love you!'

Marcia stopped and stared. She reached out and touched the combination lock, thinking about how many times Haley must have done the same thing, getting her books out, dumping her backpack onto the bottom, hanging up her coat, chatting with a friend, discussing lacrosse or maybe what boy she had a crush on.

A noise came from down the corridor. She turned and saw the principal's office door open. Pete Zecher, the high school principal, stepped out with what Marcia assumed was a set of parents. She didn't know either of them. No one spoke. Pete Zecher stuck out his hand, but neither parent took it. They turned and moved quickly toward the stairs. Pete Zecher watched them disappear, shook his head, and turned toward the locker.

He spotted her. 'Marcia?'

'Hi, Pete.'

Pete Zecher was a good principal, wonderfully accessible and willing to break the rules or piss off a teacher if it was best for the kid. Pete had grown up here in Kasselton, gone to this very high school, and his lifelong dream had been achieved when he landed the principal's job here.

He started toward her. 'Am I intruding?'

'Not at all.' Marcia forced up a smile. 'I just wanted to escape the stares for a bit.'

'I saw the dress rehearsal,' Pete said. 'Patricia is really great.'

'That's nice to hear.'

He nodded. They both looked at the locker. Marcia saw a decal with the words 'Kasselton Lacrosse' and two crossed sticks. She had one on her car's back window.

'So what was up with those two parents?' she asked.

Pete gave her a small smile. 'Confidential.'

'Oh.'

'But I could tell you a hypothetical.'

She waited.

'When you were in high school, did you ever drink alcohol?' he asked.

'I was kind of a good girl,' Marcia said, almost adding, 'like Haley.' 'But yes, we used to sneak beers.'

'How did you get them?'

'The beers? My neighbor had an uncle who owned a liquor store. How about you?'

'I had a mature-looking friend named Michael Wind,' Pete said. 'You know the type – shaving when he was in sixth grade. He'd buy the booze. That wouldn't work now. Everyone gets carded.'

'So what does that have to do with our hypothetical couple?'

'People think that the way kids get alcohol nowadays is with fake IDs. There are some examples of that, but in my years I've confiscated less than five. And yet drinking is a bigger problem now than ever.'

'So how do the kids get it?'

Pete looked toward where the couple had just been standing. 'From the parents.'

'Kids sneaking into their liquor cabinet?'

'I wish. The couple I was just talking to – hypothetically – were the Milners. Nice people. He sells insurance in the city. She has a boutique in Glen Rock. They have four kids, two in the high school. Their oldest is on the baseball team.'

'So?'

'So on Friday night these two nice, caring parents bought a keg and held a party for the baseball team in their basement. Two of the boys got drunk and egged another kid's house. One got so wasted he almost had to have his stomach pumped.'

'Wait. The parents bought the keg?'

Pete nodded.

'And that was what you were meeting about?'

'Yes.'

'What did they say in their defense?'

'They offered up the most common excuse I get: Hey, kids are going to drink anyway – might as well be sure they do it in a safe environment. The Milners don't want the kids going into New York City or someplace else unsafe, maybe driving after they drink, whatever. So they let the team get bombed in their basement, contained, where they can't get in too much trouble.'

'It makes sense on some level.'

'Would you do it?' he asked.

Marcia thought about it. 'No. But last year we took Haley and a friend of hers to Tuscany. We let them have wine at the vineyards. Was that wrong?'

'It's not against the law in Italy.'

'That seems a fine line, Pete.'

'So you don't think what these parents did was wrong?'

'I think they were dead wrong,' Marcia said. 'And their excuse also rings a little hollow – buying kids booze? That's about more than keeping their children safe. That's about wanting to be the cool, hip parents. Wanting to be the kid's friend first and parent second.'

'I agree.'

'But then again,' Marcia said, turning back to the locker, 'who am I to be giving parenting advice?'

Silence.

'Pete?'

'Yes?'

'What's the gossip?'

'I'm not sure I know what you mean.'

'Yeah, you do. When you guys talk about it – teachers,

students, whatever – do they think Haley was abducted or do they think she ran away?'

More silence. She could see he was thinking.

'No filter, Pete. And please don't humor me.'

'I won't.'

'Well?'

'I have nothing but my gut to go on.'

'I understand.'

Posters were up in the corridors now. The prom wasn't far away. Graduation too. Pete Zecher's eyes traveled back to Haley's locker. Marcia followed his gaze and spotted a photograph that made her stop. Her whole family minus her – Ted, Haley, Patricia, and Ryan – stood with Mickey Mouse at Disney World. Marcia had taken the photo with Haley's iPhone in its pink case with the purple flower decal. The vacation had taken place three weeks before Haley vanished. The police had given the trip a cursory glance, wondering whether somehow someone she had met on that trip could have followed Haley home, but that thread had gone nowhere. But Marcia remembered how happy Haley was down there, no pressure, every person just a happy kid for a few days. The picture had been a spontaneous thing. The line for Mickey was usually half an hour long, little kids queuing up with 'autograph' books for Mickey to stamp, but Haley noticed that there was no line for this particular Mickey in Epcot Center. Her face split into a smile and Haley grabbed her siblings and said, 'Come on! Let's do a quick pic!' Marcia insisted on being the photographer, and she remembered the roar of emotion she felt as her entire family, her whole world, gathered around Mickey in happy harmony. She looked at the picture now, remembered that small perfect moment, and stared at Haley's heart-splitting smile.

'You think you know a kid,' Pete Zecher said. 'But they all have secrets.'

'Even Haley?'

Pete spread his hands. 'Look down that row of lockers. I know this sounds obvious, but every one belongs to a kid with dreams and expectations, going through a hard, crazy time. Adolescence is a war, filled with pressures both imagined and real. Social, academic, athletic – and all the while you're changing and your hormones are out of whack. All those lockers, all those troubled individuals trapped for seven hours a day in this place. My background is science and whenever I'm here, I imagine those particles from the lab trapped under intense heat. How they need to escape.'

'So,' Marcia said, 'you think Haley ran away?'

Pete Zecher kept his eyes on the photograph from Disney World. He too seemed to focus on that heart-splitting smile. Then he turned away and she saw tears in his eyes.

'No, Marcia, I don't think she ran away. I think something happened to her. Something bad.'

Chapter 5

Wendy woke up in the morning and flipped on the panini maker, which was a fancy way of saying 'toasted sandwich maker' or 'George Foreman Grill.' It had quickly become the most important machine in the house, and she and Charlie pretty much lived on paninis. She put some bacon and cheese between slices of nice whole wheat bread from Trader Joe's and lowered the heated top.

As he did every morning, Charlie thudded down the stairs as if he were an overweight racing horse wearing anvil shoes. He collapsed more than sat at the kitchen table and inhaled the sandwich.

'When you going to work?' Charlie asked her.

'I lost my job yesterday.'

'Right. Forgot.'

The selfishness of teenagers. Sometimes, like right at that moment, it can be endearing.

'Can you give me a ride to school?' Charlie asked.

'Sure.'

The morning drop-off traffic by Kasselton High was ridiculously congested. Some days it drove her mad, but other days, the morning commute was the one time she and her son might talk and maybe he'd share his thoughts, not in an open gush, but if you listened, you could pick up enough. Today, though, Charlie had his head down and texted. He didn't say a word the whole ride, his fingers a blur on the tiny handheld.

When she stopped, Charlie rolled out of the passenger door, still texting.

Wendy called out to him: 'Thanks, Mom!'

'Yeah, sorry.'

As Wendy pulled back into her own driveway, she spotted the car parked in front of her house. She slowed, pulled in to park, kept her cell phone nearby. She didn't expect trouble, but you never know. She punched in 9-1-1, kept her finger near the send button, and she slid out of the car.

He was now squatting by her back bumper.

'Tire's low,' he said to her.

'Can I help you, Mr. Grayson?'

Ed Grayson, the father of one of the victims, stood, wiped his hands, squinted into the sunshine. 'I went to your TV studio today. Someone told me you were fired.'

She said nothing.

'I assume it's because of the judge's decision.'

'Is there something I can do for you, Mr. Grayson?'

'I want to apologize for what I said to you after court yesterday.'

'I appreciate that,' she said.

'And if you have a minute,' Ed Grayson continued, 'I really think we need to talk.'

After they were both inside and Ed Grayson turned down her offer of a drink, Wendy sat at her kitchen table and waited. Grayson paced a few more moments, then suddenly pulled the kitchen chair right up to her, so that he was sitting less than a yard away.

'First,' he said, 'I want to apologize again.'

'No need. I get how you feel.'

'Do you?'

She said nothing.

'My son's name is E. J. Ed Junior, of course. He was a happy kid. Loved sports. His favorite was hockey. Me, I don't know the first thing about the game. I was a basketball guy growing up. But my wife, Maggie, was born in Quebec. Her whole family plays. It's in their blood. So I learned to love it too. For my boy. But now, well, now E. J. has no interest in the sport. If I bring him near a hockey rink, he freaks out. He just wants to stay home.'

He stopped, looked off. Wendy said, 'I'm sorry.'

Silence.

Wendy tried to shift gears. 'What were you talking to Flair Hickory about?'

'His client hasn't been seen in over two weeks,' he said.

'So?'

'So I was trying to find out where he might be. But Mr. Hickory wouldn't tell me.'

'That surprise you?'

'Not really, no.'

More silence.

'So what can I do for you, Mr. Grayson?'

Grayson started playing with his watch, a Timex with one of those twist-a-flex bands. Wendy's father had one way back when. It always left a red mark on his wrist when he took it off. Funny, all these years after his death, what you remember.

'Your TV show,' Grayson said. 'You spent a year hunting down pedophiles. Why?'

'Why what?'

'Why pedophiles?'

'What's the difference?'

He tried to smile, but it didn't quite hold. 'Humor me,' he said.

'Good ratings, I guess.'

'Sure, I can see that. But there's more, isn't there?'

'Mr. Grayson—'

'Ed,' he said.

'Let's stay with Mr. Grayson. I would like you to get to the point.'

'I know what happened to your husband.'

Just like that. Wendy felt the slow burn, said nothing.

'She's out, you know. Ariana Nasbro.'

Hearing the name said out loud made her wince. 'I know.'

'Think she's all cured now?'

Wendy thought about the letters, about how they turned her stomach.

'She could be,' Grayson said. 'I've known people who've kicked it at this stage. But that doesn't really matter much to you, does it, Wendy?'

'This is none of your business.'

'That's true. But Dan Mercer is. You have a son, don't you?'

'Also none of your business.'

'Guys like Dan,' he went on. 'One thing we know for certain. They don't get cured.' He moved a little closer, tilted his head. 'Isn't that part of it, Wendy?'

'Part of what?'

'Why you liked going after pedophiles. Alcoholics, well, they can quit. Pedophiles are simpler – there really is no chance for redemption and thus forgiveness.'

'Do me a favor, Mr. Grayson. Don't psychoanalyze me. You don't know a damn thing about me.'

He nodded. 'Fair point.'

'So get to yours.'

'It's pretty simple. If Dan Mercer isn't stopped, he will hurt another child. That's a fact. We both know it.'

'You should probably be telling this to the judge.'

'She can't do me any good now.'

'And I can?'

'You're a reporter. A good one.'

'A fired one.'

'More reason to do this.'

'Do what?'

Ed Grayson leaned forward. 'Help me find him, Wendy.'

'So you can kill him?'

'He won't stop.'

'So you said.'

'But?'

'But I don't want to be part of your plans for revenge.'

'You think that's what it's about?'

Wendy shrugged.

'It's not a question of vengeance,' Grayson said, his voice low. 'Just the opposite, in fact.'

'I'm not following.'

'This decision is calculated. It's practical. It's about taking no chances. I want to make sure that Dan Mercer never hurts anyone ever again.'

'By killing him?'

'Do you know another way? This isn't about blood-lust or violence either. We are all human beings, but if you do something like this – if your own genetics or pathetic life are so messed up that you need to harm a child – well, the most humane thing you can do is put a man down.'

'Must be nice to be judge and jury.'

Ed Grayson looked almost amused by that. 'Did

Judge Howard make the right call?'

'No.'

'So who better than us – the ones in the know?'

She thought about that. 'Yesterday, after court. Why did you say I lied?'

'Because you did. You weren't worried about Mercer killing himself. You went inside because you were afraid he might destroy the evidence.'

Silence.

Ed Grayson stood, crossed the kitchen, stopped at the sink. 'Do you mind if I take some water?'

'Help yourself. The glasses are on the left.'

He took one down from the cabinet and turned on the faucet. 'I have a friend,' Grayson began, watching the water fill the glass. 'Nice guy, works as a lawyer, very successful. So a few years ago, he told me that he was a big supporter of the Iraq war. Gave me all the reasons and how the Iraqis deserve a chance at freedom. I said to him, "You have a son, right?" He says, yes, he's going to Wake Forest. I say, "Be honest, would you sacrifice his life for this war?" I asked him to really dig deep. Pretend God comes down and says, "Okay, here's the deal. The USA wins the war in Iraq, whatever that means, but in return, your son gets shot in the head and dies. Just him. No one else. Everyone else goes home safe, but your son dies." So I ask my friend: Do you make that trade?'

Ed Grayson turned and took a deep sip.

'What did he say?' she asked.

'What would you say, Wendy?'

'I'm not your lawyer friend who backed the war.'

'What a cop-out answer.' Grayson smiled. 'In truth, in those honest moments in the dark, none of us would make that trade, would we? None of us would sacrifice our own child.'

'People send their children to war every day.'

'Sure, right, you might be willing to send them to war, but not to death. There's a difference, albeit one that includes a strong dose of self-denial. You may be willing to roll the dice, to play the odds because you don't really believe your child will be the one to die. That's different. That's not a choice, like I'm talking about.'

He looked at her.

'Are you waiting for applause?' she asked.

'You don't agree?'

'Your hypothetical belittles sacrifice,' Wendy said. 'And it's nonsense.'

'Well, yes, perhaps it is unfair, I grant you that. But for us, Wendy, right now, there is an element of it that is very real. Dan isn't going to hurt my child again, and your son is too old for him. Are you going to let it go because your child is safe? Does that give you or me the right to wash our hands of this – because it's not our child?'

She said nothing.

Ed Grayson rose. 'You can't wish this away, Wendy.'

'I'm not big on vigilantism, Mr. Grayson.'

'That's not what this is.'

'Sounds like it.'

'Think about this then.' Grayson stared at her, made sure she was looking at him and giving him her full attention. 'If you could go back in time and find Ariana Nasbro—'

'Stop,' she said.

'If you could go back to her first DUI or her second or even her third—'

'You need to shut the hell up right now.'

Ed Grayson nodded, satisfied, it seemed, that he'd drawn blood. 'I think it's time I left.' He moved out of the kitchen and toward the front door. 'Think about it, okay? That's all I ask. You and I are on the same side here, Wendy. I think you know that.'

Ariana Nasbro.

After Grayson left, Wendy kept trying to forget that damn letter sitting in her waste bin.

She snapped on her iPod for a while, closed her eyes, tried to let the music calm her down. She put on her calm sound track, the one with Thriving Ivory singing 'Angels on the Moon' and William Fitzsimmons doing 'Please Forgive Me' and David Berkeley playing 'High Heels and All.' It didn't help, all these songs about forgiveness. She went the other route, changed into workout clothes, cranked up everything from childhood songs like 'Shout' by Tears for Fears to The Hold Steady doing 'First Night' to Eminem's 'Lose Yourself.'

It wasn't working. Ed Grayson's words kept chasing her. . . .

'If you could go back in time and find Ariana Nasbro . . .'

She would do it. No questions asked. Wendy would go back in time and hunt the bitch down and cut off her head and dance around Nasbro's still-twitching torso.

Nice thought, but there you are.

Wendy checked her e-mail. True to his word, Dan Mercer had sent her the meeting place for two PM: an address in Wykertown, New Jersey. Never heard of it. She got directions from Google. It would take an hour. Fine. She had almost four.

She showered and got dressed. The letter. That damn letter. She ran downstairs, dug through the garbage, and found the plain white envelope. Her eyes studied the penmanship, as though that might offer up some clue. It didn't. A knife from the kitchen block worked just fine

61

as a letter opener. Wendy pulled out two sheets of lined notebook paper, plain white, the same kind she'd used in school as a kid.

Still standing, Wendy read Ariana Nasbro's letter right there – every damn horrible word – at the kitchen sink. There were no surprises, no real insight, nothing but the all-about-me crap we are spoon-fed from day one. Every cliché, every namby-pamby sentiment, every hackneyed excuse . . . they were all present and accounted for. Each word felt like a blade ripping into her flesh. Ariana Nasbro talked about the 'seeds of my own self-image,' about 'making amends,' about 'searching for meaning' and 'hitting rock bottom.' Pathetic. She even had the nerve to talk about 'the abuse in my life and how I've learned to forgive' and 'the wonders of that – forgiveness' and how she wanted to grant that 'wonder to others like you and Charlie.'

Seeing this woman write her son's name filled Wendy with rage like nothing else ever could.

'*I will always be an alcoholic,*' Ariana Nasbro said toward the end of her diatribe. Another *I. I* will, *I* am, *I* want. The letter was full of them.

I, I, I.

I know now that I am an imperfect being worthy of forgiveness.

Wendy wanted to puke.
And then the last line of the letter.

This is my third letter to you. Please let me hear from you, so that the healing may begin. May God bless you.

Oh, man, Wendy thought, you'll hear from me. Right friggin' now.

She grabbed her keys and stormed to her car. Wendy plugged the return address into her GPS and headed toward the halfway house where Ariana Nasbro currently resided.

The halfway house was in New Brunswick, normally an hour away but with her foot pushing the pedal, Wendy made it in less than forty-five minutes. She threw the car into park and stormed through the front door. She told the woman at the desk her name and said she would like to see Ariana Nasbro. The woman at the desk asked her to take a seat. Wendy said that she would stand, thanks anyway.

A few moments later, Ariana Nasbro appeared. Wendy had not seen her in years, since the trial for vehicular manslaughter. Ariana had looked scared then, pitiful, her shoulders hunched, her hair a wild mousy brown, her eyes blinking as though she expected to be smacked unawares.

This woman, the postprison Ariana Nasbro, was different. Her hair was short and white. She stood straight and still and met Wendy's eye. She stuck out her hand and said, 'Thank you for coming, Wendy.'

Wendy ignored the outstretched hand. 'I didn't come for you.'

Ariana tried a smile. 'Would you like to take a walk?'

'No, Ariana, I don't want to take a walk. In your letters – the first two I ignored but I guess you can't take a hint – you asked me how you could make amends.'

'Yes.'

'So I'm here to tell you: Don't send me your self-involved AA nonsense. I don't care. I don't want to forgive you so you can heal or recover or whatever the hell you call it. I have no interest in your getting better. This isn't the first time you've tried AA, is it?'

'No,' Ariana Nasbro said, her head held high, 'it's not.'

'You tried it twice before you murdered my husband, isn't that right?'

'That's correct,' she said in too calm a voice.

'Have you reached Step Eight before?'

'I have. But this time it's different because—'

Wendy stopped her with a raised hand. 'I don't care. The fact that this time it might be different means nothing to me. I don't care about you or your recovery or about Step Eight, but if you truly want to make amends, I suggest you walk outside, wait by the curb, and throw yourself under the first passing bus. I know that sounds harsh, but if you had done that the last time you reached Step Eight – if whatever wronged person you sent this same me-me-me crap to had told you to do that instead of forgiving you – maybe, just maybe, you would have listened and you'd be dead and my John would be alive. I would have a husband and Charlie would have a father. That's what matters. Not you. Not your six-months-sober party at AA. Not your spiritual journey to sobriety. So if you truly want to make amends, Ariana, stop putting yourself first for once. Are you cured – totally cured, absolutely one hundred percent positive you'll never drink again?'

'You're never cured,' Ariana said.

'Right, more of that AA nonsense. We really don't know about tomorrow, do we? So that's how you should make amends. Stop writing letters, stop talking about yourself in group, stop taking it a day at a time. Instead, do the one thing that will guarantee you'll never murder another child's father: Wait for that bus and step right in front of it. Other than that, leave me and my son the hell alone. We will never forgive you. Not ever. And how selfish and monstrous of you to think we should so you, of all people, can heal.'

With that, Wendy turned around, headed back to her car, and started it up.

She was done with Ariana Nasbro. Now it was time to see Dan Mercer.

Chapter 6

Marcia McWaid sat on the couch next to Ted. Across from them was Frank Tremont, an Essex County investigator there to deliver their weekly briefing on the case of her missing daughter. Marcia already knew what he would say.

Frank Tremont wore a suit of chipmunk brown and a threadbare tie that looked like it had spent the past four months crinkled in a tight ball. He was in his sixties, near retirement, and had that seen-it-all, world-weary aura that you find in anyone who has been at the same job too long. When Marcia had first asked around, she'd heard rumors that Frank might be past his prime, might be coasting through his last few months on the job.

But Marcia never saw any of that, and at least Tremont was still here, still visiting them, still in touch. There used to be others with him, federal agents and experts in missing persons and assorted members of law enforcement. Their numbers had dwindled over the last ninety-four days until it was just this lone, aging cop with the horrible suit.

In the early days, Marcia had tried to busy herself by offering the various officers coffee and cookies. There was no such pretense anymore. Frank Tremont sat across from them, these clearly suffering parents, in their lovely suburban home, and wondered, she knew, how to tell them, yet again, that there was nothing new to report on their missing daughter.

'I'm sorry,' Frank Tremont said.

As expected. Almost on cue.

Marcia watched Ted lean back. He tilted his face up, his eyes blinking back tears. She knew that Ted was a good man, a wonderful man, a great husband and father and provider. But he was, she had learned, not a particularly strong man.

Marcia kept her eyes on Tremont. 'So what next?' she asked.

'We keep on looking,' he said.

'How?' Marcia asked. 'I mean, what else can be done?'

Tremont opened his mouth, stopped, closed it. 'I don't know, Marcia.'

Ted McWaid let the tears flow. 'I don't get it,' he said, as he had many times before. 'How can you guys not have anything?'

Tremont just waited.

'With all the technology, all the advancements and the Internet . . .'

Ted's voice trailed off. He shook his head. He didn't get it. Still. Marcia did. It didn't work that way. Before Haley, they'd been a typically naïve American family whose knowledge of (and thus faith in) law enforcement was derived from a lifetime of watching TV shows in which all cases get solved. The well-groomed actors find a hair or a footprint or a skin flake, they put it under a microscope, and presto, the answer comes to light before the hour mark. But that wasn't reality. Reality, Marcia now knew, was better found on the news. The cops in Colorado, for example, still hadn't found the killer of that little beauty queen, JonBenet Ramsey. Marcia re-membered the headlines when Elizabeth Smart, a pretty fourteen-year-old girl, had been abducted from her bed-room late one night. The media had been all over that kidnapping, the whole world transfixed, all eyes watch-ing as the police and FBI agents and all those crime scene 'experts' combed through Elizabeth's Salt Lake City home in search of the truth – and yet for more than nine months, no one thought to check out a crazy homeless man with a God complex who'd worked in the house, even though Elizabeth's sister had seen him that night? If you'd put that on *CSI* or *Law & Order* the viewer would toss the remote across the room, claiming it was 'unreal-istic.' But sugarcoat it as you might, that was the kind of thing that happened all the time.

The reality, Marcia now knew, was that even idiots get away with major crimes.

The reality was, none of us are safe.

'Do you have anything new to tell me?' Tremont tried. 'Anything at all?'

'We've told you everything,' Ted said.

Tremont nodded, his expression extra hangdog today. 'We've seen other cases like this, where a missing teenage girl just shows up. She needed to blow off steam or maybe had a secret boyfriend.'

He had tried selling this before. Frank Tremont, like everyone else, including Ted and Marcia, wanted this to be a runaway.

'There was another teenage girl from Connecticut,' Tremont continued. 'Got caught up with the wrong guy and ran away. Three weeks later, she just came back home.'

Ted nodded and turned to Marcia to have his hope bolstered. Marcia tried to muster a rosier façade, but there was simply no way. Teddy turned away as though scalded and excused himself.

It was odd, Marcia thought, that she of all people could see clearest. Of course, no parent wants to think that they are so clueless as to miss the signs of a teenager so desperately unhappy or unhinged that she'd run away for three months. The police had magnified every disappointment in her young life: Yes, Haley hadn't gotten into the University of Virginia, her first choice. Yes, she hadn't won the class essay contest or made the AHLISA honors program. And yes, she may have broken up with a boy recently. But so what? Every teen had stuff like that.

Marcia knew the truth, had known it from that first day. To echo the words of Principal Zecher, something had happened to her daughter. Something bad.

Tremont sat there, not sure what to do.

'Frank?' Marcia said.

He looked at her.

'I want to show you something.'

Marcia took out the Mickey Mouse photograph she'd found at her daughter's locker and handed it to him. Tremont took his time. He held the picture in his hand. The room was still. She could hear his wheezing breath.

'That picture was taken three weeks before Haley vanished.'

Tremont studied the photograph as though it might hold a clue to Haley's disappearance. 'I remember. Your family trip to Disney World.'

'Look at her face, Frank.'

He obeyed, his eyes resting there.

'Do you think that girl, with that smile, just decided to run away and not tell anyone? Do you really think that girl took off on her own and was savvy enough to never use her iPhone or ATM or credit cards?'

'No,' Frank Tremont said, 'I don't.'

'Please keep looking, Frank.'

'I will, Marcia. I promise.'

When people think of New Jersey's highways, they think of either the Garden State Parkway with its mix of shattered warehouses, unkempt graveyards, and worn two-family dwellings, or they think of the New Jersey Turnpike with its factories and smokestacks and mammoth industrial complexes that resemble the nightmarish future in *Terminator* movies. They don't think of Route 15 in Sussex County, the farmland, the old lake communities, the antique barns, the 4-H Fairgrounds, the old minor league baseball stadium.

Following Dan Mercer's directions, Wendy took Route 15 until it became 206, turned right on a gravel road, drove past the U-Store-It units, and arrived at the trailer park in Wykertown. The park was silent and small and had the kind of ghostly look where you half expect to see a rusted child's swing swaying in the wind. The lots were divided up in a grid. Row D, Column 7 was in the far corner, not far from the chain-link fence.

She got out of the car and was amazed by the quiet. Not a sound. No tumbleweeds blew across the dirt, but maybe they should have. The whole park looked like one of those postapocalyptic towns – the bomb dropped and the residents had evaporated. There were clotheslines, but nothing on them. Foldout chairs with torn seats littered the grounds. Charcoal barbecues and beach toys looked as though they'd been abandoned in mid-play.

Wendy checked her phone service. No bars. Terrific. She climbed the two cinder-block steps and stopped in front of the trailer door. Part of her – the rational part that knew that she was a mother, not a superhero – told her that she should back up and not be an idiot. She would have pondered that decision further, except suddenly the screen door opened and Dan Mercer was there.

When she saw his face, she took a step back.

'What happened to you?'

'Come on in,' Dan Mercer mumbled through a swollen jaw. His nose was flattened. Bruises covered his face, but that wasn't the worst of it. The worst were the clusters of burn circles on his arm and face. One looked as though it had gone all the way through his cheek.

She pointed to one of the circles. 'They do that with a cigarette?'

He managed a shrug. 'I told them my trailer was a no-smoking zone. It made them angry.'

'Who?'

'That was a joke. The no-smoking zone.'

'Yeah, I got that. Who assaulted you?'

Dan Mercer shook it off. 'Why don't you come in?'

'Why don't we stay out here?'

'Gee, Wendy, don't you feel safe with me? As you so bluntly pointed out, you're hardly my type.'

'Still,' she said.

'I really don't relish going outside right now,' he said.

'Oh, but I insist.'

'Then good-bye. Sorry to make you drive all this way for nothing.'

Dan let the door close as he disappeared inside. Wendy waited a second, trying to call his bluff. It didn't work. Forgetting the earlier warning bells – he didn't look as though he could do much damage in his current condition anyway – she opened the door and stepped inside. Dan was on the other side of the trailer.

'Your hair,' she said.

'What about it?'

Dan's once wavy brown hair was now a horrible shade of yellow some might call blond.

'You dye it yourself?'

'No, I went to Dionne, my favorite colorist in the city.'

She almost smiled at that. 'Really blends you in.'

'I know. I look like I just walked out of an eighties glam-rock video.'

Dan moved farther away from the door, toward the back corner of the trailer, almost as if he wanted to hide the bruises. Wendy let go of the door. It slammed shut. The light was dim. Sun streaks slashed across the room. The floor near her was worn linoleum, but a poorly cut rug of orange shag, like something the Brady Bunch would have considered too garish, covered the far quarter of the room.

Dan looked small in the corner, hunched over and broken. What was bizarre, what had angered her so, was that she had tried to do a story on Dan Mercer and his 'good works' about a year before her sting showed his true predilections. Before that, Dan had seemed to be that rarest of beasts – the honest-to-God do-gooder, a man who truly wanted to make a difference and, most shockingly, a man who didn't couple that desire with self-aggrandizement.

She had – dare she admit this? – fallen for it. Dan was a handsome man with that unruly brown hair and dark blue eyes, and he had that ability to look at you as though you were the only person in the world. He had focus and charm and a self-deprecating sense of humor, and she could see how these miserable kids must have loved that.

But how had she, a pathologically skeptical reporter, not seen through him?

She had even – again, dare she admit it, even to herself? – hoped that he would ask her out. There had been that great, early attraction when he looked at her, that thunderbolt, and she'd felt sure that she'd sent a bit of a lightning storm his way too.

Beyond creepy to think about that now.

From his spot in the corner, Dan tried to stare at her with that same focus, but it wasn't happening. The seemingly beautiful clarity she'd been fooled by before had been shattered. What was left in its place was pitiful, and even now, even after all she knew, Wendy's instincts told her that he simply could not be the monster that he so obviously was.

But, alas, that was crap. She'd been had by a con man – simple as that. His modesty had been a way to cover up his true self. Call it instinct or women's intuition or going with your gut – whenever Wendy had done that, she had been wrong.

'I didn't do it, Wendy.'

More *I*. Some day she was having.

'Yeah, you told me that on the phone,' she said. 'Care to elaborate?'

He looked lost, not sure how to continue. 'Since my arrest, you've been investigating me, right?'

'So?'

'You talked to the kids I worked with at the community center, right? How many?'

'What's the difference?'

'How many, Wendy?'

She had a pretty good idea of where he was going with this. 'Forty-seven,' she said.

'How many of them claimed that I abused them?'

'Zero. Publicly. But there were some anonymous tips.'

'Anonymous tips,' Dan repeated. 'You mean those

anonymous blogs that could have been written by anyone, including you.'

'Or a scared kid.'

'You didn't even believe those blogs enough to air them.'

'That's hardly evidence you're innocent, Dan.'

'Funny.'

'What?'

'I thought it worked the other way around. Innocent
until proven guilty.'

She tried not to roll her eyes. This was not a game she
wanted to play. Time to turn the tide a bit. 'You know
what else I found when I was investigating you?'

Dan Mercer seemed to move farther away, almost all
the way into the corner. 'What?'

'Nothing. No friends, no family, no real connections.
Other than your ex-wife, Jenna Wheeler, and the community center, you seem to be pretty much a ghost.'

'My parents died when I was young.'

'Yes, I know. You grew up in an orphanage in Oregon.'

'So?'

'So there are a lot of holes in your résumé.'

'I'm being set up, Wendy.'

'Right. And yet you showed up at the sting house
right on time, correct?'

'I thought I was visiting a kid in trouble.'

'My hero. And you just walked right in?'

'Chynna called out to me.'

'Her name was Deborah, not Chynna. She's an intern
for the station. What a coincidence she sounds like your
mystery girl.'

'It was from a distance,' he said. 'That's your setup,
isn't it? Like she just came out of the shower?'

'I see. You thought it was a girl named Chynna from
your community center, right?'

'Yes.'

'Of course, I looked for this Chynna, Dan. Your mystery girl. Just to cross my *t*'s and dot my *i*'s. We had you sit down with our sketch artist.'

'I know this.'

'And you know that I showed that sketch to everyone in the area – not to mention every employee and resident at your community center. No one knows her, no one saw her, nothing.'

'I told you. She came to me in confidence.'

'Convenient. And someone also used your laptop from your house to send those horrible messages?'

He said nothing.

'And – help me here, Dan – someone downloaded those photos onto it too, right? Oh, and someone – me perhaps, if we believe your lawyer – hid disgusting pictures of children in your garage.'

Dan Mercer closed his eyes, defeated.

'You know what you should do, Dan? Now that you're free, now that the law can't touch you, you should get help. See a therapist.'

Dan shook his head and managed a smile.

'What?'

He looked up at her. 'You've been catching pedophiles for two years, Wendy. Don't you know?'

'Know what?'

His voice from the corner was a whisper. 'You can't cure pedophiles.'

Wendy felt the chill. And that was when the trailer door burst open.

She jumped back, the screen nearly slamming into her. A man with a ski mask slid inside. There was a pistol in his right hand.

Dan raised his hands, took another step back. 'Don't . . .'

75

The man in the ski mask pointed the gun at him. Wendy scrambled back, out of sight, and then, just like that, the man in the ski mask fired.

There had been no warning, no telling Dan not to move or to put his hands in the air, nothing like that. Just the hissing, short boom of gunfire.

Dan spun and went down face-first.

Wendy screamed. She dropped flat behind the old couch, as though that could provide protection. From underneath she could see Dan lying on the floor. No movement. A puddle of blood spread around his head, staining the carpet. The executioner crossed the room. No rush. Casual. Taking a stroll through the park. He stopped where Dan lay. He aimed the gun down toward Dan's head.

And that was when Wendy noticed the watch.

It was a Timex with one of those twist-a-flex bands. Just like her own dad wore. Everything slowed down for a few seconds. The height, Wendy saw now, was right. So too the weight. Then you add in the watch.

It was Ed Grayson.

He fired twice more into Dan's head, a noise like cut-off thuds. Dan's body bucked from the impact. Panic grabbed hold of her. She fought through it. Clear thinking. That was what she needed now.

Two options here.

Option one, talk it out with Grayson. Convince him she was on his side.

Option two, flee. Make for the door, run to her car, get out of here.

There were problems with both options. Option one, for example: Would Grayson believe her? She had turned him away just hours ago, had in fact lied to him, and here she was, secretly meeting with Dan Mercer, a man she'd just seen shot down in cold blood. . . .

Option one wasn't sounding so good, which left . . .

She scrambled for the open door.

'Stop!'

Keeping herself low, she stumbled more than ran out the door.

'Wait!'

Not a chance, she thought. She rolled into the sunlight. Keep moving, she thought. Don't slow down.

'Help!' she screamed.

No response. The park was still abandoned.

Ed Grayson came bounding out the door behind her. The gun was in his hand. Wendy kept running. The other trailers were too far in the distance.

'Help!'

Gunshots.

The only place to duck and hide was behind her car. Wendy ran for it. Another burst of gunfire. She dived behind the car, using it as a shield.

Risk it?

What choice did she have? Stay here and let him walk around and shoot her?

She fished into her pocket and got her car remote. She unlocked the door. Even better, when Charlie had gotten his driver's permit, her son had insisted that they get one of the start remotes because on those winter mornings they could let the car warm up from the kitchen. She had bemoaned this indulgence, of course, her pampered son too soft to stand the cold for a few minutes. Now she wanted to kiss him for it.

The car turned on.

Wendy opened the driver's-side door and, head down, got inside. She glanced out the window. The gun was aimed right at the car. She ducked down.

More gunshots.

She waited for the sound of shattering glass. Nothing. No time to worry about that now. Lying on her side, she shifted into drive. The car began to move. Using her left hand, she pressed on the gas pedal and drove blindly. She hoped like hell that she wouldn't hit anything.

Ten seconds passed. How far had she driven?

Enough, she figured.

Wendy sat up and slid into the seat. The masked Grayson was in her rearview mirror, running toward her, gun raised.

She slammed on the gas pedal, her head snapping back, and drove until there was no one in the rearview mirror. She grabbed her cell phone. Still no bars. She dialed 9-1-1, hit send anyway, and got the CALL FAILED beep for her trouble. She drove a full mile away. Still no bars. She headed back toward Route 206 and tried again. Nothing.

Three miles later, the call went through.

'What's the nature of your emergency?' a voice said.

'I need to report a shooting.'

Chapter 7

By the time Wendy turned the car around and drove back to the trailer, three Sussex County squad cars were on the scene. There was an officer covering the perimeter.

'Are you the lady who called this in?' the officer asked.

'Yes.'

'Are you okay, ma'am?'

'I'm fine.'

'Do you require any medical assistance?'

'No, I'm fine.'

'You said on the phone that the perpetrator was armed?'

'Yes.'

'And that he was alone?'

'Yes.'

'Please come with me.'

He led her to a squad car and opened the back door. She hesitated.

'For your safety, ma'am. You're not under arrest or anything.'

She slid into the back. The officer closed the door and took the driver's seat. He kept the engine turned off and continued peppering her with questions. Every once in a while he would hold up his hand to stop her and radio some of what she'd said to, Wendy assumed, another officer. She told him everything she knew, including her suspicion that the perpetrator was Ed Grayson.

More than half an hour passed when another officer, this one huge, three-hundred-plus pounds, and African American, approached the vehicle. He wore an untucked Hawaiian shirt that on a normal-size person could double as a muumuu. He opened the back door.

'Ms. Tynes, I'm Sheriff Mickey Walker of the Sussex County Police Department. Would you mind stepping out of the vehicle?'

'Did you catch him?'

Walker did not reply. He waddled toward the entrance to the trailer park. Wendy hurried behind him. She saw another officer questioning a man in a wife-beater T and boxers.

'Sheriff Walker?'

He did not slow down. 'You said you believe the man wearing a ski mask was named Ed Grayson?'

'Yes.'

'And that he arrived after you did?'

'Yes.'

'Do you know what kind of car he was driving?'

She thought about it. 'I didn't see, no.'

Walker nodded as though this was the answer he'd been expecting. They arrived at the trailer. Walker pushed on the screen door and bent down to squeeze inside. Wendy trailed. Two other uniformed officers were already there. Wendy looked across the trailer where Dan had fallen.

Nothing.

She turned to Walker. 'You already removed the body?' But she knew the answer. No ambulance or crime scene vans or hearses had driven past her.

'There was no body,' he answered.

'I don't understand.'

'No Ed Grayson or anyone else either. The trailer is exactly as it was when we entered.'

Wendy pointed to the far corner. 'He was lying there. Dan Mercer. I'm not making it up.'

She stared at where the body had been, thinking, Oh no, this couldn't be. She flashed to that movie/TV scene you've seen a million times, the dead body gone, the pleading woman saying, *But you must believe me!* and nobody does. Wendy's eyes moved back toward the big cop to see his reaction. She expected skepticism, but Walker surprised her.

'I know you're not making it up,' he said.

She had been ready to launch into a prolonged argument, but now there was no need. She waited.

'Take a deep breath,' Walker said. 'Smell anything?'

She did. 'Gunpowder?'

'Yep. Fairly recent, I'd guess. More than that, there's a bullet hole in the wall over there. Went clean through. We found the slug outside in a cinder block. Looks like a thirty-eight, but we'll know more later. Now I want you to look around the room and tell me if you notice anything different from when you ran out.' He paused, gestured awkwardly. 'Except, you know, for the no dead body and all.'

Wendy spotted it right away. 'The carpet is gone.'

Again Walker nodded as though he'd already known what she'd say. 'What sort of carpet?'

'Orange shag. That's where Mercer fell after he was shot.'

'And that carpet was in the corner? Where you pointed before?'

'Yes.'

'Let me show you something.'

81

Walker took up a lot of room in the tiny trailer. They crossed the room, and Walker pointed a beefy finger at the wall. Wendy could see the bullet hole, neat and small. Walker wheezed as he bent down to where the body had fallen.

'Do you see this?'

Small curls of orange shag, like thin Cheetos, littered the floor. That was great – evidence she'd been telling the truth – but that wasn't what Walker wanted to show her. She followed his finger.

Blood.

Not a lot. Certainly not all that had poured out when Dan Mercer had been shot. But enough. More of the orange shag remnants were caught up in the sticky liquid.

'Must have bled through the carpet,' Wendy said.

Walker nodded. 'We have a witness outside who spotted a man putting a rolled-up carpet in the back of his vehicle – a black Acura MDX, New Jersey plates. We already called DMV on Edward Grayson of Fair Lawn, New Jersey. He owns a black Acura MDX.'

First they cued up the theme music. Very dramatic. *Bahdah-duuumm* . . .

Wearing a black robe, Hester Crimstein opened the door and strode lionlike toward the judge's seat. The drumbeat picked up as she grew closer. The famous voice-over, the same one who did all the 'In a world' movies before he passed away, said, 'All rise and rise now, Judge Hester Crimstein presiding.'

Smash to title: CRIMSTEIN'S COURT.

Hester took her seat. 'I've reached a verdict.'

The female chorus, the same ones who sing the quick radio call letters like, 'One oh two point seven . . . New Yoooorkkkk,' sang, *'It's verdict time!'*

Hester tried not to sigh. She had been taping her new TV show for three months now, leaving the cable-news confines of *Crimstein on Crime,* her show that dealt with 'real cases' – real cases being a euphemism for celebrity wrongdoings, missing white teens, politicians' adultery.

Her 'bailiff' was named Waco. He was a retired stand-up comic. Yes, for real. This was a TV set, not a courtroom, though it looked like one. While it was not exactly a trial, Hester did preside over a legal proceeding of a certain kind. The two parties sign a contract for arbitration. The producers pay the settlement, and both the plaintiff and the defendant are paid a hundred dollars a day. It's win–win.

Reality shows have a bad rap and deserve it, but what most ably demonstrated, especially the ones involving either courtship or courts, was that this remains a man's world. Take the defendant, Reginald Pepe. Please. Big Reg, as he liked to be called, had allegedly borrowed two grand from the defendant, Miley Badonis, his girlfriend at the time. Big Reg claimed it was a gift, telling the court, 'Chicks like to give me stuff – what can I say?' Big Reg was fifty years old, weighed a paunchy two-fifty, and wore a mesh shirt that gave his chest hairs enough room to curl through. He wasn't wearing a bra but should have been. His hair was gelled into a spike that made him look like the latest anime cartoon villain, and there were gold chains around his neck, dozens of them. Big Reg's wide face, emphasized by the sad fact that Hester's show now filmed in high def, contained enough craters to make one search for a lunar rover on his right cheek.

Miley Badonis, the plaintiff, was at least two decades younger, and while nobody would be speed-dialing the Elite modeling agency upon gazing at her, she was, well, fine. But she had been so anxious to get a man, any man, that she gave Big Reg money with nary a question.

Big Reg was twice divorced, separated from his third wife, and had two other women with him today. Both women wore navel-revealing tube tops, and neither had the figure for it. The tube tops appeared so tight they squeezed all flesh south, giving both women a gourdlike shape.

'You.' Hester pointed at the tube top on the right.

'Me?'

Somehow, despite the word being one syllable, she had managed to crack gum mid-word.

'Yes. Step forward. What are you doing here?'

'Huh?'

'Why are you here with Mr. Pepe?'

'Huh?'

Waco, her hilarious bailiff, started singing, 'If I only had a brain . . .' from *The Wizard of Oz*. Hester shot him a look. 'Timely reference, Waco.'

Waco went silent.

The tube top on the left stepped forward. 'If it pleases the court, Your Honor, we're here as friends of Big Reg.'

Hester glanced at Big Reg. 'Friends?'

Big Reg arched an eyebrow as if to say, Right, sure, friends.

Hester leaned forward. 'I'm going to give both of you ladies some advice. If this man here works hard to educate and better himself, he may one day rise to the level of total loser.'

Big Reg said, 'Hey, Judge!'

'Quiet, Mr. Pepe.' She kept her eyes on both girls. 'I don't know what your deal is, ladies, but this I do know: This isn't the way to get revenge on Daddy. Do you two know what a skank is?'

Both girls looked confused.

'Let me help you,' Hester said. 'You two are skanks.'

Miley Badonis shouted, 'Tell them, Judge!'

Hester cut her eyes toward the voice. 'Ms. Badonis, do you know anything about throwing stones and glass houses?'

'Uh, no.'

'Then shut up and listen.' Hester turned back to the tube tops. 'Do you two know the definition of a skank?'

'It's like a slut,' the tube top on the left said.

'Yes. And no. A slut is a promiscuous girl. A skank, which in my mind is far worse, is any girl who would touch a man like Reginald Pepe. In short, Ms. Badonis is proudly on her way to not being a skank. Both of you have the same opportunity. I'm begging you to take it.'

They wouldn't. Hester had seen it all before. She turned to the defendant.

'Mr. Pepe?'

'Yeah, Judge?'

'I would tell you what my grandmother used to say to me: You can't ride two horses with one behind—'

'You can if you do it right, Judge, heh heh heh.'

Oh, man.

'I *would* tell you,' Hester continued, 'but you're beyond hope. I would call you pond scum, Mr. Pepe, but really, is that fair to scum? Scum really doesn't hurt anybody while you, being a miserable excuse for a human being, will leave nothing but a lifetime of waste and destruction in your path. Oh, and skanks.'

'Hey,' Big Reg said, spreading his hands and smiling, 'you're hurting my feelings.'

Yep, Hester thought. A man's world. She turned back to the plaintiff. 'Unfortunately, Ms. Badonis, there is no crime in being a miserable excuse for a human being. You gave him the money. There is no evidence it was a loan. If the roles were reversed – if you were a butt-ugly man who gave money to a somewhat attractive albeit naïve younger woman – this wouldn't even be a case. In short, I find for the defendant. And I find him disgusting. Court adjourned.'

Big Reg whooped with delight. 'Hey, Judge, if you're not busy—'

The theme music started up again, but Hester wasn't paying attention to that. Her cell phone rang. When she saw the incoming number, she hurried offstage and picked it up.

'Where are you?' she asked.

'I'm just pulling up to my house,' Ed Grayson said. 'And from the looks of it, I'm about to get arrested.'

'You went where I suggested?' Hester asked.

'I did.'

'Okay, good. Invoke your right to counsel and shut up. I'm on my way.'

Chapter 8

Wendy was surprised to see Pops's Harley-Davidson in her driveway. Exhausted from the long questioning – not to mention confronting her husband's killer earlier in the day and watching a man being murdered – she trudged past Pops's old Hog blanketed in fading decals: the American flag, the NRA member, the VFW logo. A small smile came to her face.

She opened the front door. 'Pops?'

He lumbered out of the kitchen. 'No beer in the fridge,' he said.

'No one here drinks beer.'

'Yeah, but you never know who might visit.'

She smiled at him . . . what do you call the father of your late husband? . . . her former father-in-law. 'Truer words.'

Pops crossed the room and hugged her deep and hard. The faint smells of leather and road and cigarettes and, yep, beer wafted up. Her father-in-law – screw the 'former' – had that hairy, big-bear, Vietnam-vet thing going. He was a big man, probably two-sixty, wheezed when he breathed, had a gray handlebar mustache stained yellow from tobacco.

'Heard you lost your job,' he said.

'How?'

Pops shrugged. Wendy thought about it. Only one answer: Charlie.

'Is that why you're here?' she asked.

'Just passing through and needed a place to crash. Where's my grandson?'

'At a friend's house. He should be home any minute.'

Pops studied her. 'You look like the fifth ring of hell.'

'Sweet talker.'

'Want to tell me about it?'

She did. Pops mixed them up a couple of cocktails. They sat on the couch, and as she told him about the shooting, Wendy realized, hard as it was to admit, how much she missed having a man around.

'A murdered baby raper,' Pops said. 'Wow, I'll be mourning for weeks.'

'That's a little cavalier, don't you think?'

Pops shrugged. 'You cross certain lines, you can't go back. By the way, you dating at all?'

'Nice segue.'

'Don't duck the question.'

'No, I'm not dating.'

Pops shook his head.

'What?'

'Humans need sex.'

'I'll write that down.'

'I'm serious. You still got it all going on, girl. Get out there and get some.'

'I thought you right-wing NRA guys were against pre-marital sex.'

'No, no, we just preach that so we can clear the playing fields for ourselves.'

She smiled at that. 'Ingenious.'

Pops looked up at her. 'What else is wrong?'

Wendy had debated not saying anything about it, but the words tumbled out anyway.

'I got a couple of letters from Ariana Nasbro,' Wendy said.

Silence.

John had been Pops's only child. Hard as it was for Wendy to lose a husband, no parent wants to speculate what it might be like to lose a child. The pain in Pops's face was a living, breathing thing. It never left.

'So what did dear, sweet Ariana want?' he asked.

'She's doing the Twelve Steps.'

'Ah. And you're one of those steps?'

Wendy nodded. 'Step Eight or Nine, I forget which.'

The front door burst open, stopping the conversation. They heard Charlie rush in – he had clearly spotted the Harley in the driveway. 'Pops is here?'

'We're in the den, kiddo.'

Charlie sprinted into the room, his smile wide. 'Pops!'

Pops was Charlie's only surviving grandparent – Wendy's parents had both died before Charlie was even born, and John's mom, Rose, had passed away two years ago from cancer. The two men – Charlie was still a boy, sure, but he was now taller than his grandfather – embraced with everything they had. They both squeezed their eyes shut. That was how Pops always hugged. Nothing was held back. Wendy watched them and again felt the pang of missing a man in their lives.

When they stopped, Wendy aimed for normalcy. 'How was school?'

'Lame.'

Pops threw his arm around his grandson's neck. 'Mind if me and Charlie go for a ride?'

She was about to protest, but Charlie's expectant face

made her stop. Gone was the sulky teenager. He was a kid again.

'You have an extra helmet?' she asked Pops.

'Always.' Pops arched an eyebrow at Charlie. 'You never know when you may run into a safety-conscious biker chick.'

'Don't be out late,' Wendy said. 'Oh, and before you go, maybe we should send out a warning.'

'A warning?'

'To lock up the ladies,' Wendy said. 'The two of you on the prowl and all.'

Pops and Charlie shared a knuckle bump. 'Oooh yeah.'

Men.

She walked them to the door, shared more hugs, realized that part of what she missed was simply the physical presence of a man, the hugging and embracing and the comfort there is in that. She watched them roar off on Pops's Hog, and as she turned to head back inside, a car pulled up and parked in front of the house.

The car was unfamiliar. Wendy waited. The driver's-side door opened, and a woman stormed out. Her eyes were red, her cheeks wet from tears. Wendy recognized her right away – Jenna Wheeler, Dan Mercer's ex-wife.

Wendy had first met Jenna the morning after Dan's episode aired. She went to the Wheeler house and sat on Jenna's bright yellow couch with bright blue flowers and listened as Jenna had defended her ex – publicly and loudly – and it had cost her. People in this town – Jenna lived less than two miles from Wendy, her daughter even went to the same high school as Charlie – were, of course, shocked. Dan Mercer had spent time in the Wheeler household. He had even babysat Jenna's children from her second marriage. How, neighbors wondered, could a caring mother do that, let that monster into their community, and how could she defend him now that the truth was so obvious?

'You know,' Wendy said.

Jenna nodded. 'I'm listed as his next of kin.'

The two women stood there on the stoop.

'I don't know what to say, Jenna.'

'You were there?'

'Yes.'

'Did you set Dan up?'

'What?'

'You heard me.'

'No, Jenna, I didn't set him up.'

'Why were you there, then?'

'Dan called me. He said he wanted to meet.'

Jenna looked skeptical. 'With you?'

'He said he had new evidence he was innocent.'

'But the judge had already thrown out the case.'

'I know.'

'So why—?' Jenna stopped. 'What was the new evidence?'

Wendy shrugged, as if that said it all, and maybe it did. The sun had set. The night was warm but a breeze was blowing through.

'I have more questions,' Jenna said.

'Why don't you come in, then?'

Wendy's reasons for inviting Jenna in were not entirely altruistic. Now that the shock of witnessing horrific violence had passed, the reporter in her was coming to the forefront.

'Can I get you some tea or something?'

Jenna shook her off. 'I still don't understand what happened.'

So Wendy told her. She started with Dan's phone call and ended with her returning to the trailer with Sheriff

Walker. She didn't go into Ed Grayson's visit to her house the day before. She had told Walker about that, but there was no reason to fan the flames here.

Jenna listened with moist eyes. When Wendy finished Jenna said, 'He just shot Dan?'

'Yes.'

'He didn't say anything first?'

'No, nothing.'

'He just—' Jenna looked around the room, as though for help. 'How does a person do that to another?'

Wendy had an answer, but she said nothing.

'You saw him, right? Ed Grayson? You can give the police a positive ID?'

'He wore a mask. But, yeah, I think it was Grayson.'

'Think?'

'Mask, Jenna. He wore a mask.'

'You never saw his face?'

'I never saw his face.'

'So how did you know it was him?'

'By his watch. His height, his build. The way he carried himself.'

Jenna frowned. 'Do you think that will hold up in court?'

'I don't know.'

'The police have him in custody, you know.'

Wendy didn't know, but again she kept her mouth shut. Jenna began to cry again. Wendy had no idea what to do here. Offering words of comfort would be at best superfluous. So she waited.

'How about Dan?' Jenna asked. 'Did you see his face?'

'Pardon?'

'When you got there, did you see what they did to his face?'

'You mean the bruises? Yeah, I saw them.'

'They kicked the crap out of him.'

'Who?'

'Dan tried so hard to escape. Wherever he went, the neighbors found out and hounded him. There were phone calls and threats and graffiti and, yes, beatings. It was horrible. He would move and someone would always find him.'

'Who beat him this time?' Wendy asked.

Jenna raised her eyes, met Wendy's. 'His life was a living hell.'

'Are you trying to put that on me?'

'You think you're blameless?'

'I never wanted him beaten.'

'No, you just wanted him put in jail.'

'Are you expecting me to apologize for that?'

'You're a reporter, Wendy. You don't get to be judge and jury. But once you aired that story, well, you think it mattered that the judge dismissed the charges? Did you think Dan would just be able to go back to his life – to any life?'

'I just reported what happened.'

'That's crap, and you know it. You created this story. You set him up.'

'Dan Mercer started flirting with an underage girl. . . .' Wendy stopped. No point in rehashing this. The two of them had been here before. This woman, naïve as she might be, was in mourning. Let her do it in peace.

'Are we done?' Wendy asked.

'He didn't do it.'

Wendy did not bother with a reply.

'I lived with him for four years. I was married to the man.'

'And divorced him.'

'So?'

Wendy shrugged. 'Why?'

'Half the marriages in this country end in divorce.'

'Why did yours?'

Jenna shook her head. 'What? You think it's because I learned he was a pedophile?'

'Did you?'

'He's the godfather of my daughter. He babysits my kids. They call him Uncle Dan.'

'Right. All very special. So why did you two get divorced?'

'It was mutual.'

'Uh-huh. Did you fall out of love with him?'

Jenna took her time, mulling that one over. 'Not really.'

'So? Look, I know that you don't want to admit this, but maybe you sensed something was wrong with him.'

'Not like that.'

'Like how then?'

'There was a part of Dan I couldn't quite reach. And before you say the obvious, no, it wasn't that he was a sexual deviant. Dan had a tough childhood. He was an orphan, bounced around from foster home to foster home. . . .'

Her voice trailed off. Wendy again skipped the obvious. Orphan. Foster homes. Abuse maybe. Scratch a pedophile's past, you always find something like this in the mix. She waited.

'I know what you're thinking. And you're wrong.'

'Why? Because you knew the man so well?'

'Yes. But not just that.'

'What then?'

'It was always like . . . I don't know how to put this. Something happened to him in college. You know he went to Princeton, right?'

'Right.'

'Poor orphan, worked hard, managed to go to a big-time Ivy League school.'

'Yeah, so?'

Jenna stopped, met her eye.

'What?'

'You owe him.'

Wendy said nothing.

'Whatever you think,' Jenna said, 'whatever may or may not be the truth here, one thing is certain.'

'And that is?'

'You got him killed.'

Silence.

'Maybe you did more than that. His attorney embarrassed you in court. Dan was going to go free. That must have upset you.'

'Don't go there, Jenna.'

'Why not? You were angry. You feel the courts got it wrong. You meet with Dan and suddenly, by shocking coincidence, there's Ed Grayson. You have to be involved – an accomplice at the very least. Or maybe you're being set up.'

She stopped. Wendy waited. Then: 'You're not going to say, "Just like Dan," are you?'

Jenna shrugged. 'Hell of a coincidence.'

'I think it's time for you to leave, Jenna.'

'I think you're probably right.'

The two women walked to the door. Jenna said, 'I have one more question.'

'Go ahead.'

'Dan told you where he was, right? I mean, that's how you ended up at the trailer park?'

'Right.'

'Did you tell Ed Grayson about it?'

'No.'

'So how did he end up there – at the exact same time?'

Wendy hesitated before answering. 'I don't know. I guess he followed me.'

'How would he have known to do that?'

Wendy had no answer. She remembered checking her rearview mirrors too, on those quiet roads. There had been no other cars.

How had Ed Grayson found Dan Mercer?

'See? The most logical answer is, you helped him.'

'I didn't.'

'Right. And it would suck,' Jenna said, 'if no one believed you.'

She turned and walked away. Her question stayed in the air. Wendy watched her drive off. She started to turn around and head back inside when something made her pull up.

Her car tire. Low on air. Wasn't that what Ed Grayson said?

She ran out to the driveway. The tire was fine. She ducked down and felt alongside the back bumper. Fingerprints, she realized. In her haste, she had forgotten about them. She pulled her hand away, bent down on her haunches, took a look.

Nothing.

No choice really. She lay flat on her back like a classic grease monkey. She had installed motion-sensor lighting in the driveway. It provided enough illumination. She wiggled on the tar surface under the car. Not far. Just a little. And that was when she saw it. It was small, not much bigger than a book of matches. It was held on by a magnet, the same kind of thing people use to keep a spare set of keys hidden. But that's not what this was. It explained a lot.

Ed Grayson had not bent down to check her back tire. He had bent down to stick a magnetic GPS device under her bumper.

Chapter 9

'Does your client wish to make a statement?'

Sitting in the interrogation room at the Sussex County Police headquarters with Ed Grayson, an enormous sheriff named Mickey Walker, and a young cop named Tom Stanton, attorney Hester Crimstein replied, 'Don't take this the wrong way, but, man, this is fun.'

'I'm glad you're amused.'

'I am. Really. This arrest is laughable.'

'Your client isn't under arrest,' Walker said. 'We merely want to chat.'

'Like something on your social calendar? How nice. Yet you issued search warrants for his home and car, did you not?'

'We did.'

Hester nodded. 'Good, super. Here, before we get started.' She slid a piece of paper and pen across the table.

'What's this?' Walker asked.

'I would like you to write down your names, ranks, office addresses, home addresses, phone numbers, turn-ons, turnoffs, whatever else may help my subpoena server find and thus serve you when we sue for wrongful arrest.'

'I just told you. No one is under arrest.'

'And I just told you, handsome: Yet you issued search warrants.'

'I would think your client would like to make a statement.'

'You do?'

'We have a witness who saw your client execute a man,' Walker said.

Ed Grayson opened his mouth, but Hester Crimstein put her hand on his forearm, silencing him.

'You don't say.'

'A reliable witness.'

'And your reliable witness saw my client execute – such an impressive word, by the way, not kill or murder or shoot, but execute – a man?'

'That's correct.'

Hester smiled faux sweetly. 'Do you mind then if we take it a step at a time, Sheriff?'

'A step at a time.'

'Yes. First off, who is the man? The victim of this execution?'

'Dan Mercer.'

'The pedophile?'

'Doesn't matter who or what he was. And that particular charge was dropped.'

'Well, that last part is true. Your compadres screwed up the case. But never mind. Step by step. First step: You say Dan Mercer was executed.'

'Correct.'

'So, step one: Show us the body.'

Silence.

'Trouble with your hearing, big boy? The body. I would like my medical examiner to examine it.'

'Don't be cute, Hester. You know it hasn't been located yet.'

'Not located?' Now Hester feigned shock. 'Well, maybe you could tell me what evidence you have that Dan Mercer is even dead? Wait, never mind. I'm kind of in a rush. No body, am I right?'

'Not yet.'

'Okay, fine. Next step. You claim, even though you don't have a body, that Dan Mercer was executed?'

'Yes.'

'I assume a weapon of some sort was used? Could we examine that please?'

More silence.

Hester cupped her ear. 'Hello?'

'We haven't located it yet,' Walker said.

'No weapon?'

'No weapon.'

'No body, no weapon.' Hester spread her hands and grinned. 'Now do you see what I mean by "man, this is fun"?'

'We were hoping your client would like to make a statement.'

'About what? Solar energy and its role in the twenty-first century? Wait, I'm not done. We did the body and the weapon – what did we forget? Oh, that's right. The witness.'

Silence.

'Your witness saw my client execute Dan Mercer, correct?'

'Correct.'

'She saw his face?'

Another pause.

Hester cupped the ear again. 'Go ahead, big fella. Say it.'

'He was wearing a mask.'

'Pardon me?'

100

'He was wearing a mask.'

'As in, a mask that would cover his face?'

'That's what she testified to, yes.'

'And yet she identified my client how?'

'By his watch.'

'His watch?'

Walker cleared his throat. 'And his height and build.'

'Six foot, one-eighty. Oh, and that ever-rare Timex. Do you know why I'm no longer smiling, Sheriff Walker?'

'I'm sure you'll tell us.'

'I'm no longer smiling because this is too easy. Do you know what I get per hour? For that kind of money, I deserve a challenge. This is simply insulting. Your case, as it were, is beyond fish 'n' barrel. I don't want to hear what you *don't* have anymore. I want to hear what you do.'

She waited. So far Walker had only given up what she already knew. That was the only reason Crimstein was still there. She wanted to know what they did have.

'We are hoping your client will make a statement,' Walker said again.

'Not if that's all you have.'

'It's not.'

Pause.

'Would you like a drum roll?' Hester asked.

'We have physical evidence tying your client to both Dan Mercer and the scene of the crime.'

'Oh, goodie. Do tell.'

'Understand the tests are all preliminary. We will have details in the next few weeks. But we have a pretty good idea of what the physical evidence will show. That's why we have your client here. To help explain his part in this to us. Get ahead of it.'

'Nice of you.'

'We found blood in the trailer. We also found blood specks in Mr. Grayson's Acura MDX. While a full DNA test will take some time, the preliminary results show that the blood matches. That is, the blood found where our witness says Mr. Mercer was shot is the same as the blood found in your client's vehicle. We also typed it. O negative, the same as Mr. Mercer's. We also have carpet fibers. Without going into too much detail, the same carpet fibers were found in the trailer rented out by Mr. Mercer and in your client's Acura MDX. We also have the same fibers on the bottom of your client's sneaker. Lastly, we ran a gun residue test. There were powder marks found on your client's hands. He fired a gun.'

Hester sat there and stared. Walker stared back.

'Ms. Crimstein?'

'I'm waiting until you're finished. Because that can't be all you have.'

Walker said nothing.

Hester turned to Ed Grayson. 'Come on. We're leaving.'

'No response at all?' Walker asked.

'To what? My client is a decorated retired federal marshal. Mr. Grayson is a family man, a pillar of the community, a man with no criminal record at all – yet you waste our time with this nonsense. At best – at the very, *very* best if all the tests come back the way you hope and I don't destroy all your so-called physical evidence with my experts and my cross and my accusations about tainting and incompetence – if that all goes perfectly for you, which I highly doubt, you might, *might,* be able to show a casual link between my client and Dan Mercer. Period, the end. And that's laughable. No body, no weapon, no witness who can positively identify my client. You don't even have proof there was a crime – let alone that my client was involved.'

Walker sat back, the chair creaking with the onslaught. 'So you can explain the fibers and blood?'

'I don't need to, do I?'

'I just thought you might want to help us out. Clear your client once and for all.'

'Tell you what I'll do.' Hester scribbled down a phone number and passed it to him.

'What's this?'

'A phone number.'

'I see that. For?'

'The Gun-O-Rama shooting range.'

Walker just looked at her. The color in his face ebbed away.

'Give them a call,' Hester said. 'My client was there just this afternoon, an hour before you picked him up. Doing a little target practice.' Hester did a little finger wave. 'Bye-bye, gun residue test.'

Walker's jaw dropped. He looked at Stanton, tried to regain his composure. 'Convenient.'

'Hardly. Mr. Grayson is a decorated retired federal marshal, remember? He shoots frequently. Are we done here?'

'No statement?'

'"Don't eat yellow snow." That's our statement. Come on, Ed.'

Hester and Ed Grayson stood.

'We will keep looking, Ms. Crimstein. You should both know that. We have a timeline. We will trace Mr. Grayson's steps. We will find the body and the weapon. I understand why he did what he did. But we don't get to play executioner. So I will make that case. Make no mistake.'

'May I speak frankly, Sheriff Walker?'

'Sure.'

Hester looked at the camera above his head. 'Turn the camera off.'

Walker looked back, nodded; the red light on the camera went off.

Hester put her fists on the table and leaned down. She didn't have to lean far. Even sitting Walker was nearly her height. 'You could have the body and the weapon and, hell, a live feed of my client shooting this child rapist at Giants Stadium in front of eighty thousand witnesses – and I could still get him off in ten minutes.'

She turned. Ed Grayson had already opened the door.

'Have a nice day,' Hester said.

At ten PM, Charlie texted Wendy.

POP WANTS TO KNOW WHERE THE NEAREST TITTY BAR IS.

She smiled. His way of letting her know that he was fine. Charlie was pretty good about staying in touch.

She responded: I DON'T KNOW. AND NOBODY CALLS THEM THAT. THEY'RE GENTLEMEN'S LOUNGES NOW.

Charlie: POPS SAID HE HATES THAT POLITICALLY CORRECT SH*T.

She smiled as the home phone rang. It was Sheriff Walker returning her call.

'I found something on my car,' she said.

'What?'

'A GPS. I think Ed Grayson put it there.'

'I'm around the corner,' he said. 'I know it's late, but do you mind if I take a look now?'

'No, that's fine.'

'Give me five.'

She met him outside by her car. Walker bent down as Wendy reminded him of Ed Grayson's visit, this time adding the seemingly unimportant detail of him checking her back tire. He looked at the GPS and nodded. It took him a moment or two to get himself back upright.

'I'll send some people out here to take pictures and remove it.'

'I heard you arrested Ed Grayson.'

'Who told you that?'

'Mercer's ex-wife, Jenna Wheeler.'

'She's wrong. We brought him in for questioning. He was never arrested.'

'Are you still holding him?'

'No, he was free to go.'

'And now?'

Walker cleared his throat. 'Now we continue our investigation.'

'Wow, that sounds official.'

'You're a reporter.'

'Not anymore, but okay, let's make this conversation off the record.'

'Off the record, we don't have a case. We don't have a body. We don't have a weapon. We have one witness – that would be you – and she never saw the shooter's face, so she really can't positively ID him.'

'That's crap.'

'How so?'

'If Dan Mercer was a prominent citizen instead of a suspected pedophile—'

'And if I lost a hundred pounds and became white and good-looking, someone might mistake me for Hugh Jackman. But the truth is, until the body or weapon is found, we have nothing.'

'Sounds like you're giving up.'

'I'm not. But the brass has absolutely no interest in pursuing this. As both my boss and opposing counsel reminded me today, the best-case scenario is that we charge a retired fed whose son was sexually abused by the victim.'

'And that would be bad for any political career.'

'That's the cynical viewpoint,' Walker said.

'What other viewpoint is there?'

'The real-world one. We have a limited amount of resources. One of my colleagues, an old-timer named Frank Tremont, is still looking for that missing girl, Haley McWaid, but after this much time, well, it is all about resources, right? So who wants to divert resources away from that case, for example, to – one – find justice for an undeserving scumbag and – two – a case we can't possibly win because no jury will convict?'

'Again I repeat: Sounds like you're giving up.'

'Not quite. I plan to retrace his steps, figure out where Mercer had been living.'

'Not the trailer?'

'No. I spoke to his lawyer and ex-wife. Mercer moved around a lot – I guess it was tough for him to settle. Anyway he had just rented out the trailer that morning. There's nothing there, not even a change of clothes.'

Wendy made a face. 'So what do you expect to learn when you find his place?'

'Damn if I know.'

'What else?'

'I'll try to track down that GPS on your car, but I can't imagine that'll get us anywhere. Even if we get extra lucky and prove it belongs to Grayson, well, that shows he kept tabs on you? We'd still have a long way to go.'

'You need to find the body,' she said.

'Right, that's priority one. I need to retrace Grayson's driving route – and I think I might be able to get a rough idea. We know that two hours after leaving that trailer, Grayson stopped at a shooting range.'

'You're kidding.'

'That was my reaction. But actually it was pretty ingenious. Witnesses saw him firing a gun at targets, thereby making our gun residue test null and void. We checked the weapon he brought with him to the range, but no surprise – the slugs didn't match the ones we found at the trailer park.'

'Wow. Grayson knew to go to a range to screw up your test?'

'He's an ex–federal marshal. He knows what he's doing. Think about it. He wore a mask, got rid of the body, got rid of the weapon, destroyed our gun residue test – and he hired Hester Crimstein. Do you see what I'm up against?'

'I do.'

'We know Grayson dumped the body somewhere on the route, but there are a lot of hours unaccounted for, and that area has plenty of empty acreage.'

'And you won't get the manpower to cover it?'

'Like I said, this isn't a girl gone missing. This is the corpse of a pedophile. And if Grayson planned it well enough – which, so far, seems to be the case – he might have dug a hole before he even killed Mercer. We might never find the body.'

Wendy looked off, shook her head.

'What?'

'I was his patsy. Grayson tried to get me on his side. When he couldn't, he just followed me – and I led him right to Mercer.'

'Not your fault.'

'Doesn't matter if it is or it isn't. I don't like being used like that.'

Walker said nothing.

'It's a crap ending,' Wendy said.

'Some would say it's pretty tidy.'

'How so?'

'The pedophile escapes our legal system but not just-ice. It's almost biblical when you think about it.'

Wendy shook her head. 'It feels wrong.'

'What part?'

She kept it to herself. But the answer was, all of it. Like maybe Mercer's ex had a point. Like maybe something about this whole thing stank right from the get-go. Like maybe from the get-go she should have trusted her woman's intuition or her gut or whatever the hell you want to call it.

Suddenly it felt as though she'd helped kill an innocent man.

'Just find him,' Wendy said. 'Whatever he was, you owe him that.'

'I'll try. But understand, this case will never be a prior-ity.'

Chapter 10

B ut Walker was tragically wrong about that.

Wendy wouldn't learn about the horrible discovery until the next day when it became 'breaking news' on all the media outlets. With Pops and Charlie both sleeping in and Jenna's comment about Princeton ringing in her head, Wendy had decided to start her own investigation. First stop: Phil Turnball, Dan Mercer's college roommate. It was time, she thought, to dig seriously into Dan's past. There seemed no place better to start.

But at the exact same time that Wendy entered a Starbucks in Englewood, New Jersey, two law enforcement officials, Sussex County sheriff Walker and his rookie deputy, Tom Stanton, were twenty-five miles away, in Newark, searching room 204 at the dubiously dubbed Freddy's Deluxe Luxury Suites. Total fleabag. Freddy must have had some sense of humor, Walker thought, insomuch as the no-tell managed to be none of the three things – deluxe, luxury, or suites – listed in the moniker.

Walker had worked diligently trying to track down the last two weeks in the life of Dan Mercer. The clues were few. Using his cell phone, Dan Mercer had called only three people: his lawyer, Flair Hickory; his ex-wife, Jenna Wheeler; and yesterday, the reporter Wendy Tynes. Flair had never asked his client where he was staying –

the less he knew, the better. Jenna didn't know. Wendy, well, she wasn't in contact with him until yesterday.

Still the trail wasn't hard to follow. Dan Mercer had been hiding, yes, but according to both his lawyer and his ex, it was from threats from overly 'concerned' citizens and quasi-vigilantes, not law enforcement. No one wanted a predator in the neighborhood. So he moved from hotel to hotel, usually paying with cash he had picked up from a nearby ATM. Because of the impending trial, Mercer couldn't leave the state.

Sixteen days ago, he had checked into a Motel 6 in Wildwood. From there, he had stayed three days at the Court Manor Inn in Fort Lee followed by the Fair Motel in Ramsey, and as of yesterday, Mercer had been at Freddy's Deluxe Luxury Suites in downtown Newark, room 204.

The window looked out over a shelter nicknamed the Resort (as in Last Resort) where Dan Mercer had worked. Interesting place to end up. The manager hadn't seen Mercer in two days, but then, as the manager explained, clients didn't come here to be noticed.

'Let's see what we can find,' Walker said.

Stanton nodded. 'Okay.'

Walker said, 'Mind if I ask you something?'

'Nope.'

'No other cop wanted to work with me on this one. They figure, good riddance to a scumbag.'

Stanton nodded. 'Yet I volunteered.'

'Right.'

'And you want to know why.'

'Right.'

Stanton closed the top drawer, opened the second one. 'Maybe I'm new, maybe I'll get more jaded. But the law cleared this guy. Period, the end. If you don't like that, change the law. We in law enforcement need to be impartial referees. If the speed limit is fifty-five miles per hour, then you ticket a guy going fifty-six. If you think, nah, don't ticket until he's going sixty-five, then change the law to sixty-five. And it works the other way too. Following the rules, the judge freed Dan Mercer. If you don't like that, change the law. Don't bend the rules. Legally change them.'

Walker smiled. 'You are new.'

Stanton shrugged, still searching through the clothes. 'I guess there's a bit more to it.'

'I thought there might be. Go ahead, I'm listening.'

'I have an older brother named Pete. Great guy, terrific athlete. He was on the Buffalo Bills practice squad for two years out of school. Tight end.'

'Okay.'

'So Pete's up at camp at the start of his third season. This is his year, he thinks. He's been lifting and working out like a madman, and he has a real shot of getting on the roster. He's twenty-six years old and he's up in Buffalo. He goes out one night and meets this girl at a Bennigan's. You know. The chain restaurant?'

'I know it.'

'Okay, so Pete orders wings, and this smoldering chick saunters over and asks if she can have one. He says sure. She makes a spectacle of herself eating it. You know what I mean? Using lots of tongue and she's wearing this scoop top that's begging for an ogling. I mean, she's a total hottie. They start flirting. She sits down. One thing leads to another – and Pete takes her back to his place and gives her what for.'

Stanton made a sideways fist and gently pounds it – demonstrating what 'what for' meant, in case it wasn't clear.

111

'Turns out the girl is fifteen. A high school sophomore, but man, she doesn't look it. You know how high school girls dress nowadays. She's decked out like she's serving up drinks at Hooters – or just serving 'em up, if you know what I mean.'

Stanton looked at Walker and waited. To keep the conversation moving, Walker said, 'I know what you mean.'

'Right, so anyway, the girl's dad finds out. He goes nuts, says Pete seduced his little girl – even though she was probably banging my brother to get back at her old man. So Pete gets charged with statutory rape. Gets caught up in the system. The system I love. I get it. It's the law. He is now labeled a sex offender, a pedophile, the whole works. And that's a joke. My brother is a solid citizen, a good guy, and now no team will touch him with a ten-foot pole. Maybe this guy, this Dan Mercer, well, it was a form of entrapment, wasn't it? Maybe he deserves the benefit of the doubt. Maybe he's innocent until proven guilty.'

Walker turned away because he didn't want to admit that maybe Stanton had a point. You make so many calls in life that you don't want to make – and you want those calls to be easy. You want to put people in neat categories, make them monsters or angels, but it almost never works that way. You work in the gray and frankly that kinda sucks. The extremes are so much easier.

As Tom Stanton bent down to look under the bed, Walker tried to refocus. Right now, maybe it was best to keep this black and white and stay away from the moral relativism. A man was missing, probably dead. Find him. That was all. Doesn't matter who he is or what he did. Just find him.

Walker moved into the bathroom, checked the vanity.

Toothpaste, toothbrush, razor, shaving cream, deodorant. Fascinating stuff.

From the other room Stanton said, 'Bingo.'

'What?'

'Under the bed. I found his mobile phone.'

Walker was about to yell, 'Great,' but he stopped short.

Knowing Mercer's cell phone number and using cell tower triangulation, Walker had already learned that the last phone call from Mercer's mobile had been somewhere on Route 15 not long before the murder, approximately three miles from the trailer park and at least an hour's drive from this room.

So why would his mobile phone be in the room?

He didn't have much time to think about it. From the other room, he heard Stanton's low voice, almost a pained whisper: 'Oh no . . .'

The tone sent a chill straight up the spine. 'What?'

'Oh my God . . .'

Walker hustled back into the bedroom. 'What is it? What's wrong?'

Stanton held the phone in his hand. All color was gone from his face. He stared down at the image on the screen. Walker could see the phone with the bright pink case.

It was an iPhone. He had the same model.

'What is it?'

The screen on the iPhone went dark. Stanton didn't say anything. He raised the phone, pressed the button. The screen lit up. Walker took a step closer and took a look.

His heart sank.

The lit-up iPhone's welcome screen was a family photograph. A classic vacation group shot. Four people – three kids, one adult – smiling and laughing. In the center of the photograph was Mickey Mouse. And on Mickey's right, flashing maybe the biggest smile of them all, stood a missing girl named Haley McWaid.

Chapter 11

Wendy called the residence of Mercer's college roommate, Phil Turnball. After graduating from Princeton, Turnball had taken the express train straight to Wall Street and high finance. He lived in the tonier section of Englewood.

When the Dan episode of *Caught in the Act* first aired, she had tried to contact Turnball. He had refused to comment. She let it go. Maybe now that Mercer was dead, Phil Turnball might be more forthcoming.

Mrs. Turnball – Wendy didn't catch the first name – answered the phone. Wendy explained who she was. 'I know your husband's been blowing me off, but trust me, he's going to want to hear this.'

'He's not here now.'

'Is there a way I can reach him?'

She hesitated.

'It's important, Mrs. Turnball.'

'He's in a meeting.'

'At his office in Manhattan? I have the address here from my old notes—'

'Starbucks,' she said.

'Excuse me?'

'The meeting. It's not what you think. It's at Starbucks.'

*

Wendy found a parking space in front of Baumgart's, a restaurant she frequented as often as she could, and walked four stores down to Starbucks. Mrs. Turnball had explained that Phil had been laid off during the economic slump. His meeting, such as it was, was more of a coffee klatch for former masters of the universe – a group founded by Phil called the Fathers Club. Mrs. Turnball had told her that the club was a way for these suddenly unemployed men to 'cope and find camaraderie during these very trying times,' but Wendy couldn't help but hear the sarcasm in the woman's voice. Or maybe Wendy was projecting. A group of blood-sucking, overpaid, over-important yuppies whining about the economy they helped destroy by feasting on it parasitelike – all while enjoying a five-dollar cup of coffee.

Well, boo-friggin'-hoo.

She entered the Starbucks and spotted Phil Turnball in the right-hand corner. He wore a fresh-pressed business suit, and he sat huddled around a table with three other men. One wore tennis whites and spun a racket like he was waiting for Federer to serve. Another wore a baby sling complete with, uh, baby. He gently bounced up and down, no doubt to keep the little one content and silent. The final guy, the one the others were all intensely listening to, wore an oversize baseball cap with the flat bill precariously tilted upward and to the right.

'You don't like it?' Hat Tilt asked.

Now that she was closer, she could see that Hat Tilt looked like Jay-Z – if Jay-Z suddenly aged ten years and never worked out and was a pasty white guy trying to look like Jay-Z.

'No, no, Fly, don't get me wrong,' the guy in the tennis whites said. 'It's righteous and all. Totally righteous.'

Wendy frowned. Righteous?

'But – and this is just a suggestion – I don't think the line works. What with the puppies swinging and all.'

'Hmm. Too graphic?'

'Maybe.'

'Because I gotta be me, you know what I'm saying? Tonight at Blend. Open mike. Gotta be. Can't sell out to the man.'

'I hear you, Fly, I do. And you'll kick ass tonight, no worries. But necklace?' Tennis Whites spread his arms. 'It just doesn't fit your theme. You need another puppy reference. Dogs don't wear a necklace, am I right?'

Murmurs of agreement around the table.

The Jay-Z NeverBe – Fly? – noticed Wendy hovering. He lowered his head. 'Yo, check it. Shawty at five o'clock.'

They all turned toward her. Except for Phil, this was hardly what Wendy had expected. You'd have thought Mrs. Turnball would have warned her about this particular collection of ex–masters of the universe.

'Wait.' It was the guy in the tennis whites. 'I know you. NTC News. Wendy Something, right?'

'Wendy Tynes, yes.'

They all smiled except for Phil Turnball.

'You here to do a story on Fly's gig tonight?'

Wendy thought a story on these guys sounded like a hell of an idea. 'Maybe later,' she said. 'But right now, I'm here to see Phil.'

'I have nothing to say to you.'

'You don't have to say a word. Come on. We need to talk in private.'

As they walked out of the Starbucks and back up the block, Wendy said, 'So that's the Fathers Club?'

'Who told you about that?'

'Your wife.'

He said nothing.

'So,' Wendy continued, 'what's with Vanilla Ice back there?'

'Norm . . . well, actually, he wants us to call him Fly.'

'Fly?'

'Short for Ten-A-Fly. That's his rap handle.'

Wendy tried not to sigh. Tenafly was a New Jersey town right down the street.

'Norm . . . Fly . . . was a brilliant marketing guy at Benevisti Vance in the city. He's been out of work for, what, two years now, but he thinks he found a new talent.'

'What?'

'Rapping.'

'Please tell me you're kidding.

'This is like grief,' Phil said. 'Everyone does it a little differently. Fly thinks he's got a new market cornered.'

They arrived at Wendy's car. She unlocked the doors. 'Rapping?'

Phil nodded. 'He's the only white middle-aged New Jersey rapper on the circuit. At least, that's what he says.' They slipped into the front seats. 'So what do you want with me?'

No easy way to do it so she dived straight in.

'Dan Mercer was murdered yesterday.'

Phil Turnball listened without saying a word. He stared out the front windshield, his face pale, his eyes moist. His shave, Wendy noticed, was perfect. His hair had that perfect part and a curl in the front so that you could imagine what he looked like as a young boy. Wendy waited, let him absorb what she'd told him.

'Something I can get you?' Wendy asked.

Phil Turnball shook his head. 'I remember meeting Dan first day of orientation, freshman year. He was so funny. The rest of us were so uptight, wanting to impress. He was just so comfortable, had such a strange outlook.'

'Strange how?'

'Like he'd seen it all already and it wasn't worth getting too worked up about. Dan also wanted to make a difference. Yeah, I know how that sounds, but he really did straddle that line. He partied hard, like the rest of us, but he always talked about doing good. We had plans, I guess. All of us did. And now . . .'

His voice faded away.

'I'm sorry,' Wendy said.

'I assume you didn't track me down just to deliver this bad news.'

'No.'

'So?'

'I'm investigating Dan—'

'Seems you've already done that.' He turned toward her. 'Only thing left is to pick at the corpse.'

'That's not my intent.'

'What then?'

'I called you once before. When we first ran our exposé on Dan.'

He said nothing.

'Why didn't you return my calls?'

'And say what?'

'Whatever.'

'I have a wife, two kids. I didn't see where publicly defending a pedophile – even a wrongly accused one – would help anyone.'

'You think Dan was wrongly accused?'

Phil squeezed his eyes shut. Wendy wanted to reach out, but again it felt like the wrong move. She decided to shift gears.

'Why do you wear a suit to Starbucks?' she asked.

Phil almost smiled. 'I always hated casual Fridays.'

Wendy stared at this handsome yet thoroughly defeated man. He looked drained, bled out almost, and it was as if the gorgeous suit and shoe polish could prop him up.

Studying his face, a sudden memory flash of another face stole her breath: Wendy's beloved father, age fifty-six, sitting at the kitchen table, flannel sleeves rolled up, stuffing his rather flimsy résumé into an envelope. Fifty-six years old and suddenly, for the first time in his adult life, out of work. Her dad had been a union leader, Local 277, running a printing press for a major New York newspaper for twenty-eight years. He had negotiated fair deals for his men, striking only once in 1989, beloved by everyone on the floor.

Then there was a merger, one of those constant M&A deals of the early nineties, the kind of thing Wall Street suits like, well, Phil Turnball loved because stock portfolios go up a few points, damn what may. Her father was suddenly made superfluous and let go. Just like that, for the first time in his life, he was out of work. The next day, he started at that kitchen table with the résumés. And his face that day looked a lot like Phil Turnball's did now.

'Aren't you angry?' she'd asked her father.

'Anger is a waste.' Her father stuffed another letter. He looked up at her. 'You want some advice – or are you too old for that now?'

'Never too old,' Wendy had said.

'Work for yourself. That's the only boss you can ever trust.'

He never got the chance to work for himself. He never found another job. Two years later, at the age of fifty-eight, her father died of a heart attack at that same kitchen table, still combing classifieds and stuffing envelopes.

'You don't want to help?' Wendy asked.

'With what? Dan is dead.'

Phil Turnball reached for the door handle.

Wendy put her hand on his arm. 'One question before you go: Why do you think Dan was wrongly accused?'

He thought about it before answering. 'I guess when it happens to you, you just have a feel for it.'

'I'm not following.'

'Don't worry about it. It's not important.'

'Did something happen to you, Phil? What am I missing here?'

He chuckled, but there was no humor in it. 'No comment, Wendy.' He pulled on the handle.

'But—'

'Not now,' he said, opening the door. 'Right now I'm going to take a walk and think about my old friend for a little while. Dan deserves that, at the very least.'

Phil Turnball slid out of the car, adjusted his suit jacket, and headed north away from her, away from his friends at Starbucks.

Chapter 12

Another dead hooker.

Essex County investigator Frank Tremont hoisted up his pants by the belt and looked down at the girl and sighed. Same ol', same ol'. Newark, South Ward, not far from Beth Israel Hospital yet a lifetime away. Frank could smell the decay in the air, but it wasn't from just the body. It was always this way. No one ever cleaned up out here. No one tried. They all just bathed lazily in the decay.

And so another dead hooker.

They already had her pimp in custody for it. The hooker had 'dissed' him or whatever and he had to show what a big man he was so he slit her throat. Still had the knife on him when they picked him up. Smart guy, real genius. It took Frank about six seconds to get a confession out of him. All he had to say was, 'We heard you don't have the balls to hurt a woman.' That was enough for Genius Pimp to 'man up.'

He stared down at the dead girl, maybe fifteen years old, maybe thirty, hard to tell out here, splayed among the street debris, crushed soda cans, wrappers from McDonald's, empty forties of beer. Frank flashed back to his last dead hooker investigation. That case had exploded in his face. His bad, totally. He'd read it wrong and messed up. It might have cost more lives, but there was no point in going over that anymore. He had blown the case and lost his job over it. Forced out by the county prosecutor and the chief investigator. He'd been set to retire.

And then he'd drawn the Haley McWaid missing person case.

He'd gone to his bosses and asked to stay on, just until the case was solved. His bosses understood. But that was three months ago. Frank had worked hard looking for the high school girl. He had gotten others involved, the feds, cops who understood the Internet and tracking and profiling, anyone and everyone who could possibly help. He had no interest in glory, just finding the girl.

But the case was bone-dry.

He looked down at the dead hooker. That was what you got a lot of on this job. You see junkies and whores pissing their lives away, getting hammered and stoned and freeloading and then they get beaten up or knocked up with Lord knows how many kids with Lord knows how many different fathers and it was such a damn waste. Most skate through okay, shuffling listlessly through pathetic lives, making barely a dent in the social fabric, and if they do get noticed, it's for a bad reason. But most survive. They're a drain, but God lets them survive, sometimes to old age.

And then, because God is a freaking riot, He takes Frank's daughter instead.

A crowd had gathered behind the yellow tape, but not a very big one. A quick glance and then they moved on.

'You done, Frank?'

It was the medical examiner. Frank nodded. 'All yours.'

His little girl, Kasey. Seventeen years old. So sweet

and bright and loving. There's the old saw about a smile being able to light up a whole room. Kasey had one of those smiles. *Bam,* a beam that could slice through any darkness. She never gave anyone an ounce of trouble or hurt anyone. Not once in her whole life. Kasey never did drugs or whored or got knocked up. Meanwhile these junkies and whores roamed like wild animals – and Kasey died.

Unfair doesn't begin to get it.

Kasey was sixteen when they made the diagnosis of Ewing's sarcoma. Bone cancer. The tumors started in her pelvis and began to gnaw away. His little girl died in pain. Frank watched it. He sat there, at her bedside, dry-eyed, holding on tightly to both her frail hand and his sanity. He saw the scars from invasive surgeries and the sunken eyes of the slowly dying. He felt her body warmth spike when she had a fever. He remembered that Kasey had a lot of bad dreams as a young child, that she'd often crawl into their bed quaking, slipping between him and Maria, that she talked in her sleep, tossed and turned, but once she was diagnosed, all that stopped. Maybe her night terror fled in the face of her day terror. Either way, Kasey's sleep became quiet, a night calm, almost as though she was rehearsing for death.

He had prayed, but that was worthless. That was just how he felt. God knows what He's going to do. He's got a plan, right? If you truly want to believe that He is all-knowing and all-powerful, do you really think you and your pitiful begging are going to sway His grand plan? Tremont knew it didn't work that way. He met another family praying for their son in the hospital. Same disease. He still died. Then their other son went to Iraq and died there. How anyone could hear that and believe prayer worked was beyond him.

Meanwhile the streets out here are littered with the useless. They live – Kasey dies. So, yeah, girls with families, girls like Haley McWaid and Kasey Tremont, girls who had people who loved them and had lives in front of them, real lives, lives that would amount to more than waste, they mattered more. That was the truth. No one wanted to say it. The spineless phonies would tell you that the dead hooker being zipped up in that Hefty bag deserved the exact same consideration as a Haley McWaid or a Kasey Tremont. Except we all know that's crap. We peddle it. But we all know the truth. We tell the lie. But we know.

So let's stop pretending. The dead hooker would maybe get two paragraphs on page twelve of *The Star-Ledger*, strictly as a story for the readers to tsk-tsk over. Haley McWaid got hours on national TV. So we all know, don't we? Why can't we just say it?

The Haley McWaids of the world mattered more.

Nothing wrong with that. It's the truth, right? Didn't mean the dead hooker didn't matter. But Haley mattered more. And it wasn't a question of race or any of those other tags people tried to stick on him. Label a guy a bigot – that's the easy way out. But it's crap. White, black, Asian, Latino, whatever – lesser is lesser. Everyone gets it, even if they're afraid to say it.

Frank's mind traveled, as it often did these days, to Haley McWaid's mother, Marcia, and the shattered father, Ted. This hooker being whisked away was gone now. Maybe someone will care, but nine times out of ten, that's not the case. Her parents, if she knew who they were, had given up on her long ago. Marcia and Ted were still waiting and scared and hoping. And yeah, that mattered. Maybe that was the difference between the Dead Hookers of the world and the Haley McWaids.

Not skin color or finances or picket fences, but people who cared about you, family who'd be left devastated, fathers and mothers who would never ever be whole again.

So Frank would not quit until he found out what happened to Haley McWaid.

He thought about Kasey again, tried to conjure up the happy little girl, the one who liked aquariums more than zoos and blue more than pink. But those images had faded, were harder now to evoke, outrageous as that was, and instead, Frank remembered the way Kasey grew smaller in that hospital bed, the way she ran her hand through her hair and it came out in clumps, the way she looked down at the hair in her hand and cried while her father sat by her side, helpless, powerless.

The ME finished with the dead hooker. Two men lifted the corpse and plopped it on a gurney, as though it were a bag of peat moss.

'Easy,' Frank said.

One of the guys turned to him. 'Ain't going to hurt her.'

'Just go easy.'

As they wheeled the body away, Frank Tremont felt his mobile phone vibrate.

He blinked back the moistness and hit the answer button. 'Tremont here.'

'Frank?'

It was Mickey Walker, sheriff of nearby Sussex County. Big black guy, used to work in Newark with Frank. Solid dude, good investigator. One of Frank's favorites. Walker's office had landed the baby-raper murder case – apparently a parent had taken care of the pedophilia problem with his own gun. Seemed to Frank a damned fine example of good riddance, though he knew Walker would work it for all it had.

'Yeah, I'm here, Mickey.'

'You know Freddy's Deluxe Luxury Suites?'

'The hot sheets on Williams Street?'

'That's the one. I need you to get over here right away.'

Tremont felt a tick in his blood. He switched hands. 'Why, what's up?'

'I found something in Mercer's room,' Walker said in a voice as gray as a tombstone. 'I think it belongs to Haley McWaid.'

Chapter 13

Pops was in the kitchen scrambling up some eggs when Wendy got home.

'Where's Charlie?'

'Still in bed.'

'It's one in the afternoon.'

Pops looked at the clock. 'Yep. Hungry?'

'No. Where did you guys go last night?'

Pops, working the frying pan like a short-order lifer, arched an eyebrow.

'Sworn to secrecy?'

'Something like that,' Pops said. 'So where you been?'

'I spent a little time with the Fathers Club this morning.'

'Care to elaborate?'

She did.

'Sad,' he said.

'And maybe a little self-indulgent.'

Pops shrugged. 'A man stops being able to earn for his family – you might as well cut off his balls. Makes him feel like less of a man. That's sad. Losing your job is an earthquake for Working Joes and Yuppie Scum alike. Maybe more so for the Yuppie Scum. Society has taught them to define themselves by their job.'

'And now that's gone?'

'Yep.'

'Maybe the answer isn't in another job,' Wendy said. 'Maybe the answer is in finding new ways to define manhood.'

Pops nodded. 'Deep.'

'And sanctimonious?'

'Right on,' Pops said, sprinkling grated cheese into the pan. 'But if you can't be sanctimonious with me, well, who else is there?'

Wendy smiled. 'No one, Pops.'

He turned off the burner. 'Sure you don't want some huevos de Pops? It's my forte. And I already made enough for two.'

'Yeah, okay.'

They sat and ate. She told him more about Phil Turnball and the Fathers Club and her sense that Phil was holding something back. As they were finishing, a sleepy Charlie appeared in ripped boxers, a huge white T-shirt, and a major case of bed head. Wendy was just thinking how much he looked like a man when Charlie started plucking at his eyes and flicking his fingers.

'You okay?' she asked.

'Sleep buggers,' Charlie explained.

Wendy rolled her eyes and headed for the upstairs computer. She Googled Phil Turnball. Got very little. A political donation. There was a hit on an image search, a group shot with Phil and his wife, Sherry, a pretty petite blonde, at a charity wine tasting two years ago. Phil Turnball was listed as working for a securities firm called Barry Brothers Trust. Hoping that they hadn't already changed her password, Wendy signed on to the media database her station used. Yes, everything is supposed to be available on free search engines nowadays, but it wasn't. You still had to pay to get the goods.

She did a news search on Turnball. Still nothing. But Barry Brothers came back with more than a few unflattering articles. For one thing the company was moving out of its long-term home on Park Avenue at Forty-sixth Street. Wendy recognized the address. The Lock-Horne Building. She smiled, took out her cell phone. Yep, after two years, the number was still there. She made sure the door was closed and pressed send.

The phone was answered on the first ring.

'Articulate.'

The tone was haughty, superior, and, if you could do it in one word, sanctimonious.

'Hey, Win. It's Wendy Tynes.'

'So it says on my caller ID.'

Silence.

She could almost see Win, the ridiculously handsome face, the blond hair, the steepled hands, the piercing blue eyes with seemingly very little soul behind them.

'I need a favor,' she said. 'Some info.'

Silence.

Win – short for Windsor Horne Lockwood III – would not make this easy.

'Do you know anything about Barry Brothers Trust?' she asked.

'Yes, I do. Is that the info you need?'

'You're such a wiseass, Win.'

'Love me for all my faults.'

'Seems I did that once,' she said.

'Oh, meow.'

Silence.

'The Barry Brothers fired an employee named Phil Turnball. I'm curious why. Can you find out?'

'I will call you back.'

Click.

Win. He was often described in the society pages as an 'international playboy,' and she guessed that fit. He was blue-blooded old money, very old money, the kind of old money that disembarked from the *Mayflower* and immediately called for a caddy and a tee time. She had met him at a black-tie event two years ago. Win had been refreshingly up-front. He wanted to have sex with her. No muss, no fuss, no obligation. One night only. She had been taken aback at first, but then thought, Well, why the hell not? She had never done the one-night-stand thing, and here was this ridiculously handsome, engaging man giving her the ideal opportunity. You only live once, right? She was a single, modern woman, and as Pops had recently put it, humans need sex. So she went back to his place in the Dakota building on Central Park West. Win ended up being kind and attentive and funny and great, and when she got home the next morning, she cried her eyes out for two hours.

Her phone rang. Wendy checked her watch and shook her head. It had taken Win less than a minute.

'Hello?'

'Phil Turnball was fired for embezzling two million dollars. Have a pleasant day.'

Click.

Win.

She remembered something. Blend, right? That was the name of the place. She had gone there once to see a concert. It was in Ridgewood. She pulled up the Web site and clicked on Calendar of Events. Yep, tonight was open-mike night. It even said: 'Special Appearance by new rap sensation Ten-A-Fly.'

There was a knock on the door. She called, 'Come in,' and Pops stuck his head in the doorway. 'You okay?' he asked.

'Sure. Do you like rap?'

Pops furrowed his brows. 'You mean like the paper stuff on presents?'

'Uh, no. As in rap music.'

'I'd rather listen to a strangled cat cough up phlegm.'

'Come with me tonight. It's time we opened up your horizons.'

Ted McWaid watched his son, Ryan, at the Kasselton lacrosse field. Day had surrendered her rays, but the field, made from some newfangled artificial turf, had stadium-quality lights. Ted was at his nine-year-old son's lacrosse game because what else was he going to do, hang around the house and cry all day? His former friends – 'former' was probably unkind but Ted wasn't in the mood to be charitable – politely nodded and made no eye contact and generally avoided him, as though having a missing child was contagious.

Ryan was on Kasselton's third-grade travel team. Stick skills were, to put it kindly, somewhere between 'still developing' and 'nonexistent.' The ball spent most of the time on the ground, no boy able to keep it in the stick webbing for very long, and the game began to resemble hockey players at a rugby scrum. The boys wore helmets that looked too big on their heads, like the Great Gazoo on *The Flintstones,* and it was nearly impossible to tell which kid was which. Ted had cheered for Ryan an entire game, marveling at his progress, until the kid took his helmet off at the end and Ted realized that it wasn't Ryan.

Standing a little way from the other parents, thinking about that day, Ted almost smiled. Then reality pushed its way back in and snatched his breath. That's how it always was. You could sometimes slip into normalcy, but if you did, you paid a price.

He thought of Haley on this very field – here the day it opened – and the hours she spent working on her left. There was a lacrosse retriever in the far corner of the field, and Haley would come down and work on her left because she needed to improve her left, the scouts would be looking at her left, her weakness was her damn left, and UVA would never recruit her if she couldn't go to her left. So she worked on the left nonstop, not just down here, but walking through the house. She started using her left for other things, like brushing her teeth, writing notes for school, whatever. All the parents in this town trying to push their kids to be better, riding them day and night for better grades, better athletics, all in the hopes of getting into what someone deemed a more desirable institution of higher learning. Not Haley. She was self-driven. Too driven? Maybe. In the end UVA hadn't taken her. Her left became damn good, and she was fast for a high school team or maybe a lower-level Division I program, but not UVA. Haley had been crushed, inconsolable. Why? Who cares? What difference did it make in the long run?

He missed her so damn much.

Not so much this – going to her lacrosse games. He missed watching TV with her and the way she'd want him to 'get' her music, the YouTube videos she thought were so funny and wanted to share with him. He missed the dumb stuff, like doing his best 'moonwalk' in the kitchen while Haley rolled her eyes. Or purposely over-smooching Marcia until a mortified Haley would frown and shout, 'Helloooo, yuck, children present!'

Ted and Marcia hadn't touched each other in three months – by mutual unspoken but implied consent. It just felt too raw. The lack of physical togetherness wasn't causing tension, though he had sensed a widening chasm.

It just didn't feel that important to work on it, at least right now.

The not knowing. It weighs on you. You start to want an answer, any answer, and that just makes you feel more guilt-ridden and horrible. The guilt ate him up, kept him up every single night. Ted was not good with confrontation. It made his heart beat too fast. An argument with a neighbor last year over a property line had robbed him of weeks of sleep. He stayed up, rehashed, reargued.

It was his fault.

Man Rule Number One: Your daughter is safe in your home. You take care of your family. However you want to spin this horror, that was the plain fact: Ted hadn't done his job. Had someone broken in and snatched his Haley away? Well, that would be on him, wouldn't it? A father protects. That's job one. And if Haley had left the house on her own that night, sneaked out somehow? That was on him too. Because he hadn't been the kind of father his daughter could go to and tell what was wrong or what was going on in her life.

The rehashing never stopped. He wanted to go back, change one thing, alter the universal time structure or whatever. Haley had always been the strong child, the independent one, the competent one. He had marveled at her resourcefulness, which definitely came from her mother. Had that been part of it? Had he figured, well, Haley doesn't need as much parenting, as much supervision, as Patricia and Ryan?

Useless, constant rehashing.

He was not a depressive type, not at all, but there were days, dark, bleak days, when Ted remembered exactly where his dad kept his pistol. He pictured the whole scene now – making sure no one was home; walking into his childhood house where his parents still lived; taking the pistol from the shoebox on the top of the closet; walking down to the basement where he had first made out with Amy Stein in seventh grade; moving into the washer-dryer room because the floor there was cement, not carpet, and easier to clean. He would sit on the floor, lean against the old washer, put the pistol in his mouth – and the pain would end.

Ted would never do it. He wouldn't do that to his family, add to their suffering in any way. A father didn't do that. He took it on himself. But in his more honest, more frightening moments, he wondered what it meant that thinking about that release, that end, sounded so damn sweet.

Ryan was in the game now. Ted tried to concentrate on that, on his boy's face through the protective cage, mouth distorted by the guard, tried to find some joy in this rather pure childhood moment. He still didn't get the boys' lacrosse rules – the boys' game seemed entirely different from the girls' – but he knew that his son was playing attack. That was the position where you had the best chance of scoring a goal.

Ted cupped his hands around his mouth, forming a flesh megaphone. 'Go, Ryan!'

He heard his voice echo dully. For the past hour, other parents had called out constantly, of course, but Ted's voice sounded so awkward, so out of place. It made him cringe. He tried to clap instead, but that, too, felt awkward, as if his hands were the wrong size. He turned away for just a second, and that was when he saw him.

Frank Tremont trudged toward him as though through deep snow. A big black man, definitely another cop, walked with him. For a moment, hope spread its wings and took flight. Ted felt something inside him soar. But only for a moment.

Frank's head was down. As he drew closer, Ted could see that the body language was all wrong. Ted felt the quake begin in his knees. One buckled but he held himself upright. He started crossing the sidelines to meet up with him faster.

When they were close enough, Frank said, 'Where's Marcia?'

'She's visiting her mother.'

'We need to find her,' Frank said. 'Now.'

Chapter 14

A giant smile spread across Pops's face when they entered the Blend bar.

'What?' Wendy asked.

'More cougars on those bar stools than on the Discovery Channel.'

The bar had low lights and smoky mirrors, and everyone was dressed in black. He was right about the clientele. In a way.

'By definition,' Wendy said, 'a cougar is an older woman who frequents clubs to score with *younger* men.'

Pops frowned. 'Some of them still gotta have Daddy issues, right?'

'At your age, you should hope for a Daddy *complex*. Check that – Grandpa complex.'

Pops looked at her, disappointed, as though the line was super lame. She nodded an apology because, yeah, it was.

'Mind if I mingle?' Pops asked.

'I cramp your style?'

'You're the hottest cougar here. So, yes. Though some chicks dig that. Like they're stealing me away.'

'Just don't bring any of them home. I have an impressionable teenage son at home.'

'I always go to her place,' Pops said. 'I don't like her knowing how to find me. Plus I save her the morning walk of shame.'

'Thoughtful.'

Blend had a bar up front, restaurant in the middle, club in the back. The club was holding the open-mike night. Wendy paid the cover charge – five bucks including a drink for men, one buck including a drink for the ladies – and ducked inside. She could hear Norm, aka Ten-A-Fly, rapping:

> *Hotties, listen up,*
> *You may not be in Tenafly*
> *But Ten-A-Fly gonna be deep in you. . . .*

Oy, she thought. There were forty, fifty people gathered around the stage, cheering. Ten-A-Fly wore enough gold bling to make Mr. T envious and a trucker hat with a flat brim and forty-five-degree tilt. He held up his droopy trousers with one hand – might have been because they were too big, might have been because the guy had absolutely no ass – while the other gripped the microphone.

When Norm finished that particularly romantic ditty with the closer that Ten-A-Fly be so deep in you, you be begging for no Engle-Wood, the crowd – median age: early forties – gave him a huge ovation. A red-clad maybe-groupie in the front threw something onstage, and with something approaching horror, Wendy realized that they were panties.

Ten-A-Fly picked them up and took a deep sniff. 'Yo, yo, love to the ladies out there, the burning shawties, Ten-A-Fly and the FC in da house!'

The maybe-groupie put her hands in the air. She wore, God help her, a T-shirt that read, 'Ten-A-Fly's Main Ho!'

Pops came up behind her. He looked pained. 'For the love of all that is merciful . . .'

Wendy scanned the room. She spotted the rest of the Fathers Club – FC? – near the front, including Phil. They cheered wildly for their man. Wendy's gaze traveled back and settled on a petite blonde sitting alone near the back. Her eyes were down and on her drink.

Sherry Turnball, Phil's wife.

Wendy swam through the crowd, making her way toward her. 'Mrs. Turnball?'

Sherry Turnball turned from her drink slowly.

'I'm Wendy Tynes. We talked on the phone.'

'The reporter.'

'Yes.'

'I didn't realize that you were the one who did the story on Dan Mercer.'

'Did you know him?'

'I met him once.'

'How?'

'He and Phil lived in the same suite at Princeton. I met him at the political fund-raiser we held for Farley last year.'

'Farley?'

'Another classmate.' She took a sip of her drink. On the stage, Ten-A-Fly asked for quiet. 'Let me tell you about this next number.' A hush fell over the room. Ten-A-Fly took off his sunglasses as if they'd angered him. His scowl aimed for intimidation but seemed more in the neighborhood of constipation.

'So one day I'm sitting at Starbucks with my homies in the FC,' he began.

The Fathers Club hooted at the shout-out.

'I'm sitting there, enjoying my latte or whatnot, and this dial-nine-one-one-kickin' shawty walks by, and man-o-man she's working it up top, if you know what I'm saying.'

The cheers said, We know what you're saying.

'And I'm looking for inspiration, for a new tune and whatnot, and I'm checking out this five-alarm shawty in a halter top . . . and this phrase just comes to me: "Swing dem puppies." Just like that. She saunters by, head up, working it up top, and I think to myself, "Yeah, baby, swing dem puppies."'

Ten-A-Fly paused to let that sink in. Silence. Then someone yelled: 'Genius!'

'Thanks, brother, I mean that.' He pointed at the 'fan' in some complicated way, like his fingers were a gun turned on its side. 'Anyway, my homies in the FC helped me take this rap and bring it up to the next level. So this is for you guys. And of course, all you top-heavy shawties out there. You be Ten-A-Fly's inspiration.'

Applause.

Sherry Turnball said, 'You think this is all pretty pathetic, don't you?'

'Not my place to judge.'

Ten-A-Fly began to perform what some might consider a 'dance,' though medical experts would probably classify it as a 'seizure' or 'devastating stroke.'

Yo, girl, swing dem puppies,
Swing em like you're my favorite ho,
Swing dem puppies,
Swing dem like you're Best in Show,
Swing dem puppies,
Yo, got here a bone to feed ya,
Swing dem puppies,
Take it, girl, be no protest from PETA . . .

Wendy rubbed her eyes, blinked, opened them again.

By now, the other members of the Fathers Club were standing and joining in for the 'Swing Dem Puppies' chorus, letting Ten-A-Fly solo on the lines between:

Swing dem puppies,

Ten-A-Fly: '*No need to scream and holler.*'

Swing dem puppies.

Ten-A-Fly: '*Swing dem right, I gives you a pearl doggie collar. . . .*'

Wendy made a face. The men were up now. The guy who'd been wearing the tennis whites was all prepped out in a bright green polo. Phil had khakis and a blue button-down. He was standing and clapping and seemingly lost in the rap. Sherry Turnball stared off.

'You okay?' Wendy asked.

'It's nice to see Phil smile.'

The rap went on for a few more verses. Wendy spotted Pops talking up two ladies in the corner. The biker look was rare in suburbia – and some tony club hopper always wanted to take home the bad boy.

Sherry said, 'See the woman sitting up front?'

'The one who threw her panties onstage?'

She nodded. 'That's Norm's – uh, Ten-A-Fly's – wife. They've got three kids, and they're going to have to sell their house and move in with her parents. But she's supportive.'

'Nice,' Wendy said, but looking again, the cheering looked a little too forced, closer perhaps to classic overcompensation than true enthusiasm.

'Why are you here?' Sherry Turnball asked.

'I'm trying to find out the truth about Dan Mercer.'

'A little late, don't you think?'

'Probably. Phil said something strange to me today. He said he understood what it was like to be wrongly accused.'

Sherry Turnball played with her drink.

'Sherry?'

Her eyes rose and met Wendy's. 'I don't want him hurt anymore.'

'That's not my intent here.'

'Phil wakes up every morning at six and puts on a suit and tie. Like he's going to work. Then he buys the local papers and drives down to the Suburban Diner on Route Seventeen. He sits there alone with his coffee and goes through the classifieds. By himself, wearing a suit and tie. Every morning, alone. The exact same thing.'

Wendy flashed again on her father sitting at the table stuffing résumés into envelopes.

'I try to tell him it's okay,' Sherry said. 'But if I suggest moving down to a smaller house, Phil takes it as a personal failure. Men, right?'

'What happened to him, Sherry?'

'Phil loved his job. He was a financial adviser. A money manager. Nowadays those are negative terms. But Phil used to say, "People trust me with their life savings." Think about that. He cares for people's money. They entrust him with their toil, their kids' college education, their retirement. He used to say, "Imagine the responsibility of that – and the honor." It was all about trust with him. About honesty and honor.'

She stopped. Wendy waited for her to continue. When she didn't, Wendy said, 'I did some research.'

'I'm going back to work. Phil doesn't want that. But I'm going back.'

'Sherry, listen to me. I know about the embezzlement charge.'

She stopped as though she'd been slapped. 'How?'

'That's not important. Is that what Phil meant by wrongly accused?'

'The allegations are trumped-up nonsense. An excuse to fire one of their most highly paid. If he was guilty, why hasn't he been charged?'

'I'd like to talk to Phil about it.'

'Why?'

Wendy opened her mouth, stopped, closed it again.

Sherry said, 'It doesn't have anything to do with Dan.'

'Maybe it does.'

'How?'

Good question.

'Will you talk to him for me?' Wendy asked.

'And say what?'

'That I want to help him.'

But a thought hit Wendy, something Jenna had said, something Phil and Sherry had said too, stuff about the past, about Princeton, the name Farley. She needed to get home, get to a computer, do some research. 'Just talk to him, okay?'

Ten-A-Fly started up another song, an ode to some MILF named Charisma, plagiarizing himself with some joke about having no charisma in him but wanting to be in Charisma. Wendy rushed over to Pops.

'Come on,' she said.

Pops gestured toward the tipsy woman with the beckoning smile and plunging neckline. 'Working here.'

'Get a phone number and tell her to swing dem puppies at you later. We've got to get out of here.'

Chapter 15

Goal one for Investigator Frank Tremont and Sheriff Mickey Walker: Find a connection between molester Dan Mercer and missing girl Haley McWaid.

Haley's phone had so far provided few clues – no new texts, e-mails, or calls – though Tom Stanton, a young Sussex County cop with some techno background, was still going through it. Still, with the help of a teary Ted and steely Marcia, it didn't take long to come up with a link between Haley and Dan Mercer. Haley McWaid had been a senior at Kasselton High School. One of her classmates was a girl named Amanda Wheeler, stepdaughter of Jenna Wheeler, Dan's ex. Dan Mercer was friendly with his ex-wife and purportedly spent a great deal of time at their house.

Connection.

Jenna and Noel Wheeler sat on a couch across from Tremont in their classic split-level home. Jenna's eyes were puffy from recent tears. She was a small woman, tight body like she worked out, probably striking when her face wasn't bloated from crying. The husband, Noel, was, Tremont had learned, head of cardiac surgery at Valley Medical Center. His hair was dark, unruly, a little too long – almost like what you'd expect in a concert pianist.

Another plush couch, Frank thought, in another lovely suburban home. Like with the McWaids. Both couches were nice, probably pretty expensive. This one was bright yellow with blue flowers. Springlike. Frank pictured it, the two of them, Noel and Jenna Wheeler (or Ted and Marcia McWaid), going to some highway furniture store, probably on Route 4, testing out a bunch of couches, trying to figure out which one would go in their lovely suburban home, match both the décor and lifestyle, combine comfort and durability, how it would blend in with the designer wallpaper and Oriental carpet and the knickknacks from that trip to Europe. They had it delivered and moved it from spot to spot until it was just right, collapsed into it, called the kids to try it out, maybe even sneaked down late one night to break it in.

Sussex County sheriff Mickey Walker loomed behind him like a solar eclipse. Now that the two cases were overlapping, there would be full cooperation – no county jurisdiction bickering when you're trying to find a missing girl. They agreed that Frank would lead this line of questioning.

Frank Tremont coughed into his fist. 'Thank you for agreeing to talk with us.'

'Have you found something new about Dan?' Jenna asked.

'I wanted to ask you both about your relationship with Dan Mercer.'

Jenna looked puzzled. Noel Wheeler did not move. He leaned slightly forward, his forearms rested on his thighs, his fingers laced between his knees.

'What about our relationship?' Jenna asked.

'You were close?'

145

'Yes.'

Frank looked at Noel. 'All of you? I mean, he is your wife's ex.'

Again it was Jenna who answered. 'All of us. Dan is . . . was . . . the godfather of our daughter Kari.'

'How old is Kari?'

'What does that have to do with anything?'

Frank put a little steel in his voice. 'Please just answer the question, Mrs. Wheeler.'

'She's six.'

'Did she spend time alone with Dan Mercer?'

'If you're insinuating—'

'I'm asking a question,' Frank said, cutting her off. 'Did your six-year-old daughter spend time alone with Dan Mercer?'

'She did,' Jenna said, head high. 'And she loved him dearly. She called him Uncle Dan.'

'You have another child, don't you?'

Noel took that one. 'I have a daughter from a previous marriage, yes. Her name is Amanda.'

'Is she home right now?'

Frank had already checked on this and knew the answer.

'Yes, she's upstairs.'

Jenna looked toward the silent Walker. 'I don't see what any of this has to do with Ed Grayson killing Dan.'

Walker just stared back at her, arms folded.

Frank said, 'How often did Dan come to this house?'

'What difference does that make?'

'Mrs. Wheeler, do you have something to hide?'

Jenna's mouth dropped open. 'Excuse me?'

'Why do you keep giving me a hard time?'

'I'm not giving you anything. I just want to know—'

'Why? What's the difference why I'm asking?'

146

Noel Wheeler put a calming hand on his wife's knee. 'He visited frequently. Maybe once a week or so before' – he paused here – 'before that story on him aired.'

'And since then?'

'Rarely. Maybe once or twice.'

Frank zeroed in on Noel. 'Why less? Did you believe the charges?'

Noel Wheeler took his time. Jenna stared at him, her body suddenly stiff. Finally he said, 'I did not believe the charges, no.'

'But?'

Noel Wheeler stayed silent. He did not look at his wife.

'But better safe than sorry, is that it?'

Jenna said, 'Dan felt it was best not to come around. So the neighbors wouldn't gossip.'

Noel kept his eyes on the carpet.

'And,' she continued, 'I would still like to know what this has to do with anything.'

'We would like to talk with your daughter Amanda,' Frank said.

That got their attention. Jenna jumped first, but something made her stop. She looked toward Noel. Tremont wondered why. Stepmother syndrome, he figured. Noel Wheeler was, after all, the real parent here.

Noel said, 'Detective . . . Tremont, is it?'

Frank nodded, not bothering to correct the terminology – it was investigator, not detective, but half the time, hell, he mixed them up.

'We've been willing to cooperate,' Noel went on. 'I will answer any and every question you have. But now you're involving my daughter. Do you have a child, Detective?'

With his peripheral vision, Frank Tremont could see

147

Mickey Walker shifting his feet uneasily. Walker knew, though Tremont had never told him. Tremont never talked about Kasey.

'No, I don't.'

'If you want to talk to Amanda, I really need to know what's going on.'

'Fair enough.' Tremont took his time, let the silence make them squirm a bit. When he thought the timing was right, he said, 'Do you know who Haley McWaid is?'

'Yes, of course,' Jenna said.

'We think your ex-husband did something to her.'

Silence.

Jenna said, 'When you say "did something—"'

'Kidnapped, molested, abducted, murdered,' Frank snapped. 'Is that specific enough for you, Mrs. Wheeler?'

'I just want to know—'

'And I don't care what you want to know. I also don't give a rat's ass about Dan Mercer or his reputation or even who killed him. I only care about him insomuch as he relates to Haley McWaid.'

'Dan wouldn't hurt anyone.'

Frank felt the vein in his forehead throb. 'Oh, why didn't you say so? I might as well just take your word for it and go home then, right? Forget the mountain of evidence that he snatched your daughter, Mr. and Mrs. McWaid – his ex-wife says he wouldn't hurt anyone.'

'There's no reason to get snippy,' Noel said, in that doctor voice he probably used on patients.

'Actually, Dr. Wheeler, there is every reason to get snippy. As you pointed out so clearly earlier, you're a father, aren't you?'

'Yes, of course.'

'Well, imagine that your Amanda had been missing

for three months – and the McWaids were jerking me around like this. How would you react?'

Jenna said, 'We're just trying to understand—'

But again her husband silenced her with a hand on her knee. Noel shook his head at her and shouted, 'Amanda!'

Jenna Wheeler sat back as a sullen teen voice from upstairs called back, 'Coming!'

They waited. Jenna looked at Noel. Noel looked at the carpet.

'Question for both of you,' Frank Tremont said. 'To your knowledge, did Dan know or ever encounter Haley McWaid?'

Jenna said, 'No.'

'Dr. Wheeler?'

He shook his head with the unruly hair as his daughter appeared. Amanda was tall, skinny; her body and head seemed elongated, as though giant hands had squeezed the clay on either side. It may be a cruel word to bandy about, but the one that came to mind here was 'gawky.' She stood with her big hands in front of her, as though she were naked and being inspected and wanted to cover up. Her eyes were everywhere other than on someone else's eyes.

Her father rose and crossed the room. He put a protective arm around her and led her to the couch. He placed his daughter between Jenna and himself. Jenna too put her arm around her stepdaughter. Frank waited a few moments, letting them coo words of comfort.

'Amanda, I'm Investigator Tremont. This is Sheriff Walker. We need to ask you a few questions. You're not in any trouble, so please relax. We just need you to answer the questions as honestly and directly as you can, okay?'

Amanda did a quick nod. Her eyes darted about like

two scared birds seeking a safe perch. Her parents huddled in closer, leaned a little forward, wanting to take the hit for her.

'Do you know Haley McWaid?' Frank asked.

The teen seemed to shrink right before his eyes. 'Yeah.'

'How?'

'School.'

'Would you say that you two are friends?'

Amanda gave him the teenage shrug. 'We were lab partners in AP chemistry.'

'Was that this year?'

'Yeah.'

'How did that come about?'

Amanda seemed confused by the question.

'Did you two choose each other?'

'No. Mrs. Walsh assigns it.'

'I see. Did you two get along?'

'Yeah, sure. Haley's real nice.'

'Has she ever been to your house?'

Amanda hesitated here. 'Yeah.'

'Lots of times?'

'No, just once.'

Frank Tremont sat back, gave it a second. 'Could you tell me when?'

The girl looked to her father. He nodded. 'It's okay.'

Amanda turned back to Tremont. 'Thanksgiving.'

Frank watched Jenna Wheeler. She gave away nothing, but he could see it was an effort. 'Why was Haley here?'

Another teenage shrug. 'Just hanging out,' Amanda said.

'But on Thanksgiving? She wasn't with her family?'

Jenna Wheeler explained. 'It was after. The girls all had Thanksgiving dinner with their families and came over here late. There was no school the next day.'

150

Jenna's voice seemed to come from far away now. Flat, lifeless. Frank kept his eyes on Amanda. 'What time would that have been?'

Amanda thought about it. 'I don't know. She got here about ten.'

'How many girls were there?'

'Four. Bree and Jody were here too. We hung out in the basement.'

'After Thanksgiving?'

'Yeah.'

Frank waited. When no one volunteered, he asked the obvious question: 'Was Uncle Dan here for Thanksgiving?'

Amanda didn't answer. Jenna sat very still.

'Was he here?' Tremont asked again.

Noel Wheeler leaned forward, lowered his hands into his face. 'Yes,' he said. 'Dan was here on Thanksgiving.'

Chapter 16

Pops groused the entire way home. 'I had that shawty in the palm of my hand.'

'Sorry.' Then: 'Shawty?'

'I like to keep up on modern terms for chicks.'

'Good to keep up.'

'You should only know.'

'Please don't elaborate.'

'Oh, I won't,' Pops said. 'So this is important?'

'Yup. Sorry you lost your shawty.'

'Fish, sea.' Pop shrugged. 'You know the deal.'

'I do.'

Wendy hurried into the house. Charlie was flipping channels with two of his buds, Clark and James. They were sprawled on the den furniture as only teenage boys can, as though they'd removed their skeletons, hung them in a nearby closet, and slid to a collapse against whatever upholstery was nearby.

'Hey,' Charlie said without moving anything but his lips. 'You're home early.'

'Right, don't get up.'

He smirked. Clark and James muttered, 'Hey, Mrs. Tynes.' They didn't move their bodies, but they at least rolled their necks to get a glance. Charlie stopped on her suddenly former station. The NTC News was on. Michele Feisler, the annoying, new, and very young anchor they should have fired instead of Wendy, was reporting a follow-up to a story from a couple of days ago about a man named Arthur Lemaine who had been shot in both knees while leaving the South Mountain Arena in West Orange.

'Ouch,' Clark said.

'Like one knee wouldn't be enough.'

Arthur Lemaine, Michele recapped in that pseudo-serious newswoman inflection Wendy hoped that she didn't have, had been shot following a late-night practice. The camera now panned over the South Mountain Arena, even showing the sign that said the New Jersey Devils practiced here – like that added something important to the story.

The camera came back to a properly grim Michele Feisler at the anchor desk.

'I hate her,' James said.

'Her head is, like, way too big for her body,' Clark added.

Feisler continued in that milk-curdling voice: 'Arthur Lemaine is still not talking to authorities about the incident.' Big surprise, Wendy thought. If someone shoots you in both knees, it was probably best to see, hear, say nothing. Even James bent his nose as if to indicate mafioso. Charlie flipped stations again.

James turned around and said, 'That Michele chick isn't in your league, Mrs. T.'

'Yeah,' Clark added. 'You kick her lame ass.'

Clearly Charlie had filled them in on her recent employment woes, but she was still grateful. 'Thanks, boys.'

'Seriously,' Clark said. 'Her head looks like a beach ball.'

Charlie added nothing. He'd once explained to his mother that his friends considered her a major MILF. He said this without embarrassment or horror, and Wendy didn't know whether that was a good thing or not.

She headed upstairs to the computer. Farley was an unusual first name. Sherry Turnball had said something about holding a political fund-raiser for him. She recalled the name and remembered hearing something about a sex scandal.

The speed and thoroughness of the Internet should not shock her anymore, but sometimes it still did. Two clicks and Wendy found what she was looking for:

Six months ago, Farley Parks had been running for Congress in Pennsylvania when he was waylaid by a scandal involving prostitution. It had only gotten minor play in the press – political sex scandals were not exactly rare nowadays – but it had forced Farley out of the race. Wendy went through the first few Web sites on the search engine.

Apparently, an 'erotic dancer' (read 'stripper') named 'Desire' (maybe not her real name) had given the story to a local newspaper. The story spread from there. 'Desire' had set up a blog, describing her trysts with Farley Parks in rather horrifying detail. Wendy considered herself pretty worldly, but the specifics made her cringe and blush. Yowza. There was a video too. Eyes half shut, she clicked it. No nudity, thank goodness. 'Desire' sat in silhouette. She offered up more graphic details in a breathy, machine-altered voice. Thirty seconds in, Wendy shut it down.

Enough. Got the point. And it really wasn't a good one.

Okay, slow down. Reporters are taught to look for patterns, but there was nothing subtle about this one. Still, she needed to do the research. The search's first page of 'Farley Parks' hits was loaded up on the scandal. She clicked for the second, found a dry biography. Yep, there it was – Farley Parks had graduated from Princeton twenty years ago. Same year as Phil Turnball and Dan Mercer.

Coincidence?

Three men in the same graduating class from the same elite university ruined in the past year by scandals – the rich and powerful have a way of drawing these sorts of troubles. It could be just that. A coincidence.

Except that the three men may have been closer than classmates.

'Suitemates.' That was the word Phil Turnball had used. Phil and Dan were in the same suite. A college suite implied more than two people. If it were just Phil and Dan, you'd say roommates. Suitemates? That implied at least three, maybe more.

So how to find out if Farley Parks was in with them?

Wendy only had the Turnballs' home number. They'd probably still be at Blend. So who else would know about roommates?

Jenna Wheeler, Dan's ex, might.

It was getting late now, but this was hardly the time to worry about being phone appropriate. Wendy dialed the Wheelers' home number. A man – probably her husband, Noel – answered on the third ring.

'Hello?'

'This is Wendy Tynes. May I please speak to Jenna?'

'She's not home.'

Click.

She stared at the receiver. Hmm. That seemed rather abrupt. She shrugged and put the phone down. Turning back to the computer, a strange thought hit her: Facebook. With silly quasi–peer pressure mounting, Wendy had opened a Facebook account last year, accepted and requested a few friends – and pretty much did nothing else with it. Maybe it was an age thing, though there seemed to be plenty of folks older than her populating these social sites, but when Wendy was younger – not to sound like an old fart – when a man 'poked' you, it meant something, uh, different from what it did on Facebook. Intelligent people she respected were constantly sending her silly quizzes or throwing things at her or inviting her to Mafia Wars or posting on her wall – were the double entendres intentional? – and she felt like Tom Hanks in the movie *Big*, the part where he keeps raising his hand and saying, 'I don't get it.'

But she remembered now that her Tufts graduating class had its own page, complete with photographs old and new and information on classmates. Could there be a page for those who graduated Princeton twenty years ago?

She signed on to Facebook and did a search.

Pay dirt.

Ninety-eight members of the Princeton class had signed up. The front page had tiny photos of eight of them. There were discussion boards and links. Wendy was wondering how to join the group so she could get access to everything when her cell phone started buzzing. She checked it and saw the little logo signaling a phone message. Call must have come in while she was at Blend. She scrolled through the incoming call log and saw the most recent had come from her former place of employment. Probably something about her nearly nonexistent severance package.

But, no, the call had come in less than an hour ago. HR wouldn't call this late.

Wendy dialed in for the message and was surprised to

hear the voice of Vic Garrett, the man who'd fired her on . . . was it really just two days ago?

'Hey, sweetums, it's Vic. Call me pronto. Hugely important.'

Wendy felt a tick in her blood. Vic was not one for hyperbole. She dialed his private line in the office. If Vic was gone, he'd forward it to his mobile. He picked up on the first ring.

'Did you hear?' Vic asked.

'What?'

'You may get rehired. At the very least, freelance. Either way, I want you on this.'

'On what?'

'The cops found Haley McWaid's cell phone.'

'What's that have to do with me?'

'They found it in Dan Mercer's hotel room. Apparently your boy is responsible for whatever the hell happened to her.'

Ed Grayson lay alone in his bed.

Maggie, his wife of sixteen years, had packed up and left while he was being interrogated for the murder of Dan Mercer. No matter. Their marriage was dead, had indeed been dead for a while, he guessed, but you still go through the motions and hope, and now that hope was finally gone. Maggie wouldn't tell. He knew that. She wanted to wish problems away. That was her way. Pack the bad away in a suitcase, stick it on the top shelf of some closet in the back of your mind, close the door, and plaster on a smile. Maggie's favorite phrase, something her mom in Quebec had taught her, was 'You bring your own weather to the picnic.' So both women smiled a lot. They both had smiles so great you sometimes forgot that they were meaningless.

Maggie's smile had worked for many years. It had charmed young Ed Grayson, swept him off his proverbial feet. The smile seemed like goodness to him, and Ed wanted to be near that. But the smile was not goodness. It was a façade, a mask to fight off the bad.

When the naked pictures of their son, E. J., first surfaced, Maggie's reaction had shocked him: She wanted to ignore them. No one has to know, Maggie said. E. J. seems fine, she went on. He's only eight years old. No one actually touched him – or if someone had, there were no signs of it. The pediatrician found nothing. E. J. seemed normal, untroubled. No bed-wetting or night terrors or extra anxiety.

'Let it go,' Maggie urged him. 'He's fine.'

Ed Grayson was apoplectic. 'You don't want this scumbag put away? You want to let him keep doing this to other kids?'

'I don't care about other kids. I care about E. J.'

'And this is what you want to teach him? "Let it go"?'

'It's what's best. There's no reason the world has to know what happened to him.'

'He did nothing wrong, Maggie.'

'I know that. Don't you think I know that? But people will look at him differently. He'll be defined by it. If we just keep it quiet, not let anybody know . . .'

Maggie flashed him the smile. For the first time, it made him cringe.

Ed sat up and made himself another Scotch and soda. He flipped on ESPN and watched *SportsCenter*. He closed his eyes and thought about the blood. He thought about the pain and horror that he'd inflicted in the name of justice. He believed everything that he said to that reporter Wendy Tynes: Justice needed to be done. If not by the courts, well, then it fell to men like him. But that didn't mean there wasn't a personal price paid by those who delivered it.

You often hear that freedom isn't free. Neither is justice.

He was alone, but he could still hear Maggie's horrified whisper when he got home:

'What have you done?'

And rather than make a long defense, he kept it short and simple:

'It's over.'

He might as well have been talking about them, Ed and Maggie Grayson, and then you start to look back and you wonder whether it was ever really love. It was easy to blame what happened to E. J. for their demise – but was that accurate? Did tragedy cause fissures, open them wider – or did tragedy merely turn on the light so you could see the fissure that had always been there? Maybe we live in darkness, blinded by the smile and façade of goodness. Maybe tragedy just takes away the blinders.

Ed heard his doorbell ring. Late. The sound was immediately followed by an impatient fist pounding on the door. Reacting more than thinking, Ed jumped up and grabbed his gun from the nightstand. Another doorbell ring, more fist pounding.

'Mr. Grayson? Police, open up.'

Ed looked out the window. Two Sussex County cops in brown uniforms – neither was that big black sheriff, Walker. That was fast, Grayson thought. He was mildly surprised rather than shocked. He put the gun away, came downstairs, and opened the door.

The two cops looked about twelve years old.

'Mr. Grayson?

'It's Federal Marshal Grayson, son.'

159

'Sir, you're under arrest for the murder of Daniel J. Mercer. Please put your hands behind your back while I read you your rights.'

Chapter 17

I n something of a daze, Wendy finished her phone call with her old (and current again?) boss Vic Garrett and hung up the phone.

Haley McWaid's iPhone had been found under Dan Mercer's bed.

She tried to process this, sort through her emotions. Her first thought was also the most obvious: She was sick to her stomach for the McWaid family. She hoped like hell that it all somehow turned out okay for them. Okay, go deeper. Wendy was shocked, yes. That was what this was. Too shocked maybe. Shouldn't there be some kind of dark relief here? Wasn't this vindication, that she had been right about Dan all along? Justice of some sort had been served. She had not been a cog in some plot to take down an innocent man trying to do good.

But there, on the screen right in front of her, was the Facebook page for Dan's graduating class at Princeton. She closed her eyes and leaned back. She saw Dan's face on the day they first met, that first interview at the shelter, the enthusiasm for the kids he rescued from the streets, the way those kids looked at him with such awe, the way she'd been drawn to him. She flashed to yesterday at the damn trailer park, the horrible bruises on that same face, the dimming in those eyes, the way she wanted, despite all she knew, to reach out.

Do you just dismiss all that intuition?

The counter, of course, is that evil comes in all guises. She'd heard a dozen times the example of famed serial killer Ted Bundy. But the truth was, she had never found Bundy remotely handsome. Maybe it was hindsight, knowing what he was, but you could see the vacancy in the eyes. She would have, she was sure, found him oily, slimy, charm hiding villainy. You can feel evil. You just can. Or so she thought.

Either way, she hadn't seen or felt that with Dan. She had felt, even on the day he died, kindness and warmth. And it was more than intuition now. There was Phil Turnball. There was Farley Parks. There was something more going on here, something darker and more insidious at work.

She opened her eyes and leaned forward. Okay, Facebook. She had signed on, found the Princeton class page, but how could she join? There had to be a way.

Ask the resident Facebook expert, she supposed.

'Charlie!'

From downstairs: 'What?'

'Can you come up here?'

'Can't hear you.'

'Come up here!'

'What?' Then: 'What for?'

'Just come up please.'

'Can't you just yell down what you want?'

She grabbed her mobile and sent a text telling him she needed emergency computer help and if he didn't hurry, she would cancel all his online accounts, even though she didn't really know how to do that. A moment later, she heard a deep sigh and the sound of heavy footsteps as he

162

ascended the stairs. Charlie poked his head in the door.

'What?'

She pointed to the computer screen. 'I need to join this group.'

Charlie squinted at the page. 'You didn't go to Princeton.'

'Thanks for that in-depth analysis. I had no idea.'

Charlie smiled. 'I love when you go all sarcastic on me.'

'Like mother, like son.' God, she loved this kid. Wendy had one of those waves, the ones that sneak up on parents and crush them and make them just want to wrap their arms around their kid and never let him go.

'What?' Charlie said.

She shook it off. 'So how do I join this group if I didn't actually go to Princeton?'

Charlie made a face. 'You're kidding, right?'

'Do I look like I'm kidding?'

'Hard to say, what with your sarcasm and all.'

'I'm not kidding or being sarcastic. How do I get in?'

Charlie sighed, bent over, and pointed to the right side of the page. 'You see that link that says "Join Group"?'

'Yes.'

'You click it.'

He stood upright.

'And then?'

'That's it,' her son said. 'You're in.'

Now Wendy made a face. 'But, as you so wisely pointed out, I didn't go to Princeton.'

'Doesn't matter. It's an open group. Closed groups say "Request To Join." This one is open to anyone. Click and you're in.'

Wendy looked dubious.

Charlie sighed again. 'Just do it,' he said.

'Okay, wait.' Wendy clicked it – and just like that, voilà, she became a member of a Princeton graduating class, albeit the Facebook version. Charlie gave her a told-you-so glance, shook his head, and clumped his way back downstairs. She thought again about how much she loved him. She thought about Marcia and Ted McWaid getting word from the police about that iPhone, one Haley probably really wanted and squealed with delight when she got, being found under a strange man's bed.

Not helpful.

The page was up, so back to work. First Wendy scanned through the ninety-eight members. No Dan, no Phil, no Farley. Made sense. All three were probably keeping a low profile. If they had ever joined, they were probably off Facebook now. None of the other names were familiar.

Okay, now what?

She checked the discussion boards. One about a sick class member, offering support. Another about regional gatherings of class members. Nothing there. Another about the upcoming reunion. She clicked around that page and landed on a link that held promise:

'Dorm Pics – Freshman Year!'

She found the three of them in the fifth photograph of the slideshow. The caption read 'Stearns House' and featured about a hundred students posing in front of a brick building. She spotted Dan first. He had aged well, the curls shorter as an adult, but otherwise, he looked the same. No question about it – he'd been a good-looking guy.

The names were listed on the bottom. Farley Parks, ever the politician, was front and center. Phil Turnball stood on the right. While Dan was wearing jeans and a T-shirt, both Farley and Phil were decked out for the cover shot of *Snooty Prep Monthly*. Khakis, collared shirts, loafers without socks – the only thing missing was a sweater tied around their necks.

Okay, so she knew the name of the dorm. Now what?

She could Google every other guy in the picture – the names were listed below – but that could take a while and might not give her what she needed. It wasn't like people listed their freshman roommates on the Web.

Back to it: Wendy started scouring through the Facebook page again. Ten minutes later, she hit pay dirt:

'Our Freshman Face Book on Facebook!'

She clicked the link, downloaded a PDF file, and opened it with Adobe Acrobat. The freshman face book – Wendy smiled at the memory. She had one at Tufts, of course. Your high school yearbook picture along with your town of origin, high school, and – best of all for her purposes tonight – your freshman room assignment. Wendy clicked the *M* button, jumped two more pages, and found Dan Mercer. There it was, his freshman picture:

Daniel J. Mercer
Riddle, Oregon
Riddle High School
Stearns Suite 109

Dan grinned in the photograph, his whole life supposedly in front of him. Wrong. Probably eighteen years old when this picture was taken. His smile said he was ready to take on the world, and yep, he'd graduate from Princeton, marry, divorce . . . and what?

Become a pedophile and die?

Did that add up? Was Dan already a pedophile then, at the age of eighteen? Had he abused anybody? Were there tendencies as a college student – or more than that? Had he really kidnapped a teenage girl?

Why was she not buying that?

Didn't matter. Focus. The entry gave her the room number in Stearns. Suite 109. She clicked to the *P*s to double-check. Sure enough, Farley Parks of Bryn Mawr, P.A., and Lawrenceville School was also in Stearns 109. Philip Turnball of Boston, M.A., and Phillips Academy Andover looking very much as he did today – yep, Stearns 109 too.

Wendy hit the search button and put in 'Stearns Suite 109.'

Five hits.

Philip Turnball, Daniel Mercer, Farley Parks – and now the two new ones: Kelvin Tilfer, an African-American with a cautious smile, and Steven Miciano, who wore one of those ropey necklaces with a big bead in the middle.

The two new names meant nothing to her. She opened another browser, typed 'Kelvin Tilfer' into the search engine.

Nothing. Almost literally. One hit from a list of Princeton graduates – and that was about it. No LinkedIn. No Facebook. No Twitter. No MySpace.

Wendy wondered what to make of that. Most people, even the most innocuous, you can find something about them online. Kelvin Tilfer, especially when you consider his roommates, was a ghost.

So what did that mean?

Maybe nothing. Too early to hypothesize. Gather more information first.

Wendy typed 'Steven Miciano' into the search engine. When she saw the results, even before she clicked on any of them for details, she knew.

'Damn,' she said out loud.

From behind her: 'What?'

It was Charlie. 'Nothing, what's up?'

'Do you mind if we head over to Clark's?'

'I guess it's okay.'

'Cool.'

Charlie left. Wendy turned back to the computer. She clicked the first hit, a news article from four months ago from a paper called the *West Essex Tribune*:

Local resident Steven Miciano, an orthopedic surgeon at St. Barnabas Medical Center in Livingston, NJ, was arrested last night and charged with possession of illegal narcotics. Police, working on a tip, found what was described as a 'large haul of illegally obtained prescribed painkillers' in the trunk of the doctor's car. Dr. Miciano was released on bail pending a hearing. A spokesman for St. Barnabas Medical Center said Dr. Miciano would be put on leave until the matter was investigated fully.

That was it. Wendy searched the *West Essex Tribune* for follow-ups. Nothing. She went back to the Web and found hits on blogs and even on Twitter. The first was from a former patient talking about how Miciano sneaked him drugs. Another was from a 'drug supplier' who had turned state's evidence in nailing Dr. Miciano. Still another blog entry came from a patient who said Miciano had been 'inappropriate' and 'definitely seemed high on something.'

Wendy started taking notes, checking the blog sites, checking the Tweets, the postings on various boards, the links to MySpace and Facebook.

This was too crazy.

Five freshman roommates from Princeton. Nothing on one. Okay, subtract Kelvin Tilfer out for a second. The other four: a financial consultant, a politician, a social worker – and now a physician. All four had been taken down by scandals within the past year.

That was a hell of a coincidence.

Chapter 18

With his one call, Ed Grayson woke up his attorney, Hester Crimstein. He told her that he'd been arrested.

Hester said, 'This sounds like so much bull that I would normally send an underling out.'

'But?' Ed said.

'But I don't like the timing.'

'Me neither,' Ed said.

'I mean, I just ripped Walker a new hole a few hours ago. So why pick you up and actually arrest you?' She paused. 'Unless I've lost my touch?'

'I don't think that's it.'

'Neither do I. So that means that they have something new.'

'The blood test?'

'That shouldn't be enough.' Hester hesitated. 'Ed, you're sure there is no way they found, uh, anything more incriminating?'

'No way.'

'You're certain?'

'Absolutely.'

'Okay, you know the drill. Don't talk. I'll have my driver take me out. Shouldn't be more than an hour this time of night.'

'One more troubling thing,' he said.

'What?'

'I'm not at the Sussex County police station this time. I'm in Newark. That's Essex County, a different jurisdiction.'

'Any idea why?'

'Nope.'

'Okay, sit tight. Let me throw on some clothes. I'm bringing my A game this time. No mercy on these asswipes.'

Forty-five minutes later, Hester sat with her client Ed Grayson in a small interrogation room with Formica floors and a bolted-down table. They waited. They waited a long time. Hester grew furious.

Finally the door opened. Sheriff Walker entered, wearing his uniform. Another guy – potbellied, around sixty, in a squirrel gray suit that looked as if it had been intentionally wrinkled – was with him.

'Sorry for the wait,' Walker said. He leaned against the far wall. The other man took the chair across the table from Grayson. Hester was still pacing.

'We're leaving,' she said.

Walker gave her a finger wave. 'Bye, Counselor, we'll miss you. Oh, but your client is going nowhere. He's under arrest. He's going through the system – being processed and held. It's late. We'll probably have the bail hearing first thing in the morning, but don't worry, we have cozy accommodations.'

Hester was having none of it. 'Excuse me, Sheriff, but aren't you an elected official?'

'I am.'

'So imagine when I put my full resources into getting your ass canned. I mean, how hard will this be? Arresting a man whose son was a victim of a heinous—'

The other man finally spoke. 'Can we just cut through the threats for a moment?'

Hester looked at him.

'Do whatever the hell you want, Ms. Crimstein, okay? I don't care. We have questions. You're going to answer them or your client is going to get very lost in the system. Do you get me?'

Hester Crimstein squinted at him. 'And you are?'

'My name is Frank Tremont. I'm an Essex County investigator. And really, if we could cut the posturing for a minute, maybe you'll get why you're here.'

Hester looked as though she was ready to attack, but she pulled back. 'Okay, big boy, what you got?'

Walker took that one. He slapped a file down on the table. 'A blood test.'

'Saying?'

'As you know, we found blood in your client's car.'

'So you said.'

'The blood in the car is a perfect match with the victim, Dan Mercer.'

Hester faked a big yawn.

Walker said, 'Maybe you could tell us why that would be?'

Hester shrugged. 'Maybe they took a ride together. Maybe Dan Mercer got a bloody nose on his own.'

Walker folded his arms. 'Is that really the best you can offer up?'

'Oh no, Sheriff Walker. I can offer up much better, if you'd like.' Hester batted her eyes and put on a fake girlie voice. 'May I give you a hypothetical?'

'I'd rather have facts.'

'Sorry, handsome, that's the best I can do.'

'Fine, go for it.'

'Well, here's one hypothetical, if I may. You have a

witness to the alleged murder of Dan Mercer, isn't that correct?'

'That's correct.'

'Now hypothetically, let's say I've read the statement made by your witness, that TV reporter Wendy Tynes.'

'That would be impossible,' Walker said. 'The witness's statement and identity are both confidential.'

'Gasp oh gasp, my bad. The *hypothetical* statement made by a *hypothetical* TV reporter. May I continue?'

Frank Tremont said, 'Go ahead.'

'Super. Now according to her hypothetical statement, when she encountered Dan Mercer at this trailer, before any shooting took place, there were clear signs that he'd suffered a recent beating.'

Nobody spoke.

'I like feedback,' Hester said. 'One of you nod.'

'Pretend we both did,' Frank said.

'Okay, good. Now let's say – again hypothetically – Dan Mercer met up with one of his victims' fathers a few days earlier. Let's say that a fight ensued. Let's say a little bit of blood was spilled. Let's say that little bit of blood ended up in a car.'

She stopped, spread her hands, and arched her eyebrow. Walker looked at Tremont.

Frank Tremont said, 'Well, well.'

'Well, well what?'

He tried to smile through the strain. 'If a hypothetical fight started, that would certainly give your client motive, now wouldn't it?'

'I'm sorry, what's your name again?'

'Frank Tremont, Essex County investigator.'

'You new on the job, Frank?'

Now he spread his hands. 'Do I look new?'

'No, Frank, you look like a hundred years of bad

172

decisions, but your statement about motive would be the kind of thing some oxygen-deficient rookie might try on a brain-dead paralegal. First off – pay attention here – the loser of the fight is usually the one who seeks retribution, correct?'

'Most of the time.'

'Well' – Hester gestured to her client as if she were a hostess on a game show – 'take a look at this strapping hunk of manhood I call a client. Do you see any bruises or abrasions on him? No. So it would seem that if there was a physical altercation, my boy got the better of it, don't you think?'

'That's proof of nothing.'

'Trust me, Frank, you don't want to get into a proof argument with me. But either way, win or lose a fight, it's irrelevant. You're talking about finding motive, like that's innovative or helpful. You're new to the case, Frank, so let me help you here – Dan Mercer took nude pictures of my client's eight-year-old son. That's motive already. See? When a man sexually assaults your child, that would be motive to seek revenge upon him. Write that down. Experienced investigators need to know stuff like this.'

Frank made a grumbling noise. 'That's hardly the point.'

'Unfortunately, Frank, that's exactly the point. You claim some big breakthrough with this blood test. You drag us down here in the middle of the night because you're so impressed by it. I'm telling you, your so-called evidence – and I'll skip the part about how I'll tear apart your crime scene guys and the chain of handling because Walker can play you the tape from our first tête-à-tête – means absolutely bubkes and can easily be explained away.'

Hester looked over at Walker. 'I don't mean to make bold threats, but are you really going to use this dumb-ass blood test to falsely arrest my client for murder?'

'Not for murder,' Tremont said.

That made Hester pull back a bit. 'No?'

'No. Not for murder. My thinking is, an accessory after the fact.'

Hester turned to Ed Grayson. He shrugged. She looked back at Tremont. 'Let's pretend I gasped and move straight on to what you mean by accessory after the fact.'

'We searched Dan Mercer's motel room,' Frank Tremont said. 'We found this.'

He slid an eight-by-ten photograph across to them. Hester looked at it – a pink iPhone. She showed it to Ed Grayson, her hand on his forearm as though warning him not to react. Hester said nothing. Grayson did the same. Hester understood certain basic tenets. There were times that called for attack and times that called for silence. She had a habit, big surprise, of leaning too much toward the attack – of talking too much. But they wanted a reaction here. Any reaction. She would not give them one. She would wait them out.

Another minute passed before Frank Tremont said, 'That phone was found under Mercer's bed in his hotel room in Newark, not far from where we now sit.'

Hester and Grayson stayed silent.

'It belongs to a missing girl named Haley McWaid.'

Ed Grayson, retired federal marshal who should have known better, actually groaned. Hester turned to him. Grayson's face drained of color as though someone had opened a spigot and let out all the blood. Hester grabbed his arm again, squeezed, tried to bring him back.

Hester tried to buy some time. 'You can't possibly think that my client—'

'You know what I think, Hester?' Frank Tremont interrupted. He was gaining confidence, his voice full of bluster. 'I think your client killed Dan Mercer because Mercer was getting off for what he did to your client's son. That's what I think. I think your client decided to take the law into his own hands – and on one level, I can't blame him. If someone did that to my kid, yeah, sure, I'd go after him. Honest to God, I would. And then I'd hire the best lawyer I could because the truth is, the victim here is so unsympathetic – such a bucket of scum – that he could indeed get shot in front of the home crowd at a Giants game and no one would convict.'

He glared at Hester. Hester folded her arms and waited.

'But that's the problem with taking the law into your own hands. You don't know where it will lead. So now – oh, and this is all hypothetically speaking, right? – your client killed the only man who may have told us what happened to a seventeen-year-old girl.'

'Oh God,' Grayson said. He dropped his face in his hands.

Hester said, 'A moment with my client.'

'Why?'

'Just get the hell out.' Then, thinking better of it, she leaned into Grayson's ear and whispered, 'Do you know something about this?'

Grayson leaned away and looked at her in horror. 'Of course not.'

Hester nodded. 'Okay.'

'Look, we don't think your client hurt Haley McWaid,' Frank continued. 'But we're pretty damn sure Dan Mercer did. So now we need to know everything we can to find Haley. Everything. Including where Mercer's body is. And we're running against the clock here. For all we know, Dan was holding her someplace secret.

Haley could be tied up, scared, hurt, who knows? We're digging up his yard. We are asking neighbors, coworkers, friends, even his ex about places he liked to go. But the clock is ticking – and that girl may be alone, starving or trapped or worse.'

'And,' Hester said, 'you think a corpse might tell you where she is?'

'It could, yes. He may have a clue on his body or in his pockets, something. Your client needs to tell us where Dan Mercer is.'

Hester shook her head. 'Do you really expect me to allow my client to incriminate himself?'

'I expect your client to do the right thing here.'

'For all I know you're making this all up.'

Frank Tremont stood. 'What?'

'I've dealt with cops and their tricks before. Confess and we can save the girl.'

He leaned down. 'Take a close look at my face. Do you really think this is a ploy?'

'Could be.'

Walker said, 'It's not.'

'And I'm supposed to take your word for it?'

Both Walker and Tremont just looked at her. They all knew – this was real. De Niro couldn't give this good a performance.

'Still,' Hester said, 'I won't let my client incriminate himself.'

Tremont got up, his face red. 'Is that how you feel, Ed?'

'Talk to me, not my client.'

Frank ignored her. You're a law enforcement officer.' He leaned right into Ed Grayson's lowered face. 'By killing Dan Mercer, you may be responsible for killing Haley McWaid.'

'Back off,' Hester said.

'You can live with yourself, Ed? With your conscience? If you think I'm going to waste time on legal maneuvers—'

'Wait,' Hester said, her voice suddenly calm. 'You're basing this connection simply on this phone?'

'What?'

'That's all you have? This phone in his hotel room?'

'What, you don't think that's enough?'

'That's not what I asked you, Frank. I asked, what else have you got?'

'Why do you care?'

'Just tell me.'

Frank Tremont looked back at Walker. Walker nodded. 'His ex-wife,' Frank said. 'Mercer used to visit her house. Apparently so did Haley McWaid.'

'You think that's where Mercer met this girl?'

'We do.'

Hester nodded. Then: 'Let my client go now, please.'

'You're joking, right?'

'Right now.'

'Your client killed our only lead!'

'Wrong,' Hester snapped. Her voice boomed through the room. 'If what you're saying is true, Ed Grayson *gave* you your only lead.'

'What the hell are you talking about?'

'How did you bumbling idiots finally find this phone?'

No one answered.

'You searched Dan Mercer's room. Why? Because you thought that my client had murdered him. So without that, you'd have nothing. Three months of investigating and you had nothing. Until today. Until my client handed you your only clue.'

Silence. But Hester wasn't done.

177

'And while we're on the subject, Frank, I know who you are. Essex County investigator Frank Tremont, who botched up that high-profile murder case a few years back. Washed-up has-been ridden out by his boss Loren Muse because of his lazy-ass incompetence, right? And here you are, on your last case, and what happens? Rather than redeem yourself and your pitiful career, you never bother to even look at a well-known pedophile who crossed paths with the victim in a fairly obvious way. How the hell did you miss that, Frank?'

Now it was Frank Tremont who was losing color in his face.

'And now, lazy cop that you are, you have the nerve to come raining down on my client as an accessory? You should be thanking him. All these months on the case and you found nothing. Now you're closer than you've ever been to finding this poor girl *because* of what you allege my client did.'

Frank Tremont deflated right in front of them.

Hester nodded at Grayson. They both started to rise.

Walker said, 'Where do you think you're going?'

'We're leaving.'

Walker looked to Tremont to protest. Tremont was still reeling. Walker picked up the ball. 'Like hell you are. Your client is under arrest.'

'I want you to listen to me,' Hester said. Her voice was softer now, almost apologetic in tone. 'You're wasting your time.'

'How do you figure?'

She looked him dead in the eye. 'If we knew something that could help that girl, we would tell you.'

Silence.

Walker tried for bravado, but it wasn't there anymore. 'Why don't you let us decide what might help?'

'Yeah,' Hester said, standing all the way up now, flicking a glance at Tremont, then back to Walker. 'You've both done so much to inspire confidence so far. What you need to do is concentrate on finding that poor girl – not on prosecuting a man who may be the only hero in all this.'

There was a knock on the door. A young cop opened it and leaned in. All eyes turned toward him. Walker said, 'What's up, Stanton?'

'I found something on her phone. I think you're going to want to see this.'

Chapter 19

Frank Tremont and Mickey Walker followed Stanton down the corridor. 'Hester Crimstein is an amoral shark with scruples that would shame a street hooker,' Walker said to him. 'You know all that incompetency stuff was just to throw us off our game.'

'Uh-huh.'

'You've been all over this case. You've done more than anyone could.'

'Right.'

'So have the FBI and the big-time profilers and your entire office. Nobody could have foreseen this.'

'Mickey?'

'Yeah.'

'If I need to get stroked,' Frank said, 'I'll find someone a lot hotter and more feminine than you, okay?'

'Yeah, okay.'

Stanton led them to a corner room in the basement where the tech guys hung out. Haley McWaid's iPhone was plugged into a computer. Stanton pointed at the screen. 'This is basically her cell phone blown up for you to see on this bigger monitor.'

'Okay,' Frank Tremont said. 'So what's up?'

'I found something in an app.'

'A what?'

'An app. A phone application.'

Tremont hoisted up his pants by the belt. 'Pretend I'm an old fossil who still can't program his Betamax.'

Stanton pressed a button. The screen turned black with small icons neatly aligned in three rows. 'These are apps for the iPhone. See, she had iCal, which is where Haley kept her appointments, like lacrosse games and homework, on a calendar; Tetris – that's a game, and so is Moto Chaser; Safari is her Web browser; iTunes so she could download songs. Haley loves music. There's this other music app program called Shazam. It—'

'I think we get the gist,' Walker said.

'Right, sorry.'

Frank stared at Haley's iPhone. What song, he wondered, had she listened to last? Did she like faster rock or heartbreaking ballads? Typical old fart, Frank had made fun of these devices, kids texting and e-mailing and walking around with earbuds, but in a sense, the device was a life. Her friends would be listed in her address book, her school schedule in the calendar, her favorite songs in some playlist, photos that made her smile – like the one taken with Mickey Mouse – in her photo file.

Hester Crimstein's accusation was there. True, Dan Mercer had no history of violence or rape, seemed to be into girls younger than this, and really, the fact that his ex-wife lived in the same large town was hardly a big warning sign. But Crimstein's words about incompetence hammered him, and in them, Frank feared that he heard the echo of a truth.

He should have seen it.

'Anyway,' Stanton said, 'I don't mean to go into too much detail, but this is a little weird. Haley downloaded a bunch of songs like every teenager, but none since her disappearance. Same with surfing the Web. I mean, you know every place she visited on her iPhone because you got the server to show you. So what I saw in the browser won't surprise you much. She had done some searches on University of Virginia – I guess she was bummed that she didn't get in, right?'

'Right.'

'So there was also a search for some girl named Lynn Jalowski, who's from West Orange, a lacrosse player who got into UVA, so I guess maybe she was looking up a rival.'

'We know all this,' Frank said.

'Right, the server – so you also know about the instant messages, the texts, stuff like that, though I have to say, Haley did a lot less of it than most of her friends. But see, there's a separate app we didn't really know about for Google Earth. You probably know what that is.'

'Humor me,' Frank said.

'Watch this. It's basically a built-in GPS feature.'

Stanton picked up Haley's iPhone and tapped a picture of the earth. The giant globe spun and then the satellite camera zoomed down, the planet growing bigger – first the United States, then the East Coast, then down to New Jersey – until it stopped about a hundred yards above the building where they now stood. It read: '50 W Market Street, Newark, NJ.'

Frank's jaw dropped. 'Will this tell you everyplace this iPhone went?'

'I wish,' Stanton said. 'No. You have to turn the feature on. Haley didn't. But you can look up any address or place and see a satellite photo of it on the map. Anyway, I'm having some experts figure out exactly why, but I guess Google Earth is self-contained so you never saw her searches on the server. The history also can't tell when a search was made, just that it was and where.'

'And Haley looked up places?'

'Only two since she downloaded the app.'

'Well?'

'One was her own home. My guess is, when she first downloaded it, she turned it on and it showed where she was. So that really doesn't count.'

'And the other?'

Stanton clicked and the giant Google Earth globe spun again. They watched it zoom in on New Jersey again. It stopped in a wooded area with one building in the middle.

'Ringwood State Park,' Stanton announced. 'It's about forty miles away from here. The heart of the Ramapo Mountains. That building is the Skylands Manor in the middle of the park. It's surrounded by at least five thousand acres of woods.'

There was a second, maybe two, of silence. Frank could feel his heart beating in his chest. He looked at Walker. No words were exchanged. They knew. When something like this lands in your lap, you just know. The park was pretty big. Frank remembered a few years ago when some survivalist had hidden in the surrounding woods for more than a month. You could build a small lodging, hide it under trees and bush, lock someone up there.

Or, of course, you could bury someone where they'd never be found.

Tremont was the first to check the time. Midnight. Hours more of darkness. Panic set in. He quickly called Jenna Wheeler. If she didn't answer, he'd drive his car through her front door to get the answer.

'Hello?'

'Dan liked to hike, didn't he?'

'Right.'

'Any favorite spots?'

'I know he used to like the trail in Watchung.'

'How about Ringwood State Park?'

Silence.

'Jenna?'

A moment passed before she spoke.

'Yeah,' she said, her voice faraway. 'I mean, years ago, when we were married, we used to take the Cupsaw Brook Loop up there all the time.'

'Get dressed. I'll have a car pick you up.' Frank Tremont hung up and turned to Walker and Stanton. 'Helicopters, dogs, bulldozers, lights, shovels, rescue squads, park rangers, every available man, local volunteers. Let's get moving.'

Walker and Stanton both nodded.

Frank Tremont flipped open his phone again. He took a deep breath, felt the punch from Hester Crimstein's earlier words, and then he dialed Ted and Marcia McWaid.

At five AM, Wendy was jarred awake by the phone. She had only fallen asleep two hours earlier. She had stayed up and surfed and started to put things together. Nothing on Kelvin Tilfer. Was he the exception that proved the rule? She didn't know yet. But the more she surfed the other four – the further she dug into their histories – the stranger the Princeton suitemate scandals became.

Wendy reached blindly for the phone and croaked out a hello.

Vic skipped the niceties. 'Do you know Ringwood State Park?'

'No.'

'It's in Ringwood.'

'You must have been an insightful reporter, Vic.'

'Get up there.'

'Why?'

'That's where cops are looking for that girl's body.'

She sat up. 'Haley McWaid's?'

'Yep. They think Mercer dumped her in the woods.'

'What pointed them in that direction?'

'My source said something about Google Earth on her iPhone. I'll get a camera crew to meet you.'

'Vic?'

'What?'

Wendy put her hand through her hair, tried to quiet her racing mind. 'I don't know if I have the stomach for this one.'

'Boo-friggin'-hoo. Get moving.'

He hung up. Wendy got out of bed, showered, and dressed. She had her TV makeup case always at the ready, which was pretty sick when you thought about where she was headed. Welcome to the world of television news. As Vic had so poetically put it, boo-friggin'-hoo.

She walked past Charlie's room. It was a wreck, yesterday's shirt and shorts balled up on the floor. When you lose a husband, you learn not to waste time on stuff like that. She looked past it, at her sleeping son, and thought about Marcia McWaid. Marcia had woken up like this, looked into her child's room like this, and found the bed empty. Now, three months later, Marcia McWaid was waiting for word as law enforcement officers scoured a state park for her missing daughter.

That was what people like Ariana Nasbro didn't quite get. The fragility of it all. The ripples one horror can unleash. How any carelessness can plummet you down that pit of despair. How it can all be irreparable.

Yet again, Wendy said the silent prayer of every parent:

185

Don't let anything harm him. Please just keep him safe.

Then she got into her car and drove to the state park where the police were searching for the girl who hadn't been in that bed in the morning.

Chapter 20

The sun rose at five forty-five AM.

Patricia McWaid, Haley's younger sister, stood in the middle of the activity storm and didn't move. Since the police found Haley's iPhone, it felt as though they had gone back to those numbing first days – stapling up posters, calling all her friends, visiting her favorite spots, updating her missing-girl Web site, handing out her photograph at the local malls.

Investigator Tremont, who had been so nice to her family, seemed to have aged about ten years in the last few days. He forced up a smile for her and said, 'How you doing, Patricia?'

'Fine, thank you.'

He patted her shoulder and moved on. People did that a lot with Patricia. She didn't stand out. She wasn't particularly special. That didn't bother her. Most people aren't particularly special, though they may think they are. Patricia was content with her situation – or at least she had been. She missed Haley. Patricia did not relish attention. Unlike her big sister, she hated competition and avoided the limelight. Now she was a 'pity celebrity' at school, the popular girls acting friendly, wanting to get close to her so they could say at parties, 'Oh, that missing girl? Well, I'm friends with her sister!'

Patricia's mother was helping to organize the search parties. Mom was pure strength, like Haley, a panther-like power to their walks, as if even a stroll was a challenge to those around them. Haley led. Always. And Patricia followed. Some people thought that bothered her. It didn't. Her mother would sometimes get on her, tell her, 'You need to be more decisive,' but Patricia never saw the need. She didn't like making decisions. She was just as happy seeing the movie Haley liked. She didn't care whether they ate Chinese or Italian. What was the big deal? When you think about it, what's so great about being decisive?

News vans were being corralled into a roped-off area like she'd seen cowboys do with cattle in the movies. Patricia spotted that shrill-voiced, frosted-hair woman from that cable station. One of the reporters sneaked past the barricade and called out Patricia's name. He gave her a toothy smile and showed her a microphone, as if it were candy he was using to lure her into his car. Tremont walked over to the reporter and told him to get the f-something behind the barricade.

A crew from another news van started setting up a camera. Patricia recognized the beautiful reporter with them. Her son, Charlie Tynes, went to their high school. Charlie's dad had been killed by a drunk driver when he was young. Her mom had told her that story. Whenever they'd see Mrs. Tynes at a game or the supermarket or whatever, Patricia and Haley and Mom would all go a little quiet, as if in respect or maybe fear, wondering, Patricia guessed, what her life would be like if a drunk driver did something like that to her dad.

More police arrived. Her dad greeted them, forcing up a smile, shaking hands like he was running for office. Patricia was more like her father – go with the flow. But her father had changed. They all had, she guessed, but something inside of her dad had shattered, and she wasn't sure whether, even if Haley came home, it would ever be right again. He still looked the same, smiled the same, tried to laugh and act goofy and do those little things that made him, well, him, but it was as if he were empty, like everything inside of him had been scooped out or like some movie in which the aliens replace people with soulless clones.

There were police dogs, Great Danes, and Patricia walked over to them.

'Is it okay if I pet them?' she asked.

'Sure,' the officer said after a brief hesitation.

Patricia scratched one behind the ears. His tongue flopped out in appreciation.

People talk about how much parents shape you, but Haley was the most dominant person in her life. When girls in second grade started picking on Patricia, Haley beat up one as a warning to the others. When some guys catcalled at them by Madison Square Garden – Haley had taken her little sister to see Taylor Swift – Haley had slid in front of her and told them to shut the hell up. At Disney World, their parents had let Haley and Patricia go out alone one night. They ended up meeting some older boys and getting drunk in the All-Star Sports Resort. The good girl could get away with stuff like that. Not that she wasn't good – Haley was – but she was still a teenager. That night, after having her first beer, Patricia had made out with a guy named Parker, but Haley made sure that Parker went no further.

'We'll start deep in the woods,' she overheard Investigator Tremont say to the officer handling the dogs.

'Why deep?'

'If she's alive, if the bastard has built some kind of

shelter to hide her, it has to be pretty far off the path or someone would have noticed already. But if she's near the trail . . .'

His voice trailed off as he realized, Patricia was sure, that she was in earshot. She looked off into the woods and petted the dog and pretended that she didn't hear. For the past three months, Patricia had blocked everything out. Haley was strong. She would survive. It was as though her big sister had just gone on some weird adventure and would be home soon.

But now, looking out in the woods and petting this dog, she pictured the unfathomable: Haley, alone, scared, hurt, crying. Patricia squeezed her eyes shut. Frank Tremont walked toward her. He stood in front of her, cleared his throat, waited for her to open her eyes. After a few moments she did. She waited for his words of comfort. But he didn't offer any. He just stood there, shuffling his feet, indecisive.

So Patricia closed her eyes again and kept petting that dog.

Chapter 21

Wendy stood in front of the crime scene tape and spoke into the microphone with the NTC News logo near the mouthpiece. 'And so we wait for some word,' she said, trying to add gravitas to her voice without that TV-news melodrama. 'From Ringwood State Park in northern New Jersey, this is Wendy Tynes, NTC News.'

She lowered the microphone. Sam, her cameraman, said, 'We should probably do that again.'

'Why?'

'Your ponytail is loose.'

'It's fine.'

'Come on, tighten the band. It'll take two minutes. Vic will want another take.'

'Screw Vic.'

Sam rolled his eyes. 'You're kidding, right?'

She said nothing.

'Hey, you're the one who gets all pissed when we air a take with a makeup smudge,' he went on. 'All of a sudden you got religion? Come on, let's do one more take.'

Wendy handed him the microphone and walked away. Sam was right, of course. She was a television news reporter. Anyone who thinks looks don't matter in this industry is somewhere between naïve and brain-dead. Of course looks matter – and Wendy had primped for the camera and done repeated takes in equally grim situations.

In short, add 'hypocrite' to her growing list of failures.

'Where you going?' Sam asked.

'I have my cell. Call me if something happens.'

She headed to her car. She had planned on calling Phil Turnball, but then she remembered that his wife, Sherry, had said that Phil spent every morning alone with the classifieds at the Suburban Diner on Route 17. It was only about twenty minutes from here.

The classic New Jersey diners of yore had these wonderful shiny aluminum walls. The newer ones – 'newer' meaning circa 1968 – had a faux stone façade that made Wendy long for, well, aluminum. The interiors had, however, changed very little. There were still small jukeboxes at every table; a counter with spin stools; doughnuts under Batphone-style glass covers; signed, sun-faded autographed photos of local celebrities you never heard of; a surly guy with hairy ears behind the cash register; and a waitress who called you 'hon' and you loved her for it.

The jukebox played the eighties hit 'True' by Spandau Ballet, a curious six AM song selection. Phil Turnball sat in a corner booth. He wore a gray pinstripe suit with a yellow tie they used to call a 'power tie.' He was not reading the paper. He stared down at his coffee as though it hid an answer.

Wendy approached and waited for him to look up. He didn't.

Still looking down: 'How did you know I was here?' Phil asked.

'Your wife mentioned you hang out here.'

He smiled but there was no joy in it. 'Did she now?'

Wendy said nothing.

'Tell me, how did that conversation go exactly – oh,

pathetic Phil goes to this diner every morning and feels sorry for himself?'

'Not at all,' Wendy said.

'Right.'

This was not a subject worth mining. 'Do you mind if I sit down?'

'I have nothing to say to you.'

The newspaper was open to the story on Haley's iPhone being found in Dan Mercer's motel room. 'You read about Dan?'

'Yep. You still here to defend him? Or was that a crock from the beginning?'

'I'm not following.'

'Did you know about Dan abducting this girl before yesterday? Did you figure I wouldn't talk if you told me your real agenda, so you pretended you were going to restore his reputation?'

Wendy slid in across the table from him. 'I never said I wanted to restore his reputation. I said I wanted to find out the truth.'

'Very noble,' he said.

'Why are you being so hostile?'

'I saw you talking to Sherry last night.'

'Yeah, so?'

Phil Turnball took the coffee with both hands, one finger in the handle, the other for balance. 'You wanted her to persuade me to cooperate.'

'And again I say: Yeah, so?'

He took a sip, gently put the coffee back down. 'I didn't know what to think. I mean, some of what you said about Dan being set up made sense. But now' – he pointed with his chin toward the article on Haley's iPhone – 'what's the point?'

'Maybe you can help find a missing girl.'

He shook his head and closed his eyes.

'What?'

The waitress, what Wendy's father used to call a 'floozy' – a big, badly bottled blonde with a pencil tucked behind her ear – said, 'Get you anything?'

Damn, Wendy thought. She didn't call her 'hon.'

'Nothing, thanks,' Wendy said.

She sauntered away. Phil still had his eyes closed.

'Phil?'

'Off the record?' he said.

'Okay.'

'I don't know how to put this without making it sound like something it's not.'

Wendy waited, tried to give him space.

'Look, Dan and this sex stuff . . .'

His voice drifted off. Wendy was about to go after him. Sex stuff? Trying to meet up with an underage girl and maybe kidnapping another – that isn't something to dismiss as 'sex stuff.' But now was hardly the time for a morality play. So again she said nothing and waited.

'Don't get me wrong. I'm not saying Dan was a pedophile. It wasn't like that.'

He stopped again and this time Wendy wasn't sure that he'd start up again without some prompting. 'So what was it like?' she asked.

Phil started, stopped, shook his head. 'Let's say that Dan didn't mind getting them when they were young, if you know what I mean.'

Wendy's heart dropped.

'When you say getting them when they were young . . . ?'

'There were times – now keep in mind this was more than twenty years ago, okay? – but there were times when Dan preferred the company of younger girls. Not like a pedophile or anything. Nothing sick. But he liked

194

going to high school parties. He'd invite young girls to campus events, that kind of thing.'

Wendy's mouth felt dry. 'How young?'

'I don't know. It's not like I asked for ID.'

'How young, Phil?'

'Like I said, I don't know.' He squirmed. 'Keep in mind we were freshmen in college. All of eighteen, nineteen years old ourselves. So maybe these girls were in high school. Not a big deal, right? I think Dan was maybe eighteen. So the girls were like two, maybe three or four years younger.'

'Four? That would make a girl fourteen.'

'I don't know. I'm just saying. And you know how it is too. Some fourteen-year-old girls look a lot older. The way they dress and stuff. It's like they want to appeal to older guys.'

'Don't go there, Phil.'

'You're right.' He rubbed his face with both hands. 'God, I have daughters that age. I'm not defending him. I'm trying to explain. Dan wasn't a pervert or a rapist, but still, okay, the idea that he could hit on a younger girl? That I could maybe get. But that he would kidnap one, that he'd grab and harm a young girl . . . ? That, no, I can't see at all.'

He stopped talking and leaned back. Wendy sat very still. She thought back to what she knew about Haley McWaid's disappearance: No break-in. No violence. No calls. No texts. No e-mails. No signs of abduction. Not even an unmade bed.

Maybe they had this all wrong.

A theory started forming in her head. It was incomplete, based on a lot of innuendo and assumptions, but she needed to follow up. Next step: Go back to the woods and find Sheriff Walker. 'I have to go.'

He looked up at her. 'Do you think that Dan hurt that girl?'

'I don't have a clue anymore. I really don't.'

Chapter 22

Wendy called Walker from the car. The call got routed three different ways before Walker picked up.

'Where are you?' she asked.

'In the woods.'

Silence.

'Anything yet?'

'No.'

'You got five minutes for me?'

'I'm on my way back to the manor now. There's a guy named Frank Tremont. He's in charge of the Haley McWaid case.'

The name rang a bell. She had covered a few cases he'd handled in the past. The guy was a lifer, fairly smart, overly cynical. 'I know him.'

'Cool. We can meet you there.'

She hung up. She drove back to Ringwood, parked with the other reporters, and approached the cop guarding the crime scene entrance. Sam grabbed the camera and started to follow. Wendy stopped him with a head shake. Sam pulled up, puzzled. Wendy gave the cop her name and was waved through. The other reporters didn't like that. They hurried over and started demanding access. Wendy never turned around.

When she got to the tent, another officer said, 'Sheriff

Walker and Investigator Tremont said you should wait here.'

She nodded and sat on a foldout canvas chair, the same kind parents used on the sidelines at soccer games. There were dozens of law enforcement cars – some marked, some not – parked every which way. There were uniformed cops, cops in street clothes, and several officers sporting nifty FBI windbreakers. Many were on laptops. In the distance, Wendy could hear the clacking whir of a helicopter.

Standing by herself on the edge of the woods was a young girl Wendy recognized as Patricia McWaid, Haley's younger sister. Wendy debated whether this was the right time or not – but the debate didn't last long. Opportunity knocking and all that. She started toward the girl, telling herself that this was not about nailing a big story but about finding out what really happened to Haley and Dan.

A new theory had wormed its way into her brain. Patricia McWaid might have information that could prove or disprove it.

'Hi,' Wendy said to the young girl.

The girl gave a little startled jump. She turned and faced Wendy. 'Hello.'

'My name is Wendy Tynes.'

'I know,' Patricia said. 'You live in town. You're on TV.'

'That's right.'

'You also did a story on the man who had Haley's phone.'

'Yes.'

'Do you think he hurt her?'

Wendy was surprised by the girl's directness. 'I don't know.'

'Pretend you had to guess – do you think he hurt her?'

Wendy thought about it. 'I don't think he hurt her, no.'

'Why not?'

'Just a thought. I have no reason for believing that. Like I said, I really don't know.'

Patricia nodded. 'Fair enough.'

Wendy debated how to approach this. Start with something small like, 'Were you and your sister close?' Normally that was the way to go with any interview. Open with some softball questions. Get them relaxed, develop a rapport, get them in the rhythm. But even without the time constraint – Tremont and Walker could pop up any second – that felt like the wrong track. This girl had been direct with her. She might as well try the same.

'Did your sister ever mention Dan Mercer?'

'The police asked me that.'

'And?'

'No. Haley never mentioned him.'

'Did Haley have a boyfriend?'

'The police asked me that too,' Patricia said. 'First day she vanished. Investigator Tremont must have asked me that a million times since. Like I was hiding something.'

'Were you?'

'No.'

'So did she have a boyfriend?'

'I think so, yeah. But I don't know. It was like a secret or something. Haley could be private with stuff like that.'

Wendy felt her pulse pick up a bit. 'Private how?'

'She'd sneak out and meet up with him sometimes.'

'How did you know about it?'

'She told me. To, you know, cover if our parents asked.'

'How often did she do this?'

'Maybe two, three times.'

'Did she ask you to cover for her the night she vanished?'

'No. The last time was like a week before that.'

Wendy considered this. 'And you told the police all this?'

'Sure. Day one.'

'Did they ever find the boyfriend?'

'I think so. I mean, they said they found him.'

'Can you tell me who it was?'

'Kirby Sennett. A guy in our school.'

'Do you think it was Kirby?'

'You mean, was he her boyfriend?'

'Yes.'

Patricia shrugged. 'I guess so, yeah.'

'You don't sound certain.'

'Like I said, she never told me. I was just supposed to cover for her.'

The helicopter flew overhead. Patricia cupped a hand over her eyes and looked up. She swallowed deep and hard. 'It still doesn't feel real. Like she's just away on a trip and one morning she'll be back home.'

'Patricia?'

She lowered her gaze.

'Do you think Haley ran away?'

'No.'

Just like that.

'You seem pretty certain.'

'Why would she run away? Sure, maybe she liked to sneak a drink every once in a while, stuff like that. But Haley was happy, you know? She liked school. She liked lacrosse. She liked her friends. And she loved us. Why would she run away?'

Wendy considered that.

'Ms. Tynes?' Patricia said.

'Yes?'

'What are you thinking?'

She didn't want to lie to this girl. She also didn't want to tell her. Looking off, Wendy hesitated just long enough.

'What's going on here?' They both turned. County Investigator Frank Tremont stood with Sheriff Walker. He did not look happy. He cut a glance at Walker. Walker nodded and said, 'Patricia, why don't you come with me?'

Walker and Patricia headed toward the police tent, leaving Tremont alone with Wendy. He frowned at her. 'Man, I hope this wasn't a ploy to talk to the family.'

'It's not.'

'So what have you got?'

'Dan Mercer liked younger girls.'

Tremont gave her flat eyes. 'Wow, that's helpful.'

'Something about the whole Dan Mercer case has rubbed me wrong from day one,' she went on. 'No reason to go into details right now, but I've just never been able to buy him as a purely evil predator. I just spoke to an old classmate of his from Princeton. He can't believe Dan would abduct anyone.'

'Wow, that's also helpful.'

'But he did confirm that Dan liked younger girls. I'm not saying the guy wasn't a scum bucket. Sounds like he was. But my point is, he seemed to do it on a more consensual, less, I don't know, violent basis.'

Tremont did not look impressed. 'So?'

'So Patricia says Haley had a secret boyfriend.'

'Not so secret. It's a local punk-wannabe named Kirby Sennett.'

'Are you sure?'

'Sure about what?' Tremont paused. 'Wait, what are you saying?'

'According to Patricia, Haley sneaked out a few times – the last time a week before she vanished. She said that Haley asked her to cover for her.'

'Right.'

'And you guys figure she met up with this Kirby kid?'

'Right.'

'Did Kirby confirm it?'

'Not fully, no. Look, there's evidence they were an item. Some texts, e-mails, stuff like that. Seems like Haley liked the idea of keeping it a secret, probably because the kid was a punk. No big deal. The kid lawyered up. Not unusual, even if you're innocent. Rich parents, spoiled brat of a kid, you know the deal.'

'And this was Haley's boyfriend?'

'Seems so, yeah. But Kirby told us that he and Haley broke up about a week before she vanished. That matches when she last sneaked out.'

'And you obviously looked at Kirby?'

'Sure, but the kid is a small-time asshat. Don't get me wrong. We looked at Kirby hard and long. But he was in Kentucky when she disappeared. His alibi is completely solid. We checked him out six ways to Sunday. There's no way he had anything to do with it, if that's where you're going with this.'

'That's not where I'm going at all,' Wendy said.

Tremont hoisted his pants by the buckle. 'You want to share with the class then?'

'Dan Mercer dates younger girls. Haley McWaid leaves her house – no signs of violence, a break-in, nothing. What I'm saying is that maybe the mysterious boyfriend wasn't Kirby Sennett. Maybe it was Dan Mercer.'

202

Tremont took his time with that one. He chewed at something in his mouth, something that apparently tasted bad. 'So you think, what, Haley ran away with this perv on her own accord?'

'I'm not willing to go that far yet.'

'Good,' Tremont said, and there was steel in his voice. 'Because this is a good kid. A really good kid. I don't want her parents hearing crap like this. They don't deserve that.'

'I'm not casting any aspersions here.'

'Okay. Just so we're clear.'

'But for the sake of argument,' Wendy said, 'let's say Haley did run away with Mercer. It would explain why there was no evidence of foul play. And maybe it also explains the iPhone in the motel room.'

'How?'

'Haley runs away with Dan Mercer. He ends up getting killed. So she hurries out of the motel room – never looks back. I mean, think about it. If Dan Mercer had grabbed and killed her, why would he hold on to her iPhone?'

'As a trophy?'

Wendy frowned. 'Do you really buy that?'

Tremont said nothing.

'You found this state park on her Google Earth, right?'

'Right.'

'Pretend you're Haley. You wouldn't look up the place a kidnapper was going to hold you or bury you or what-ever.'

'But,' Tremont finished for her, 'you might look up a place where you were going to meet up with your boy-friend to run away.'

Wendy nodded.

Tremont sighed. 'She's a good kid.'

'We're not making a moral judgment here.'

'No?'

Wendy let that go.

'So let's say you're right,' Tremont said. 'Where would Haley be now?'

'I don't know.'

'And why would she leave her phone in the motel?'

'Maybe she had to rush out. Maybe she couldn't go back to the room for some reason. Maybe she's scared because Dan was killed and she's hiding.'

'So she had to rush out,' Tremont repeated, cocking his head. 'And so she, what, left her iPhone under the bed?'

Wendy thought about that. No answer came to her.

'Let's take it step by step,' Tremont said. 'First, I'll send some guys down to the motel – to all the crap holes where Dan stayed – and see if anyone remembers him being with a teenage girl.'

'Good,' Wendy said. Then: 'One other thing.'

'What?'

'When I saw Dan before he was shot, someone had beaten him pretty good.'

Tremont saw where she was going with this. 'So you figure that maybe Haley McWaid, if she was with him, might have seen that beating.' He nodded. 'Maybe that's why she ran.'

But now that he said it out loud, that didn't sound right to Wendy. There was a false note here. She tried to think it through. There was still more – like how did the scandals involving Stearns 109 fit in? She was about to present that angle to Tremont, but right now it still seemed too far out there. She needed to look into it more. That meant going back to Phil and Sherry Turnball, maybe calling Farley Parks and Steven Miciano, trying to find Kelvin Tilfer.

'So maybe you should look into who assaulted Dan Mercer,' she said.

A half-smile crossed Tremont's face. 'Hester Crimstein had an interesting theory on that.'

'Hester Crimstein, the TV judge?'

'Right. She's also Ed Grayson's attorney. According to her hypothetical, her client gave Dan Mercer that beating.'

'How does she figure?'

'See, we found Dan Mercer's blood in Grayson's car. We said that, along with your testimony, was clear evidence Grayson murdered Mercer.'

'Okay.'

'But Crimstein – God, she's good – she says, well, your witness, you, said Mercer had been beaten. So, she says, maybe Grayson and Mercer got into a fight a day or two earlier. And maybe that's how the blood ended up in the car.'

'You buy that?'

Tremont shrugged. 'Not really, no, but that's not the point.'

'It's pretty brilliant on her part,' Wendy said.

'Yep. Crimstein and Grayson pretty much figured a way to negate all the evidence. We have blood DNA – but a fight gives that a plausible explanation. Yes, Grayson had gun residue on his hand, but the owner of the Gun-O-Rama shooting range confirmed that he was there an hour after you saw him shoot Mercer. The owner says Grayson is one of the best shots he's ever seen, so he remembers him well. You witnessed him killing Dan Mercer – but there's no body, no gun, and he wore a mask.'

Something was niggling the back of Wendy's brain. It was there, just out of sight, but she couldn't quite get to it.

Tremont said, 'You know what I'm going to ask of you now, right?'

'I think so.'

'The McWaids have been through hell. I don't want to put them through more. You can't report this yet.'

Wendy said nothing.

'We have nothing, anyway, but a few whacked-out theories,' he went on. 'I promise to let you have anything we learn first. But for the sake of the investigation – for the sake of Haley's parents – you can't say anything yet. Deal?'

The niggling was still there. Tremont was waiting. 'Deal,' she said.

Back behind the crime scene tape, Wendy was only mildly surprised to see Ed Grayson leaning against her car. He tried to look casual, but he wasn't pulling it off. His finger toyed with a cigarette. He put it in his mouth and sucked on it as though he were deep underwater and it was a breathing tube.

'Sticking another GPS on my back bumper?' she asked.

'I have no idea what you mean.'

'Sure. You were just checking for a flat, right?'

Grayson took another deep drag. His face hadn't seen a razor, but that was true of more than half the men who'd gotten up here at such an early hour. His eyes were bloodshot. He looked a lot worse than the man who had just yesterday confidently explained to her his theories on vigilantism. She thought about that, about his visit to her house.

'Did you really think I'd help you kill him?' she asked.

206

'Truth?'

'That'd be nice, yeah.'

'You might've agreed with what I said in theory. You maybe even started to waver a little when I raised Ariana Nasbro. But no, I never thought you'd help.'

'So you were just giving it a shot?'

He didn't reply.

'Or was your visit all an excuse to put that GPS on my car?'

Ed Grayson slowly shook his head.

'What?' she asked.

'You don't have a clue, do you, Wendy?'

She stepped closer to the driver's door. 'Why are you here, Ed?'

He looked off toward the woods. 'I wanted to help with the search.'

'They wouldn't let you?'

'What do you think?'

'Sounds like you feel guilty.'

He took another drag. 'Do me a favor, Wendy. Skip the analysis.'

'So what do you want with me?'

'Your opinion.'

'On?'

He pinched the cigarette between his fingertips and studied it as though it held an answer. 'Do you think Dan killed her?'

She wondered how to answer that. 'What did you do with his body?'

'You talk first. Did Dan kill Haley McWaid?'

'I don't know. Maybe he just locked her up, and right now, because of what you did, she's starving to death.'

'Nice try.' He scratched at his cheek. 'But the cops laid that guilt trip on me already.'

'Didn't work?'

'Nope.'

'Are you going to tell me what you did with the body?'

'My. My.' He spoke in pure monotone. 'I. Have. No. Idea. What. You're. Talking. About.'

This was getting her nowhere – and she had places to go. The niggling had something to do with her research on the Princeton group. Dan and Haley running away together – okay, maybe. But what about all those scandals involving his old roommates? Could be nothing. Probably was. But she was missing something huge here.

'So what do you want from me?' she asked.

'I'm trying to figure out whether Dan really kidnapped this girl.'

'Why?'

'Trying to help the investigation, I guess.'

'So you can sleep better at night?'

'Maybe.'

'So what answer will make you sleep better?' she asked.

'I don't follow.'

'Well, if Dan killed Haley, would you feel better about what you did? Like you said before, he was bound to do it again. You stopped him – albeit a little late. And if Dan did not kill her, well, you're still convinced he would have hurt someone else, right? So either way, killing him was the only way to stop him. Seems the only way you lose sleep is if Haley is alive somewhere and you put her in further danger.'

Ed Grayson shook his head. 'Just forget it.' He started to walk away.

'Am I missing something?' she asked.

'Like I said before.' Grayson tossed the cigarette and never broke stride. 'You don't have a clue.'

Chapter 23

So now what?

Wendy could keep looking for clues that proved Dan and Haley were involved in some kind of consensual, albeit wrong, relationship, but what was the point? The police now had that theory. They would run with it. She needed to attack from another angle.

The five Princeton roommates.

Four out of five had been felled by scandals in the past year. The fifth, well, maybe he had too, but it just wasn't online. So she headed back to the Starbucks in Englewood to continue her investigation. When she entered, even before she spotted the Fathers Club, the sound of Ten-A-Fly's rapping blew forth from the overhead speakers.

Charisma Carpenter, I love you
You ain't no carpenter's dream, you ain't flat as board,
And you ain't easy to screw. . . .

'Yo, hey.'

It was Ten-A-Fly. She stopped. 'Hi.'

Ten-A-Fly was decked out in a Grass Roots zip-up blue hoodie. On his head he wore the hood over a red baseball cap with a brim so big a trucker in 1978 would have been embarrassed to wear it while on the CB. Behind him Wendy could see the guy with the tennis whites. He was typing madly on a laptop. The younger father with the baby sling was walking back and forth and making cooing noises.

Ten-A-Fly jiggled a bling bracelet that looked like a Halloween prop. 'Saw you at my gig last night.'

'Yep.'

'You likey?'

Wendy nodded. 'It was, uh, phat, dawg.'

That pleased him. He held up his fist for a knuckle pound. She obliged. 'You're a TV reporter, right?'

'Right.'

'So are you here to do a story on me?'

Tennis Whites on the laptop added, 'You should.' He pointed to the screen. 'We're getting a lot of action here.'

Wendy circled around and looked at the laptop. 'You're on eBay?'

'It's how I make a living now,' Tennis Whites said. 'Since I got laid off—'

'Doug here was at Lehman Brothers,' Ten-A-Fly interrupted. 'He saw the bad coming, but nobody would listen to him.'

'Whatever,' Doug said, waving a hand with modesty. 'Anyway, I stay solvent with eBay. First, I sold pretty much everything I owned. Then I started going to garage sales, buying things, fixing them up, reselling them.'

'And you can make a living at that?'

He shrugged. 'No, not really. It's something to do.'

'Like tennis?'

'Oh, I don't play.'

She just looked at him.

'My wife does. Second wife actually. Some would call her a trophy wife. She kept whining about how she gave up this wonderful career to watch the kids, but really, she plays tennis all day. When I lost my job, I suggested that she go back to work. She told me that it was too late now. So she still plays tennis every day. And she hates me now. She can barely look at me. So I wear the tennis whites too.'

'Because . . . ?'

'I don't know. A protest, I guess. I dumped a good woman – hurt her horribly – for a hottie. Now the good woman has moved on and doesn't even have the good sense to be mad at me anymore. I guess I got what I deserved, right?'

Wendy had no interest in going there. She looked at the screen. 'What are you selling now?'

'Ten-A-Fly souvenirs. I mean, we're selling his CD, of course.'

There were copies on the table. Ten-A-Fly dressed like Snoop Dogg on a bender making gangsta hand signs that made one think not so much of intimidation as an unusual state of palsy. The CD was titled *Unsprung in Suburbia.*

'Unsprung?' Wendy asked.

'Ghetto slang,' Doug of the Tennis Whites explained.

'For?'

'You don't want to know. Anyway, we're selling those CDs, T-shirts, caps, key chains, posters. But now I'm putting up one-of-a-kind items. Like, see here, that's the actual bandana Ten-A-Fly wore onstage last night.'

Wendy looked and couldn't believe the bidding. 'It's up to six hundred dollars?'

'Six-twenty now. Like I said, a lot of action. The panties a fan threw up onstage are also a hot item.'

Wendy looked back at Fly. 'Wasn't the fan your wife?'

'Your point?'

Good question. 'Absolutely none. Is Phil here?'

As she asked the question, Wendy spotted him behind the counter talking to the barista. He was smiling when he turned and saw her. The smile anvil-dropped off his face. Phil hurried toward her. Wendy met him halfway.

'What are you doing here?'

'We need to talk.'

'We already talked.'

'We need to talk more.'

'I don't know anything.'

She took a step closer to him. 'Do you not get that there is still a girl missing?'

Phil closed his eyes. 'Yeah, I get it,' he said. 'It's just . . . I don't know anything.'

'Five minutes. For Haley's sake.'

Phil nodded. They moved over to a table in the corner. It was rectangular and had a handicap logo with the words 'Please offer this table to our disabled customers.'

'During your freshman year at Princeton,' Wendy said, 'who else did you and Dan room with in college?'

Phil frowned. 'What could that possibly matter?'

'Just answer, okay?'

'There were five of us. Besides Dan and me, there was Farley Parks, Kelvin Tilfer, and Steve Miciano.'

'Did you guys room together other years?'

'Are you serious?'

'Please.'

'Yeah. Well, sophomore year – or maybe junior – Steve did a semester in Spain. Barcelona or Madrid. And junior year, I think, Farley lived in a frat house.'

'You didn't join a fraternity?'

'No. Oh, and I was gone first semester senior year. Did a program in London. Happy?'

'Do you guys stay in touch?'

'Not really.'

'How about Kelvin Tilfer?'

'I haven't heard from him since graduation.'

'Do you know where he lives?'

Phil shook his head. A barista brought over a cup of coffee and placed it in front of Phil. Phil looked toward Wendy, seeing if she wanted one, but she shook him off. 'Kelvin was from the Bronx. Maybe he's back there, I don't know.'

'How about the others? You ever talk to them?'

'I hear from Farley, though it's been a while. Sherry and I held a fund-raiser for him last year. He was running for Congress, but it didn't work out.'

'Well, Phil, that's the thing.'

'What is?'

'It didn't work out for any of you.'

He put his hand on the cup but didn't lift it. 'I'm not following.'

She took the printouts from a manila envelope and laid them on the desk.

'What's this?' he asked.

'Let's start with you.'

'What about me?

'A year ago, you go down for embezzling over two million dollars.'

His eyes widened. 'How do you know that number?'

'I have my sources.'

'The charges are total crap. I didn't do it.'

'I'm not saying you did. Just bear with me, okay? First, you go down for embezzling.' She opened another folder. 'Two months later, Farley gets ruined by a political scandal involving a prostitute.' The next file. 'A month or so after that, Dan Mercer gets nailed on my TV show.

213

And then, skip ahead another two months, Dr. Steve Miciano gets arrested for illegally possessing prescription drugs.'

The files with various online printouts sat on the table. Phil stared at them, his hands down as though afraid to touch them.

'Don't you think it's a hell of a coincidence?' she asked.

'What about Kelvin?'

'I don't have anything on him yet.'

'You found this all out in one day?'

'It didn't take much. I just did a simple Web search.'

From behind her, Ten-A-Fly said, 'May I see those?'

She turned. They were all there – the rest of the Fathers Club. 'You were eavesdropping?'

'Don't take offense,' Doug said. 'People come in here and talk about the most personal things in the loudest of voices. It's like they think someone lowered a cone of silence around them. You just get used to listening in. Phil, this trumped-up embezzling charge – is that the reason they fired you?'

'No. That was the excuse. I was laid off like the rest of you.'

Ten-A-Fly reached out and picked up the sheets. He slipped on a pair of reading glasses and started studying them.

Phil said, 'I still can't see what any of this has to do with that missing girl.'

'Maybe nothing,' Wendy said. 'But take it step by step. You get caught up in a scandal. You claim you're innocent.'

'I am innocent. Why do you think I'm free right now? If my firm had any real proof, I'd be in jail. They know the charges were trumped-up.'

'But don't you see? That kind of adds up. Take Dan. He ended up getting off. And to the best of my knowledge, neither Steve Miciano nor Farley Parks is in jail. None of the charges against you guys have been proven – yet the accusations alone were ruinous.'

'So?'

Doug said, 'Are you kidding, Phil?'

Wendy nodded. 'Four guys, all in the same Princeton class, lived together in college, all involved in scandals within a year of each other.'

Phil thought about it. 'But not Kelvin.'

'We don't know that yet,' Wendy said. 'We need to find him to know for sure.'

Owen, still with baby in tow, said, 'Maybe this Kelvin is the one who set this all up.'

'Set what up?' Phil said. He looked at Wendy. 'You're joking, right? Why would Kelvin want to hurt us?'

'Whoa,' Doug said. 'I saw a movie like this once. Like, Phil, were you guys in the Skull and Bones or some secret society?'

'What? No.'

'Maybe you guys killed a girl and buried her body and now she's getting revenge on you. I think that's what happened in the movie.'

'Stop it, Doug.'

'But they have a point,' Wendy said. 'I mean, forgetting all the melodrama, could something have happened back at Princeton?'

'Like what?'

'Like something that would make someone come after you years later.'

'No.'

He said it too fast. Ten-A-Fly was looking down his half-moon reading glasses – a bizarre look on a rapper – still studying her printouts. 'Owen,' Fly said.

The guy with the baby sling came over. Fly ripped off

a piece of paper. 'This is a video blog. Look it up online, see what you can come up with.'

Owen said, 'Sure.'

'What are you thinking?' Wendy asked him.

But Ten-A-Fly was still going through the pages. She looked back at Phil. His eyes were on the floor.

'Think, Phil.'

'There was nothing.'

'Did you guys have any enemies?'

Phil frowned. 'We were just a bunch of college kids.'

'Still. Maybe you guys got into a fight. Maybe one of you stole someone's girlfriend.'

'No.'

'You can't think of anything?'

'There isn't anything. I'm telling you. You're barking up the wrong tree.'

'How about Kelvin Tilfer?'

'What about him?'

'Did he ever feel slighted by you guys?'

'No.'

'He was the only black guy in the group.'

'So?'

'I'm just taking stabs in the dark here,' Wendy said. 'Did something happen to him maybe?'

'At school? No. Kelvin was weird, a math genius, but we all liked him.'

'What do you mean, weird?'

'Weird – different, funky, out there. He kept strange hours. He liked taking late-night walks. He talked out loud when he worked on math problems. Weird – mad genius weird. That plays well at Princeton.'

'So you can't think of any incident at school?'

'That would make him do something like this? No, nothing.'

'How about something more recent?'

'I haven't spoken to Kelvin since graduation. I told you.'

'Why not?'

Phil answered the question by asking one of his own. 'Where did you go to college, Wendy?'

'Tufts.'

'Do you still talk to everyone you graduated with?'

'No.'

'Neither do I. We were friends. We lost touch. Like ninety-nine percent of college friends.'

'Did he ever come to reunions or homecoming or anything like that?'

'No.'

Wendy mulled that one over. She would try to contact Princeton's alumni office. Maybe they'd have something.

Ten-A-Fly said, 'I found something.'

Wendy turned to him. Yes, the outfit was still ridiculous, what with the baggy jeans, the cap with the bill the size of a manhole cover, the Ed Hardy shirt, but it was amazing how much of a persona is indeed the attitude. Ten-A-Fly was gone now. Norm was back. 'What?'

'Before I got laid off, I was a marketing guy for several start-ups. Our main task was to get our company noticed in a positive way. Create buzz, especially online. So we got heavily into viral marketing. Do you know anything about it?'

'No,' she said.

'It is getting big to the point of irrelevancy – meaning everyone is doing it so no one will be heard over the din. But for now it still works. We even do some of it with my rap persona. Let's say a movie comes out. Right away, you'll see great reviews or positive comments posted on the YouTube trailers, bulletin boards, blogs about how great the movie is, all that. Most of the early comments aren't real. They are done by a marketing group hired by the movie studio.'

'Okay, so how does that fit with this?'

'In short, someone did that here in reverse – with this Miciano guy and Farley Parks, for sure. They set up blogs and Tweets. They paid search engines so that when you perform a search on these guys, your viral feeds get seen first and foremost – right at the top of the page. This is like viral marketing – but designed to destroy rather than build up.'

'So,' Wendy said, 'if I were, for example, to want to know about Dr. Steve Miciano and looked him up online . . .'

'You'd be flooded with negativity,' Ten-A-Fly finished for her. 'Pages and pages of it. Not to mention Tweets, social networking posts, anonymous e-mail—'

'We had something like that when I was at Lehman,' Doug said. 'Some guys would go on boards and say positive stuff about an IPO – anonymously or with a fake name, but it was always someone who had a vested interest. And the opposite, of course. You'd post rumors about a strong competitor going bankrupt. Oh, and I remember once there was an online financial columnist who posted that Lehman was going down, and guess what? Suddenly the blogosphere was filled with fake accusations about him.'

'So these charges are all made up?' Wendy asked. 'Miciano never got arrested?'

'No,' Fly said, 'that one is real. From a legit newspaper on a legit site. But the rest on him, I mean, look at this blog about the drug dealer. And now look at this blog from the prostitute involved with Farley Parks. Both plain pages from Blogger – and the author didn't write

218

any other blog entries, just the ones condemning these guys.'

'These are just smear jobs,' Wendy said.

Ten-A-Fly shrugged. 'I'm not saying that they didn't do it. They all might be guilty – not you, Phil, we know better. But what I am saying is that someone wanted the world to know about the scandals.'

Which, Wendy knew, played into her scandal-to-ruin conspiracy theory.

Ten-A-Fly looked behind him. 'You got anything, Owen?'

Without glancing away from the laptop, he said, 'Soon maybe.'

Ten-A-Fly continued to study the printouts. A barista shouted out a complicated order involving ventis and half-cafs and one percent and soy. Another barista jotted notes on a cup. The espresso machine sounded like a train whistle, drowning out the *Unsprung* sound track.

'What about the pedophile you caught?' Ten-A-Fly asked.

'What about him?'

'Did someone viral-market him?'

'I never thought to check.'

'Owen?' Ten-A-Fly said.

'On it. Dan Mercer, right?' Wendy nodded. Owen clicked a few keys. 'Not much, maybe a few posts on Dan Mercer, but no need. The dude was all over the news.'

'Good point,' Ten-A-Fly said. 'Wendy, how did you find out about Mercer?'

Wendy was already going there in her own mind – and she wasn't crazy about the path her mind was taking. 'I got an anonymous e-mail.'

Phil shook his head slowly. The rest of the guys just stared for a moment.

'What did it say?' Ten-A-Fly asked.

She took out her BlackBerry. The e-mail was still in the saved file. She found it, brought it up, and handed it to Ten-A-Fly:

Hi. I've seen your show before. I think you should know about this creepy guy I met online. I'm thirteen and I was in the SocialTeen chat room. He acted like he was my age, but it turned out he was way older. I think he's like forty. He is the same height as my dad so that's six feet and has green eyes and curly hair. He seemed so nice so I met him at a movie and he made me go back to his house. It was horrible. I'm scared he's done this to other kids too because he works with kids. Please help so he doesn't hurt more kids.

Ashlee (not my real name – sorry!)

PS Here is a link to the SocialTeen chat room. His screen name is DrumLover17.

They all read the e-mail in silence, one at a time. Wendy stood there stunned. When Ten-A-Fly handed her back the phone, he said, 'I assume you tried to write her back?'

'No one replied. We tried to trace it down, but it got us nowhere. But I didn't rely just on this e-mail,' Wendy added, trying not to sound too defensive. 'I mean, that was just the start. We acted on it, but that's what we do. We go into chat rooms and pretend to be young girls and see what pervert comes out of the woodwork. So we went into this SocialTeen chat room like we always do. DrumLoverSeventeen was in there. He pretended to be, well, a seventeen-year-old drummer. We set up a meet. Dan Mercer showed up.'

Ten-A-Fly nodded. 'I remember reading about the case. Mercer claimed that he thought he was meeting some other girl, right?'

'Right. He worked for a homeless shelter. He claimed a girl he was helping had called him to the location of our sting house. But keep in mind we had solid evidence: DrumLoverSeventeen's chat logs and the sexually explicit e-mails to our fake thirteen-year-old girl all came from a laptop found in Dan Mercer's home.'

No one responded to that. Doug took a swing with his air tennis racket. Phil looked like someone had whacked him with a two-by-four. Ten-A-Fly was keeping his wheels in motion. He looked back at Owen. 'Done yet?'

'I'll need my desktop computer for a fuller analysis of the videos,' Owen said.

Wendy was ready to move to a new subject. 'What are you looking for?'

The baby against Owen's chest was asleep, head tilted in that way that always made her nervous. Wendy had another flash – to John carrying Charlie in a baby sling. She wondered again what John would make of his son now, nearly a man, and wanted to cry for all that he missed. That was what always got to her – at every birthday or back-to-school night or just hanging out watching TV together, whatever. Not just how much Ariana Nasbro had taken from her and Charlie, but how much she had taken from John. All she had made him miss.

'Owen worked as a tech specialist on a daytime TV show,' Phil explained.

'Let me simplify this as much as I can,' Owen said. 'You know how your digital camera has a megapixels setting?'

'Yes.'

'Okay, so let's say you take a picture and post it on-line. Let's say it's four by six. The more megapixels, the bigger the file. But for the most part, a, say, five-mega-pixel picture of the same size will be roughly the same size as another – especially if taken by the same camera.'

'Okay.'

'The same is true for digital videos uploaded like these. When I get home I can look for special effects and other telltale signs. Right here, I can only see file size and then I can divide up the time. Put simply, the same type of video recorder was used to make both of these videos. That in and of itself doesn't mean much. There are hundreds of thousands of video cameras sold that would fit the bill. But it's worth noting.'

They were all there now, the Fathers Club – Norm, the Ten-A-Fly Rapper, Doug of the Tennis Whites, Owen of the Baby Sling, and Phil of the Power Suit.

Ten-A-Fly said, 'We want to help.'

'How?' Wendy asked.

'We want to prove Phil's innocent.'

'Norm . . . ,' Phil said.

'You're our friend, Phil.'

The others mumbled their agreement.

'Let us, okay? We got nothing else to do. We hang here and feel sorry for ourselves. I say enough with wallowing in failure. Let's do something constructive again – put our expertise to use.'

'I can't ask you to do that,' Phil said.

'You don't have to ask,' Norm continued. 'You know we want to. Heck, maybe we need this more than you do.'

Phil said nothing.

'We can start by looking into this viral marketing, see

if we can figure out where it came from. We can help you find that last roommate, Kelvin. We all have kids, Phil. If my daughter was out there, missing, I'd want any help I could get.'

Phil nodded. 'Okay.' Then: 'Thank you.'

We all have talents. That was what Ten-A-Fly said. Put our expertise to use. Something about those phrases stuck with Wendy. Expertise. We have a tendency to gravitate to what we are good at, don't we? Wendy saw the scandals through the eyes of a reporter. Ten-A-Fly saw them through the eyes of a marketing guru, Owen through a camera lens. . . .

A few minutes later, Ten-A-Fly walked Wendy to the door. 'We'll stay in touch,' he said.

'I wouldn't be so hard on yourself,' she said.

'How's that?'

'That failure talk.' Wendy nodded toward the laptop. 'A failure doesn't get someone to bid six hundred dollars on a used bandana.'

Ten-A-Fly smiled. 'That impressed you, eh?'

'Yes.'

He leaned closer and whispered, 'Do you want to know a little secret?'

'Sure.'

'The bidder is my wife. In fact, she has two online personas and bids against herself to make it look good. She thinks I don't know.'

Wendy nodded. 'Proves my point,' she said.

'How's that?'

'A man whose wife loves him that much,' Wendy said. 'How can you call that guy a failure?'

Chapter 24

The clouds had darkened over Ringwood State Park. Marcia McWaid trudged through the thick woods, her husband, Ted, a few steps in the lead. Marcia hoped rain was not on the way, but the cloud cover was an improvement over the morning's pounding sun.

Neither Ted nor Marcia was much for hiking or camping or pretty much anything that one might categorize as 'outdoors.' Before – there was always a 'before' now, a shattered world of wonderful naïveté from a dead age – the McWaids enjoyed museums and bookstores and dinners out at trendy restaurants.

When Ted looked to his right, Marcia could see his profile – and what she saw surprised her. There was, despite the fact that they were performing the grimmest task imaginable, a small smile on his handsome face.

'What are you thinking about?' Marcia asked her husband.

He kept walking. The small, wistful smile stayed in place. His eyes brimmed with tears, but that was pretty much how they had been for the past three months. 'Do you remember Haley's dance recital?'

There had been only one. Haley had been six years old. Marcia said, 'I think it's the last time I saw her in pink.'

'Do you remember that getup?'

'Sure,' Marcia said. 'They were supposed to be cotton candy. Strange memory. I mean, it was so not her.'

'Very true.'

'So?'

Ted stopped in front of an incline. 'Do you remember the actual recital?'

'It was in the middle school auditorium.'

'Right. We parents sit there and the show is like three hours long and it's so damn boring and you're just waiting for the two minutes your own kid is onstage. And I remember Haley's cotton-candy dance was maybe the eighth or ninth act out of, what, twenty-five, maybe thirty, and she comes on and we start nudging each other. I remember smiling then, you know, and I'm looking at my daughter and for a few moments you feel such a pure joy. It's like there's this light in my chest and I'm looking at Haley and her little face is all scrunched up because you know her – even then Haley was Haley. She didn't want to get anything wrong. Every step is exact and precise. I mean, there is no rhythm or expression, but Haley makes no mistakes. And I'm looking at this little wonder and I'm almost bursting.'

Ted looked at her as though to confirm the memory. Marcia nodded and maybe now, despite the grimmest of tasks, there was a small smile on her face too.

'And,' he continued, 'you're sitting there and you have tears in your eyes and you think about the wonder of this moment, and then – and this is the amazing thing – you look around the auditorium, at the other parents, and you realize that every one of them feels exactly the same away about their own kid. I mean, that's so obvious and simple and yet something about it overwhelms me. I can't believe this tremendous feeling, this wave of love, doesn't belong to us alone, that what we're experiencing isn't unique – and that just made it somehow greater. I remember watching the other parents in the audience. You see the wet eyes and the smiles. You see the wives reach for their husband's hand, no words exchanged. And I remember being just awed. Like, I don't know, like I couldn't believe one room, this school auditorium, could be so full of pure love and not just take off from the ground.'

Marcia wanted to say something, but no words came to her. Ted shrugged, turned, and started up the incline. He dug his foot into the ground, took hold of a thin tree, and powered his way up. Finally Marcia said, 'I'm so scared, Ted.'

'We'll be okay,' he said.

The smiles were gone now. The clouds continued to darken. A helicopter flew overhead. Ted reached his hand back. Marcia took it. He pulled her up. And the two of them resumed their search for their daughter.

Two days later, in a shallow grave on the outskirts of Ringwood State Park, the canine unit found the body of Haley McWaid.

PART TWO

Chapter 25

Funeral services are always pretty much the same. The same prayers, the customary biblical readings, the words of supposed comfort that, especially in situations like this, sound to an outsider's ear like either the most ridiculous rationalizations or obscene justifications. What occurs on the pulpit is pretty much a constant; only the reaction of the mourners alters the mood.

The funeral of Haley McWaid had been a dark, leaden blanket thrown over the entire community. Grief weighed you down, made your limbs heavy, put glass shards in your lungs so that even breathing was agony. Everyone in the community hurt right now, but Wendy knew that would not last. She had seen it with John's premature death. Grief is devastating, all-consuming. But grief merely visits friends, even the closest. It stays much longer, probably forever, with the family, but that was probably how it should be.

Wendy had stood in the back of the church. She came in late and left early. She never looked at Marcia or Ted. Her mind would not let her – would not 'go there' as Charlie, who was alive and breathing, liked to say. It was a defense mechanism, pure and simple. That was okay too.

The sun shone bright. It always seemed to be that way

229

on funeral days. Her mind again wanted to go to John, to the closed casket, but again she fought it off. She walked down the street. She stopped at the corner, closed her eyes, and tilted her face toward the sun. Her watch read eleven AM. It was time to meet Sheriff Walker at the medical examiner's office.

Located on a depressing stretch of Norfolk Street in Newark, the medical examiner's office handled Essex, Hudson, Passaic, and Somerset counties. Newark had indeed enjoyed some revitalization of late, but that was a few blocks east of here. Then again, what would be the point of putting an ME office in a trendy spot? Sheriff Walker met her on the street. He always looked a little uneasy with his size, slouching his big shoulders. She half expected him to crouch down and speak to her, the way you would to put a small child at ease, and this somehow made him more endearing.

'Been a busy few days for us both, I guess,' Walker said.

The death of Haley McWaid had exonerated Wendy and then some. Vic rehired her and promoted her to the weekend anchor spot. Other news agencies wanted to interview her, to talk about Dan Mercer and how she, the heroic reporter, had brought down not only a pedophile but a killer.

'Where is Investigator Tremont?' she asked.

'Retired.'

'He's not finishing up the case?'

'What's there to finish up? Haley McWaid was murdered by Dan Mercer. Mercer is dead. That pretty much ends the case, don't you think? We will continue to look for Mercer's body, but I have other cases too – and who wants to try Ed Grayson for stamping out that scumbag anyway?'

'You're certain Dan Mercer did it?'

Walker frowned. 'You're not?'

'I'm just asking.'

'First off, it's not my case. It's Frank Tremont's. He seems pretty sure. But it's not totally over. We're digging into Dan Mercer's life. We're looking at any other missing-girl cases. I mean, if it wasn't for Haley's phone found in the room, we'd probably have never tied her to Dan. He could have been doing it for years, with many girls. Maybe other missing kids crossed his path, we just don't know. Still, I'm a county sheriff – and the crimes weren't even committed in my jurisdiction. The feds are on this.'

They entered the rather pedestrian office of Tara O'Neill, the medical examiner. Wendy was grateful that they were in a room that looked more like a vice principal's office than anything having to do with human corpses. The two women had met before when Wendy covered local murders. Tara O'Neill was dressed in a sleek black dress – much better than scrubs – but what always surprised her about Tara was that she was shockingly gorgeous, albeit with a Morticia Addams vibe. Tara was tall with long, straight, too-black hair and a pale, calm, luminous face – a look that could be described as sort of ethereal goth.

'Hello, Wendy.'

She reached from behind her desk to shake hands. Her grip was stiff and formal.

'Hi, Tara.'

'I'm not exactly sure why we need to talk privately like this,' Tara said.

'Consider it a favor,' Walker said.

'But, Sheriff, you don't even have jurisdiction here.'

Walker spread his hands. 'Do I really need to go through those channels?'

231

'No,' Tara said. She sat down and invited them to do likewise. 'What can I do for you?'

The chair was wood and designed for anything other than comfort. Tara sat with her back straight and waited, ever the consummate professional with a bedside manner that clearly worked best on the dead. The room could use a paint job, but as the old joke goes, Tara's patients never complained.

'Like I said on the phone,' Walker said. 'We want to hear all you have on Haley McWaid.'

'Of course.' Tara looked at Wendy. 'Should we start with the identification process?'

'That would be great,' Wendy said.

'First off, there is no doubt that the body found in Ringwood State Park belonged to the missing girl Haley McWaid. There was serious decay, but the skeleton was intact, as was the hair. In short, she looked very much like herself but with the skin gone. Would you like to see a photograph of the remains?'

Wendy flicked a glance at Walker. Walker looked like he might be sick.

'Yes,' Wendy said.

Tara slid the photographs across her desk as if they were dinner menus. Wendy braced herself. She did not have a strong stomach when it came to gore. Even R-rated movies made her queasy. She risked one quick glance and turned away, but even in that second, horrible as it was, she could still see Haley McWaid's features in the horror of decay.

'Both parents, Ted and Marcia McWaid, insisted on seeing their daughter's body,' O'Neill continued in a perfect monotone. 'They both recognized their daughter and gave us positive identifications. We took it several steps further. The height and size of the skeleton matched.

232

Haley McWaid had broken her hand when she was twelve – the metacarpal bone below what we commonly call the ring finger. The injury had healed but we could still see signs of it on an X-ray. And of course, we ran a DNA test from a sample provided by her sister, Patricia. The match was made. In short, there is no doubt about identification.'

'How about a cause of death?'

Tara O'Neill folded her hands and put them on her desk. 'Undetermined at this juncture.'

'When do you think you'll know?'

Tara O'Neill reached across the desk and took back the photographs. 'In truth,' she said, 'probably never.'

She carefully slid the pictures back into the folder, closed it, put it to her right.

'Wait, you don't think that you'll ever determine a cause of death?'

'That's correct.'

'Isn't that unusual?'

Tara O'Neill finally smiled. It was radiant and sobering at the same time. 'Not really, no. Our society unfortunately is being raised on television shows where a medical examiner can work miracles. They look through a microscope and find all the answers. Sadly, that's not reality. For example, let's ask the question, was Haley McWaid shot? First – and this comes more from the crime scene technicians – no bullets were found at the scene. No bullets were found in the body either. I also ran X-rays and visuals to see if there were any unusual nicks or marks on the bones that might indicate a bullet wound. There were none. If that isn't complicated enough, I still can't definitely rule out a shooting. The bullet might not have struck bone. Since most of the body had decomposed, we wouldn't necessarily see any sign if it just passed through tissue. So the most I can say is that there is no evidence of a shooting and that a shooting is unlikely. Are you following me?'

'Yes.'

'Good. I would also conclude the same about a knife stabbing, but we just don't know for sure. If, for example, the perpetrator pierced an artery—'

'Yeah, I think I get that.

'And of course there are many more possibilities. The victim may have been suffocated – the classic pillow over the face. Even in cases where the body is found after a few days rather than a few months it can be hard to determine suffocation for certain. But in this case, after spending most likely three months buried, it is virtually impossible. I am also running some specific drug tests to see if there is anything in her system, but when a body breaks down like this, the blood enzymes get released. It throws many tests out of whack. In lay terms, the body almost turns into something like alcohol as it breaks down. So even those drug tests on remaining tissue may prove unreliable. Haley's vitreous humor – that's the gel between the retina and the lens of the eye – had disintegrated, so we couldn't use that to look for drug traces either.'

'So you can't even say for sure it's a murder?'

'I, as medical examiner, can't, no.'

Wendy looked at Walker. He nodded. 'We can. I mean, think about it. We don't even have a body on Dan Mercer. I've seen cases go to court where no body was found, and like Tara said, this is hardly uncommon with bodies found after this much time.'

O'Neill rose, clearly indicating their dismissal. 'Anything else?'

234

'Was she sexually assaulted?'

'Same answer: We just don't know.'

Wendy stood. 'I appreciate your time, Tara.'

After another stiff, formal handshake, Wendy found herself back on Norfolk Street with Sheriff Walker.

'Did any of that help?' Walker asked her.

'No.'

'I told you there was nothing here.'

'So that's it? It's over?'

'Officially for this sheriff? Yeah.'

Wendy looked down the street. 'I keep hearing Newark is coming back.'

'Just not here,' Walker said.

'Yeah.'

'How about you, Wendy?'

'What about me?'

'Is this case over for you?'

She shook her head. 'Not quite yet.'

'You want to tell me about it?'

She shook her head again. 'Not quite yet.'

'Fair enough.' The big man shuffled his feet, his eyes on the pavement. 'Can I ask you something else?'

'Sure.'

'I feel like an ass. I mean, the timing and all.'

She waited.

'When this is over, when this all passes in a few weeks' – Walker tried to raise his eyes to meet hers – 'do you mind if I call you?'

The road suddenly seemed even more deserted. 'You weren't kidding about timing.'

Walker jammed his hands in his pockets and shrugged. 'I've never been the smoothest.'

'Smooth enough,' Wendy said, trying not to smile in spite of herself. This was life though, wasn't it? Death made you crave life. The world is nothing but a bunch of thin lines separating what we think are extremes. 'No, I wouldn't mind you calling at all.'

Hester Crimstein's law office, Burton and Crimstein, was in a midtown Manhattan high-rise and offered fantastic views of downtown and the Hudson River. She could see the military-carrier-ship-turned-museum the *Intrepid* and the enormous 'fun' cruise ships packed with three thousand vacationers and figured that she'd rather give birth than actually go on one. The truth was, this view, like almost any view, just became a view. Visitors were stunned by it, but when you see it every day, much as you never wanted to admit it, the extraordinary becomes commonplace.

Ed Grayson was standing by the window now. He looked out but if he was enjoying the view, he was keeping it pretty hidden. 'I don't know what to do here, Hester.'

'I do,' she said.

'I'm listening.'

'Listen to my professional legal advice: Do nothing.'

Still staring out the window, Grayson smiled. 'No wonder you get the big bucks.'

Hester spread her hands.

'So it's that simple?'

'In this case, yep.'

'You know my wife left me. She wants to move back to Quebec with E. J.'

'I'm sorry to hear it.'

'This whole mess is my fault.'

'Ed, don't take this the wrong way, but you know I'm bad at hand-holding or false platitudes, right?'

'Oh yes.'

'So I'll make it clear for you: You messed up big-time.'

'I never beat up someone before.'

'And now you have.'

'I never shot someone either.'

'And now you have. Your point?'

They both went quiet. Ed Grayson was comfortable with silence. Hester Crimstein was not. She started rocking in her desk chair, played with a pen, sighed theatrically. Finally she got up and crossed the room.

'See this?'

Ed turned around. She was pointing at a statue of Lady Justice. 'Yes.'

'You know what it is?'

'Sure.'

'What?'

'Are you kidding?'

'Who is this?'

'Lady Justice.'

'Yes and no. She is known by many names. Lady Justice, Blind Justice, the Greek goddess Themis, the Roman goddess Justitia, the Egyptian goddess Ma'at – or even the daughters of Themis, Dike and Astraea.'

'Uh, your point?'

'Have you ever taken a good look at the statue? Most people see the blindfold first and, well, that's an obvious reference to impartiality. It's also nonsense since everybody is partial. You can't help it. But take a look at her right hand. That's a sword. That's a kick-ass sword. That's supposed to represent swift and often brutal, even deadly punishment. But you see, only she – the system – can do that. The system, as messed up as it is, has the right to use that sword. You, my friend, do not.'

'Are you telling me I shouldn't have taken the law into my own hands?' Grayson arched an eyebrow. 'Wow, Hester, that's deep.'

'Look at the scales, numb nuts. In her left hand. Some people think the scales are supposed to represent both sides of the argument – prosecution and defense. Others claim it is about fairness or impartiality. But think about it. Scales are really about balance, right? Look, I'm an attorney – and I know my rep. I know people think I subvert the law or use loopholes or bully or take advantage. That's all true. But I stay within the system.'

'And that makes it okay?'

'Yep. Because that's the balance.'

'And I, to keep within your metaphor, disturbed the balance?'

'Exactly. That's the beauty of our system. It can be tweaked and twisted – Lord knows I do it all the time – but when you keep within it, right or wrong, it somehow works. When you don't, when you lose balance even with the best of intentions, it leads to chaos and catastrophe.'

'That,' Ed Grayson said with a nod of his head, 'sounds like an enormous load of self-rationalization.'

She smiled at that. 'Perhaps. But you also know I'm right. You wanted to right a wrong. But now the balance is gone.'

'So maybe I should do something to set it right again.'

'It doesn't work like that, Ed. You know that now. Let it be and the balance has a chance to return.'

'Even if it means the bad guy goes free?'

She held out her hands and smiled at him. 'Who's the bad guy now, Ed?'

Silence.

He wasn't sure how to say it, so he dived right in. 'The police don't have a clue about Haley McWaid.'

Hester mulled that one over. 'You don't know that,' she said. 'Maybe we're the ones without a clue.'

Chapter 26

The home belonging to retired Essex County investigator Frank Tremont was a two-bedroom Colonial with aluminum siding, a small but perfectly manicured lawn, and a New York Giants flag hanging to the right of the door. The peonies in the flower boxes burst with so much color that Wendy wondered whether they were plastic.

Wendy took the ten steps up from the sidewalk to the front door and knocked. A curtain in the bay window moved. A moment later the door opened. Though the funeral had ended hours ago, Frank Tremont still wore the black suit. The tie was loosened, the top two buttons of his dress shirt undone. He had missed spots shaving. His eyes were rummy, and Wendy got a whiff of drink coming off him.

Without a word of greeting, he stepped to the side with a heavy sigh and nodded for her to come inside. She ducked into the house. Only one lamp illuminated the dark room. She spotted a half-empty bottle of Captain Morgan on the worn coffee table. Rum. Yuck. Several open newspapers lay strewn across the couch. There was a cardboard box on the floor, loaded with what she figured were the contents of his work desk. The television played some exercise-equipment infomercial, featuring a too-enthusiastic trainer and many young, beautiful, waxed six-pack stomachs. Wendy looked back at Tremont. He shrugged.

'Now that I'm retired I figured I should get some washboard abs.'

She tried to smile. There were photographs of a teenage girl on a side table. The girl's hairstyle had been in vogue maybe fifteen, twenty years ago, but the first thing you noticed was her smile – big and wide, pure dynamite, the kind of smile that rips into a parent's heart. Wendy knew the story. The girl was undoubtedly Frank's daughter who died of cancer. Wendy looked back at the bottle of Captain Morgan and wondered how he'd ever crawled out of it.

'What's up, Wendy?'

'So,' she began, trying to buy a moment, 'you're officially retired?'

'Yep. Went out with a bang, don't you think?'

'I'm sorry.'

'Save it for the victim's family.'

She nodded.

'You've been in the papers a lot,' he said. 'This case has made you quite the celebrity.' He lifted the glass in mock salute. 'Congratulations.'

'Frank?'

'What?'

'Don't say something stupid you'll regret.'

Tremont nodded. 'Yeah, good point.'

'Is this case officially closed?' she asked.

'From our perspective, pretty much. The perp is dead – probably buried out in the woods, which I guess someone smarter than me would find ironic.'

'Did you pressure Ed Grayson again to give up the body?'

'As much as we could.'

'And?'

'He won't talk. I wanted to offer him blanket immunity if he told us where Mercer's body was, but my big boss, Paul Copeland, wouldn't agree to that.'

Wendy thought about Ed Grayson, wondered about trying to approach him again, see if maybe now he'd talk to her. Tremont knocked the newspapers off the couch and invited Wendy to sit. He fell into the BarcaLounger and picked up the remote.

'Do you know what show is on soon?'

'No.'

'*Crimstein's Court*. You do know that she's repping Ed Grayson, right?'

'You told me.'

'Right, I forgot. Anyway, she made some interesting points when we questioned him.' He picked up the Captain Morgan and poured some in his glass. He offered her some, but she shook him off.

'What sort of points?'

'She made the argument that we should give Ed Grayson a medal for killing Dan Mercer.'

'Because it was justice?'

'No, see, that would be one thing. But Hester was trying to make a larger point.'

'That being?'

'If Grayson hadn't killed Mercer, we would never have found Haley's iPhone.' He pointed the remote at the television and turned it off. 'She noted that in three months of investigating, we had made no progress and that Ed Grayson had now provided us with the only clue to Haley's whereabouts. She further made the point that a good detective might have looked into a well-known pervert who had connections to the victim's neighborhood. And you know what?'

Wendy shook her head.

'Hester was right – how did I overlook an indicted sex offender with ties to Haley's town? Maybe Haley was alive for a few days. Maybe I could have saved her.'

Wendy looked at the confident, if not creepy, depiction of Captain Morgan on the bottle's label. What a frightening companion to be alone with while you drank. She opened her mouth to argue his point, but he stopped her with a wave of his hand.

'Please don't say something patronizing. It'd be insulting.'

He was right.

'So I doubt you came here to watch me wallow in self-pity.'

'I don't know, Frank. It's pretty entertaining.'

That made him almost smile. 'What do you need, Wendy?'

'Why do you think Dan Mercer killed her?'

'You mean motive?'

'Yeah, that's exactly what I mean.'

'Do you want the list in alphabetical order? As you somewhat proved, he was a sexual predator.'

'Okay, I get that. But in this case, well, so what? Haley McWaid was seventeen years old. The age of consent in New Jersey is sixteen.'

'Maybe he was afraid she'd talk.'

'About what? She was legal.'

'Still. It would be devastating to his case.'

'So he killed her to keep it quiet?' She shook her head. 'Did you find any sign of a previous relationship between Mercer and Haley?'

'No. I know you tried to peddle that at the park – that maybe they met at his ex's house and started something up. Maybe, but there is absolutely no evidence of that, and I'm not sure I want to go there for the parents' sake. Best bet is that, yeah, he saw her at the Wheeler house, became obsessed with her, grabbed her, did whatever, and killed her.'

Wendy frowned. 'I just don't buy that.'

'Why not? You remember the maybe-boyfriend Kirby Sennett?'

'Yes.'

'After we found the body, Kirby's lawyer let him be more, shall we say, forthcoming. Yes, they dated secretly, though it was rocky. He said she was really wound up, especially when she didn't get into Virginia. He thought that she might have even been on something.'

'Drugs?'

He shrugged. 'The parents don't need to hear about this either.'

'I don't get it though. Why didn't Kirby tell you all this right from the get-go?'

'Because his lawyer was afraid if we knew the nature of his relationship with her, we'd look at the kid hard. Which, of course, is true.'

'But if Kirby had nothing to hide?'

'First, who said he has nothing to hide? He is a low-level drug dealer. If she was on something, my guess is, he provided it. Second, most lawyers will tell you that innocence doesn't necessarily mean anything. If Kirby had said, yeah, we had this rocky romance and she was maybe popping or smoking something I gave her, we would have crawled straight up his ass and built a tent. And when the body was found, well, we'd have really started probing, if you know what I mean. Now that Kirby is in the clear, it makes sense he'd talk.'

'Nice system,' she said. 'Not to mention anal analogy.'

He shrugged.

'Are you sure this Kirby didn't have anything to do with it?'

'And, what, planted her phone in Dan Mercer's hotel room?'

She thought about that. 'Good point.'

'He also has an airtight alibi. Look, Kirby is a typical rich-kid punk – the kind who thinks he's badass because maybe he toilet-papers a house on Mischief Night. He didn't do anything here.'

She sat back. Her gaze found the picture of Tremont's dead daughter, but it didn't stay there long. She looked away fast, maybe too fast. Frank saw it.

'My daughter,' he said.

'I know.'

'We're not going to talk about it, okay?'

'Okay.'

'So what's your problem with this case, Wendy?'

'I guess I need more of a why.'

'Take another look at that picture. The world doesn't work that way.' He sat up. His eyes bore into hers. 'Sometimes – most times maybe – there isn't any why.'

When she got back to her car, Wendy saw a message from Ten-A-Fly. She called him back.

'We may have something on Kelvin Tilfer.'

The Fathers Club had spent the last several days working on locating the Princeton classmates. The easiest to find, of course, was Farley Parks. Wendy had called the former politico six times. Farley had not called her back. No surprise. Farley lived in Pittsburgh, making a drop-by difficult. So for right now, he was sort of out.

Second, Dr. Steve Miciano. She had reached him by phone and asked for a meeting. If she could help it, Wendy didn't want to tell them what it was about over the phone. Miciano hadn't asked. He said that he was on shift and would be available tomorrow afternoon. Wendy figured that she could wait.

But third, and in Wendy's view, the big priority, was the elusive Kelvin Tilfer. There was nothing on him so far. As far as the Internet was concerned, the man had simply dropped off the planet.

'What?' she asked.

'A brother. Ronald Tilfer works deliveries for UPS in Manhattan. He's the only relative we've been able to locate. The parents are dead.'

'Where does he live?'

'In Queens, but we can do you one better. See, when Doug worked at Lehman they did big business with UPS. Doug called his old contact in sales and got the brother's delivery schedule. It's all computerized now, so we can pretty much track his movements online if you want to find him.'

'I do.'

'Okay, head into the city toward the Upper West Side. I'll e-mail you updates as he makes deliveries.'

Forty-five minutes later, she found the brown truck double-parked in front of a restaurant called Telepan on West Sixty-ninth Street off Columbus. She parked her car in an hour space, threw in some quarters, leaned against the fender. She looked at the truck, flashing to that UPS commercial with that guy with long hair drawing on a white-board, and while the message 'UPS' and 'Brown' did indeed come through, she didn't have a clue what the guy was drawing about. Charlie would always shake his head when that commercial came on, usually during a crucial time in a football game, and say, 'That guy needs a beat-down.'

Funny what occupies the mind.

Ronald Tilfer – at least, she assumed the man in the

brown UPS uniform was him – smiled and waved behind him as he exited from the restaurant. He was short with tightly cropped salt 'n' pepper hair and, as you noticed in these uniforms with shorts, nice legs. Wendy pushed herself off her car and cut him off before he reached the vehicle.

'Ronald Tilfer?'

'Yes.'

'My name is Wendy Tynes. I'm a reporter for NTC News. I'm trying to locate your brother, Kelvin.'

He narrowed his gaze. 'What for?'

'I'm doing a story about his graduating class at Princeton.'

'I can't help you.'

'I just need to talk to him for a few minutes.'

'You can't.'

'Why not?'

He started to move around her. Wendy slid to stay in front of him. 'Let's just say Kelvin is unavailable.'

'What's that supposed to mean?'

'He can't talk to you. He can't help you.'

'Mr. Tilfer?'

'I really need to get back to work.'

'No, you don't.'

'Excuse me?'

'That's your last delivery today.'

'How do you know that?'

Let him dangle, she thought. 'Let's stop wasting time with the cryptic "he's unavailable" or can't talk or whatever. It is hugely important I talk to him.'

'About his graduating class at Princeton?'

'There's more to it. Someone is harming his old roommates.'

'And you think it's Kelvin?'

247

'I didn't say that.'

'It can't be him.'

'You can help me prove that. Either way, lives are being ruined. Your brother may even be in danger.'

'He's not.'

'Then maybe he can help some old friends.'

'Kelvin? He's in no position to help anyone.'

Again with the cryptic. It was starting to piss her off. 'You talk like he's dead.'

'He may as well be.'

'I don't want to sound melodramatic, Mr. Tilfer, but this really is about life and death. If you don't want to talk to me, I can bring the police in on it. I'm here alone but I can come back with a big news crew – cameras, sound, the works.'

Ronald Tilfer let loose a deep sigh. Her threat was an empty one, of course, but he didn't have to know that. He gnawed on his lower lip. 'You won't take my word he can't help you?'

'Sorry.'

He shrugged. 'Okay.'

'Okay what?'

'I'll take you to see Kelvin.'

Wendy looked at Kelvin Tilfer through the thick, protective glass.

'How long has he been here?'

'This time?' Ronald Tilfer shrugged. 'Maybe three weeks. They'll probably let him back out in a week.'

'And then where does he go?'

'He lives on the street until he does something dangerous again. Then they bring him back in. The state doesn't believe in long-term mental hospitals anymore. So they release him.'

Kelvin Tilfer was writing furiously in a notebook, his nose just inches from the page. Wendy could hear him shouting through the glass. Nothing that made sense. Kelvin looked a lot older than his classmates. His hair and beard were gray. Teeth were missing.

'He was the smart brother,' Ronald said. 'A freaking genius, especially in math. That's what that book is filled with. Math problems. He writes them all day. He could never turn his mind off. Our mom worked so hard to make him normal, you know? The school wanted him to skip grades. She wouldn't let him. She made him play sports – tried everything to keep him normal. But it was like we always knew he was heading in this direction. She tried to hold the crazy back. But it was like holding back an ocean with your bare hands.'

'What's wrong with him?'

'He's a raging schizophrenic. He has terrible psychotic episodes.'

'But, I mean, what happened to him?'

'What do you mean, what happened? He's ill. There is no why.' There is no why – the second time someone had said that to her today. 'How does someone get cancer? It wasn't like Mommy beat him and he became like this. It's a chemical imbalance. Like I said, it was always there. Even as a kid, he never slept. He couldn't turn off his brain.'

Wendy remembered what Phil had said. Weird. Math-genius weird. 'Do meds help?'

'They quiet him, sure. The same way a tranquilizer gun quiets an elephant. He still doesn't know where he is or who he is. When he graduated from Princeton he got a job with a pharmaceutical company but he kept disappearing. They fired him. He took to the streets. For eight years we didn't know where he was. When we finally found him in a cardboard box filled with his own feces, Kelvin had broken bones that hadn't healed properly. He'd lost teeth. I can't even imagine how he survived, how he found food, what he must have gone through.'

Kelvin started screaming again: 'Himmler! Himmler likes tuna steaks!'

She turned to Ronald. 'Himmler? The old Nazi?'

'You got me. He never makes any sense.'

Kelvin went back to his notebook, writing even faster now.

'Can I talk to him?' she asked.

'You're kidding, right?'

'No.'

'It won't help.'

'And it won't hurt.'

Ronald Tilfer looked through the window. 'Most times, he doesn't know who I am anymore. He looks right through me. I wanted to bring him home, but I have a wife, a kid. . . .'

Wendy said nothing.

'I should do something to protect him, don't you think? I try to lock him up, he gets angry. So I let him go and worry about him. We'd go to Yankee games when we were kids. Kelvin knew every player's statistics. He could even tell you how they changed after an at-bat. My theory: Genius is a curse. That's how I look at it. Some think that the brilliant comprehend the universe in a way the rest of us can't. They see the world how it truly is – and that reality is so horrible they lose their minds. Clarity leads to insanity.'

Wendy just stared straight ahead. 'Did Kelvin ever talk about Princeton?'

'My mom was so proud of him. I mean, we all were. Kids from our neighborhood didn't go to Ivy League schools. We were worried he wouldn't fit in, but he made friends fast.'

'Those friends are in trouble.'

'Look at him, Ms. Tynes. You think he can help them?'

'I'd like to take a shot at it.'

He shrugged. The hospital administrator made her sign some releases and suggested they keep their distance from him. A few minutes later they brought Wendy and Ronald into a glass-enclosed room. An orderly stood by the door. Kelvin sat at a desk and continued scribbling into his notebook. The table was wide, so that Wendy and Ronald were at a pretty good distance.

'Hey, Kelvin,' Ronald said.

'Drones don't understand the essence.'

Ronald looked at Wendy. He gestured for her to go ahead.

'You went to Princeton, didn't you, Kelvin?'

'I told you. Himmler likes tuna steaks.'

He still had his eyes on his notebooks. 'Kelvin?'

He didn't stop writing.

'Do you remember Dan Mercer?'

'White boy.'

'Yes. And Phil Turnball?'

'Unleaded gas gives the benefactor headaches.'

'Your friends from Princeton.'

'Ivy Leagues, man. Some guy wore green shoes. I hate green shoes.'

'Me too.'

'The Ivy Leagues.'

'That's right. Your friends from the Ivy League. Dan, Phil, Steve, and Farley. Do you remember them?'

Kelvin finally stopped scribbling. He looked up. His eyes were blank slates. He stared at Wendy but clearly didn't see her.

'Kelvin?'

'Himmler likes tuna steaks,' he said, his voice an urgent whisper. 'And the mayor? He could not care less.'

Kelvin slumped. Wendy tried to get him to look her in the eye.

'I want to talk to you about your college roommates.'

Kelvin started laughing. 'Roommates?'

'Yes.'

'That's funny.' He started cackling like, well, a madman. 'Roommates. Like you mate with a room. Like you and a room have sex and you get it pregnant. Like you mate, get it?'

He laughed again. Well, Wendy figured, this was better than Himmler's fish preferences.

'Do you remember your old roommates?'

The laugh stopped as though someone had flicked an off switch.

'They're in trouble, Kelvin,' she said. 'Dan Mercer, Phil Turnball, Steve Miciano, Farley Parks. They're all in trouble.'

'Trouble?'

'Yes.' She said the four names again. Then again. Something started to happen to Kelvin's face. It crumbled before their eyes. 'Oh God, oh no . . .'

Kelvin started crying.

Ronald was up. 'Kelvin?'

Ronald reached for his brother, but Kelvin's scream stopped him. The scream was sudden and piercing. Wendy jumped back.

His eyes were wide now. 'Scar face!'

'Kelvin?'

He stood quickly, knocking over his chair. The orderly started toward him. Kelvin screamed again and ran for the corner. The orderly called for backup.

'Scar face!' Kelvin screamed again. 'Gonna get us all. Scar face!'

'Who's scar face?' Wendy shouted back at him.

Ronald said, 'Leave him alone!'

'Scar face!' Kelvin squeezed his eyes shut. He put his hands on either side of his head, as though he were trying to stop his skull from splitting in two. 'I told them! I warned them!'

'What's that mean, Kelvin?'

'Stop!' Ronald said.

Kelvin lost it then. His head rocked back and forth. Two orderlies came in. When Kelvin saw them, he screamed. 'Stop the hunt! Stop the hunt!' He dropped to the ground and started scuttling across the floor on all fours. Ronald had tears in his eyes. He tried to calm his brother. Kelvin scrambled to his feet. The orderlies tackled Kelvin as if this were a football game. One hit him low, the other got him up top.

'Don't hurt him!' Ronald shouted. 'Please!'

Kelvin was down on the ground. The orderlies were putting some kind of restraint on him. Ronald begged them not to hurt him. Wendy tried to get closer to Kelvin – tried to somehow reach him.

From the ground, Kelvin's eyes finally met hers. Wendy crawled closer to him as he struggled. One orderly shouted at her, 'Get away from him!'

She ignored him. 'What is it, Kelvin?'

'I told them,' he whispered. 'I warned them.'

'What did you warn them, Kelvin?'

Kelvin started crying. Ronald grabbed at her shoulder, trying to pull her back. She shrugged him off.

'What did you warn them, Kelvin?'

A third orderly was in the room now. He had a hypodermic needle in his hand. He shot something into Kelvin's shoulder. Kelvin looked her straight in the eye now.

'Not to hunt,' Kelvin said, his voice suddenly calm. 'We shouldn't hunt no more.'

'Hunt for what?'

But the drug was taking effect. 'We should have never gone hunting,' he said, his voice soft now. 'Scar face could tell you. We should have never gone hunting.'

Chapter 27

Ronald Tilfer had no clue what 'scar face' meant or what hunt his brother might have been talking about. 'He's said that stuff before – about hunts and scar face. Like he does with Himmler. I don't think it means anything.'

Wendy headed home, wondering what to do with this quasi-information, feeling more lost than when the day began. Charlie was watching television on the couch.

'Hi,' she said.

'What's for dinner?'

'I'm fine, thanks. How about you?'

Charlie sighed. 'Aren't we past fake niceties?'

'And general human courtesy, so it seems.'

Charlie didn't move.

'You okay?' she asked him, her voice registering more concern than maybe she intended.

'Me? I'm fine, why?'

'Haley McWaid was a classmate.'

'Yeah, but I didn't really know her.'

'Lots of your classmates and friends were at the funeral.'

'I know.'

'I saw Clark and James there.'

'I know.'

'So why didn't you want to go?'

'Because I didn't know her.'

'Clark and James did?'

'No,' Charlie said. He sat up. 'Look, I feel terrible. It's a tragedy. But people, even my good friends, get off on being involved, that's all. They didn't show up to pay their respects. They showed up because they thought it'd be cool. They wanted to be part of something. It's all about them, you know what I mean?'

Wendy nodded. 'I do.'

'Most of the time, that's fine,' Charlie said. 'But when it comes to a dead girl, sorry, I'm not into that.' Charlie put his head back on the pillow and went back to watching television. She stared at him for a moment.

Without so much as glancing in her direction, he sighed again and said, 'What?'

'You sounded like your father there.'

He said nothing.

'I love you,' Wendy said.

'Do I sound like my father when I ask yet again: What's for dinner?'

She laughed. 'I'll check the fridge,' she said, but she knew that there'd be nothing there and so she'd order. Japanese rolls tonight – brown rice so as to make them healthier. 'Oh, one more thing. Do you know Kirby Sennett?'

'Not really. Just in passing.'

'Is he a nice guy?'

'No, he's a total tool.'

She smiled at that. 'I hear he's a small-time drug dealer.'

'He's a big-time douche bag.' Charlie sat up. 'What's with all the questions?'

'I'm just covering another angle on Haley McWaid.

256

There's a rumor the two of them were an item.'

'So?'

'Could you ask around?'

He just looked at her in horror. 'You mean like I'm your undercover cub reporter?'

'Bad idea, huh?'

He didn't bother answering – and then Wendy was struck with another idea that on the face of it seemed like a pretty good one. She headed upstairs and signed on to the computer. She did a quick image search and found the perfect picture. The girl in the photograph looked about eighteen, Eurasian, librarian glasses, low-cut blouse, smoking body.

Yep, she'd do.

Wendy quickly created a Facebook page using the girl's picture. She made up a name by combining her two best friends from college – Sharon Hait. Okay, good. Now she needed to friend Kirby.

'What are you doing?'

It was Charlie.

'I'm making up a fake profile.'

Charlie frowned. 'For what?'

'I'm hoping to lure Kirby into friending me. Then maybe I can start up a conversation with him.'

'For real?'

'What, you don't think it'll work?'

'Not with that picture.'

'Why not?'

'Too hot. She looks like a spam advertising bot.'

'A what?'

He sighed. 'Companies use photographs like this to spam people. Look, just find a girl who is good-looking but real. You know what I mean?'

'I think so.'

'And then make her from, say, Glen Rock. If she's from Kasselton, he'd know her.'

'What, you know every girl in this town?'

'Every hot girl? Pretty much. Or I'd have heard of her, at least. So try a town close but not too close. Then say you heard about him from a friend or saw him at the Garden State Plaza mall or something. Oh, maybe give her a real name of a girl in that town, just in case he asks someone or looks up her number or something. Make sure no other picture of her shows up on a Google image search though. Say you just signed up for Facebook and are starting to friend people or he'll wonder why you have no other friends yet. Put in a couple of details under info. Give her a few favorite movies, favorite rock groups.'

'Like U2?'

'Like someone less than a hundred years old.' He listed some bands she'd never heard of. Wendy wrote them down.

'Think it will work?' she asked.

'Doubtful, but you never know. At the least he'll friend you.'

'And what will that do for me?'

Another sigh. 'We already discussed this. Like with that Princeton page. Once he friends you, you can see his entire page. You can see his online pics, his wall postings, his friends, his posts, what games he plays, whatever.'

The Princeton page reminded her of something else. She clicked on it, found the 'Admin' link, and hit the button to e-mail him. The administrator's name was Lawrence Cherston, 'our former class president,' according to his little write-up. He wore his Princeton orange-and-black tie in his profile pic. Oy. Wendy typed out a simple message:

Hi, I'm a television reporter doing a story on your class
at Princeton and would very much like to meet. Please
contact me at any of the below at your convenience.

As she hit send, her cell phone buzzed. She checked
and saw an incoming text. It was from Phil Turnball: WE
NEED TO TALK.

She typed a reply: SURE, CALL NOW.

There was a delay. Then: NOT ON THE PHONE.

Wendy wasn't sure what to make of that, so she typed:
WHY NOT?

MEET IN 30 MIN AT ZEBRA BAR?

Wendy wondered why he'd avoided the question.
WHY CAN'T WE TALK ON PHONE?

Longer delay. DON'T TRUST PHONES RIGHT NOW.

She frowned. That seemed a little cloak-and-dagger,
but to be fair, Phil Turnball hadn't hit her as the type to
overreact. No sense in trying to guess. She'd see him
soon enough. She typed in 'OK' and then looked back at
Charlie.

'What?' he said.

'I have to run to a meeting. Can you order yourself
dinner?'

'Uh, Mom?'

'What?'

'Tonight is Project Graduation orientation, remember?'

She nearly smacked herself on the forehead. 'Damn, I
totally forgot.'

'At the high school in, oh' – Charlie looked at his wrist
though he wore no watch – 'less than thirty minutes.
And you're on the snack committee or something.'

She had, in fact, been put in charge of bringing both
sugar/artificial sweetener and milk/nondairy alternatives

for the coffee, though modesty prevented her from bragging about it.

Blowing it off was a possibility, but the school took this Project Graduation thing pretty seriously, and she had been, at best, neglectful of her son lately. She picked up the cell phone and texted Phil Turnball:

CAN WE MAKE IT @ 10P?

No immediate reply. She headed into her bedroom and changed into a pair of jeans and a green blouse. She took off her contact lenses and slipped on a pair of glasses, threw her hair back in a ponytail. The casual woman.

Her phone buzzed. Phil Turnball's reply: OK.

She headed downstairs. Pops was in the den. He had a red bandana on his head. Bandanas – or mandanas, as they were sometimes called when men wore them – were a look that worked on very few men. Pops got away with it, but just barely.

Pops shook his head when he saw her approach. 'You're wearing old-lady glasses?'

She shrugged.

'You're never going to land a man that way.'

Like she wanted to at high school orientation. 'Not that it is any of your business, but it just so happens I got asked out today.'

'After the funeral?'

'Yep.'

Pops nodded. 'I'm not surprised.'

'Why?'

'I had the best sex of my life after a funeral. Total mindblower in the back of a limo.'

'Wow, later will you fill me in on all the details?'

'Are you being sarcastic?'

'Very.'

She kissed his cheek, asked him to make sure Charlie

ate, and made her way to the car. She stopped at the su-permarket to pick up the coffee accoutrements. By the time she arrived at the high school, the lot was full. She managed to find a spot on Beverly Road. The spot tech-nically may have been within fifty feet of the stop sign, but she didn't feel like breaking out a measuring tape. Tonight Wendy Tynes would live dangerously.

The parents were already milling around the accoutre-ment-free coffee urn when Wendy entered. She rushed over, making her apologies as she put out the various coffee-companion products. Millie Hanover, the HSA president, the mother who always had the perfect after-school arts and crafts activity on well-scheduled play-dates, quietly scowled her disapproval. In contrast, the fathers were extra-forgiving of Wendy's tardiness. A little too forgiving, in fact. This was part of the reason Wendy wore the blouse buttoned high, the jeans not too tight, the not-too-flattering glasses on, the hair up. She never engaged the married men in extended conversations. Nev. Ah. Let them call her stuck-up or a bitch, but that was, in her view, better than a flirt, harlot, or worse. The wives in this town treated her with enough suspicion, thank you very much. On nights like this, she was tempted to don a T-shirt that read, 'Really, I Have No Interest in Stealing Your Husband.'

The main topic of conversation was college; more specifically, whose child had gotten and not gotten into what schools. Some parents bragged, some joked, and, Wendy's personal favorite, some performed 'spin' like postdebate politicians, suddenly singing the praises of the 'safety' school as though it were better than their original first choice. Or maybe she was being unchar-itable. Maybe they were just trying to make the best out of their disappointment.

The bell mercifully sounded, jarring Wendy back to her own school days, and everyone headed into the campus center. One booth invited parents to post speed-limit signs that read, PLEASE DRIVE SLOWLY – WE ♥ OUR CHILDREN, which, she guessed, was effective, though the implication seemed to be that you, the driver, don't really love yours. Another handed out window decals letting neighbors know that this house was indeed 'Drug-Free,' which was nice, if not superfluous, in a 'Baby on Board' obvious way. There was a booth run by the International Institute for Alcohol Awareness and its campaign against parents hosting drinking parties called 'Not in Our House.' Still another booth passed out drinking-pledge contracts. The teen pledges never to drive drunk or get in a car with someone who's been drinking. The parent, in turn, agrees that the teen can call at any hour to be picked up.

Wendy found a seat toward the back. An overly friendly father with a sucked-in gut and game-show-host smile sat next to her. He gestured toward the booths. 'Safety overkill,' he said. 'We're so overprotective, don't you think?'

Wendy said nothing. The man's frowning wife took the seat next to him. Wendy made sure to say hello to the frowning wife, introducing herself and saying that she was Charlie's mother, studiously avoiding eye contact with the antisafety Guy Smiley.

Principal Pete Zecher took the podium and thanked everyone for coming during this 'very difficult week.' There was a moment of silence for Haley McWaid. Some had wondered why tonight hadn't been postponed, but the school activity calendar was so overwhelmingly crowded there were simply no other free dates. Besides, how long do you wait? Another day? Another week?

So, after another awkward moment or two had passed, Pete Zecher introduced Millie Hanover, who excitedly announced that this year's Project Graduation theme would be 'Superheroes.' In short, Millie explained in long, they would decorate the middle school gymnasium to look like various comic-book places. The Batcave. Superman's Fortress of Solitude. The X-Men's X-Mansion or whatever it was called. The Justice League of America's headquarters. Past years had seen the school decorated in Harry Potter theme, in the mode of the TV show *Survivor* (maybe that was more than a few years ago, Wendy thought now), even the Little Mermaid.

The idea behind Project Graduation was to give graduates a safe place to party after both the prom and commencement activities. Buses brought the students in, and all chaperones stayed outside. No drinking or drugs, of course, though in past years, some teens had sneaked them in. Still, with the chaperones on hand and buses providing transportation, Project Graduation seemed a great alternative to old-fashioned partying.

'I would love to recognize my hardworking committee chairs,' Millie Hanover said. 'When I call your name, please stand.' She introduced her decorating chair, her beverage chair, her food chair, her transportation chair, her publicity chair, each standing to a smattering of applause. 'For the rest of you, please volunteer. We can't do this without you, and it's a wonderful way to help make your child's graduation experience a positive one. Let's remember that this is for your children and you shouldn't rely on others.' Millie's voice could have been more patronizing, but it was hard to imagine how. 'Thank you for listening. The sheets are out for sign-up.'

Principal Zecher next introduced Kasselton police officer Dave Pecora, the town safety commissioner, who proceeded to give the lowdown on the dangers associated with postprom, postgraduation parties. He talked about how heroin was making a comeback. He talked about pharm parties, where kids steal prescription drugs from their homes, put them in a big bowl, and partake in experimentation. Wendy had wanted to do a story about those last year, but she couldn't find any real-world examples, just anecdotal evidence. One DEA official told her that pharm parties were more likely urban myth than reality. Officer Pecora continued to warn against the dangers of underage drinking: 'Four thousand kids per year die of alcohol overdose,' though he didn't say whether that was worldwide or just the USA or what age those kids might be. He also reiterated the fact that 'no parent is doing his kid a favor' by hosting a drinking party. With a stern look, he cited specific cases in which hosting adults were convicted of manslaughter and served jail time. He actually started describing the prison experience in some detail – like the parental version of *Scared Straight*.

Wendy surreptitiously checked the clock, again like when she was actually in school. Nine thirty. Three thoughts kept running through her head. One, she wanted to get out of here and see what was up with the suddenly cryptic Phil Turnball. Two, she should probably sign up for some committee or another. Even though she was dubious about this whole Project Graduation – part of it seeming like yet another way we cater to our child's every whim, part of it seeming more about the parents than the kids – it would be unfair, per Millie's condescending comment, to make others do all the work for something in which Charlie would partake.

And third, maybe most, she couldn't help but think about Ariana Nasbro and how alcohol and driving killed John. She couldn't help but wonder if perhaps Ariana Nasbro's parents should have attended one of these over-the-top orientations, if maybe all of this apparent safety overkill would indeed save a life during the next few weeks, so that some other family wouldn't have to deal with what she and Charlie had.

Zecher was back at the podium, finishing up with a thank-you-for-coming-out-tonight before breaking up the meeting. Wendy glanced around, looking for some familiar faces, disappointed in herself that she knew so few of her son's classmates' parents. Naturally the McWaids weren't there. Neither were Jenna or Noel Wheeler. Defending her scandalized ex-husband had cost Jenna Wheeler's family greatly in the suburban standings – but the murder of Haley McWaid must have made life here fairly untenable.

Parents started heading to the designated committee sign-in spots. Wendy remembered that Brenda Traynor, the publicity committee chair, was both friendly with Jenna Wheeler and a total gossip – a winning suburban combination. Wendy headed that way.

'Hi, Brenda.'

'It's nice to see you, Wendy. Are you here to volunteer?'

'Uh, sure. I was thinking that I could help with publicity.'

'Oh, that would be great. I mean, who better than a renowned TV reporter?'

'Well, I wouldn't say renowned.'

'Oh, I would.'

Wendy forced up a smile. 'So where do I sign in?'

Brenda showed her the sheet. 'We have committee

meetings every Tuesday and Thursday. Would you be up for hosting one?'

'Sure.'

She signed her name, keeping her head low. 'So,' Wendy said, aiming for the subtle and not getting anywhere close, 'do you think Jenna Wheeler would make a good member of the publicity team?'

'You're joking, of course.'

'I think she has a background in journalism,' Wendy said, totally making that up.

'Who cares? After what she did, letting that monster into our community – I mean, that family is gone.'

'Gone?'

Brenda nodded, leaned forward. 'There's a For Sale on their house.'

'Oh.'

'Amanda isn't even coming to graduation. I feel bad for her – it's not her fault, I guess – but really, it's the right decision. It would spoil it for everyone.'

'So where are they going?'

'Well, I heard that Noel got a job at some hospital in Ohio. Columbus or Canton or maybe Cleveland. All those Cs in Ohio, it's confusing. Come to think of it, I think it's Cincinnati. Another C. A soft C they call it, right?'

'Right. Have the Wheelers moved out there already?'

'No, I don't think so. Okay, Talia told me – do you know Talia Norwich? Nice woman? Daughter's name is Allie? A little overweight? Anyway, Talia said that she heard that they were staying at a Marriott Courtyard until they could relocate.'

Bingo.

Wendy thought about what Jenna had said, about Dan, about the part of him she could never reach – but mostly, how had she put it? Something had happened to him in college. Maybe it was time to have another chat with Jenna Wheeler.

She said her good-byes, mingled on her way to the exit, and headed toward her meeting with Phil Turnball.

Chapter 28

P hil sat in a relatively quiet spot in the back of a sports bar – relatively, of course, because sports bars are not designed for privacy, conversations, or contemplation. There were no guys at the bar with ruddy noses or slumped shoulders, no beaten men drowning sorrows on a stool. No one chose to stare at their emptying glass when there were a seemingly infinite number of wide-screen televisions broadcasting a potpourri of sports and quasi-sports craving their attention.

The bar was called Love the Zebra. It smelled more of barbecue wings and salsa than beer. The place was loud. Company softball teams were enjoying an after-game celebration. The Yankees were playing. Several young women wore Jeter jerseys, whooping it up with a little too much enthusiasm, their dates noticeably cringing at the spectacle.

Wendy slid into the booth. Phil wore a lime green golf shirt with both buttons undone. Tufts of gray chest hair peeked out. He sported a half smile and a thousand-yard stare. 'We had a company softball team,' he said. 'Years ago. When I first started. We'd come to a bar like this after the game. Sherry would come too. She would wear one of those sexy softball shirts, you know the tight white ones with dark three-quarter sleeves?'

Wendy nodded. There was a slur in his speech.

'God, she looked so beautiful.'

She waited for him to say more. Most people did. The secret in any interview was the ability to not fill the silence. A few seconds passed. Then a few more. Okay, so much for silence. Sometimes you need to goose your subject too.

'Sherry is still beautiful,' Wendy said.

'Oh yes.' The half smile remained frozen on Phil's face. His beer was empty. His eyes were glossy, his face red from drink. 'But she doesn't look at me the same anymore. Don't get me wrong. She's supportive. She loves me. She says and does all the right things. But I can see it in her eyes. I'm less of a man to her now.'

Wendy wondered what to say here, what wouldn't sound patronizing, but 'I'm sure that's not true' or 'I'm sorry' didn't make the cut. She again opted for silence.

'Do you want a drink?' he asked.

'Sure.'

'I've been pounding down Bud Lights.'

'Sounds good,' she said. 'But let me just have a plain Budweiser.'

'How about some nachos?'

'Have you eaten?'

'No.'

She nodded, thinking he could use something in his stomach. 'Nachos sounds like a good idea.'

Phil waved over a waitress. She was dressed in a low-cut referee shirt, ergo the bar name Love the Zebra. Her name tag informed them that her name was Ariel. There was a whistle around her neck and, to complete the look, black greasepaint under her eyes. Of course, Wendy had never seen a referee with the black greasepaint, only players, but the mixed metaphor in the outfit seemed to be a mild issue at best.

They placed the order.

'You know something?' Phil said, watching the waitress leave.

Again she waited.

'I worked in a bar like this. Well, not exactly like this. It was one of those chain restaurants with a bar in the middle. You know the ones. They always have green trim and wall decorations that are supposed to reflect a more innocent time.'

Wendy nodded. She knew.

'It's where I met Sherry. I worked as a bartender. She was that bubbly waitress who introduced herself right away and asked if you wanted to start with whatever appetizer corporate was pushing.'

'I thought you were a rich kid.'

Phil gave a half chuckle, tilted back the already-empty Bud Light to drain out the last sip. She half expected him to hit the side of the bottle. 'My parents believed we should work, I guess. Where were you tonight?'

'My kid's high school.'

'Why?'

'A graduation orientation,' she said.

'Did your kid get accepted to college yet?'

'Yes.'

'Where?'

She shifted in her seat. 'Why did you want to see me, Phil?'

'Was that too personal? I'm sorry.'

'I'd just like to get to the point. It's late.'

'I was just being contemplative, I guess. I see these kids today, and they're sold the same stupid dream we were. Study hard. Get good grades. Prepare for the SATs. Play a sport, if you can. Colleges love that. Make sure you have enough extracurricular activities. Do all these

270

things so you can matriculate at the most prestigious school possible. It's like the first seventeen years of your life are just an audition for the Ivy Leagues.'

It was true, Wendy knew. You live in any of the suburbs around here and during the high school years, the world becomes a ticker-tape parade of collegiate acceptance and rejection letters.

'And look at my old roomies,' Phil went on, the slur more prominent now. 'Princeton University. The crème de la crème. Kelvin was a black kid. Dan was an orphan. Steve was dirt-poor. Farley was one of eight kids – big Catholic blue-collar family. All of us made it – and all of us were insecure and unhappy. The happiest guy I knew in high school went down the road to Montclair State and dropped out his sophomore year. He still bartends. Still the most content son of a bitch I know.'

The shapely young waitress dropped off the beers. 'The nachos will be a few more minutes.'

'No problem, dear,' Phil said with a smile. It was a nice smile. A few years ago, it might have been returned, but nope, not today. Phil kept his eyes on her for maybe a second too long, though Wendy didn't think the girl noticed. Once the waitress was out of sight, Phil lifted his bottle toward Wendy. She picked up hers and clinked bottles and decided to stop this dance.

'Phil, what's the term "scar face" mean to you?'

He tried very hard not to show anything. He frowned to buy time, even went so far as to say, 'Huh?'

'Scar face.'

'What about it?'

'What does it mean to you?'

'Nothing.'

'You're lying.'

'Scar face?' He scrunched up his face. 'Wasn't that a

271

movie? With Al Pacino, right?' He threw on a horrible accent and did a terrible impression: '"Say hello to my little friend."'

He tried to laugh it off.

'How about going on a hunt?'

'Where are you getting this from, Wendy?'

'Kelvin.'

Silence.

'I saw him today.'

What Phil said next surprised her. 'Yeah, I know.'

'How?'

He leaned forward. Behind them came a happy whoop. Someone shouted, 'Go! Go!' Two Yankee runners sprinted for home off a hit to shallow center. The first made it easy. There was a throw to the plate for the second, but he slid safely under the tag. Another whoop from the partisan crowd.

'I don't understand,' Phil said, 'what you're trying to do.'

'What do you mean?'

'That poor girl is dead. Dan is dead.'

'So?'

'So it's done. It's over, right?'

She said nothing.

'What are you still after?'

'Phil, did you embezzle money?'

'What difference does that make?'

'Did you?'

'Is that what you're trying to do – prove I'm innocent?'

'In part.'

'Don't help me, okay? For my sake. For your sake. For everyone's sake. Please drop this.'

He looked away. His hands found the bottle, brought

272

it up to his lips quickly; he took a deep, hard gulp. Wendy looked at him. For a moment she saw maybe what Sherry saw. He was something of a shell. Something inside of him – a light, a flicker, whatever you want to come up with – had dimmed. She remembered what Pops said, about men losing their jobs and how it affected them. There was a line in a play she saw once, about how a man who has no job can't hold his head up, can't look his kids in the eye.

His voice was an urgent hush. 'Please. I need you to let this go.'

'You don't want the truth?'

He started peeling the label off the beer bottle. His eyes studied his handiwork as though he were an artist working with marble. 'You think they've hurt us,' he said, his voice low. 'They haven't. This stuff so far – it's just a slap down. If we let it go, it will all stop. If we keep pushing – if *you* keep pushing – it will get much, much worse.'

The label came all the way off and slid toward the floor. Phil watched it fall.

'Phil?'

His eyes rose toward her.

'I don't understand what you are talking about.'

'Please listen to me, okay? Listen closely. It will get worse.'

'Who's going to make it worse?'

'It doesn't matter.'

'Like hell it doesn't.'

The young waitress appeared with a plate of nachos piled so high it looked like she was carrying a small child. She dropped it on the table and said, 'Can I get you guys anything else?' They both declined. She spun and left them alone. Wendy leaned across the table.

273

'Who is doing this, Phil?'

'It's not like that.'

'Not like what? They may have killed a girl.'

He shook his head. 'Dan did that.'

'Are you sure?'

'Positive.' He raised his eyes to hers. 'You need to trust me on this. It is over if you let it be.'

She said nothing.

'Wendy?'

'Tell me what's up,' she said. 'I won't tell a soul. I promise. It will be just between you and me.'

'Leave it alone.'

'At least tell me who is behind it.'

He shook his head. 'I don't know.'

That made her sit up. 'How can you not know?'

He threw two twenties on the table and started to rise.

'Where are you going?'

'Home.'

'You can't drive.'

'I'm fine.'

'No, Phil, you're not.'

'Now?' he shouted, startling her. 'Now you're interested in my well-being?'

He started to sob. In a normal bar, this might have drawn a few curious glances, but what with the blaring televisions and the focus on the games, it barely made a blip.

'What the hell is going on?' she asked.

'Drop this. Do you hear me? I'm telling you this not just for our sake – but yours too.'

'Mine?'

'You're putting yourself in harm's way. Your son too.'

She gripped his arm hard. 'Phil?'

He tried to stand, but the drinks had weakened him.

'You just sort of threatened my kid.'

'You got it backward,' he said. 'You're putting mine in danger.'

She let go of him. 'How?'

He shook his head. 'You just need to leave this alone, okay? All of us do. Stop trying to reach Farley and Steve – they won't talk to you anyway. Leave Kelvin alone. There is nothing to gain here. It's over. Dan is dead. And if you keep pressing, more people will die.'

Chapter 29

She tried to press Phil for more information, but he just shut down. She ended up giving him a ride home. When she arrived back at her house, Pops and Charlie were watching TV.

'Time for bed,' she said.

Pops groaned. 'Aww, can't I just stay up till the end?'

'Funny.'

Pops shrugged. 'Not my best work, but it's late.'

'Charlie?'

He kept his eyes on the screen. 'I thought it was pretty funny.'

Great, she thought. A comedy team. 'Bed.'

'Do you know what movie this is?'

She looked. 'It looks like the wildly inappropriate *Harold and Kumar Go to White Castle*.'

'Exactly,' Pops said. 'And in our family, we don't stop in the middle of *Harold and Kumar*. It's disrespectful.'

He had a point, and she did love this movie. So she sat with them and laughed and for a little while she tried to forget about dead girls and possible pedophiles and Princeton roommates and threats to her son. The last one, selfish as it sounded, would not leave. Phil Turnball did not hit her as an alarmist, yet he had been willing to – again to quote the teenage vernacular – 'go there.'

Maybe Phil had a point. Her story had been on Dan Mercer and maybe Haley McWaid. That part of the story was indeed over. She had her job back. She had come out of the whole thing rather well, in fact – the reporter who had exposed not only a pedophile but a murderer. Follow up on that angle maybe. Work with the police to see if there were other victims.

She looked at Charlie lounging on the couch. He laughed at something Neil Patrick Harris playing Neil Patrick Harris said. She loved the sound of his laugh. What parent doesn't? She stared at him for a few more moments and thought about Ted and Marcia McWaid and how they would never hear Haley laugh again and then her mind made her stop.

When the alarm went off in the morning – seemingly after eight minutes of sleep – Wendy dragged herself out of bed. She called for Charlie. No answer. She called again. Nothing.

She hopped out of bed. 'Charlie!'

Still no answer.

Panic gripped her, made it hard to breathe. 'Charlie!' She ran down the corridor, her heart beating wildly against her rib cage. She turned the corner, opening the door without knocking.

He was there, of course, still in bed, the covers pulled over his head.

'Charlie!'

He groaned. 'Go away.'

'Get up.'

'Can't I sleep in?'

'I warned you last night. Now get up.'

'First period is health class. Can't I skip it? Please?'

'Get. Up. Now.'

'Health class,' he said again. 'They teach sex stuff to

us impressionable youngsters. It makes us more promiscuous. Really, I think for my moral well-being you should let me stay in bed.'

She tried not to smile. 'Get. The. F. Up.'

'Five more minutes? Please?'

She sighed. 'Okay, five more minutes. No more.'

An hour and a half later, as health class ended, she drove him to school. What the heck. Senior year and he'd already been accepted to college. It was okay to coast a little, she reasoned.

When she got back home, she checked her e-mail. There was a message from Lawrence Cherston, the administrator of the Princeton class Web site. He would be 'delighted' to meet with her at her 'earliest convenience.' His address: Princeton, New Jersey. She called him back and asked him whether they could meet today at three PM. Lawrence Cherston again said that he'd be 'delighted.'

After hanging up, Wendy decided to check her fake Facebook profile, Sharon Hait. Of course, whatever had spooked Phil had nothing to do with the Kirby Sennett side of the case. Then again what did this have to do with anything?

Still, no harm in checking Facebook. She signed in and was pleased to see that Kirby Sennett had friended her. Okay, good. Now what? Kirby had also sent her an invitation to a Red Bull party. She clicked the link. There was a photograph of a smiling Kirby holding up a big can of Red Bull.

There was an address and a time and a brief note from ol' Kirby. 'Hi, Sharon, would love you to come!'

So much for mourning. She wondered what a Red Bull party was. Probably just that – a party that served the 'energy drink' Red Bull, though maybe spiked with something stronger – but she would ask Charlie.

So now what? Should she start up a relationship, see if she could get him to open up? No. Too creepy. It was one thing to pretend you're a young girl to trap a depraved pervert. It was another for the mother of a teenage boy to pretend to be a teenager to get one of his classmates to talk.

So what was the point here?

No idea.

Her phone rang. She checked the caller ID and saw it was coming from the NTC Network office.

'Hello?'

'Ms. Wendy Tynes?' The voice was pinched and female.

'Yes.'

'I'm calling from human resources and legal. We'd like you to come in today at twelve sharp.'

'What's this regarding?'

'We are located on the sixth floor. Mr. Frederick Montague's office. Twelve sharp. Please don't be tardy.'

Wendy frowned. 'Did you just say "tardy"?'

Click.

What on earth could this be about? And who uses the term 'tardy' outside of high school? She sat back. Probably not a big deal. Probably needed to fill out some paperwork now that she'd been rehired. Still, why does HR always have to be so damn officious?

She considered her next move. Last night she had learned that Jenna Wheeler had moved into a nearby Marriott. Time to put on her reporter hat and figure out where. She checked online. The three closest Marriott Courtyards were in Secaucus, Paramus, and Mahwah. She called the Secaucus one first.

'Could you patch me through to a guest named Wheeler, please?'

She figured that they wouldn't think to check in under a pseudonym.

The operator asked for a spelling. Wendy gave it.

'We have no guest by that name.'

She hung up and tried Paramus next. Again she asked for a guest named Wheeler. Three seconds later, the operator said, 'Please hold while I connect you.'

Bingo.

The phone was picked up on the third ring. Jenna Wheeler said, 'Hello?'

Wendy hung up and headed to her car. The Marriott Courtyard in Paramus was only ten minutes away. Better to do this in person. When Wendy was only two minutes away she called the room again.

Jenna's voice was more tentative this time. 'Hello?'

'It's Wendy Tynes.'

'What do you want?'

'To meet.'

'I don't want to meet.'

'I'm not looking to hurt you or your family, Jenna.'

'Then leave us alone.'

Wendy pulled the car into the Courtyard's parking lot. 'No can do.'

'I've got nothing to say to you.'

She found a spot, pulled in, turned off the engine. 'Too bad. Come down. I'm in the lobby. I'm not leaving until you do.'

Wendy hung up. The Paramus Marriott Courtyard was scenically located on both Route 17 and the Garden State Parkway. Room views featured either a P. C. Richard electronics store or a windowless warehouse store called Syms, with a quasi-bragging sign that read: AN EDUCATED CONSUMER IS OUR BEST CUSTOMER.

A vacation spot this was not.

Wendy entered the hotel. She waited in a lobby of beige – a sea of beige walls really, countered by a dull forest green carpet, a room enmeshed in the blandest of bland colors, hues so plain they screamed that the hotel was competent and fine, but expect absolutely no frills. Issues of *USA Today* were scattered about the coffee table. Wendy glanced at the headline and checked out a reader survey.

Jenna appeared five minutes later. She wore an over-size sweatshirt. Her hair was pulled back in a severe ponytail, making her already-high cheekbones look sharp enough to slice.

'Did you come here to gloat?' Jenna asked.

'Yes, Jenna, that's exactly why I came here. I was sitting at home this morning, thinking about a dead girl found in the woods, and I said to myself, "You know what would be great right now? The icing on the cake? A little gloating." So that's why I'm here. Oh, and after this I'm going to go to the pound to kick a puppy.'

Jenna sat down. 'I'm sorry. That was uncalled for.'

Wendy thought about last night, about something as inane as Project Graduation, and how Jenna and Noel Wheeler should have been there, how much they probably wished now that they could have attended. 'I'm sorry too. I imagine this has all been hard on you.'

Jenna shrugged. 'Every time I want to feel sorry for myself, I think about Ted and Marcia. You know what I mean?'

'I do.'

Silence.

'I heard you're moving,' Wendy said.

'Who did you hear that from?'

'It's a small town.'

Jenna smiled without a trace of joy. 'Aren't they all?

281

Yes, we're moving. Noel is going to be chief of cardiac surgery at Cincinnati Memorial Hospital.'

'That was quick.'

'He's very much in demand. But the truth is, we started planning this months ago.'

'When you first started defending Dan?'

Again she tried to smile. 'Let's just say that didn't help our standing in the community,' she said. 'We hoped to stay until the end of the school year – so Amanda could graduate with her class. But I guess that's not meant to be.'

'I'm sorry.'

'Again, Ted and Marcia. This isn't that big of a deal.'

Wendy guessed not.

'So why are you here, Wendy?'

'You defended Dan.'

'Yep.'

'I mean, from start to end. When the show first aired. You seemed so sure that he was innocent. And last time we talked you said that I destroyed an innocent man.'

'So what do you want me to say – my bad? I was wrong, you were right?'

'Were you?'

'Was I what?'

'Were you wrong?'

Jenna just stared at her. 'What are you talking about?'

'Do you think Dan killed Haley?'

The lobby fell silent. Jenna looked as though she was about to respond but she shook her head instead.

'I don't understand. You think he's innocent?'

Wendy wasn't sure how to reply to that one. 'I think there are still some pieces missing.'

'Like what?'

'That's what I'm here to find out.'

Jenna looked at her as though expecting more. Now it was Wendy who looked away. Jenna deserved a better answer. So far, Wendy had handled this whole case as a reporter. But maybe she was more than that here. Maybe it was time to come clean, admit the truth, say it out loud.

'I'm going to confess something to you, okay?'

Jenna nodded, waited.

'I work with facts, not intuition. Intuition usually just screws me up. Do you know what I mean?'

'More than you can imagine.'

There were tears in Jenna's eyes now. Wendy imagined that they were in hers too.

'Factually I knew that I had Dan nailed. He tried to seduce my imaginary thirteen-year-old girl online. He showed up at the house. There was all that stuff in his house and on his computer. Even his job – I can't tell you how many of these creeps work with teenagers, supposedly helping them. It all added up. And yet my intuition kept screaming that something was wrong.'

'You sounded pretty certain when we spoke.'

'Almost too certain, don't you think?'

Jenna considered that and a small smile came to her face. 'Like me, when you think about it – both of us so sure. Of course, one of us had to be wrong. But now I think the truth is, you can never be certain about another person. Obvious, but I think I needed a reminder. Do you remember how I said that Dan was secretive?'

'Yes.'

'Maybe you were right about why. He kept something from me. I knew that. We all do that, don't we? No one knows us entirely. In the end, it's kind of a cliché, but maybe you never really know a person.'

'So you were wrong this whole time?'

Jenna chewed on her lip for a moment. 'I look back now. I think about his secretiveness. I thought it had something to do with being an orphan, you know? The obvious trust issues. I thought that's what ultimately drove us apart. But now I wonder.'

'Wonder what?'

A tear rolled down her cheek. 'I wonder if it was more, if something bad happened to him. I wonder if there was a darkness there, inside of him.'

Jenna stood and crossed the room. There was a coffee urn. She grabbed a Styrofoam cup and filled it. Wendy rose and followed her. She got some coffee too. When they returned to their seats, it was as though the moment had passed. Wendy was okay with that. She had dealt with the intuition part. It was time to return to the facts.

'When we met last time, you said something about Princeton. That something happened to him when he was there.'

'Right, so?'

'So I'd like to look into that.'

Jenna looked confused. 'You think Princeton has something to do with all this?'

Wendy really didn't want to get into it. 'I'm just following up.'

'I don't understand. What could his college years have to do with anything?'

'It's just an aspect of the case I need to know about.'

'Why?'

'Can you just trust me on this one, Jenna? You were the one who raised it last time we talked. You said something happened to him in college. I want to know what.'

She didn't answer for a few moments. Then: 'I don't know. That was part of the secretiveness – maybe the biggest part, now that I think about it. That's why I mentioned it to you.'

'And you have no idea what it was?'

'Not really. I mean, it ended up not making much sense.'

'Could you at least tell me about it?'

'I don't see the point.'

'Humor me, okay?'

Jenna brought the coffee up to her mouth, blew on it, took a small sip. 'Okay, when we first started going out, he'd disappear every other Saturday. I don't want to make it sound as cryptic as all that. But he'd just take off and not say where he was going.'

'I assume you asked?'

'I did. He explained to me early in the relationship that this was something he did and that it was his private time. He said it was nothing to worry about, but he wanted me to understand he needed to do it.'

She stopped talking.

'What did you make of that?'

'I was in love,' Jenna said simply. 'So at first, I rationalized it. Some guys play golf, I told myself. Some guys bowl or meet the boys in a bar or whatever. Dan was entitled to his time. He was so attentive in every other way. So I simply let it go.'

The lobby door opened. A family of five staggered in and approached the front desk. The man gave their name and handed the receptionist his credit card.

'You said "at first,"' Wendy said.

'Yes. Well, more than simply at first. I think we'd been married a year when I pushed him on it. Dan said not to worry, it was no big deal. But now it was, of course. The curiosity was eating me up. So one Saturday, I followed him.'

Her voice drifted off and a small smile came to her face.

'What?'

'I've never told anyone this. Not even Dan.'

Wendy sat back, gave her room. She took a sip of her coffee and tried to make herself look as nonthreatening as possible.

'Anyway there isn't that much more to the story. I followed him for about an hour, hour and a half. He got off at the exit for Princeton. He parked in town. He went into a coffee shop. I felt so silly following him. He sat by himself for maybe ten minutes. I kept waiting for the other woman to show up. I imagined she was some sexy college professor, you know, with glasses and dark black hair. But nobody showed up. Dan finished his coffee and got up. He started walking down the block. It was so weird, following him like that. I mean, I loved this man. You have no idea how much. And yet, like I said, there was something about him I couldn't reach and now I'm skulking around, trying to keep out of sight, and I'm feeling like now, finally, I'm close to learning the truth. And it's terrifying me.'

Again Jenna lifted the cup to her lips.

'So where did he go?'

'Two blocks away, there was a lovely old Victorian home. It was in the heart of faculty housing. He knocked on the door and entered. He stayed an hour and left. He walked back to town, got in his car, and drove back.'

The hotel receptionist told the family that check-in wasn't until four PM. The father pleaded for an earlier time. The receptionist remained firm.

'So whose house was it?'

'That's the funny thing. It belonged to the dean of students. A man named Stephen Slotnick. He was divorced at the time. He lived there with his two kids.'

'So why would he visit him?'

'I have no idea. I never asked. That was it. I never raised it with him. He wasn't having an affair. It was his secret. If he wanted to tell me, he would.'

'And he never did?'

'Never.'

They drank coffee, both lost in their own thoughts.

'You have nothing to feel guilty about,' Jenna said.

'I don't.'

'Dan is dead. One thing we had in common, neither of us believed in an afterlife. Dead is dead. He wouldn't care about being rehabilitated now.'

'I'm not trying to do that either.'

'Then what are you trying to do?'

'Damned if I know. I guess I need answers.'

'Sometimes the most obvious answer is the right one. Maybe Dan was everything people think he was.'

'Maybe, but that doesn't answer one key question.'

'That being?'

'Why was he visiting the dean of students at his alma mater?'

'I have no idea.'

'Aren't you curious?'

Jenna thought about it. 'You plan on finding out?'

'I do.'

'It might have destroyed our marriage.'

'Might have.'

'Or it might have nothing to do with anything.'

'More likely,' Wendy agreed.

'I think Dan killed that girl.'

Wendy did not reply to that. She waited for Jenna to say more, but she didn't. Admitting that had sucked the energy out of her. She sat back, seemingly unable to move.

After some time had passed, Wendy said, 'You're probably right.'

'But you still want to know about the dean?'

'I do.'

Jenna nodded. 'If you find out what it was, will you let me know?'

'Sure.'

Chapter 30

Wendy got off the elevator and headed to Vic's office. On her way, she passed Michele Feisler – the new young anchorwoman – working at her cubicle. The cubicle had photographs of Walter Cronkite, Edward R. Murrow, Peter Jennings. Again Wendy thought, Oy.

'Hi, Michele.'

Michele was busy typing. She gave a half-wave, no more. Wendy peered over the woman's shoulder. She was Tweeting on Twitter. In this case, someone had commented: 'Your hair looked great on last night's broadcast!' Michele was re-Tweeting it to her followers with a 'Using a new conditioner – will tell more soon. Stay tuned!'

Edward R. Murrow would be so proud.

'How's that guy who got both knees shot?' Wendy asked.

'Yeah, it's your kind of story,' Michele said.

'How's that?'

'Seems he's something of a perv.' She turned away from her computer, but only for a moment. 'Isn't that your specialty – pervs?'

Nice to have a specialty, Wendy thought. 'What do you mean "pervs"?'

'Well, you're our resident sex perv, aren't you?'

'Meaning?'

'Oops, can't talk now,' Michele said, back typing away. 'Busy.'

Standing there, Wendy couldn't help but notice that Clark had been right: Michele did indeed have a gigantic head, especially in contrast to that wisp of a body. It looked like a helium balloon on the end of a string. It looked like her neck might collapse under the weight.

Wendy checked her watch. Three minutes until twelve sharp. She hurried down the corridor to Vic's office. His secretary, Mavis, was there.

'Hey, Mavis.'

This woman too barely looked up at her. 'What can I do for you, Ms. Tynes?'

First time she'd called her that. Maybe someone had sent down a directive to be more formal since her firing. 'I'd like to speak to Vic for a second.'

'Mr. Garrett is not available.' Her tone, usually so friendly, was pure ice.

'Will you tell him I'm headed up to the sixth floor? I should be back soon.'

'I will let him know.'

She made her way to the elevator. Maybe it was her imagination but there seemed to be a weird tension in the air.

Wendy had been in this building – the network offices – a zillion times, but she had never been on the sixth floor before. Now she sat in an office of startling white, a cubist wonder, with a little waterfall running in the corner. One wall was dominated by a painting of black-and-white swirls. The other walls were empty. The swirls were facing her and very distracting. Across the glass table, in front of the swirls, sat three suits. Two men, one

290

woman – all lined up against her. One man was black. The woman was Asian. Nice balance, though the one in charge, the one who sat in the middle and did all the talking, was the white man.

'Thank you for coming in to see us,' the man said. He had introduced himself – had, in fact, introduced all three – but she hadn't been paying attention to names.

'Sure thing,' she said.

Wendy noticed that her chair was at least two inches lower than the others. Classic – albeit amateur – intimidation move. Wendy crossed her arms and actually slid lower. Let them think they have the advantage.

'So,' Wendy said, trying to cut through this, 'what can I do for you folks?'

The white man looked at the Asian woman. She took out a sheet of paper and slid it across the glass tabletop. 'Is this your signature?'

Wendy looked at it. It was her original employment contract. 'Looks like it.'

'Is that your signature or not?'

'It is.'

'And you've read this document, of course.'

'I guess.'

'I don't want you to guess—'

She stopped him with a wave of her hand. 'I read it. So what's the problem?'

'I would like you to refer to section seventeen point four on page three.'

'Okay.' She started turning pages.

'It references our strict policy about romantic and/or sexual relationships in the workplace.'

That made her pull up. 'What about it?'

'You've read it?'

'Yes.'

'And you understand it?'

'Yes.'

'Well,' the white man said, 'it has come to our attention that you broke this rule, Ms. Tynes.'

'Uh, no, I assure you that I did not.'

The white man sat back, crossed his arms, and tried to look judgmental. 'Do you know a man named Victor Garrett?'

'Vic? Sure, he's the news manager.'

'Have you ever had sexual relations with him?'

'With Vic? Come on now.'

'Is that a yes or no?'

'It's a big-time no. Why don't you bring him in here and ask him yourself?'

The three of them started conferring with one another. 'We plan on doing that.'

'I don't understand. Where did you hear that Vic and I . . .' She tried not to look disgusted.

'We've received reports.'

'From?'

They didn't answer right away – and suddenly the answer was obvious. Hadn't Phil Turnball warned her?

'We aren't at liberty to say,' the white man said.

'Too bad. You are leveling a serious accusation. Either you have some evidence to show me or you don't.'

The black man looked at the Asian woman. The Asian woman looked at the white man. The white man looked at the black man.

Wendy spread her hands. 'Do you guys rehearse this?'

They bent toward one another and whispered like senators during a hearing. Wendy waited. When they finished, the Asian woman opened another file and slid it across the glass surface.

'Perhaps you should read this.'

Wendy opened the file. It was a printout from a blog. Wendy felt her blood boil as she read:

I work at NTC. I can't say my real name because I'll get fired. But Wendy Tynes is horrible. She is a no-talent prima donna who rose to the top the old-fashioned way: She slept her way there. Currently she is screwing our boss Vic Garrett. Because of that, she gets to do whatever she wants. She was, in fact, fired last week for incompetence, but got hired back because Vic is afraid of a harassment suit. Wendy has had tons of plastic surgery, including nose, eyes, and boobs . . .

On and on it went. Again Wendy remembered Phil's warning. She remembered what these viral psychos had done to Farley Parks, to Steve Miciano – and now to her. The implications were beginning to sink in: her career, her livelihood, her ability to take care of her son. Rumors always hardened to facts. Accusations are convictions in the public mind. You are guilty until proven innocent.

Hadn't Dan Mercer told her something like that?

Eventually the white man cleared his throat and said, 'Well?'

With as much bravado as she could muster, Wendy stuck out her chest. 'They're real. You can squeeze one if you want.'

'This isn't funny.'

'And I'm not laughing. But I am offering you proof these are lies. Go ahead. Quick squeeze.'

The white man made a *harrumph* noise and gestured toward the file. 'Maybe you should look at the comments. They're on the second page.'

Wendy tried to keep up the confident façade, but she

felt as though her world was starting to teeter. She turned the paper over and scanned down to the first comment.

Comment: I worked with her at her last job and I totally agree. Same thing happened there. Our married boss got canned and divorced. She's trash.
   Comment: She slept with at least two college professors, one when she was pregnant. Broke up his marriage.

Now Wendy felt her face burn. She had been married to John when she was at that job. He had, in fact, been killed during her last weeks working there. That lie, in particular, enraged her more than any others. It was so obscene, so unfair.

'Well?' the white man asked.

'These,' she said, through gritted teeth, 'are total lies.'

'It's all over the Web. Some of these blogs have been sent to our sponsors. They were threatening to pull their ads.'

'It's all lies.'

'And furthermore we would like you to sign a release.'

'What kind of release?'

'Mr. Garrett is your superior. While I don't think you have a case, you could sue for sexual harassment.'

'Are you kidding?' Wendy said.

He pointed toward the file. 'One of those blogs mentioned that you once sued a superior for sexual harassment. Who's to say you won't do it again?'

Wendy actually saw red. She tightened her hands into fists and fought hard to keep her tone even. 'Mr. . . . I'm sorry, I forgot your name . . .'

'Montague.'

'Mr. Montague.' Deep breath. 'I want you to listen to

294

me very closely. Try to pay attention here because I want to make sure you understand.' Wendy lifted the file in the air. 'These are all lies. Do you get that? Fabrications. The part about me suing an old employer? That's a lie. The accusation that I slept with a superior or a professor? More lies. The accusation that I slept with anyone other than my husband while I was pregnant? Or that I got plastic surgery, for that matter? They are all lies. Not exaggerations. Not distortions. Bald-faced lies. Do you understand?'

Montague cleared his throat. 'We understand that's your position.'

'Anyone can go online and say anything about any-one,' Wendy continued. 'Don't you get that? Someone is cyber-lying about me. Look at the date on the blog, for crying out loud. It was posted yesterday and already has all these comments. It's all fake. Someone is intentionally trying to ruin me.'

'Be that as it may,' Montague began, a phrase that meant absolutely nothing but irritated Wendy like few others, 'we feel it would be best if you take a temporary leave of absence while we investigate this charge.'

'I don't think so,' Wendy said.

'Pardon me?'

'Because if you make me do that, I will make a stink that you'll never get off your shiny suits. I will sue the network. I will sue the studio. I will sue each one of you personally. I will send our beloved sponsors blogs that claim that you two' – she pointed to the white man and the black man – 'enjoy having monkey sex on the office furniture while she' – now she pointed to the Asian woman – 'likes to watch and spank herself. Is it true? Well, it will be in a blog. Several blogs, in fact. Then I'll go to other computers and add comments, stuff like

Montague likes it rough or with toys or small farm animals. Get PETA on your ass. Then I'll send those blogs to your families. Do you get my drift?'

No one spoke.

She rose. 'I'm going back to work.'

'No, Ms. Tynes, I'm afraid you're not.'

The door opened. Two uniformed security guards entered.

'We will have security escort you out. Please do not get in contact with anyone at this company until we have had a chance to look into the matter. Any attempt to communicate with anyone involved in this case will be viewed as possible tampering. Also, your threats directed at myself and my colleagues will be noted in the record. Thank you for your time.'

Chapter 31

Wendy called Vic, but Mavis wouldn't put her through. Fine. It would be like that. Princeton was about a ninety-minute ride. She spent the drive time both fuming and thinking about what this all meant. It was easy to scoff at ridiculous and unsubstantiated gossip, but she knew that, whatever happened now, these rumors would throw a dark and probably permanent shadow over her career. There had been whispered innuendos before – pretty much a given when even a semi-attractive female rose to prominence in this industry – but now, because some moron had posted them on a blog, they suddenly took on more credence. Welcome to the computer age.

Okay, enough.

As she neared her destination, Wendy started thinking about the case again, about the continuing links to Princeton, about the fact that four men – Phil Turnball, Dan Mercer, Steve Miciano, Farley Parks – had all been set up within the past year.

One question was, how?

The bigger question was, who?

Wendy figured that she might as well start with Phil Turnball because she had something of an in there. She jammed the hands-free phone cord into her ear and dialed Win's private line.

Once again Win answered in a voice too haughty for this one word: 'Articulate.'

'Can I ask another favor?'

'*May* I ask another favor? Yes, Wendy, you *may*.'

'I can't tell you how much I needed that grammar lesson right about now.'

'You're welcome.'

'Do you remember I asked you about Phil Turnball, the guy who got fired for embezzling two million dollars?'

'I recall, yes.'

'Let's say Phil was set up and didn't really take the money.'

'Okay, let's.'

'How would someone go about setting him up?'

'I have no idea. Why do you ask?'

'I'm pretty sure he didn't steal the money.'

'I see. And, pray tell, what makes you "pretty sure"?'

'He told me he's innocent.'

'Oh, well, that settles it.'

'There's more to it than that.'

'I'm listening.'

'Well, why, if Phil stole two million dollars, isn't he in jail or even asked to pay the money back? I don't want to go into details right now, but there are other guys – his college roommates, actually – who've been involved in bizarre scandals recently too. In one case, I may have been a patsy.'

Win said nothing.

'Win?'

'Yes, I heard you. I love the word "patsy," don't you? It denotes or at least suggests giving feminine characteristics to the act of being duped.'

'Yeah, it's great.'

Even his sigh was haughty. 'What would you like me to do to help?'

'Could you look into it a little? I need to know who set Phil Turnball up.'

'Will do.'

Click.

The abruptness didn't surprise her quite as much this time, though she wished there'd been time for a follow-up, a crack about quick endings being his specialty, but alas, there was no one on the other line. She held the phone in her hand for another second, half expecting him to call right back. But that didn't happen this time.

Lawrence Cherston's home was washed stone and white shutters. There was a circular rose garden surrounding a flagpole. A black pennant with a large orange *P* hung from it. Oh, boy. Cherston greeted her at the door with a two-hand shake. He had one of those fleshy, ruddy faces that make you think of fat cats and smoke-filled back rooms. He wore a blue blazer with a Princeton logo on the lapel and the same Princeton tie he'd had in his profile pictures. His khakis were freshly pressed, his tasseled loafers shined, and of course he wore no socks. He looked as though he'd started for school chapel this morning and aged twenty years on the walk. Stepping inside, Wendy pictured a closet with a dozen more matching blazers and khaki pants and absolutely nothing else.

'Welcome to my humble abode,' he said. He offered her a drink. She passed. He had laid out finger sandwiches. Wendy took one just to be polite. The finger sandwich was awful enough to make her wonder whether the moniker was also an ingredient list. Cherston was already jabbering on about his classmates.

'We have two Pulitzer Prize winners,' he said. Then

leaning forward, he added, 'And one's a woman.'

'A woman.' Wendy froze a smile and blinked. 'Wow.'

'We also have a world-famous photographer, several CEOs of course, oh, and one Academy Award nominee. Well, okay, it was for best sound and he didn't win. But still. Several of our classmates work for the current administration. One was drafted by the Cleveland Browns.'

Wendy nodded like an idiot, wondering how long she could keep the smile on her face. Cherston broke out scrapbooks and photo books and the graduation program and even the freshman face book. He was talking about himself now, his total commitment to his alma mater, as though this might surprise her.

She needed to move this along.

Wendy picked up a photograph album and started paging through it, hoping to spot any of her Princeton Five. No such luck. Cherston droned on. Okay, time to make something happen. She took hold of the freshman face book and flipped through it, heading straight for the Ms.

'Oh, look,' she said, interrupting him. She pointed to the picture of Steven Miciano. 'That's Dr. Miciano, right?'

'Why, yes, it is.'

'He treated my mother.'

Cherston may have squirmed a bit. 'That's nice.'

'Maybe I should talk to him too.'

'Maybe,' Cherston said. 'But I don't have a current address on him.'

Wendy went back to the face book, summoning up another fake gasp of surprise. 'Well, well, look at this. Dr. Miciano roomed with Farley Parks. Isn't he the one who was running for Congress?'

Lawrence Cherston smiled at her.

'Mr. Cherston?'

'Call me Lawrence.'

'Okay. Isn't Farley Parks the one who was running for Congress?'

'May I call you Wendy?'

'You *may*.' Shades of Win.

'Thank you. Wendy, perhaps we could both stop playing this game?'

'What game?'

He shook his head, as though disappointed in a favorite student. 'Search engines work both ways. Did you really think I wouldn't, at least out of curiosity, Google the name of a reporter who wanted to interview me?'

She said nothing.

'So I know you already signed up for the Princeton class page. And more to the point, I know you covered the stories on Dan Mercer. Some might even say you created them.'

He looked at her.

'These finger sandwiches are awesome,' she said.

'My wife made them and they're dreadful. Anyway, I assume the purpose of this ruse was to gather some background information.'

'If you knew that, why did you agree to see me?'

'Why not?' he countered. 'You're doing a story involving a Princeton graduate. I wanted to be sure that your information is correct, so as not to create innuendo where none belongs.'

'Well, thank you for seeing me then.'

'You're welcome. So what can I do for you?'

'Did you know Dan Mercer?'

He picked up a finger sandwich and took the smallest bite. 'I did, yes, but not well.'

'What was your impression?'

'Do you mean, did he seem like a pedophile and murderer?'

'That might be a good place to start.'

'No, Wendy. He didn't seem like the kind. But I confess that I'm rather naïve. I see the best in everyone.'

'What can you tell me about him?'

'Dan was a serious student – bright, hardworking. He was a poor kid. I'm the son of alumni – fourth generation at Princeton, in fact. It put us in different circles. I love this school. I'm hardly subtle about that. But Dan seemed awed by it.'

Wendy nodded as though this offered her some great insight. It didn't. 'Who were his close friends?'

'You mentioned two already, so I assume you already know that answer.'

'His roommates?'

'Yes.'

'Do you know them all?'

'In passing perhaps. Phil Turnball and I were in glee club together freshman year. It is interesting. As you probably know, freshman roommates are assigned by the school. That could lead to disaster, of course. My freshman roommate was an idiot savant who smoked dope all day. I moved out within the month. But these five all got along for years.'

'Is there anything you can tell me about their time here?'

'Like what?'

'Were they weird? Were they outcasts? Did they have any enemies? Were they involved in any strange activities?'

Lawrence Cherston put down the sandwich. 'Why would you ask something like that?'

Wendy aimed for vague. 'It's part of the story.'

'I can't see how. I understand why you'd inquire about

Dan Mercer. But if your goal here is to somehow link his college roommates with whatever demons plagued him—'

'That's not my goal.'

'Then what is?'

She didn't really want to say much more. To stall for time she picked up the graduation program, started paging through it. She felt his eyes upon her. She flipped more pages and found a photograph of Dan with Kelvin and Farley. Dan stood between them. All three had big smiles on their faces. Graduation. They had made it.

Lawrence Cherston was still looking at her. What's the harm, she thought.

'All of them – his roommates – have had trouble recently.'

He said nothing.

'Farley Parks had to drop out of his congressional race,' she said.

'I am aware of that.'

'Steve Miciano was arrested on drug charges. Phil Turnball lost his job. And you know about Dan.'

'I do.'

'You don't find that odd?'

'Not particularly.' He loosened his tie as though it had suddenly become a noose. 'So is that the angle you're taking on this story? Roommates from Princeton all having troubles?'

She didn't really want to answer that one, so she shifted gears. 'Dan Mercer used to come down here a lot. To Princeton, I mean.'

'I know. I used to see him in town.'

'Do you know why?'

'No.'

'He would visit the dean's house.'

'I had no idea.'

It was then, glancing at the program, at the list of students, that Wendy noticed something odd. She had gotten used to searching for the five names – or maybe that picture had set her off. The list was in alphabetical order. And under the *T*s, the last name on the list was Francis Tottendam.

'Where's Phil Turnball?' she asked.

'Pardon?'

'Phil Turnball's name isn't on this list.'

'Phil didn't graduate with our class.'

Wendy felt a strange tick in her veins. 'He took a semester off?'

'Uh, no. He was forced to leave school early.'

'Wait. Are you saying that Phil Turnball didn't graduate?'

'To the best of my knowledge, well, yes, that's exactly what I'm saying.'

Wendy felt her mouth go dry. 'Why not?'

'I don't know for sure. There were rumors, of course. The whole deal was kept hush-hush.'

She stayed very still, very calm. 'Could you tell me about it?'

'I'm not sure that's a good idea.'

'It could be very important.'

'How? It was years ago – and really, I think the school probably overreacted.'

'I won't report it. This is off the record.'

'I don't know.'

This was no time for subtlety. She had offered the carrot. Time to bring out the stick. 'Look, I already said it's off the record, but if you don't come clean, I will go back on it. And I will dig. I will dig up every skeleton I can find to learn the truth. And then it will all be on the record.'

'I hate being threatened.'

'And I hate being stalled.'

He sighed. 'Like I said, it wasn't a big deal. And I don't really know for sure.'

'But?'

'But, okay, it sounds worse than it is, but the rumor is Phil got caught off-hours in a building where he didn't belong. In short, a campus breaking-and-entering.'

'He was stealing?'

'Heavens no,' he said, as if that was the most ridiculous thing he ever heard. 'It was for fun.'

'You guys break into buildings for fun?'

'I have a friend who went to Hampshire College. Do you know it? Anyway, he got fifty points for stealing a campus bus. Some professors wanted to expel him, but like with Phil, it was all part of a game. He just got a two-week suspension. I confess that I participated too. My team spray-painted a professor's car. Thirty points. A friend of mine stole a pen off the desk of a visiting poet laureate. The game ran campus-wide. I mean, all the dorms competed.'

'Competed in what?' she asked.

Lawrence Cherston smiled. 'The hunt, of course,' he said. 'The scavenger hunt.'

Chapter 32

'*We shouldn't hunt no more. . . .*'

That was what Kelvin Tilfer had told her.

Now, maybe, that made some sense. She asked Lawrence Cherston some more about it, about scar face and all the rest, but there was nothing more to learn here. Phil Turnball had been caught where he wasn't supposed to be during a scavenger hunt. He had been expelled for it. The end.

When Wendy got back to her car, she took out her phone to call Phil.

There were sixteen messages.

Her first thought made her heart slam into her throat: *Something happened to Charlie.*

She quickly pressed down on the *V* to get her voice mail. As soon as she heard the first message, the grip of fear slackened. A different sort of sick feeling washed over her. It wasn't Charlie. But it wasn't good either.

'*Hi, Wendy, this is Bill Giuliano from ABC News. We would like to talk to you about accusations of inappropriate behavior on your part. . . .*' BEEP.

'*We're writing a story about your affair with your boss and we'd love to hear your side of the story. . . .*' BEEP.

'*One of the alleged pedophiles you exposed on your show is using the recent reports on your sexually aggressive behavior to ask for a new trial. He now claims you were a scorned lover and set him up. . . .*' BEEP.

She hit the cancel button and stared at her phone. Damn. She wanted to rise above it, dismiss the whole thing.

But oh man. She was so screwed.

Maybe she should have listened to Phil and stayed out of it. Now there was no way – no matter what she did – that she'd escape these allegations unscathed. No friggin' way. She could catch the asswipe who posted all this crap, have him (or her) admit during live coverage of the Super Bowl that it was all a pack of lies, and it still wouldn't scrub her clean. Unfair or not, the stink would linger, probably forever.

So no use crying over spilled milk, right?

Another thought hit her: Couldn't the same be said about the men she nailed on her show?

Even if these guys were ultimately proven innocent, would the stink of being a televised predator ever wash off them? Maybe this was all some kind of cosmic payback. Maybe this was karma being a total bitch.

No time to worry about it now. Or maybe it was all one and the same. Somehow it all seemed connected – what she'd done, what happened to the men she exposed, what happened to these guys at Princeton. Solve one and the rest would fall into place.

Like it or not, her life was enmeshed in this mess. She couldn't walk away.

Phil Turnball had been expelled for participating in a scavenger hunt.

That meant, at best, he lied to her when she told him about Kelvin ranting about the hunt. At worst . . . well, she wasn't sure yet what the worst was. She dialed Phil's mobile. No answer. She dialed the house. No answer. She called Phil's cell again, this time leaving a message:

'I know about the scavenger hunt. Call me.'

Five minutes later, she pounded on the dean's door. No answer. She pounded some more. Still no answer. Oh no. No way. She circled the house, peering in windows. The lights were out. She pressed her face to the window, trying to get a better look. If campus police came by, she'd try not to quake in fear.

Movement.

'Hey!'

No reply. She looked again. Nothing. She knocked on the window. No one came to it. She went back to the front door, started pounding again. From behind her a man said, 'May I help you?'

She turned toward the voice. When she saw who had spoken, the first word that came to mind was 'fop.' The man's wavy hair was a tad too long. He wore a tweed jacket with patched sleeves and a bow tie – a look that could only thrive or even exist in the rarified air of upscale educational institutions.

'I'm looking for the dean,' Wendy said.

'I'm Dean Lewis,' he said. 'What can I do for you?'

No time for games or subtlety, she thought. 'Do you know Dan Mercer?'

He hesitated as though thinking about it. 'The name rings a bell,' the dean said. 'But . . .' He spread his hands and shrugged. 'Should I?'

'I would think so,' Wendy said. 'For the past twenty years, he's visited your house every other Saturday.'

'Ah.' He smiled. 'I've only lived here for four years. My predecessor Dean Pashaian was here before then. But I think I know who you mean.'

'Why did he visit you?'

'He didn't. I mean, yes, he came to this house. But it wasn't to see me. Or Dean Pashaian for that matter.'

'Why then?'

He stepped past her and unlocked the door with the key. He pushed the door open. It actually creaked. He leaned his head in. 'Christa?'

The house was dark. He waved for her to follow him inside. She did so. She stood in the foyer.

A woman's voice called out, 'Dean?'

Footsteps started toward them. Wendy turned toward the dean. He gave her a look that offered up something akin to a warning.

What the . . . ?

'I'm in the foyer,' he said.

More footsteps. Then the female voice – Christa's? – again: 'Your four o'clock canceled. You also need—'

Christa entered from their left via the dining room. She stopped. 'Oh, I didn't know you had company.'

'She's not here to see me,' Dean Lewis said.

'Oh?'

'I think she's here to see you.'

The woman turned her head to the side, almost like a dog does when trying to contemplate a new sound. 'Are you Wendy Tynes?' she asked.

'Yes.'

Christa nodded as though she'd been expecting Wendy for a very long time. She took another step foward. Now there was some light on her face. Not much. But enough. When Wendy saw her face, she nearly gasped out loud – not because of the sight, though that would have been enough under normal circumstances. No, Wendy nearly gasped because another piece of the puzzle had just fallen into place.

Christa wore sunglasses, even though she was inside. But that wasn't the first thing you noticed.

The first thing you noticed about Christa – the one thing you couldn't help but notice, really – were the thick, red scars that crisscrossed her face.

Scar face.

She introduced herself as Christa Stockwell.

She looked about forty, but it was hard to get an age on her. She was slender, maybe five-eight, with delicate hands and a strong bearing. They sat at the kitchen table.

'Do you mind if I keep the lights low?' Christa asked.

'Not at all.'

'It's not why you think. I know people will stare. It's natural actually. I don't mind it. It's better than those people who try too hard to pretend they don't see the scars. My face becomes the elephant in the room, you know what I mean?'

'I guess so.'

'Since the incident, my eyes are sensitive to light. It's more comfortable for me in the dark. How apropos, right? The philosophy and psych majors at this school would have a field day with that one.' She stood. 'I'm going to have some tea. Would you like some?'

'Sure. Can I help?'

'No, I'm fine. Peppermint or English Breakfast?'

'Peppermint.'

Christa smiled. 'Good choice.'

She flicked on the electric kettle, got out two mugs, put the tea bags in them. Wendy noticed that she kept tilting her head to the right as she went about the task. When she sat back down, Christa just stood still for a moment as if giving Wendy the chance to examine the damage. Her face was, quite simply, horrific. The scars blanketed her from forehead to neck. Ugly, angry lines, purple and red, tore across her skin, raised up as though on a relief map. In the few spots with no lines there were instead splotches of deep red, badly abraded, as if someone had taken steel wool to the skin.

'I'm contractually obligated to never discuss what happened,' Christa Stockwell said.

'Dan Mercer is dead.'

'I know. But that doesn't change the contract.'

'Whatever you say to me will be held in the strictest confidence.'

'You're a reporter, aren't you?'

'Yes. But you have my word.'

She shook her head. 'I can't see why it matters now.'

'Dan is dead. Phil Turnball has been fired from his job, accused of stealing. Kelvin Tilfer is in an asylum. Farley Parks has had recent troubles too.'

'Am I supposed to feel sorry for them?'

'What did they do to you?'

'Isn't the evidence clear enough? Or should I turn up the lights a little?'

Wendy leaned across the table. She put her hand on the other woman's. 'Please tell me what happened.'

'I can't see what good it will do.'

The kitchen clock above the sink ticked. Wendy could look out the window and see the undergrads walking to class, all animated, young, with the clichéd rest of their lives waiting around the corner. Next year, Charlie would be one of them. You could tell these kids that it will go faster than they think, that they will blink and college will be gone and then ten years and another ten, but they won't listen, can't listen, and maybe that's a good thing.

311

'I think whatever happened here – whatever those guys did to you – started this all.'

'How?'

'I don't know. But somehow I think it could all be traced back to it. Somehow, whatever it was took on a life of its own. It is still claiming victims. And I'm caught up in it now. I'm the one who nailed Dan Mercer – rightly or wrongly. So now I'm part of it.'

Christa Stockwell blew on the tea. Her face looked as though someone had turned it inside out, like the veins and cartilage had all been dragged to the surface. 'It was their senior year,' she said. 'I'd graduated the year before and was getting my master's in comparative literature. I'd been a financial hardship case. Like Dan actually. We both had jobs while going to school. He worked doing laundry in the men's phys ed department. I worked here, in this house, for Dean Slotnick. I babysat his children, did some household chores, filing, that kind of thing. He was divorced, and I got along great with his kids. So while I got my master's, I was actually living here, in a room in the back. As a matter of fact, I still live there.'

Outside the window two students walked by and one laughed. The sound crossed the room, melodic and rich and so out of place.

'Anyway, it was March. Dean Slotnick was out of town for a speaking engagement. The children were staying with their mother in New York City. I'd gone out to dinner that night with my fiancé. Marc was in med school, second year. He had a big test in chemistry the next day, otherwise, well, there are so many what-ifs, aren't there? If he hadn't had that test, we would have gone back to his place or maybe, with the house empty, he would have stayed here. But no. Marc had taken enough time off for dinner. So anyway he dropped me

312

off and went to the med library. I had some schoolwork to do myself. So I brought my notebook right here – I mean, I placed it right on this kitchen table.'

She stared at the tabletop as though the notebook might still be there.

'I made myself tea. Just like today. I sat here and was about to start my essay when I heard a noise coming from upstairs. Like I said, I knew no one was home. I should have been scared, right? I remember one time I heard this English professor asking the class what the world's scariest noise is. Is it a man crying out in pain? A woman's scream of terror? A gunshot? A baby crying? And the professor shakes his head and says, "No, the scariest noise is, you're all alone in your dark house, you know you're all alone, you know that there is no chance anyone else is home or within miles – and then, suddenly, from upstairs, you hear the toilet flush."'

Christa smiled at Wendy. Wendy tried to smile back.

'Anyway, I wasn't scared. Maybe I should have been. Another what-if. What if I had just called the campus police? Well, it would have changed everything, wouldn't it have? I would be living an entirely different life. On that night, I was engaged to the most wonderful, handsome man. Now he's married to someone else. They have three kids. They're very happy. That'd be me, I guess.'

She took a sip of tea, holding the cup in both hands, letting that what-if roll over. 'So anyway, I heard the noise and headed toward it. I could hear whispers now, giggles even. Well, now I knew, didn't I? Students. If there had been any fear, it was gone now. It was just some mischief makers, playing a prank on the dean. Something like that. So I went up the stairs. It was silent now. Earlier the voices had sounded like they were coming from the dean's bedroom. So I headed that way. I entered the bedroom and looked around. I couldn't see anyone. I waited for my eyes to adjust to the dark. Then I thought, What are you doing? Just turn on the lights. So I reached for the light switch.'

Something caught in her voice. Christa Stockwell stopped talking. The scars on her face, the red ones, they seemed to darken. Wendy reached out again, but something in the way Christa stiffened made her pull up short.

'I don't even know what happened next. At least, I didn't then. I do now. But then, right then, well, simply put, I heard a loud crash and then my face exploded. That's what it felt like. Like a bomb had gone off on my face. I put my hands to my cheeks, and I could feel the jagged edge of glass there. I actually cut my hands. Blood was streaming down, going in my nose and mouth, choking me. I couldn't breathe. For a second, maybe two, there was no pain. And then it came in like a rush, like my face had been stripped raw. I screamed again and fell to the ground.'

Wendy felt her own pulse quicken. She wanted to ask questions, have her back up and offer up details, but she kept still, letting Christa tell the story in her own way.

'So I'm on the ground, screaming, and I hear someone run past. I reached out blindly and tripped him. He fell hard and cursed. I grabbed his leg. I'm not sure why. I was working by instinct more than anything else. And that was when he kicked out to get free.' Her voice dropped to a near whisper. 'See, I didn't realize it at the time but there were shards of glass – a shattered mirror – all in my face. So when he kicked to get free, his heel shoved the shards farther into my skin, slicing right down to the bone.' She swallowed. 'But the biggest shard was near my right eye. I might have lost the eye anyway, but that kick plunged the shard like a knife. . . .'

314

Mercifully she stopped right there.

'That's the last thing I remember. I passed out then. I didn't wake up for three days and when I did, well, I spent the next few weeks in and out of consciousness. There were constant surgeries. The pain was intolerable. I was pretty drugged up. But I'm getting ahead of myself. Let me go back a little. Campus police heard me scream that night. They caught Phil Turnball in the dean's front yard. My blood was all over his shoes. We all knew that other students were there too. See, there was a scavenger hunt. The dean's boxer shorts were a big prize. Sixty points. That's what Phil Turnball had been after – a pair of boxers. Like I said, a prank. Nothing more.'

'You said you heard others. Whispers and giggles.'

'Right, but Phil claimed that he'd been alone. His friends, of course, backed up that story. I was in no condition to counter what he said, and really, what did I know?'

'Phil took full blame?' Wendy asked.

'Yes.'

'Why?'

'I don't know.'

'I still don't understand. What did he do to you exactly? I mean, what caused all the cuts?'

'When I came in the room, Phil hid behind the bed. When he saw me reaching for the light switch, well, I guess the idea was to try to draw my attention away. A big glass ashtray got thrown near me. It was supposed to make noise so I'd turn and then Phil could run, I guess. But there was an antique mirror there. It shattered right into my face. Freak injury, right?'

Wendy said nothing.

'I spent three months in the hospital. I lost an eye. My other one was also severely damaged – the retina got severed. For a while I was totally blind. My sight came

315

back gradually in the one eye. I'm still legally blind, but I can make out enough. Everything is blurry and I have tremendous trouble with any sort of bright light – especially sunlight. Again, apropos, don't you think? According to the doctors, my face had literally been sliced off, piece by piece. I've seen early pictures. If you think this is bad . . . it looked like raw ground chuck. That's the only way I can describe it. Like a lion had eaten my face away.'

'I'm sorry,' Wendy said, because she didn't know what else to say.

'My fiancé, Marc, he was great. He stuck by me. I mean, he was heroic when you think about it. I had been beautiful. I can say that now. It doesn't sound immodest anymore. But I was. And he was so damn handsome. So Marc stuck by me. But he also kept diverting his gaze. It wasn't his fault. He hadn't signed up for this.'

Christa stopped.

'So what happened?'

'I made him go. You think you know love, right? But that's the day I learned what love really was. Even though it cut me deeper than any shard ever could, I loved Marc enough to make him go.'

She stopped again, took a sip of tea.

'You can probably guess the rest. Phil's family paid me to keep silent. A generous sum, I guess you'd say. It's in trust, paid out to me every week. If I speak about what happened, the payments stop.'

'I won't say anything.'

'Do you think that worries me?'

'I don't know.'

'It doesn't. I have pretty modest needs. I still live here. I kept working for Dean Slotnick, though not with his children. My face scared them. So I became his assistant.

When he died, Dean Pashaian was kind enough to keep me on. Now it's Dean Lewis. I mostly donate the money to various charities.'

Silence.

'So how does Dan fit into this?' Wendy asked.

'How do you think?'

'I assume he was in the house that night?'

'Yes. They all were. All five. I found out later.'

'How?'

'Dan told me.'

'And Phil took the fall for all of them?'

'Yes.'

'Any idea why?'

'He was a stand-up guy, I guess. But there might have been more. He was wealthy. The others weren't. Maybe he figured, what good would it do him to tell on his friends?'

That made sense, Wendy thought.

'So Dan visited you?'

'Yes.'

'Why?'

'To offer comfort. We talked. He felt horrible about that night. About running out. That was how it started. I was furious when he first came by. But we became friends. We talked for hours at this very table.'

'You said you were furious?'

'You have to understand. I lost everything that night.'

'Right, so you were justifiably angry.'

Christa smiled. 'Oh, I see.'

'What?'

'Let me guess. I was angry. I was furious. I hated them all. So I plotted my revenge. I, what, bided my time for twenty years and then I struck. Is that what you're thinking?'

Wendy shrugged. 'It is as though someone is paying them all back.'

'And I'm the most likely suspect? The scarred chick with the ax to grind?'

'Don't you think so?'

'Sounds like a bad horror movie, but I guess. . . .' She tilted her head again. 'Are you buying me as the bad guy, Wendy?'

Wendy shook her head. 'Not really, no.'

'And there is one other thing.'

'What?'

Christa spread her hands. She still had the sunglasses on, but a tear escaped from the one eye she had left. 'I forgave them.'

Silence.

'They were just college kids on a scavenger hunt. They never meant to hurt me.'

And there it was. There is such wisdom in the simple – a truth you can hear in the tone, unmistakable for anything else.

'You live in this world, you collide with others. That's the way it is. We collide and sometimes someone gets hurt. They just wanted to steal a silly pair of boxers. It went wrong. For a short time, I hated them. But when you think about it, what good does that do? It takes so much to hold on to hate – you lose your grip on what's important, you know?'

Wendy felt tears push into her eyes now. She picked up the tea and sipped it. The peppermint felt good sliding down her throat. Let the hate go. She couldn't reply to that.

'Maybe they hurt someone else that night,' Wendy said.

'I doubt it.'

318

'Or maybe someone else wants revenge for you.'

'My mother is dead,' Christa said. 'Marc is happily married to another woman. There is no one else.'

Dead end. 'What did Dan tell you when he first came?'

She smiled. 'That's between us.'

'There has to be a reason why they're all being ruined.'

'Is that the main reason why you're here, Wendy? To help them get their lives back?'

Wendy said nothing.

'Or,' Christa continued, 'are you here because you're worried that you inadvertently set up an innocent man?'

'Both, I guess.'

'You're hoping for absolution?'

'I'm hoping for answers.'

'Do you want my take on it?' Christa asked.

'Sure.'

'I got to know Dan pretty well.'

'Sounds like it.'

'We talked about everything at this table. He told me about his work, about meeting his first wife, Jenna, about how it was his fault the marriage didn't work, about how they remained close, about his loneliness. It was something we both shared.'

Wendy waited. Christa adjusted her sunglasses. For a moment Wendy thought that she was going to take them off, but she didn't. She adjusted them and it seemed as though she was trying somehow to look Wendy in the eye.

'I don't think Dan Mercer was a pedophile. And I don't think he killed anyone. So, yes, Wendy, I think you set up an innocent man.'

Chapter 33

Wendy blinked as she stepped out of the darkness of that kitchen and onto the lawn of the dean's house. She watched the students in the sunshine. They walked past this house every day, probably having no idea how thin the line was between them and the scarred woman in that house. Wendy stood there for another moment. She tilted her face up to the sun. She kept her eyes open, let them water from the rays. It felt damn good.

Christa Stockwell had forgiven those who hurt her.

She had made it sound so easy. Wendy pushed away the larger philosophical underpinnings – the obvious link to her own situation with Ariana Nasbro – to concentrate on the matter at hand: If the person most wronged had forgiven and moved on, who hadn't?

She checked her cell phone. More messages from reporters. She ignored them. There was a hang-up from Pops. She called him back. Pops answered on the first ring. 'A bunch of reporters keep stopping by,' he said.

'I know.'

'Now you know why I'm against gun control.'

For the first time in what seemed like forever, Wendy laughed.

'So what do they want?' he asked.

'Someone is spreading bad rumors about me.'

'Like?'

'Like I'm sleeping with my boss. Stuff like that.'

'And reporters give a crap about that stuff?'

'Apparently.'

'Any of them true?'

'No.'

'Damn.'

'Yeah. Could you do me a favor?'

'Rhetorical question,' Pops said.

'I'm in a pretty bad mess here. Some people may be after me.'

'And I'm heavily armed.'

'No need for that,' she said, hoping it wasn't true. 'But I want you to take Charlie somewhere for the next couple of days.'

'You think he's in danger?'

'I don't know. Either way these rumors will start rippling through town. The kids in school may give him a hard time.'

'So what? Charlie can take a little razzing. He's a strong kid.'

'I don't want him to be strong right now.'

'Yeah, okay, I'll take care of it. We'll stay at a motel, okay?'

'Someplace decent, Pops. Nothing with hourly rates or mirrored ceilings.'

'Got it, no worries. If you need my help—'

'Goes without saying,' Wendy said.

'Okay, take care. I love you.'

'I love you too.'

When they hung up, she called Vic again. Still no answer. Bastard was starting to piss her off. So where to now? Well, now she knew the secret of the Princeton Five, but she still didn't have a clue why it had come back after twenty years. There was, of course, one person to ask.

Phil.

She tried his phone again. Waste of time. So she drove straight to his house. Sherry answered the door. 'He's not here.'

'Did you know?' Wendy asked.

Sherry said nothing.

'About Princeton. Did you know what happened there?'

'Not for a long time.'

Wendy was going to ask a follow-up, but she stopped herself. It didn't matter when or what Sherry knew. She needed to talk to Phil. 'Where is he?'

'With the Fathers Club.'

'Don't warn him I'm coming, okay?' Carrot and stick time again. Well, stick time anyway. 'If you do, it will just mean I'll have to come back to your house. And the next time I'll be angry. I will bring cameras and other reporters and make enough noise to attract your neighbors and even your kids. Do you get my meaning?'

'You're not exactly being obtuse,' Sherry said.

Wendy didn't relish threatening this woman, but enough with the lies and getting jerked around.

'Don't worry,' Sherry said. 'I won't call him.'

Wendy turned to leave.

'One thing,' Sherry said.

'What?'

'He's fragile. Be careful, okay?'

Wendy wanted to add something about Christa Stockwell, how fragile her flesh had been, but it wasn't her place. She drove over to the Starbucks and pulled into a spot that required 'Quarters Only' for the meter. She didn't have any. Too bad. Again she'd live life on the edge.

She felt on the verge of tears again. She stopped at the door of Starbucks and gathered herself.

They were all there. Norm, aka Ten-A-Fly, was in full rap-wannabe gear. Doug had on his tennis whites. Owen had the baby. Phil was in the suit and tie. Even now. Even at this hour. They were all huddled over a round table, leaning in and whispering. Their body language, Wendy could see, was all wrong.

When Phil spotted her, his face fell. His eyes closed. She didn't care. She made her way to the table and glared down at him. He seemed to deflate in front of her eyes.

'I just talked to Christa Stockwell,' she said.

The rest of the guys just watched in silence. Wendy met Norm's eye. He shook his head, asking her to stop. She didn't.

'They're going after me now too,' Wendy said to him.

'We know,' Norm said. 'We've been following the cyber-rumors online. We've managed to get rid of a lot of the viral sites but not all of them.'

'So it's my battle too now.'

'It doesn't have to be.' Phil still had his head down. 'I warned you. I begged you to stay out of it.'

'And I didn't listen. My bad. Now tell me what's going on.'

'No.'

'No?'

Phil rose to his feet. He started for the door. Wendy blocked his path.

'Get out of my way,' he said.

'No.'

'You talked to Christa Stockwell?'

'Yes.'

323

'What did she tell you?'

Wendy hesitated. Hadn't she promised Christa not to say anything? Phil used the moment to scoot around Wendy. He headed for the door. Wendy started for him, but Norm stopped her with a hand on her shoulder. She turned angrily toward him.

'What are you going to do, Wendy? Tackle him on the street?'

'You don't have a clue what I learned.'

'He got expelled from Princeton,' Norm said. 'He never graduated. We know. He told us.'

'Did he tell you what he did?'

'Do you think it matters?'

That stopped her. She thought about what Christa said, about forgiving them, about them just being kids on a scavenger hunt.

'Did he tell you who is after them?' she asked.

'No. But he asked us to stay out of it. We're his friends, Wendy. Our loyalty is to him, not you. And I think he's suffered enough, don't you?'

'I don't know, Norm. I don't know who is after him and his old roommates – and now me. And more than that, I don't even know whether Dan Mercer killed Haley McWaid. Maybe her killer is still out there. Do you get what I'm saying?'

'I do.'

'And?'

'And our friend asked us to stay out of it. It's not our fight anymore.'

'Fine.'

Fuming, she started for the door.

'Wendy?'

She turned back to him. He looked so ridiculous in that getup, the damn black cap over a red bandana, the white belt, the wristwatch with a face the size of a satellite dish. Ten-A-Fly. For crying out loud. 'What, Norm?'

'We do have that photograph.'

'What photograph?'

'The still of the girl in the video. The hooker who accused Farley Parks of soliciting her. Owen was able to freeze the screen and enhance it around the shadow. It wasn't easy, but he got a pretty clear picture. We have it, if you want it.'

She waited. Owen handed the eight-by-ten to Norm. Norm brought it to her. She looked down at the girl in the photograph.

Norm said, 'She looks young, don't you think?'

Wendy's world, already wobbly, teetered off its axis.

Yes, the girl in the photograph did look young. Very young.

She also looked exactly like the artist sketch of Chynna, the girl Dan claimed that he was supposed to meet at the sting house.

So now she knew. The photograph was the kicker. Someone had set them up.

But still no why or who.

When Wendy got home, there was only one news van still parked outside. She couldn't believe what station it belonged to. The damn nerve – it was from her own network. NTC. Sam, her cameraman, stood outside with – deep breaths – the balloon-headed Michele Feisler.

Michele was fixing her hair. The NTC microphone was jammed into the crook of her arm. Wendy was tempted to veer her car to the right and take her out, watch that big melon head splatter onto the curb. Instead she hit the automatic garage door and headed inside. The electric door slid closed behind her and she stepped out.

'Wendy?'

It was Michele. She knocked on the garage door.

'Get off my property, Michele.'

'There's no camera or microphone. It's just me.'

'My friend inside has a gun that he's dying to use.'

'Just listen to me a second, okay?'

'No.'

'You need to hear this. It's about Vic.'

That made her pause. 'What about Vic?'

'Open the door, Wendy.'

'What about Vic?'

'He's selling you out.'

Her stomach dropped. 'What do you mean?'

'Open the door, Wendy. No cameras, no microphones, all off the record. I promise.'

Damn. She debated what to do, but really, what was the harm? She wanted to know what Michele had to say. If it meant letting Blockhead into her house, so be it. She stepped over Charlie's bike – conveniently abandoned, as always, to block her access – and turned the knob. Unlocked. Charlie always forgot to lock it.

'Wendy?'

'Come around back.'

She entered the kitchen. Pops was gone. He'd left a note that he'd picked up Charlie. Good. She opened the back door for Michele.

'Thanks for letting me in.'

'So what's this about Vic?'

'The brass want blood. They came down hard on him.'

'So?'

'So Vic is being pressured big-time to say you hit on him – to imply that you're somewhat obsessed with him.'

Wendy didn't move.

'The station released this statement.'

Michele handed her a piece of a paper.

We at NTC have no comment on the matter of Wendy Tynes though we would like to make it very clear that our news manager Victor Garrett did nothing illegal or unethical and has refused any and all advances made in his direction by any person in his employ. Stalking is a serious problem in this country today, and there are many innocent victims made to suffer.

'Stalking?' Wendy looked up. 'Is this for real?'

'Nicely done, don't you think? Couched in enough vagaries so that no one can sue.'

'So what do you want, Michele? You don't really think I'm going to go on air, do you?'

Michele shook her head. 'You're not that stupid.'

'So why are you here?'

She took back the statement and held it up. 'This isn't right. We aren't good friends. I know how you feel about me. . . .' Michele pursed her over-glossed lips and closed her eyes, as though weighing her next sentence in her mind.

'Do you believe this statement?'

The eyes snapped open. 'No! I mean, come on. You? Stalking Vic? Gag me with a soup ladle.'

Right then, if Wendy hadn't been so stunned and emotionally raw, she might have hugged Michele.

'I know it's corny, but I became a reporter because I wanted to find truths. And this is crap. You're being set up. So I wanted to let you know what the deal was.'

Wendy said, 'Wow.'

'What?'

'Nothing. I'm surprised, I guess.'

'I have always admired you, the way you handle yourself, the way you cover a story. I know how that sounds, but it's true.'

Wendy just stood there. 'I don't know what to say.'

'Nothing to say. If you need any help, I'm here for you. That's all. I'm going now. We're covering that story I told you about – the perv Arthur Lemaine who had both knees shot.'

'A new development?'

'Not really. The guy hopefully got what he deserved, but it's still pretty amazing – a convicted child pornographer coaching a kids' hockey team.'

Wendy felt the hair stand up on the back of her neck. Hockey?

She remembered now watching the story with Charlie and his friends. 'Wait, he was shot in front of South Mountain Arena, right?'

'Right.'

'But I don't get it. I remembered reading that the arena does background checks on the coaches.'

Michele nodded. 'Yes. But in Lemaine's case, the convictions didn't show up.'

'Why not?'

'Because the background checks only turn up crimes committed on U.S. soil,' Michele said. 'But see, Lemaine is Canadian. From Quebec, I think.'

Chapter 34

It didn't take Wendy long to put it together.

Michele Feisler helped. She already had plenty of background on sex criminal Arthur Lemaine, including a family tree. Wendy was impressed with the work Michele had put in already. And okay, maybe Michele's head was a little on the large side, but that was probably accentuated by the fact that she had really narrow shoulders.

'What now?' Michele asked her.

'I think we should get in touch with Sheriff Walker. He's in charge of the Dan Mercer murder.'

'Okay, why don't you make the call? You know him.'

Wendy found Walker's cell phone number and hit send. Michele sat next to her. She dutifully took out her little reporter pad, pen poised. Walker answered on the fourth ring. Wendy heard him clear his voice and say, 'Sheriff Mickey Walker.'

'It's Wendy.'

'Oh, uh, hi. How are you?'

Oh, uh, hi? His voice sounded stiff. And now that Wendy thought of it, wouldn't he have seen it was her on his caller ID?

'I see you've heard those new stories about me,' Wendy said.

'Yep.'

'Super.' This was not the time to go into it. It didn't matter anyway – screw him, right? – but she still felt the pang. 'Have you heard about this case of Arthur Lemaine? The guy who got shot in both kneecaps?'

'Yes,' he said. 'But it's not my jurisdiction.'

'Did you hear that Arthur Lemaine is a convicted child pornographer?'

'I think I heard that, yes.'

'Did you also hear that Arthur Lemaine is Ed Grayson's brother-in-law?'

There was a brief pause. Then Walker said, 'Whoa.'

'Whoa indeed. Want more whoa? Lemaine coached his nephew's hockey team. For those who aren't good at family trees, that would be E. J., Ed Grayson's son, the victim of child pornography.'

'That is another whoa,' Walker agreed.

'And – maybe "whoa" here – whoever shot Lemaine's knees did so from a distance.'

'The work of an expert marksman,' Walker said.

'Isn't that what the owner of the Gun-O-Rama said about Grayson?'

'He did indeed. My God. But I don't get it. I thought you saw Grayson kill Dan Mercer because Mercer took the pictures of his son.'

'I did.'

'So he shot both guys?'

'Well, yes, I think so. Remember how Ed Grayson showed up at Ringwood State Park to help find Haley McWaid's body?'

'Yes.'

'He said I didn't get it. But I think I do now. The guilt is haunting him, because he killed an innocent man.'

Michele was steadily taking notes – on what, Wendy couldn't imagine.

'Here is how I think it went,' Wendy continued. 'Dan Mercer is freed. Ed Grayson goes nuts. He kills Mercer and gets rid of the evidence. When he gets home, his wife, Maggie, sees what he's done. I don't know what happens then exactly. Maybe Maggie freaks out. Maybe she says, "What did you do, it wasn't Dan, it was my brother." Or maybe E. J. now tells him the truth about his uncle. I don't know. But imagine what must have gone through Grayson's mind. For months he has shown up at every hearing, talking to the media, putting a face to the victims, demanding that Dan Mercer be punished.'

'And then he finds out that he killed the wrong guy.'

'Right. Plus he now knows that Arthur Lemaine, his brother-in-law, will never be brought to justice. And if he is somehow brought to trial, well, that might destroy his family.'

'The scandal of that,' Walker said. 'Putting his family through it all again. Having to admit to the world that he'd been wrong this whole time. So, what, Grayson maims him instead?'

'Yes. I don't think he was strong enough to murder again. Not after what happened the first time.'

'And like it or not, it's his wife's brother.'

'Right.'

Wendy looked across the table at Michele. She was on her cell now, talking low into the phone.

Walker said, 'Word is, Grayson's wife left him. She took the kid.'

'Maybe it was because of what he did to Dan.'

'Or maybe because he shot her brother.'

'Right.'

Walker sighed. 'So how do we prove any of this?'

'I don't know. Lemaine probably isn't going to talk, but maybe you guys can push him.'

331

'Even so. He was shot in the dark. No other witnesses. And we already know that Grayson is damn good about getting rid of evidence.'

They sat in silence. Michele hung up. She took some more notes, drew big long arrows. She stopped, looked at the pad, and frowned.

Wendy asked, 'What is it?'

Michele started writing again. 'I'm not sure yet. But there's something wrong with this theory.'

'What?'

'It might not be a big deal but the timeline is off. Lemaine was shot the day before Dan Mercer.'

Wendy's phone vibrated. Call waiting. She checked the incoming number. It was Win. 'I have to go,' she said to Walker. 'Another call coming.'

'I'm sorry about my tone before.'

'Don't worry about it.'

'I still want to call you when this is over.'

She tried not to smile. 'When this is over,' she repeated. Then she clicked over to the other line. 'Hello?'

'Per your request,' Win said, 'I looked into the matter of Phil Turnball's termination.'

'Do you know who set him up?'

'Where are you?'

'Home.'

'Come to my office. I think you may need to see this.'

Win was rich. Superrich.

Example: 'Win' was short for Windsor *Horne* Lockwood III. His office was located on Forty-sixth Street and Park Avenue in the *Lock-Horne* high-rise.

You do the math.

Wendy parked in the lot in the MetLife Building. Her father had worked not far from here. She thought about him now, the way he always rolled up his sleeves to the elbow, the act doubly symbolic – he was always ready to pitch in and never wanted to be thought of as a suit. Her father had tremendous forearms. He made her feel safe. Right now, even though he'd been dead for years, she wanted to collapse in her father's big arms and hear him tell her that everything would be all right. Do we ever outgrow that need? John had done that too – made Wendy feel safe. That may seem antifeminist – this warm feeling of security coming from a man – but there it was. Pops was great, but this wasn't his job. Charlie, well, he would always be her little boy and it would always be her job to take care of him, not the other way around. The two men who had made her feel safe were both dead. They had never failed her, but now, with all the trouble swirling around her, she wondered whether a little voice wasn't whispering that she had failed them.

Win had moved his office down a floor. The elevator opened up to a sign reading MB REPS. The receptionist said in a high-pitched squeal: 'Welcome, Ms. Tynes.'

Wendy nearly stepped back into the elevator. The receptionist was the size of an NFL nose tackle. She was squeezed into a coal black unitard that was like the nightmare version of Adrienne Barbeau's in *Cannonball Run*. Her makeup looked as though it had been layered on with a snow shovel.

'Uh, hi.'

An Asian woman in a tailored white suit appeared. She was tall and slender and model attractive. These two women stood next to each other for a moment, and Wendy couldn't help but picture a bowling ball about to crash into a pin.

The Asian woman said, 'Mr. Lockwood is waiting for you.'

Wendy followed her down the corridor. The woman opened the office door and said, 'Ms. Tynes is here.'

Win rose from behind his desk. He was a remarkably good-looking man. Though he was not really her type, what with the blond locks, the almost delicate features, the whole pretty-boy persona, there was a quiet strength there, an ice in his blue eyes, a coil in his almost too-still body, as though he might make a deadly strike at any moment.

Win spoke to the Asian woman. 'Thank you, Mee. Would you mind telling Mr. Barry that we're ready?'

'Of course.'

Mee left. Win crossed the room and bussed Wendy's cheek. There was that small delay, that awkward hesitation. Six months ago, they had knocked boots and it had been beyond awesome and pretty-boy features or not, that always stays in a room.

'You look spectacular.'

'Thank you. I don't feel it.'

'I gather that you're going through a rough spell.'

'I am.'

Win sat back down, spread his arms. 'I'm willing to offer comfort and support.'

'And by comfort and support, you mean . . . ?'

Win made his eyebrows dance. 'Coitus with no inter-ruptus.'

She shook her head in amazement. 'You're picking the worst time to hit on me.'

'No such thing. But I understand. Would you care for a brandy?'

'No thanks.'

'Do you mind if I have one?'

'Suit yourself.'

Win had an antique globe that opened up to reveal a

crystal decanter. His desk was thick cherrywood. There were paintings of men on a foxhunt and a rich Oriental carpet. An artificial putting green covered the far corner. A big-screen TV hung on one wall. 'So tell me what this is about,' Win said.

'Is it okay if I don't? I really just need to know who set up Phil Turnball.'

'Of course.'

The office door opened. Mee entered with an old man wearing a bow tie.

'Ah,' Win said. 'Ridley, thank you for coming. Wendy Tynes, meet Ridley Barry. Mr. Barry is the cofounder of Barry Brothers Trust, your Mr. Turnball's former employer.'

'Nice to meet you, Wendy.'

Everyone sat. Win's desk was clear except for one huge pile of what looked like files. 'Before we begin,' Win said, 'Mr. Barry and I both need to know that nothing we discuss here will leave this room.'

'I'm a reporter, Win.'

'Then you'd be familiar with the phrase "off the record."'

'Fine. It's off the record.'

'And,' Win said, 'as a friend, I want your word that you won't divulge anything we say to anyone else.'

She looked at Ridley Barry, then slowly back toward Win. 'You have my word.'

'Fine.' Win looked toward Ridley Barry. Mr. Barry nodded. Win put his hand on the tall pile. 'These are the files on Mr. Phil Turnball. He was, as you know, a financial adviser for Barry Brothers Trust.'

'Yes, I know.'

'I spent the last several hours going through them. I took my time. I also examined the computer trades made by Mr. Turnball. I studied his trading patterns, his buying

335

and selling – his ins and outs, if you will. Because I hold you in high regard, Wendy, and respect your intelligence, I diligently scrutinized his work history with an eye toward how Phil Turnball may have been set up.'

'And?'

Win met her eyes, and Wendy felt the cold gust. 'Phil Turnball did not steal two million dollars. My estimate would be that the number is closer to three. In short, there is no doubt. You wanted to know how Turnball was set up. He wasn't. Phil Turnball orchestrated a fraud that dates back at least five years.'

Wendy shook her head. 'Maybe it wasn't him. He didn't work in a vacuum, did he? He had partners and an assistant. Maybe one of them . . .'

Still meeting her eye, Win picked up a remote control and pressed the button. The television came on.

'Mr. Barry was also kind enough to let me go through the surveillance tapes.'

The TV screen lit up to reveal an office. The camera had been placed up high, shooting downward. Phil Turnball was feeding documents into a shredder.

'This is your Mr. Turnball destroying his clients' account statements before they get mailed out.'

Win hit the remote. The screen jumped. Now Phil was at his desk. He stood and moved toward a printer. 'Here is Mr. Turnball printing out the fake replacement statements, which he will subsequently mail out. We could go on and on here, Wendy. But there is no doubt. Phil Turnball defrauded his clients and Mr. Barry.'

Wendy sat back. She turned to Ridley Barry. 'If Phil is this big-time thief, why hasn't he been arrested?'

For a moment, no one said anything. Ridley Barry looked toward Win. Win nodded. 'Go ahead. She won't tell.'

He cleared his throat and adjusted his bow tie. He was a small man, wizened, the kind of old man some might call endearing or cute. 'My brother Stanley and I founded Barry Brothers Trust more than forty years ago,' he began. 'We worked side-by-side for thirty-seven years. In the same room. Our desks faced each other. Every single working day. The two of us managed to build a business with gross outsets that exceed a billion dollars. We employ more than two hundred people. Our name is on the masthead. I take that responsibility very seriously – especially now that my brother is gone.'

He stopped, looked down at his watch.

'Mr. Barry?'

'Yes.'

'This is all very sweet, but why isn't Phil Turnball being prosecuted if he stole from you?'

'He didn't steal from me. He stole from his clients. My clients too.'

'Whatever.'

'No, not "whatever." That's much more than a question of semantics. But let me answer it two ways. Let me answer as, first, a cold businessman and, second, as an old man who believes that he is responsible for his clients' well-being. The cold businessman: In this post-Madoff environment, what do you think will happen to Barry Brothers Trust if it gets out that one of our top financial advisers ran a Ponzi scheme?'

The answer was obvious, and Wendy wondered why she didn't see that before. Funny. Phil had used that question to his advantage, hadn't he? He kept using that as proof he'd been set up – 'Why haven't they arrested me?'

'On the other hand,' he went on, 'the old man feels responsible to those who put their trust in him and his

337

company. So I'm going through the accounts myself. I will reimburse all clients from my personal finances. In short, I will take the hit. The clients who were defrauded will be compensated in full.'

'And will be kept in the dark,' Wendy said.

'Yes.'

Which was why Win had sworn her to secrecy. She sat back and suddenly more pieces came together. Lots of them.

She knew now. She knew most of it – maybe all of it.

'Anything else?' Win asked.

'How did you catch him?' she asked.

Ridley Barry shifted in his seat. 'You can only keep up a Ponzi scheme for so long.'

'No, I get that. But what made you first start looking into him?'

'Two years ago, I hired a firm to examine the background of all our employees. This was a routine thing, nothing more, but a discrepancy in Phil Turnball's personal file came to our attention.'

'What discrepancy?'

'Phil lied on his résumé.'

'About?'

'About his education. He said he graduated from Princeton University. That wasn't true.'

Chapter 35

So now she knew.

Wendy called Phil's cell phone. Once again there was no answer. She tried his home. Nothing. On the way back from Win's office, she stopped at his home in Englewood. No one was there. She tried the Starbucks. The Fathers Club was gone.

She debated calling Walker or maybe, more likely, Frank Tremont. He was the one who handled the case of Haley McWaid. There was a good chance that Dan Mercer had not killed Haley. She thought that maybe she now knew who did, but it was still speculation.

After Ridley Barry left his office, Wendy had run it all by Win. There were two reasons for this. One, she wanted an intelligent outside ear and opinion. Win could provide that. But, two, she wanted someone else to know what she knew as, well, backup – to protect both the information and herself.

When she finished, Win opened his bottom drawer. He pulled out several handguns and offered her one. She declined.

Charlie and Pops were still gone. The house was silent. She thought about next year, Charlie gone to college, the house always this still. She didn't like it – the thought of being alone in a house like that. Might be time to down-size.

Her throat was parched. She downed a full glass of water and refilled the glass. She headed upstairs, sat down, and flipped on the computer. Might as well start testing out her theory. She did the Google searches in reverse-Princeton-scandal order: Steve Miciano, Farley Parks, Dan Mercer, Phil Turnball.

It made sense to her now.

She then Googled herself, read the reports on her 'sexually inappropriate' behavior, and shook her head. She wanted to cry, not for herself, but for all of them.

Had this all really started with a college scavenger hunt?

'Wendy?'

She should have been scared, but she wasn't. It just reconfirmed what she already knew. She turned around. Phil Turnball stood in her doorway.

'Other people know,' she said.

Phil smiled. His face had that shine from too much drink. 'You think I mean to hurt you?'

'Haven't you already?'

'I guess that's true. But that's not why I'm here.'

'How did you get in?'

'The garage was open.'

Charlie and that damn bike. She wasn't sure what the right move was here. She could try to be subtle, hit her cell phone, dial 9-1-1 or something. She could try to send an e-mail, an electronic SOS of some kind.

'Don't be afraid,' he said.

'Do you mind if I call a friend then?'

'I'd rather you didn't.'

'And if I insist?'

Phil took out a gun. 'I have no intention of hurting you.'

Wendy froze. When a gun comes out, it becomes the

340

only thing you see. She swallowed, tried to stay strong. 'Hey, Phil?'

'What?'

'Nothing says you have no intention of hurting someone better than whipping out a handgun.'

'We need to talk,' Phil said. 'But I'm just not sure where to start.'

'How about how you kicked that mirror shard into Christa Stockwell's eye?'

'You really have done your homework, haven't you, Wendy?'

She said nothing.

'You're right too. That is where it began.' He sighed. The gun hung down by his thigh. 'You know what happened though, don't you? I was hiding and then Christa Stockwell screamed. I ran for the door, but she tripped me and grabbed my leg. I never meant to hurt her. I was just trying to get away, and I panicked.'

'You were in the dean's house because of a scavenger hunt?'

'We all were.'

'Yet you took the fall alone.'

For a moment Phil looked off, lost. She considered making a run for it. He wasn't pointing the gun at her. It might be her best chance. But Wendy didn't move. She just sat there until he finally said, 'Yes, that's true.'

'Why?'

'It seemed like the right thing to do at the time. You see, I came into that school with every advantage. Wealth, family name, a prep school education. The others struggled and scraped. I was drawn to that. They were my friends. Besides, I was going to get in trouble anyway – why drag them into it?'

'Admirable,' Wendy said.

'Of course, I didn't know the extent of the trouble I was in. It was dark in the house. I thought Christa was just screaming out of fear. I had no idea when I confessed that she'd been hurt that badly.' He cocked his head to the right. 'I like to think that I still would have done the same thing. Taken the hit for my friends, that is. But I don't know.'

She tried to glance at the computer, tried to see if there was something she could click to get help. 'So what happened then?'

'You know already, don't you?'

'You were expelled.'

'Yes.'

'And your parents paid Christa Stockwell for her silence.'

'My parents were aghast. But maybe, I don't know, maybe I knew they would be. They paid my debt and then told me to go away. They gave the family business to my brother. I was out. But again maybe that was a good thing.'

'You felt free,' Wendy said.

'Yes.'

'You were now like your roommates. The guys you admired.'

He smiled. 'Exactly. And so, like them, I struggled and scraped. I refused any help. I got a job with Barry Brothers. I put together a client list, worked hard to keep everyone happy. I married Sherry, a spectacular woman in every way. We made a family. Beautiful kids, nice house. All on my own. No nepotism, no help . . .'

His voice drifted off. He smiled.

'What?'

'You, Wendy.'

'What about me?'

342

'Here we are, the two of us. I have a gun. I'm telling you all about my nefarious deeds. You're asking questions to stall me, hoping for the police to arrive just in the nick of time.'

She said nothing.

'But I'm not here for me, Wendy. I'm here for you.'

She looked at his face, and suddenly, despite the gun and the situation, the fear left her. 'How so?' she asked.

'You'll see.'

'I'd rather—'

'You want the answers, don't you?'

'I guess.'

'So where was I?'

'Married, job, no nepotism.'

'Right, thank you. You said you met Ridley Barry?'

'Yes.'

'Nice old man, right? Very charming. He comes across as honest. And he is. I was too.' He looked down at the gun in his hand as though it had just materialized out of thin air. 'You don't start off as a thief. I bet even Bernie Madoff didn't. You're doing the best you can for your clients. But it's a cutthroat world. You make a bad trade. You lose some money. But you know you'll get it back. So you move some other money into that account. Just for a day, maybe a week. When the next trade comes in, you'll make it up and then some. It isn't stealing. In the end, your clients will be better off. You just start small like that, a little crossing of the line – but then what can you do about it? If you admit what you've done, you're ruined. You'll get fired or go to jail. So what other choice do you have? You have to keep borrowing from Peter to pay Paul and hope that something will click, some Hail Mary pass will work, so you can get out from under.'

'Bottom line,' Wendy said, 'you stole from your clients?'

'Yes.'

'Gave yourself a decent salary?'

'It was part of keeping up appearances.'

'Right,' Wendy said. 'I see.'

Phil smiled. 'You're right, of course. I'm just trying to give you the mind frame, justified or not. Did Ridley tell you why they first started looking at me?'

She nodded. 'You lied on your résumé.'

'Right. That night in the dean's house – it came back to haunt me again. All of a sudden, because of what happened all those years ago, my whole world began to disintegrate. Can you imagine how I felt? I took the fall for those guys, even though I wasn't really to blame, and now, well, after all these years, I was still suffering.'

'What do you mean, you weren't to blame?'

'Just what I said.'

'You were there. You kicked Christa Stockwell in the face.'

'That's not what started it. Did she tell you about the ashtray?'

'Yes. You threw it.'

'Did she tell you that?'

Wendy thought about it. She had assumed, but had Christa Stockwell actually said it was Phil?

'It wasn't me,' he said. 'Someone else threw an ashtray at her. That's what shattered the mirror.'

'You didn't know who?'

He shook his head. 'The other guys who were there that night all denied it was them. That's what I meant about not being to blame. And now I had nothing again. When my parents heard about my firing, well, that was the final blow. They disowned me entirely. Sherry and

344

my kids – they started looking at me differently. I was lost. I was at rock bottom – all because of that damned scavenger hunt. So I went to my old roommates for help. Farley and Steve, they were grateful to me for taking the fall, they said, but what could they do about it now? I started thinking, I shouldn't have taken that hit alone. If all five of us had come forward, we could have shared the load. I wouldn't be alone in this. The school would have gone easier on me. And I'm looking at them, my old friends who won't help, and they're all doing great now, all well-off and successful. . . .'

'So,' Wendy said, 'you decided to take them down a peg.'

'Do you blame me? I'm the only one who paid a price for what happened, and now it was like I was finished in their eyes. Done. Like I wasn't worth saving. My family was rich, they said. Ask them for help.'

Phil couldn't escape his family, Wendy thought – their wealth, their position. He could want to be like his struggling friends, but he was never really one of them in their eyes – because when push came to shove, he simply didn't belong with the poor any more than they belonged with the rich.

'You learned about viral marketing from the Fathers Club,' she said.

'Yes.'

'That should have tipped me off. I just looked again. Farley was trashed. Steve was trashed. I was trashed. And there was already enough about Dan online. But you, Phil. There isn't a word about your embezzling crimes online. Why? If someone was out to get all of you, why didn't he blog about your stealing from the company? In fact, nobody knew about it. You told the Fathers Club that you were laid off. It wasn't until my friend Win informed me that you'd actually been fired for stealing two million dollars that you suddenly opened up about it. And when you knew I was down at Princeton, you even got in front of that one too – telling the guys you got expelled.'

'All true,' Phil said.

'So let's get to your setups. First, you got some girl to play Chynna, Dan's teenage girl, and Farley's hooker.'

'That's right.'

'Where did you find her?'

'She's just a hooker I hired to play two roles. It wasn't all that complicated. As for Steve Miciano, well, how hard is it to plant drugs in a man's trunk and tell the police to take a look? And Dan . . .'

'You used me,' Wendy said.

'It was nothing personal. One night I saw your TV show and figured, wow, what better way to get back at someone?'

'How did you do it?'

'What was so complicated about it, Wendy? I wrote that first e-mail from Ashlee, the thirteen-year-old girl in the SocialTeen room. Then I posed as Dan in the room. I hid the photographs and the laptop in his house when I visited him. My hooker pretended to be a troubled teen named Chynna. When you told me in my online persona as "pedophile Dan"' – he made quote marks with his fingers – 'to show up at a particular time and place, Chynna simply asked Dan to meet her at the same time and place. Dan showed up, your cameras were rolling . . .' He shrugged.

'Wow,' she said.

'I'm sorry you got involved. And I'm even sorrier I started all those rumors about you. I went too far there. That was a mistake. I feel terrible about that. That's why I'm here now. To make it up to you.'

346

He kept saying that – that part about being here for her. It was maddening. 'So you did all that,' she said, 'you went after all these guys, just for revenge?'

He lowered his head. His answer surprised her. 'No.'

'Don't be easy on yourself, Phil. You lost everything, so you decided to take down the innocent with you.'

'The innocent?' For the first time, anger crept into his voice. 'They weren't innocent.'

'You mean because of what they did that night at the dean's house.'

'No, that's not what I mean. I mean, because they were guilty.'

Wendy made a face. 'Guilty of what?'

'Don't you get it? Farley did sleep with hookers. He was a horrible womanizer. Everyone knew. And Steve did use his standing as a medical doctor to illegally sell and dispense prescription drugs. Ask the cops. They couldn't nail him for it. But they knew. See, I didn't set them up. I exposed them.'

There was silence now, a deep hum, and Wendy felt her body shake. They were coming to it now. He waited, knowing that she would prompt him.

'And what about Dan?' Wendy asked.

His breathing got a little funny. He tried to get himself under control, but the past was coming at him fast now. 'That's why I'm here, Wendy.'

'I don't understand. You just said Farley was a womanizer and that Steve was a drug pusher.'

'Yes.'

'So I'm asking the obvious question – was Dan Mercer really a pedophile?'

'Do you want the truth?'

'No, Phil, after all this I want you to lie to me. Did you set him up so he could be brought to justice?'

'With Dan,' he said slowly, 'I guess nothing went as planned.'

'Please stop with the semantics. Was he a pedophile, yes or no?'

He looked to the left and summoned up something inside him. 'I don't know.'

That was not the answer she'd been expecting. 'How can that be?'

'When I set him up, I didn't think he was. But now, I'm not so sure.'

The answer made her head spin. 'What the hell does that mean?'

'I told you I went to Farley and Steve,' he said. 'And that they weren't interested in helping me.'

'Yes.'

'Then I went to Dan.' Phil lifted the gun, switched it to his other hand.

'How did he react?'

'We sat in his crappy house. I mean, I didn't even know why I bothered. What could he do? He had absolutely no money. He worked with the poor. So Dan asked me if I wanted a beer. I took one. Then I told him what had happened to me. He listened with a sympathetic ear. When I finished Dan looked me in the eye and said he was so glad I came by. Why, I asked him. He told me how he'd visited Christa Stockwell all these years. I was shocked. And then he told me the final truth.'

Wendy saw it now – what Christa Stockwell had kept from her.

'What did Dan tell you when he first came?'

'That's between us.'

Wendy looked up at him. 'Dan threw the ashtray.'

Phil nodded. 'He saw me duck down behind the bed. The other guys – Farley, Steve, and Kelvin – they had

348

started sneaking out already. They were halfway down the stairs by the time Christa Stockwell started reaching for that light switch. Dan just wanted to distract her. Give me a chance to run. So he threw the ashtray.'

'And it smashed the mirror into her face.'

'Yes.'

She imagined the moment. She imagined Dan confessing and Christa merely accepting it. They were college kids on a scavenger hunt, after all. Was it all that easy to forgive? For Christa, maybe it was.

'And all these years,' Wendy said, 'you never knew.'

'I never knew. Dan lied about it. He tried to explain why. He was a poor kid, he said. He was on scholarship and scared. It wouldn't help me anyway. It would just destroy him – and for what?'

'So he kept quiet.'

'Like the others, he figured I had money. I had family and connections. I could pay off Christa Stockwell. So he never said a word. He just let me take the fall for what he'd done. So you see, Wendy, Dan wasn't so innocent. In fact, in many ways, he was the guiltiest of all.'

She thought about it, about the rage Phil must have felt when he learned that he had paid for the crime committed by Dan.

'But he wasn't a child molester, was he?'

Phil thought about that one. 'I didn't think so, no. At least, I didn't at first.'

She tried to sort through it, tried to make sense of it. And then she remembered Haley McWaid.

'My God, Phil. What did you do?'

'Those guys are right. I'm done. Whatever else was left of me – whatever good was there – it's gone now too. That's what revenge does to you. It eats away at your soul. I should have never opened that door.'

349

Wendy didn't know what door he meant anymore – the one to the dean's house all those years ago or the one to the hatred that made him seek revenge. Wendy remembered what Christa Stockwell had said about hatred, how holding on to it makes you let go of everything else.

But they still weren't done. There was still the matter of Haley McWaid.

'So when Dan got off,' Wendy began, 'I mean, when the judge let him go . . .'

The smile on his face chilled her. 'Go on, Wendy.'

But she couldn't. She tried to follow it, but suddenly none of it made sense.

'You're wondering about Haley McWaid, aren't you? You're wondering how she fits in.'

Wendy couldn't speak.

'Go on, Wendy. Say what you were going to say.'

But she saw it now. It made no sense.

His expression was calmer now, almost serene. 'I hurt them, yes. Did I break the law? I'm not even sure. I hired a girl to lie about Farley and play a part with Dan. Is that a crime? A misdemeanor maybe. I pretended I was someone else in a chat room – but isn't that what you do? You said that the judge let Dan go. That's true, but so what? I wasn't necessarily trying to send them to jail. I just wanted them to suffer. And they did, didn't they?'

He waited for an answer. Wendy managed a nod.

'So why then would I set him up for murder?'

'I don't know,' she managed.

Phil leaned forward and whispered, 'I didn't.'

Wendy couldn't breathe. She tried to slow it down, think it through, take a step back somehow. Haley McWaid had been murdered three months before she was found. Why? Did Wendy think, what, that Phil had killed her

350

just in case Dan got off so Phil could pin it on him?

Did that make sense?

'Wendy, I'm a father. I couldn't kill a teenage girl. I couldn't kill anyone.'

It was, she realized, a huge leap between viral trashing and murder, between getting back at some old classmates and killing a teenage girl.

The truth started to sink in, numbing her.

'You couldn't have planted the iPhone in his room,' Wendy said slowly. 'You didn't know where he was.' Her head wouldn't stop spinning. She tried to focus, tried to make sense of this, but the answer was now so obvious. 'It couldn't have been you.'

'That's right, Wendy.' He smiled, and the look of peace returned to his face. 'That's why I'm here. Remember? I told you that I came here for you, not me. That's my final gift to you.'

'What gift? I don't understand. How did that iPhone get in Dan's room?'

'You know the answer, Wendy. You're worried you ruined an innocent man. But you didn't. There's only one explanation why that phone was in his hotel room: Dan had it the whole time.'

She just looked at him. 'Dan killed Haley?'

'Of course,' he said.

She couldn't move, couldn't breathe.

'And now you know everything, Wendy. You're free. I'm sorry for it all. I don't know whether it makes up for what I did to you, but it will have to do. Like I said in the beginning, that's why I came here – to help you.'

Phil Turnball lifted his gun then. He closed his eyes and looked almost peaceful. 'Tell Sherry I'm sorry,' he said. Wendy raised her hands, shouted at him to stop, started toward him.

But she was too far away.

He placed the muzzle under his chin, aimed up, and pulled the trigger.

Chapter 36

The police cleaned up the mess.

Both Walker and Tremont came by to check up on her and hear the story. She tried to be as detailed as possible. The media, too, took a pretty big interest. Farley Parks released a statement condemning those who had 'rushed to judgment' but did not reenter the race. Dr. Steve Miciano refused any interviews and announced that he was stepping down from practicing medicine to 'pursue other interests.'

Phil Turnball had been right about them.

Life returned to quasi-normal in quick order. Wendy was cleared by NTC of any sort of sexual misconduct, but work had become an impossible place. Vic Garrett couldn't look her in the eye. He gave all his assignments to her via his personal assistant, Mavis. So far, the assignments had been crap. If that didn't change, she would take a more aggressive stand.

But not quite yet.

Pops announced that he would be hitting the road by the weekend. He had stayed on to make sure Wendy and Charlie were okay, but as Pops noted, he was 'a ramblin' man, a rolling stone.' Staying in one place didn't suit him. Wendy understood, but God, she'd miss him.

Amazingly, while her workplace had accepted that the rumors online about her were not true, many of her fellow Kasseltonians did not. She was ignored in the supermarket. The mothers kept away from her during school pickup. On day five, two hours before Wendy was to head out to her PR committee meeting for Project Graduation, Millie Hanover called: 'For the sake of the children, I suggest you step down from serving on any committee.'

'For the sake of the children,' Wendy replied, 'I suggest you suck eggs.'

She slammed the phone down. From behind her she heard clapping. It was Charlie. 'All right, Mom.'

'That woman is so narrow-minded.'

Charlie laughed. 'Remember I told you how I wanted to skip health class because it promotes promiscuity?'

'Yes.'

'Cassie Hanover gets excused because her mother's afraid it might corrupt her morals. Funny thing is, her nickname is "Hand Job" Hanover. I mean, the girl's a total slut.'

Wendy turned and watched her lanky son approach the computer. He sat down and started typing, keeping his eyes on the screen.

'Speaking of total sluts,' Wendy began.

He looked up at her. 'Huh?'

'There are some rumors going around about me. They were put in blogs online.'

'Mom?'

'Yes?'

'Do you think I live in a cave?'

'You've seen them?'

'Of course.'

'Why didn't you say anything?'

Charlie shrugged, went back to typing.

'I want you to know they aren't true.'

'You mean you don't sleep around to get ahead?'

'Don't be a wiseass.'

He sighed. 'I know it's not true, Mom. Okay? You don't have to tell me that.'

She was trying very hard not to cry. 'Are your friends giving you a hard time about it?'

'No,' he said. Then: 'Well, okay, Clark and James want to know if you dig younger men.'

She frowned.

'Kidding,' he said.

'Good one.'

'Lighten up.' He started typing.

She started to head out of the room, give him his privacy. If she had done that, it would all have been over now. They had the answers. Phil set up his friends. Dan had snapped and killed Haley. The fact that they couldn't find a motive was irksome but life works that way sometimes.

But she didn't leave the room. She was feeling teary and alone and so she asked her son, 'What are you doing?'

'Going through my Facebook.'

That reminded her of her fake profile, the Sharon Hait one, the one she'd used to 'friend' Kirby Sennett.

'What's a Red Bull party?' she asked.

Charlie stopped typing. 'Where did you hear that term?'

Wendy reminded him of how she'd used the fake profile to get in touch with Kirby Sennett. 'Kirby invited "Sharon" to a Red Bull party.'

'Show me,' he said.

Charlie logged out and stepped away from the computer. Wendy sat down, signed in as 'Sharon Hait.' It took her a second to remember the password ('Charlie') before she got in. She brought up the invitation and showed it to him.

'Lame,' Charlie said.

'What?'

'Okay, you know how the school has these strict zero-tolerance rules, right?'

'Right.'

'And Principal Zecher is like a Nazi on this stuff. I mean, if a kid is seen drinking, he can't play for any sports teams, can't be in the New Players shows, he reports it to the college admissions people, the whole works.'

'Yes, I know.'

'And you know how teens are idiots and always posting pictures of themselves drinking on stuff like, well, Facebook?'

'Yes.'

'So anyway, someone came up with the idea of Red Bulling the photos.'

'Red Bulling?'

'Yeah. So let's say you go to a party and you're drinking a can of Bud and because you're a loser with self-esteem issues, you think, wow, I'm so cool, I want everyone to see how cool I am. You ask someone to take your picture drinking this Bud so you can put it online so you can show off to your lame-o friends. Thing is, suppose Principal Zecher or his Third Reich minions stumble across it? You're screwed. So what you do is, you photoshop a Red Bull over your beer can.'

'You're kidding.'

'I kid not. Makes sense when you think about it. Here.'

He leaned over her and clicked the mouse. A bunch of photos of Kirby Sennett popped up. He started clicking through them. 'See? Look how many times he, his pals, and their various skanks drink Red Bull.'

'Don't call them skanks.'

'Whatever.'

Wendy started clicking through them. 'Charlie?'

'Yeah.'

'Have you ever been to a Red Bull party?'

'Destination: Loserville.'

'Does that mean no?'

'It means no.'

She looked at him. 'Have you ever been to a party where people drank alcohol?'

Charlie rubbed his chin. 'Yes.'

'Did you drink?'

'Once.'

She turned back to the computer, kept clicking, kept watching Kirby Sennett and his red-faced companions with the Red Bulls. In some of the pictures, you could see the photoshopping. The can of Red Bull was too big or too small or over the fingers or slightly askew.

'When?' she asked.

'Mom, it's okay. It was once. Sophomore year.'

She was debating how far to take the conversation when she saw the photograph that changed everything. Kirby Sennett sat front and center. There were two girls behind him, both with their backs to the cameras. Kirby had a wide smile. He held the Red Bull in his right hand. He wore a New York Knicks T-shirt and a black baseball cap. But what drew her eyes, what made her stop and take another look, was the couch he sat on.

It was bright yellow with blue flowers.

Wendy had seen that couch before.

Alone – just the photograph – it would have meant nothing to her. But now she remembered Phil Turnball's last words, about how he was offering her a 'gift,' that she wouldn't have to blame herself for setting up an innocent man. Phil Turnball believed it – and Wendy had wanted to believe it too. That was the thing. It let her off the hook. Dan had been a killer. She hadn't set up an innocent man. She had, in fact, brought down a murderer.

So how come she still wasn't totally buying it?

The early intuition, the one that said she'd somehow wronged Dan Mercer, the one that had been nibbling at her subconscious from the moment he first opened that red door and walked into the sting house – she had let it go dormant over the past few days.

But it had never gone away.

Chapter 37

The moving truck was parked in front of the Wheeler home.

There was a little ramp running up to the open front door. Two men wearing dark gloves and leather weightlifter belts rolled a credenza down it, one repeating the words, 'Steady, steady,' as though it were a mantra. The FOR SALE sign was still in the yard. There was no UNDER CONTRACT or anything else hung beneath it.

Wendy let the credenza pass and then she headed up the ramp, leaned her head in the doorway, and said, 'Anyone home?'

'Hey.'

Jenna came from the den. She too wore dark gloves. She had on blue jeans. A bulky flannel shirt hung over her white T. The sleeves of the flannel were rolled up to her wrists, but she practically swam in the fabric. Her husband's, Wendy thought. As a kid, you might use your dad's old dress shirts as smocks. As an adult, you use your husband's for household errands or sometimes, just to feel close to him. Wendy had done the same, loving the smell of her man on them.

'Did you find a buyer?' Wendy asked.

'Not yet.' Jenna's hair was tied back, but some strands

had come loose. She tucked it back behind her ear. 'Noel starts in Cincinnati next week though.'

'Fast.'

'Yes.'

'Noel must have started looking for that job right away.'

Jenna hesitated this time. 'I guess so.'

'Because of the stigma of defending a pedophile?'

'That's right.' Jenna put her hands on her hips. 'What's going on, Wendy?'

'Have you ever been to Freddy's Deluxe Luxury Suites in Newark?'

'Freddy's what?'

'It's a no-tell motel in the middle of Newark. Have you been?'

'No, of course not.'

'Funny. I showed the front desk manager your picture. He said he saw you there the day Dan was killed. In fact, he said you asked for a key to his room.'

This was, Wendy knew, a semi-bluff. The front desk manager had recognized Jenna Wheeler and said she'd been there within the past two weeks, but he couldn't say exactly when. He also remembered giving her a key without asking questions – when nice-looking suburban women show up at Freddy's, you never ask for ID – but he didn't remember what room.

'He was mistaken,' Jenna said.

'I don't think so. More important, when I tell the police, the police won't think so.'

The two women stood there, toe-to-toe, staring each other down.

'You see, that was what Phil Turnball missed,' Wendy said. 'You heard about his suicide, I assume?'

'Yes.'

360

'He thought Dan killed Haley because, in his mind, there were no other suspects. Dan was in hiding at the motel. No one knew where he was, ergo nobody could have planted Haley's iPhone. He forgot about you, Jenna. So did I.'

Jenna took off the leather gloves. 'That doesn't mean anything.'

'How about this then?'

Wendy handed her the photograph of Kirby Sennett. The bright yellow couch with blue flowers was behind them, wrapped in plastic, ready to be loaded for Cincinnati. Jenna looked at the photograph a little too long.

'Has your daughter told you what Red Bulling is?'

Jenna handed it back to her. 'This still proves nothing.'

'Sure it does. Because now we know the truth, don't we? Once I give this information to the police, they'll go after the kids harder. They'll get the untouched photographs. I know Kirby was here. He and Haley had a big fight and broke up. When I got him alone, he told me that there'd been a drinking party here, in your house, the night Haley vanished. He said only four kids showed. The police will pressure them now. They'll talk.'

Again this was not exactly true. Walker and Tremont had gotten Kirby alone in a room. They threatened everything under the sun to get him to talk. It wasn't until his lawyer got a waiver of confidentiality, not just no prosecution, that he told them about the party.

Jenna crossed her arms. 'I don't know what you're talking about.'

'Do you know what amazed me? None of the kids came forward after Haley went missing. But again there were only a few kids here. Kirby said he asked your step-daughter, Amanda, about it. Amanda told him that Haley had left here fine right after he did. What with Principal Zecher's zero-tolerance policy, no one wanted to admit to drinking if they didn't have to. Kirby was worried about being thrown off the baseball team. He said another girl was on the wait-list to Boston College and she'd never get in once Zecher told them. So they kept quiet about it, the way kids can do. And really, it was no big deal since Amanda told them Haley had been fine when she left the party. Why would they have doubted that?'

'I think you should leave now.'

'I plan to. I also plan to head straight to the police. You know they'll be able to reconstruct that night now. They'll give the other kids at the party immunity. They'll find out you were at the motel, maybe go through the nearby surveillance tapes. They'll realize you planted the phone. The medical examiner will take another look at Haley's corpse. Your web of lies will fall apart with ease.'

Wendy turned to leave.

'Wait.' Jenna swallowed. 'What do you want?'

'The truth.'

'Are you wearing a wire?'

'A wire? You watch too much TV.'

'Are you wearing a wire?' she asked again.

'No.' Wendy spread her arms. 'Do you want to – what's the correct terminology? – pat me down?'

The two moving men came back into the house. One said, 'It okay if we clear out the teenager's bedroom next, Mrs. Wheeler?'

'Fine,' Jenna said. She looked back at Wendy. There were tears in her eyes. 'Let's talk out back.'

Jenna Wheeler led the way. She slid open the glass door. There was a pool in the back. A blue float drifted alone on the water. Jenna stared at it for a moment. She lifted her eyes and let them travel around the yard, as though she were the prospective buyer.

'It was an accident,' Jenna said. 'When you hear what happened, I'm hoping you'll understand. You're a mother too.'

Wendy felt her heart sink.

'Amanda isn't a popular kid. Sometimes that's okay. You find other interests or you make friends with other unpopular kids. You know how it is. But Amanda wasn't like that. She got picked on a lot. No one ever invited her to parties. It became worse for her after I defended Dan, but really, I'm not sure that was much of a factor. Amanda was the type who cared too much. She sat up in her room and cried all the time. Noel and I didn't know what to do.'

She stopped.

'So you decided to throw a party,' Wendy said.

'Yes. I won't go into all the details, but it seemed the smart move for all involved. Did you know that all that week, the seniors had been driving to the Bronx because they found someplace that served underage teens? Ask Charlie, he'll tell you.'

'Leave my son out of this.'

Jenna put up both hands in mock surrender. 'Fine, whatever. But that's the truth. They'd all go to this club and get wasted and then they'd drive home. So Noel and I figured we could host something in the house. We would stay upstairs, out of the way, and, well, we would just leave a cooler of beer out. It wasn't like we would push it on them, but come on, you were in high school once. Kids drink. We figured at least we could channel it toward the safest possible environment.'

Wendy flashed on that Project Graduation booth with

the 'Not in Our House' campaign, the one against parents hosting parties. 'Safety overkill,' that father had called it, and maybe, on one level, she had agreed.

'I assume that Haley McWaid was there?' Wendy said.

Jenna nodded. 'She didn't really like Amanda. She'd only been to the house once before. She was just using her for the alcohol, I guess. I mean, only a handful of kids showed up. And Haley McWaid was upset. She was heartbroken about not getting into the University of Virginia. She had a big fight with Kirby. That's why he left early.'

Her voice faded away. Jenna looked at the pool water again.

'So what happened?' Wendy asked.

'Haley died.'

She said it just like that.

The moving men clunked down the stairs. One cursed. Wendy stood there with Jenna Wheeler. The sun beat down upon them. The yard was hushed, holding its breath.

'She drank too much,' Jenna said. 'Alcohol overdose. Haley was a small girl. She found an unopened bottle of whiskey in the cabinet. She drank it all. Amanda thought she had just passed out.'

'You didn't call nine-one-one?'

She shook her head. 'Noel is a doctor. He tried everything to revive that poor girl. But it was too late.' Jenna finally turned away from the pool. She looked at Wendy with imploring eyes. 'I need you to put yourself in our position for a moment, okay? The girl was dead. Nothing could bring her back.'

'Dead is dead,' Wendy said, echoing what Jenna had said about her ex-husband during their last meeting.

'You're being sarcastic, but yes, dead is dead. Haley

was gone. It was a terrible accident, but there was no bringing her back. So we stood over her body. Noel kept trying to do CPR, but it was useless. Think about it. You're a reporter. You've covered stories on these parties, haven't you?'

'I have.'

'You know that parents have ended up going to jail, right?'

'Right. It's called manslaughter.'

'But it was an accident. Don't you see? She drank too much. It happens.'

'Four thousand times a year,' Wendy said, remembering Safety Officer Pecora stating that statistic.

'So Haley is lying there. She's dead. And we don't know what to do. If we call the police, we go to prison. An open-and-shut case. Our lives would be ruined.'

'Better than being dead,' Wendy said.

'But what good would that do? Don't you get that? Haley was already dead. Destroying our lives wouldn't bring her back. We were terrified. Don't get me wrong. We felt horrible about Haley. But there is nothing to do for the dead. We were scared – you get that, right?'

Wendy nodded. 'I do.'

'I mean, put yourself in our shoes. Your whole family is about to be destroyed. What would you have done?'

'Me? I probably would have buried her body in a state park.'

Silence.

'That's not funny,' Jenna said.

'But that's what you did, isn't it?'

'Imagine it's your home. Imagine that Charlie came up to you in your bedroom and brought you downstairs and one of his friends was lying dead. You didn't make the kid drink. You didn't force the alcohol down his throat. And now you might go to jail for this. Or Charlie might. What would you have done to protect your family?'

This time, Wendy said nothing.

'We didn't know what to do, so, yes, we panicked. Noel and I put the body in the trunk of our car. I know how it sounds, but again, we saw no other alternative. If we called the police, we were done – and the girl would still be dead. That's what I kept telling myself. I would have sacrificed my own life to bring her back – but that wasn't possible.'

'So you buried her in the woods?'

'That wasn't the initial plan. We were going to drive to Irvington or some city, and just, well, we were going to leave her somewhere so she could be found right away – but then we realized that the autopsy would show alcohol poisoning. The police would be able to trace it back to us. So we knew that we had to hide her. I felt horrible about this – about Ted and Marcia not knowing. But I didn't really know what else to do. And then when people started assuming Haley had run away, well, wasn't that better than knowing for certain that your child is dead?'

Wendy did not reply.

'Wendy?'

'You said to put myself in your shoes.'

'Yes.'

'Now I'm putting myself in Ted's and Marcia's shoes. Was it your hope that they'd never find out the truth? That one day their daughter was there and the next she vanished and so for the rest of their lives they'd rush to every doorbell and wonder about every phone call?'

'Is that worse than knowing your daughter is dead?'

Wendy did not bother giving an answer.

'And you have to understand,' Jenna continued. 'We were living in a sort of suspended hell too. Every time our doorbell or the phone rang, we wondered if it was the police.'

'Wow,' Wendy said, 'I feel horrible for you.'

'I'm not telling you that to gain your sympathy. I'm trying to explain what happened next.'

'I think I know what happened,' Wendy said. 'You were Dan's next of kin. When the police came to you and told you he was dead, well, it was fortuitous, wasn't it?'

Jenna looked down. She pulled the large flannel shirt tighter against her, as though it might offer protection. She looked even smaller now. 'I loved that man. I was devastated.'

'But like you said, dead is dead. Dan had already been branded a pedophile, and well, you told me that Dan wouldn't care about being rehabilitated. He didn't believe in an afterlife.'

'That's all true.'

'The phone records showed the only people Dan called were you and his lawyer, Flair Hickory. You were the only one he trusted. You knew where he was. You still had Haley's iPhone. So why not? Pin it on a dead man.'

'He couldn't be hurt anymore. Don't you see that?'

In a terrible way, this part made sense. You can't hurt a dead man.

'You plugged Ringwood State Park into Google Earth on Haley's iPhone. That was another clue. Why, if Dan killed her and buried her there, would she have looked up that park? There'd be no reason. The only conclusion I could draw was that Haley's killer wanted her body found.'

'Not her killer,' Jenna said. 'It was an accident.'

'I'm really not up for a semantics lesson here, Jenna. But why did you put Ringwood State Park into Google Earth?'

'Because despite what you think, I'm not a monster. I saw Ted and Marcia – the torment they were going through. I saw what the not knowing was doing to them.'

'You did it for them?'

Jenna turned to her. 'I wanted to give them some measure of peace. I wanted their daughter to have a true burial.'

'Nice of you.'

'Your sarcasm,' Jenna said.

'What about it?'

'It's a cover. What we did was bad. It was wrong. But you also understand it on some level. You're a mother. We do what we have to do to protect our children.'

'We don't bury dead girls in the woods.'

'No? So you wouldn't, no matter what? Suppose Charlie's life was at stake. I know you lost your husband. Suppose he was there, on his way to jail for an accident. What would you have done?'

'I wouldn't have buried a girl in the woods.'

'Well, what would you have done? I want to know.'

Wendy did not answer. For a moment she let herself imagine it. John still alive. Charlie coming upstairs. The girl dead on the floor. She didn't have to wonder what she would have done. There was no reason to take it that far.

'Her death was an accident,' Jenna said again, her voice soft.

Wendy nodded. 'I know.'

'Do you understand why we did what we did? I'm not saying you have to agree. But do you understand?'

'I guess on some level I do.'

Jenna looked at her with a tearstained face. 'So what are you going to do now?'

'What would you do if you were me?'

'I would let it be.' Jenna reached out and took Wendy's hand. 'Please. I beg you. Just let it be.'

Wendy thought about that. She had come here feeling one way. Had her opinion shifted? Again she pictured John alive. She pictured Charlie coming up the stairs. She pictured the girl dead on the floor.

'Wendy?'

'I'm not up for being judge and jury,' she said, flashing now on Ed Grayson, on what he'd done. 'It's not my place to punish you. But it's not my place to absolve you either.'

'What does that mean?'

'I'm sorry, Jenna.'

Jenna stepped back. 'You can't prove any of this. I'll deny this whole conversation took place.'

'You could try, but I don't think that will help you.'

'It will be your word against mine.'

'No, it won't,' Wendy said. She gestured toward the gate. Frank Tremont and two other police detectives came around the corner.

'I lied before,' Wendy said, opening up her shirt. 'I am wired.'

Chapter 38

That night, when it was all done, Wendy sat alone on the porch of her house. Charlie was upstairs on the computer. Pops came out and stood by her chair. They both stared up at the stars. Wendy drank white wine. Pops had a bottle of beer.

'I'm ready to go,' he said.

'Not if you have a beer.'

'Just having this one.'

'Still.'

He sat. 'We need to have a little talk first anyway.'

She took another sip of the wine. Odd. Alcohol had killed her husband. Alcohol had killed Haley McWaid. Yet here they both were, sitting on a cool, clear spring evening drinking. Some other time, maybe when she was stone-cold sober, Wendy would search for the deeper meaning in that.

'What's up?' she asked.

'I didn't come back to New Jersey just to visit you and Charlie.'

She turned to him. 'Why then?'

'I came,' he said, 'because I got a letter from Ariana Nasbro.'

Wendy just stared at him.

'I met with her this week. More than once.'

'And?'

'And I'm forgiving her, Wendy. I don't want to hold on to it anymore. I don't think John would want me to. If we don't have compassion, what have we got?'

She said nothing. She thought back to Christa Stockwell, how she had forgiven the college boys who had done her wrong. She said that if you hold on to hate, you lose your grip on so much more. Phil Turnball had learned that lesson the hard way, hadn't he? Revenge, hate – if you hold on to them too tightly, you could lose the important stuff.

On the other hand, Ariana Nasbro wasn't a college kid playing a harmless prank. She had been a drunk driver, a repeat offender, who had killed her husband. Still, Wendy couldn't help but wonder: If Dan Mercer were alive, would he forgive? Were the situations comparable? Did it matter if they were?

'I'm sorry, Pops,' she said. 'I can't forgive her.'

'I'm not asking you to. I respect that. And I want you to respect what I'm doing. Can you do that?'

She thought about it. 'Yeah, I think I can.'

They sat in comfortable silence.

'I'm waiting,' Wendy said.

'For what?'

'For you to tell me about Charlie.'

'What about him?'

'Did you tell him why you came back?'

'Not my place,' Pops said. He rose and finished packing. An hour later, Pops left. Wendy and Charlie flipped on the television. Wendy sat there for a moment, the images flickering before her. Then she rose and went into the kitchen. When she came back, the envelope was in her hand. She handed it to Charlie.

'What's this?' he asked.

'It's a letter to you from Ariana Nasbro. Read it. If you want to talk about it, I'll be upstairs.'

Wendy got ready for bed and left her door open. She waited. Eventually she heard Charlie making his way up the stairs. She braced herself. He poked his head in the doorway and said, 'I'm heading to bed.'

'You okay?'

'Fine. I don't want to talk about it right now, okay? I just want to think a little on my own.'

'Okay.'

'Good night, Mom.'

'Good night, Charlie.'

Two days later, right before Kasselton High School girls played Ridgewood for the county championship in lacrosse, a memorial service was held at midfield. A big sign that read HALEY MCWAID'S PARK was hoisted up on the scoreboard during a moment of silence.

Wendy was there. She watched at a distance. Ted and Marcia were there, of course. Their remaining children, Patricia and Ryan, stood with them. Wendy looked at them and felt her heart break all over again. Another sign was hoisted below Haley's name. This one said NOT IN OUR HOUSE, and reminded parents not to host drinking parties. Marcia McWaid looked away as the sign went up. She scanned the crowd then, and her eyes landed on Wendy. She gave Wendy a small nod. Wendy nodded back. That was all.

When the game began, Wendy turned and walked away. Now-retired county investigator Frank Tremont was there too, way in the back, wearing the same rumpled suit he'd worn to the funeral. It had helped for him to know that Haley McWaid was dead before he ever got the case. But right now, it didn't seem to help a lot.

Walker wore his full sheriff uniform for the ceremony, complete with gun and holster. He stood on the blacktop talking to Michele Feisler. Michele was covering the event for NTC. She moved away when she saw Wendy approach, leaving the two of them alone. Walker started shifting his feet nervously.

Walker said, 'You okay?'

'I'm fine. Dan Mercer was innocent, you know.'

'I do.'

'So that means Ed Grayson murdered an innocent man.'

'I know.'

'You can't just let him get away with that. He needs to be brought to justice too.'

'Even if he thought Mercer was a pedophile?'

'Even if.'

Walker said nothing.

'Did you hear what I said?'

'I did,' Walker said. 'And I will do my best.'

He didn't add 'but.' He didn't have to. Wendy was doing all she could to rehabilitate Dan's name, but nobody much cared. Dead is dead, after all. Wendy turned toward Michele Feisler. Michele had that pad out again, watching the crowd, jotting down notes like the last time they'd been together.

That reminded her of something.

'Hey,' Wendy said to her. 'What was that thing about the timeline again?'

'You got the order wrong,' Michele said.

'Oh, right. Ed Grayson shot his brother-in-law Lemaine before Mercer.'

'Yes. I don't think that changes anything, does it?'

Wendy thought about it, ran it through her head now that she had time.

Actually it changed everything.

She turned toward Walker and saw the gun in his holster. For a moment she just stared at it.

Walker saw what she was doing. 'What's wrong?'

'How many slugs did you find at the trailer park?'

'Excuse me?'

'Your crime-tech guys went through the park where Dan Mercer was shot, right?'

'Of course.'

'How many slugs did they find?'

'Just the one in that cinder block.'

'The one that made the hole in the trailer?'

'Yes. Why?'

Wendy started for her car.

Walker said, 'Wait, what's going on?'

She didn't reply. She walked back to her car and looked it over. Nothing. Not a mark, not a scratch. Her hand fluttered up toward her mouth. She bit back the scream.

Wendy got in her car and drove to Ed Grayson's house. She found him out back, pulling weeds. He was startled by her sudden approach.

'Wendy?'

'Whoever killed Dan,' she said, 'shot at my car.'

'What?'

'You're an expert shot. Everyone says so. I saw you aim at my car and fire several rounds. Yet there isn't a mark on it. In fact, the only slug found in the whole park was the one that went through the wall – the first shot you took. The most obvious place.'

Ed Grayson looked up from the dirt. 'What are you talking about?'

'How could an expert marksman miss Dan from such close range? How could he miss my car? How could he miss the damn ground? Answer: He couldn't. It was all a ruse.'

'Wendy?'

'What?'

'Let it go.'

They just looked at each other for a moment.

'No way. Dan's death is still on me.'

He said nothing.

'And it's ironic when you think about it. When I first got to the trailer, Dan was all bruised from a beating. The cops thought Hester Crimstein had been so clever. She used my testimony to claim that you beat him up – that's how the blood got in your car. What the cops didn't realize was, she was telling the truth. You found Dan. You beat him up because you wanted him to confess. But he didn't, did he?'

'No,' Ed Grayson said. 'He didn't.'

'In fact, you started believing him. You realized that maybe he was innocent.'

'Maybe.'

'So help me here. You came home. What then – did you push E. J. for the truth?'

'Leave it alone, Wendy.'

'Come on. You know I can't. Did E. J. come clean and tell you it was his uncle who took the pictures?'

'No.'

'Who then?'

'My wife, okay? She saw me covered in blood. She told me that I had to stop. She told me what happened, that it was her brother who took those pictures. She begged me to let it go. E. J. was moving past it, she said. Her brother was getting help.'

'But you weren't going to let it slide.'

'No, I wasn't. But I wasn't going to make E. J. testify against his own uncle.'

'So you shot him in the kneecaps.'

'I'm not dumb enough to answer that one.'

'Doesn't matter. We both know you did. And then, what, you called Dan to apologize? Something like that?'

He didn't reply.

'It didn't matter that the judge had thrown the case out,' she continued. 'My show had destroyed Dan's life. Even now – even after I've come forward and publicly exonerated him – people still think he's a pedophile. Where there's smoke, there's fire, right? He had no chance right then. His life was over. You probably blamed yourself some too, the way you hounded him. So you wanted to make things right.'

'Let it go, Wendy.'

'And even better, you were a federal marshal. Those are the guys who handle the witness protection program, don't they? You know how to make people disappear.'

He did not reply.

'So the solution was pretty simple now. You had to fake his death. You couldn't really find another body or make up a fake police report like you could with your federal subjects. And without a body, you needed a reliable witness – someone who would never side with Dan Mercer. Me. You left enough evidence so the police would believe my story – the one round, his blood, the witness who saw you carry out a carpet, your car at the scene, putting the GPS on my car, even going to the shooting range – but not enough evidence so you could be convicted. You had one real bullet in the gun. That's the first one you shot into the wall. The rest were blanks. Dan probably gave you a blood sample or just intentionally cut himself – that explains the blood left behind. Oh, and even smarter – you found a trailer park where you knew there would be no cell phone service. Your witness would have to drive off. That would give you enough time to sneak Dan out. And when they found that iPhone in his motel room, well, you freaked out for a moment, didn't you? That's why you came up to the park. That's why you wanted information. You were afraid, just for a moment, that maybe you had helped a real killer run away.'

She waited for him to say anything. For a moment he just studied her face.

'That's a whale of a tale, Wendy.'

'Now, I can't prove any of this—'

'I know,' he said. 'Because it's nonsense.' He almost smiled now. 'Or are you hoping to get me on your wire too?'

'I don't have a wire.'

He shook his head and started toward his house. She followed him.

'Don't you see? I don't want to prove any of it.'

'So why are you here then?'

Tears filled her eyes. 'Because I'm responsible for what happened to him. I'm the one who set him up on that television show. I'm the reason the world thinks he's a pedophile.'

'I guess that's true.'

'And if you killed him, that's on me. Forever. I don't get a do-over. It's my fault. But if you helped him escape, maybe, just maybe, he's okay now. Maybe he'd even understand and . . .'

She stopped. They were inside the house.

'And what?'

She had trouble getting the words out of her mouth. The tears were coming faster now.

'And what, Wendy?'

'And maybe,' she said, 'he'd even forgive me.'

Ed Grayson lifted the phone then. He dialed a long telephone number. He said some kind of code into the line. He listened for a click. Then he handed the phone to her.

Epilogue

'Mr. Dan?'

I am in a tent that doubles as the school, teaching these kids to read via a program called LitWorld. 'Yes?'

'The radio. It's for you.'

There is no phone in the village. You can only reach this part of the Cabinda Province of Angola via a radio. I had served not far from here years ago, after I graduated from Princeton and worked for the Peace Corps. You've heard that saying that when God closes a door, he opens another. Or something like that. So when I opened that red door, I had no idea another one would open.

Ed Grayson is the one who saved my life. He has a friend, a woman named Terese Collins, who works in a village like this on the other side of the mountain. She and Ed are the only ones who know the truth. To everyone else, Dan Mercer is indeed dead.

That isn't really a lie.

I told you before that the life of Dan Mercer was over. But the life of Dan Mayer – not a big name change, but big enough – has begun. Funny thing. I don't really miss my old life. Something had happened to me along the way – maybe it was a cruel foster family, maybe it was what I had done to Christa Stockwell, maybe it was the fact that I let Phil Turnball take the fall alone – that made this kind of work my calling. I guess that you'd call it atonement. That might be it. But I think it somehow works on a genetic level, like some people are born to be doctors or to like fishing or to shoot baskets with great skill.

For a long time I fought this. I married Jenna. But like I told you in the beginning, my destiny is to be alone. Now I embrace that. Because – and I know this will sound corny – when you see the smiles on these kids' faces, you aren't really ever alone.

I don't look back. If the world thinks Dan Mercer is some kind of pedophile, so be it. We don't have the Internet out here, so I can't check on what's going on at home. I don't think I'd be tempted anyway. I miss Jenna and Noel and the kids, but that's okay. I am tempted to tell her the truth. Jenna is the only one who will really, truly mourn for me.

I don't know. Maybe someday I will.

I pick up the radio receiver. In my short time here, I have never gotten a call. Only Terese Collins and Ed Grayson have this number, so I'm surprised when I hear the familiar voice say, 'I'm so sorry.'

I guess that I should hate the sound of her voice. I should be angry with her, but I'm not. I smile. In the end, in a way, she's made me happier than I've ever been.

She is talking fast now, crying too, explaining herself. I listen with half an ear. I don't need to know any of this. Wendy has called to hear three words. I wait. And when she finally gives me the chance, I am more than happy to say them to her:

'I forgive you.'

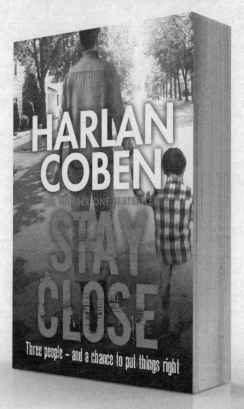

Chapter 1

Sometimes, in that split second when Ray Levine snapped a picture and lost the world in the strobe from his flashbulb, he saw the blood. He knew, of course, that it was only in his mind's eye, but at times, like right now, the vision was so real he had to lower his camera and take a good hard look at the ground in front of him. That horrible moment—the moment Ray's life changed completely, transforming him from a man with a future and aspirations into this Grade-A loser you see in front of you—never visited him in his dreams or when he sat alone in the dark. The devastating visions waited until he was wide-awake, surrounded by people, busy at what some might sarcastically dub work.

The visions mercifully faded as Ray continuously snapped pictures of the bar mitzvah boy.

"Look this way, Ira," Ray shouted from behind his lens. "Who are you wearing? Is it true Jen and Angelina are still fighting over you?"

Someone kicked Ray's shin. Someone else pushed him. Ray kept snapping pictures of Ira.

"Where is the after-party, Ira? What lucky girl is getting the first dance?"

Ira Edelstein frowned and shielded his face from the camera lens. Ray surged forward undaunted, snapping pictures from every angle. "Get out of the way!" someone shouted. Someone else pushed him. Ray tried to steady himself.

Snap, snap, snap.

"Damn paparazzi!" Ira shouted. "Can't I have a moment of peace?"

Ray rolled his eyes. He did not back off. From behind his camera lens, the vision with the blood returned. He tried to shake it off, but it would not go. Ray kept his finger pressed down on the shutter. Ira the Bar Mitzvah Boy moved in a slow-motion strobe now.

"Parasites!" Ira screamed.

Ray wondered if it was possible to sink any lower.

Another kick to the shins gave Ray his answer: Nope.

Ira's "bodyguard"—an enormous guy with a shaved head named Fester—swept Ray aside with a forearm the size of an oak. The sweep was with a bit too much gusto, nearly knocking him off his feet. Ray gave Fester a "what gives" look. Fester mouthed an apology.

Fester was Ray's boss and friend and the owner of Celeb Experience: Paparazzi for Hire—which was just what it sounded like. Ray didn't stalk celebrities hoping to get compromising shots to sell to tabloids like a real paparazzo. No, Ray was actually beneath that— Beatlemania to the Beatles—offering the "celebrity experience" to wannabes who were willing to pay. In short, clients, most with extreme self-esteem and probably erectile dysfunction issues, hired paparazzi to

2

follow them around, snapping pictures to give them, per the brochure, the "ultimate celebrity experience with your very own exclusive paparazzi."

Ray could sink lower, he supposed, but not without an extreme act of God.

The Edelsteins had purchased the A-List Mega-Package—two hours with three paparazzi, one bodyguard, one publicist, one boom-mike handler, all following around the "celebrity" and snapping pictures of him as though he were Charlie Sheen sneaking into a monastery. The A-List MegaPackage also came with a souvenir DVD for no extra charge, plus your face on one of those cheesy-fake gossip magazine covers with a custom-made headline.

The cost for the A-List MegaPackage?

Four grand.

To answer the obvious question: Yes, Ray hated himself.

Ira pushed past and disappeared into the ballroom. Ray lowered his camera and looked at his two fellow paparazzi. Neither one of them had the loser *L* tattooed on their forehead because, really, it would have been redundant.

Ray checked his watch. "Damn," he said.

"What?"

"We still have fifteen minutes on the clock."

His colleagues—both barely bright enough to write their names in the dirt with a finger—groaned. Fifteen more minutes. That meant going inside and working the introduction. Ray hated that.

The bar mitzvah was being held at the Wingfield Manor, a ridiculously gauche banquet hall that, if scaled back a tad, could have doubled as one of Saddam Hussein's palaces. There were chandeliers and mirrors

3

and faux ivory and ornate woodwork and lots and lots of shimmering gold paint.

The image of the blood came back to him. He blinked it away.

The event was black-tie. The men looked worn and rich. The women looked well kept and surgically enhanced. Ray pushed through the crowds, wearing jeans, a wrinkled gray blazer, and black Chuck Taylor Hi-Tops. Several guests stared at him as though he'd just defecated on their salad fork.

There was an eighteen-piece band plus a "facilitator" who was supposed to encourage guest frolicking of all sorts. Think bad TV-game-show host. Think Muppets' Guy Smiley. The facilitator grabbed the microphone and said, "Ladies and gentlemen," in a voice reminiscent of a boxing ring announcer, "please welcome, for the first time since receiving the Torah and becoming a man, give it up for the one, the only . . . Ira Edelstein!"

Ira appeared with two . . . Ray wasn't sure what the right terminology was but perhaps the best phrase would be "upscale strippers." The two hot chicks escorted little Ira into the room by the cleavage. Ray got the camera ready and pushed forward, shaking his head. The kid was thirteen. If women who looked like that were ever that close to him when he was thirteen, he'd have an erection for a week.

Ah youth.

The applause was rapturous. Ira gave the crowd a royal wave.

"Ira!" Ray called out. "Are these your new goddesses? Is it true you may be adding a third to your harem?"

"Please," Ira said with a practiced whine, "I'm entitled to my privacy!"

Ray managed not to vomit. "But your public wants to know."

Fester the Sunglassed Bodyguard put a large mitt on Ray, allowing Ira to brush past him. Ray snapped, making sure the flash worked its magic. The band exploded—when did weddings and bar mitzvahs start playing music at a rock-stadium decibel?—into the new celebration anthem "Club Can't Handle Me." Ira dirty-danced with the two hired helpers. Then his thirteen-year-old friends joined in, crowding the dance floor, jumping straight up and down like pogo sticks. Ray "fought" through Fester, snapped some more pictures, checked his watch.

One more minute on the clock.

"Paparazzi scum!"

Another kick to the shins from some little cretin.

"Ow, damn it, that hurt!"

The cretin scurried away. Note to self, Ray thought: Start wearing shin guards. He looked over at Fester as though begging for mercy. Fester let him off the hook with a head gesture to follow him toward the corner. The corner was too loud so they slipped through the doors.

Fester pointed back into the ballroom with his enormous thumb. "Kid did a great job on his haftorah portion, don't you think?"

Ray just stared at him.

"I got a job for you tomorrow," Fester said.

"Groovy. What is it?"

Fester looked off.

Ray didn't like that. "Uh-oh."

"It's George Queller."

"Dear God."

"Yes. And he wants the usual."

5

Ray sighed. George Queller tried to impress first dates by overwhelming and ultimately terrifying them. He would hire Celeb Experience to swarm him and his date—for example, last month it was a woman named Nancy—as he entered a small romantic bistro. Once the date was safely inside, she would be presented with—no, this was for real—a custom-made menu that would read, "George and Nancy's First Date of Many, Many" with the address, month, day, and year printed beneath. When they left the restaurant, the paparazzi for hire would be there, snapping away and shouting at how George had turned down a weekend in Turks and Caicos with Jessica Alba for the lovely and now-terror-stricken Nancy.

George considered these romantic maneuvers a pre-quel to happy-ever-after. Nancy and her ilk considered these romantic maneuvers a prelude to a ball gag and secluded storage unit.

There had never been a second date for George.

Fester finally took off his sunglasses. "I want you to work lead on the job."

"Lead paparazzo," Ray said. "I better call my mother, so she can brag to her mahjong group."

Fester chuckled. "I love you, you know that."

"Are we done here?"

"We are."

Ray packed away his camera carefully, separating the lens from the body, and threw the case over his shoulder. He limped toward the door, not from the kicks but the hunk of shrapnel in his hip—the shrapnel that started his downward slide. No, that was too simple. The shrapnel was an excuse. At one time in his miserable life, Ray had fairly limitless potential. He'd graduated from Columbia University's School of Journalism with what one professor called "almost supernatural talent"—now being wasted—in the area of photojournalism. But in the end, that life didn't work out for him. Some people are drawn to trouble. Some people, no matter how easy the path they are given on the walk of life, will find a way to mess it all up.

Ray Levine was one of those people.

It was dark out. Ray debated whether he should just head home and go to bed or hit a bar so seedy it was called Tetanus. Tough call when you have so many options.

He thought about the dead body again.

The visions came fast and furious now. That was understandable, he supposed. Today was the anniversary of the day it all ended, when any hope of happy-ever-after died like . . . Well, the obvious metaphor here would involve the visions in his head, wouldn't it?

He frowned. Hey, Ray, melodramatic much?

He had hoped that today's inane job would take his mind off it. It hadn't. He remembered his own bar mitzvah, the moment on the pulpit when his father bent down and whispered in his ear. He remembered how his father had smelled of Old Spice, how his father's hand cupped Ray's head so gently, how his father with tears in his eyes simply said, "I love you so much."

Ray pushed the thought away. Less painful to think about the dead body.

The valets had wanted to charge him—no professional courtesy, he guessed—so Ray had found a spot three blocks down on a side street. He made the turn, and there it was—his piece-o-crap, twelve-year-old Honda Civic with a missing bumper and duct tape holding together a side window. Ray rubbed his chin.

Unshaven. Unshaven, forty years old, piece-o-crap car, a basement apartment that if heavily renovated might qualify as a crap hole, no prospects, drank too much. He would feel sorry for himself, but that would involve, well, caring.

Ray was just taking out his car key when the heavy blow landed on the back of his head.

What the . . . ?

He dropped to one knee. The world went dark. The tingle ran up his scalp. Ray felt disoriented. He tried to shake his head, tried to clear it.

Another blow landed near his temple.

Something inside his head exploded in a flash of bright light. Ray collapsed to the ground, his body splayed out. He may have lost consciousness—he wasn't sure—but suddenly he felt a pulling in his right shoulder. For a moment he just lay limp, not able or wanting to resist. His head reeled in agony. The primitive part of his brain, the base animal section, had gone into survivor mode. Escape more punishment, it said. Crawl into a ball and cover up.

Another hard tug nearly tore his shoulder out. The tug lessened and began to slip away, and with it, a realization made Ray's eyes snap open.

Someone was stealing his camera.

The camera was a classic Leica with a recently updated digital-send feature. He felt his arm lift in the air, the strap running up it. In a second, no more, the camera would be gone.

Ray didn't have much. The camera was the only possession he truly cherished. It was his livelihood, sure, but it was also the only link to old Ray, to that life he had known before the blood, and he'd be damned if he'd give that up without a fight.

"Help!" Ray shouted.

No one appeared.

Panic seized Ray—followed quickly by a primitive survival instinctive reaction. Flee. He tried to stand, but, nope, that was simply not happening yet. Ray was already a weakened mess. One more shot, one more hard blow with that baseball bat . . .

"Help!"

The attacker took two steps toward him. Ray had no choice. Still on his stomach he scrambled away like a wounded crab. Oh, sure, that would work. That would be fast enough to keep away from the damn bat. The assuwipe with the baseball bat was practically over him. He had no chance.

Ray's shoulder hit something, and he realized that it was his car.

Above him he saw the bat coming up in the air. He was a second, maybe two, away from having his skull crushed. Only one chance and so he took it.

Too late.

The strap was off his arm now. He wondered whether he'd have another opportunity, whether the mugger would go for the fourteen bucks in his wallet and give Ray a chance. Couldn't wait to find out.

With his head still swimming and his knees wobbling, Ray shouted, "No!" and tried to launch himself at his attacker. He hit something—legs maybe—and tried to wrap his arms around them. He didn't get much of a grip, but the impact was enough.

The attacker fell down. So did Ray, landing on his stomach. Ray heard the clacking of something falling and hoped like hell that he hadn't just shattered his own camera. He tried to blink his eyes open, managed to get them into slits, and saw the camera case a few feet away. He tried to scramble toward it, but as he did, he saw two things that made his blood freeze.

The first was a baseball bat on the pavement. The second—and more to the point—was a gloved hand picking it up.

Ray tried to look up, but it was useless. He flashed back to the summer camp his father ran when he was a kid. Dad—the campers all called him Uncle Barry—used to lead a relay race where you hold a basketball directly over your head and spin as fast as you can, staring up at the ball, and then, dizzy beyond words, you had to dribble the length of the court and put the ball in the basket. The problem was, you got so dizzy from the spinning that you'd fall one way while the ball would go the other way. That was how he felt now, as though he were tumbling to the left, while the rest of the world teetered to the right.

The camera thief lifted the baseball bat and started toward him.